SUING THE VATICAN

BALANCING THE SCALES OF JUSTICE

S.M. SEBASTIAN

Published by: Make a Difference Publications
ISBN: 978-0-9765246-4-9

DEDICATION

This book is dedicated to all the victims of sexual abuse
of any kind.

Please know the trauma you've experienced can be put to
rest with one simple act—forgiveness. While I understand
how difficult that may sound, know that forgiveness led
me to write this book. Forgiveness freed my soul.
Forgiveness can do the same for you.

So read this book with the love intended—
and when finished, feel your soul lighten, knowing
you are finally free.

All my love to each and every one of you.

A Personal Note from the Author

THIS BOOK HAS BEEN 55 years in the making.

It began the day I found the courage to say *enough*—after being sexually abused by a clergy member and then expelled from high school for speaking up.

I can still recall the sky that day in April 1969, as I stepped out onto Lincoln Avenue in my small New England town: clear, wide, and blue. No clouds above me—for the first time in years, the cloud had lifted from within.

What lay ahead terrified me. I didn't know where I'd go, or how my father would react when he found out. But even then, something stirred. A sense that my story was no longer being written for me.

My father did what many did in the 1960s: he believed the Church without question. He kicked me out of the house without knowing why I'd been expelled. Back then, priests were treated as infallible. Untouchable. I was just a kid.

Homelessness followed. I look upon it now as the beginning of my real education. I learned how to survive, how to think independently, how to plan a future from scratch.

I found work in a factory. Rented a room at the YMCA. Finished high school. Then college. I left the tiny one-square-mile town I'd grown up in and moved to the big city. I started a company that's still thriving four decades later.

And yet, something always felt missing.

Part of that was discovering, at the age of 45, that I had been born an identical twin—he died at birth. But the bigger piece was buried much deeper: the truth I couldn't—or wouldn't—face for decades.

That changed one morning during meditation. In a moment of stillness, the memories came. And not long after, during a Christmas Eve 2017 conversation with a former classmate, I learned my abuser—the man who expelled me—had been quietly transferred to Rome just weeks later. The following year, the Vatican reassigned him to another all-boys Catholic school—where he abused again.

I began to investigate.

What I found was horrifying: a long, documented history of abusive priests being shuffled from parish to parish, leaving shattered lives behind them—while those in power, all the way to the Vatican City, looked the other way.

No accountability. No justice. No end.

And I kept asking myself: *Why hasn't anyone taken them to trial?* Not for headlines. Not for hush money settlements. But truly, to trial for crimes against humanity. Crimes some say have harmed over 1.2 million children worldwide.

So I wrote this book. Because if no one else will hold them accountable, maybe this small offering can help spark something. A conversation. A movement. A reckoning.

To anyone who has ever been hurt, silenced, or cast aside—I wrote this with you in my heart. With love. With sorrow. And with a fierce hope that justice can be more than a dream.

Please read this book with compassion—for yourself, for survivors, and even for those who still can't face the truth. But most of all, read it with the courage to believe that justice—real, unflinching justice—is possible.

Because it is. And it's long overdue.

— S.M. SEBASTIAN

A NOTE TO THE READER

EXPECTATION IS EVERYTHING WHEN OPENING to the first page of a book. Expectation sets the mood for the reader.

Below is a link to a song the author wrote and performed. A song that sets the mood for this story.

It is suggested that you listen to this song before you begin your journey of discovery in *Suing The Vatican:*

Go to www.SuingTheVatican.com/song or scan the QR code below.

PRELUDE

1

Sexual abuse in the Catholic Church dates back to the 11th century when Cardinal and now Saint Peter Damian wrote a treatise titled *The Book of Gomorrah* that addressed sexual abuse of young boys and girls as well as adults. He warned Popes Leo IX and Nicholas II that something needed to be done.

2

In 1985 a report, *The Problem of Sexual Molestation by Roman Catholic Clergy*, was presented to the Vatican by Thomas Doyle, a canon lawyer at the Vatican embassy. Pope John Paul II read the report, but nothing was done and Mr. Doyle's embassy role was not renewed.

3

United Nation's Committee Against Torture condemned sexual abuse in the Catholic Church, recognizing it as a form of torture under international law. The committee's stance is based on multiple reports, investigations, and hearings that have examined the Vatican's role in covering up cases of sexual abuse.

4

A formal complaint was filed in the International Criminal Court, asking it to investigate Pope Benedict XVI and three Cardinals for alleged crimes against humanity, claiming they bore responsibility for systematic cover-ups of the sexual abuse of children by Catholic clergy worldwide.

5

Pope Francis and several Cardinals received a letter alleging that Gabriele Martinelli, the rector of the youth seminary that handed out papal assignments, was sexually abusing boys at the seminary. Pope Francis knew about the abuse in 2013 but ignored it.

In 2017 Gabriele Martinelli was ordained a priest by Pope Francis.

Gabriele Martinelli was formally convicted of sexual abuse in January 2024.

Despite these obvious connections, along with many more, between sexual abuse and the Vatican, no one has ever made an effort to sue the Vatican on behalf of the estimated 1.2 million innocent victims.

One has to wonder *why?*

DISCLAIMER

This is a work of fiction. It uses the justice system as a dramatic framework to explore themes of accountability and moral complexity. All characters, dialogues, and incidents are either the product of the author's imagination or used in a fictionalized manner. This novel does not assert legal conclusions. Depictions within are dramatized for narrative purposes and do not constitute verifiable claims unless supported by sources referenced in the end notes. The Vatican and related entities are referenced within the bounds of protected literary expression.

Some events and statements in this novel are meant to provoke reflection rather than present courtroom evidence. That said, references to real-world abuses and cover-ups are drawn from publicly available research and journalistic investigations listed in the end notes.

∞   ∞   ∞

This book is not only about accountability and seeking justice for crimes against humanity, but also about the power of forgiveness, with a look at what the Church could be, if someone only had the courage to move in that direction.

To be read with an open mind and a loving heart.

SUING THE VATICAN

BALANCING THE SCALES OF JUSTICE

S.M. SEBASTIAN

PROLOGUE

Innocence is the light that flickers, even in the darkest of cages.

D ARNELL "DRIZZLE" ARCENEAUX, 22, AT one o'clock in the afternoon on Day 5 of his three-year incarceration at Folsom State Maximum Security Prison for Men, sat by the southern wall in the Visitor's Room facing a steel door, waiting for the arrival of his family. Ahead of Drizzle sat a roomful of other inmates, men waiting for their wives and children, their brothers and sisters, in-laws, cousins and outlaw friends.

Drizzle, a strapping young black kid from New Orleans—six-foot-two and fighting one-seventy-five—had been transferred to California from Angola, Louisiana's toughest prison, in mid-December, convicted of a minor crime: selling stolen TVs on the black market when his family was out of food and homeless. It would be Drizz's first Christmas in prison.

Outside, the wind was blowing hot. Drizzle watched with fascination as the families of other prisoners entered the cramped Visitor's Room. He cast a glum eye at the holiday decorations strung everywhere: the plastic reindeer, glittery holly and gold tinsel, the sounds of Yuletide music being piped in, and the white-bearded, chubby old man in orange prison garb and red Santa hat, grumpily plopping candy cane ornaments one-by-one on a lopsided Christmas tree.

Where are they? Drizzle wondered gloomily. Where was Jada, his wife, and Jamal, his five-year-old son? Drizzle's eyelids drooped as he waited.

Before Angola, Drizz had never been in prison—not even a small-town jailhouse. He'd mentioned this to the guard, the youngest officer in Folsom, a calm blue-eyed dude from Detroit said to be a prior member of Young Boys Incorporated, who'd sold drugs on the street until he turned his life around. Drizzle thought the guy looked easy to talk to. But the guard said move your ass, telling Drizzle to keep his damn mouth shut and take a seat.

Plopping into a chair in the corner, Drizzle got hard, unforgiving stares from the other inmates. He smiled back, but smiling made him feel fearful. *You make eye contact with summa these thugs,* he'd been warned, *you dead.* Instead, he prayed silently for mercy over all the other felons.

Drizz waited, drumming his fingers on the table, anxious to see his wife and child. He kept staring at the door, about to give up on his family ever coming. Just then the door opened, the guard stood aside, and Drizzle was looking at his wife and son, both of them smiling, waving their arms.

Drizzle almost fell out of his chair laughing. He stood, beaming a big smile. Tiny Jamal raced over for a hug, yelling, "Daddy! Daddy!"

Drizz watched his wife step inside and creep forward through the room, holding her coat collar tight around her throat as she studied the other inmates, side-stepping the bearded old man in the Santa hat grumbling, griping and bitching as he slapped his wooden cane at the fake tree.

Kissing the boy on both cheeks, Drizzle hoisted Jamal halfway to the ceiling. Then he and his son started boxing, sparring with both fists, the five-year-old swaying like a little cobra, throwing playful uppercuts to his father's jaw. "Bam, bam!"

Drizzle chuckled. "You a good little fighter, Jamal!" he said, getting bammed in the nose by the child's whirling punches. Seeing his little boy for the first time in a year delighted him. "Damn, slow down! I'm too old to go 10 rounds with you, tiger!"

"You looking good, Pops," smiled Jamal. Drizz swallowed hard. He bent down to his son and hugged him tight. Then he turned to his wife and looked at her oddly.

"Damn, girl, you cut your hair."

Jada ran her hand carefully over her head. She smiled. "Mama shaved the dreads off before we came out here. Don't get sore."

"I ain't sore. It looks nice."

A delicate and graceful woman of 21, Jada in New Orleans had sported collarbone-grazing cornrows, with beads at the tail of the long braids. Now she had a tightly-cropped buzzcut, which Drizzle grinned at, running his hand over her scalp and rubbing it almost in worship.

Shying away, Jada pulled out a tissue and wiped her nose. "Drizz, it's good to see you." She jammed her hands in her pockets and looked frightened.

Behind them, the white-bearded, pot-bellied little old man grit his teeth and bitched about the pre-lit tree lights not working. For a moment, Drizzle thought of asking the guards for another table, not so close to the guy. Instead, the three of them smiled and sat, Drizz keeping his gaze on the crazy old-timer with the crumpled Santa hat slanted over one eye.

"How you doin', baby?" Jada asked.

Turning to face his wife, Drizzle felt a warmth spread through him. He saw a twinkle in her eye, though he could tell it was forced. His heart went out to her. Then a glint of worry showed on her face. "What you looking at, Jada?"

"I'm looking at those bruises on your neck. Jesus, Drizz, what the *hell?*"

Drizzle tried to stay cool. His gaze lowered to Jamal, seated quietly beside him. Jamal was squinting now, looking his father over.

"Baby, where you get those bruises from?" Jada said. "Honey, what happened?"

The smile evaporated from Drizzle's face. He shifted his weight uneasily, gripping his orange shirt lapels tight at the throat, so the bruises and marks on his neck couldn't be seen.

"Got worked over back in Angola," Drizzle confessed. "Couple of big guys, doing time for runnin' guns and dealin' meth. Bad dudes, Jada. Took me in the shower, knocked me down, got on top of me and drug my pants down and—"

There was a silence. Jada could see the tears in his eyes. She reached across and touched Drizzle's left hand. "Oh, Drizz!" she moaned.

"Wasn't the first time it happened, either. That's why I begged the warden for a transfer. Angola the scariest place I ever been in."

Jada wiped his eyes with the back of her hand, mopped his cheeks with her coat sleeve. Drizzle looked at his scared wife and child, and held out his hand. "Don't be crying now, Jada."

"You get them punks back?"

"Get 'em back? I *forgave* 'em."

"Say what?"

"I forgave 'em."

"Why you do that?"

"Jada, you ain't gonna believe this. But I found God in that prison in Louisiana." Drizzle paused and looked tenderly at his son. "I forgave 'em because God says to. Says the law of Karma will get 'em. God is loving, and He makes certain the scales of justice are balanced. So yeah, baby, I coulda kicked their ass, maybe make a win for me. But forgiving them? That's a win for God."

Jada remained very still, staring at her husband. Drizzle watched Jamal chew at the corner of his lip. He looked into the boy's beautiful eyes and took his hand. "Anyway, they going to move me out of isolation to the general population today. Don't know who my cellmate gonna be."

Jada sat back in her chair and stared. Her eyes were wide, hurt and worried. She held that gaze as she studied Drizzle. Then she shook her head and brightened. "You seem like a changed man," she smiled, and her voice cracked.

Drizzled stared down at the table in front of him. "This is the path I gotta walk," he sighed. "The path of forgiveness. Lord says forgiveness is for me, not for them. It's time to live God's way."

Somewhere deep within Drizzle, Jada saw a heavy weight being lifted, carried away. Drizzle reached out and touched her cheek. He looked down at his puzzled son, then at the bearded old man hobbling on the other side of the room, scowling and grumbling as he hung Christmas stockings on the tree. He saw a tiredness in the old man, a deep and hidden sorrow that seemed to sink into the fellow's bones.

Jamal watched the chubby old man, curious. The white tip of the dented Santa hat bobbed up and down as the old guy whacked again at the broken Christmas bulbs with his cane.

"Dad," Jamal whispered, tugging on Drizzle's orange pantleg, "I thought Santa was s'posed to be a jolly old man."

Drizz leaned in and ruffled his son's hair, happy to tear his eyes away from the other prisoner. "Old man probably got dementia," he said. "Or just crazy. Wandering 'round prison looking like some crazy-ass Santy Claus. But my heart goes out to him, son. He deserves that. As does every man," he said, looking gently at his wife, "and every woman."

Jamal pursed his lips. "Maybe he's lonely," the child said. "Maybe he just needs a hug."

"You leave that man alone now, Jamal," Drizzle said, playfully tugging on his son's ear and smiling. "Listen to your father."

Jamal leaned back, pouting, moving in closer to his mother. Still he continued watching the red-hatted old-timer, the young boy's eyes alive in wonder.

Jada shook her head at their son. She put a hand on her husband's wrist.

"The church been good to us, Drizz," she said, and her face brightened. "Donations from the elders got us out here. I told your story to the whole parish. Said Drizz's a good man, couldn't find a job, had a marijuana cigarette conviction from years back. One of the deacons heard that, offered you a job over in Baton Rouge, soon as you're released. The church janitor's retiring. Maybe counseling kids in the Catholic school there, too."

Drizzle stared at his wife and frowned. "Baby, that's three years from now. Three years I be behind these iron bars, Jada." He sank down into his chair.

Jada shut her eyes and took a deep breath. "Jamal misses you. The boy *needs* you. Child needs his daddy taking him on walks in the park, taking him to ballgames and movies. You know how young boys are…"

"Yeah," Drizzle grimaced. He looked down at his son, then at the old man the boy was watching, seeing the flash of a hopeful smile on Jamal's face.

Jada could see her words hurt. They rocked Drizz back to growing up in the Desire neighborhood of New Orleans, their tiny home near the cypress swamp and the city dumping ground, his father always unemployed and hustling for odd jobs, mother trying to raise her babies but holding on for hope that better days for the family lay ahead. Jada knew those better days never came. She pressed her warm hand tight around her husband's.

"Be careful in here, Drizzle," she said.

Drizzle turned to her. A magnetic smile spread across his face. He reached across and set one hand on his wife's shoulder. Jada turned her head away, and Drizzle could feel all the goodwill and faith she was holding onto evaporate.

"I will, baby," he said. "I promise. And you, Slugger—" Drizzle turned to his son—"you be—"

Drizzle looked for Jamal. But the boy was gone, his chair empty. Drizzle and Jada exchanged glances.

"Jada? Where that boy go?"

Drizzle slapped the table in front of him. He leaned back, head twisting on his neck, eyes scanning the room. Looking, looking, finally he saw his child on the other side of the Visitor's Room, jumping up and down and hugging the chubby Santa Claus's knee.

"Santa! Santa!" Jamal squealed with delight. "Are you comin' to my house tonight?"

Annoyed, the old man tried to shove the child off, to knee him away. But the kid wasn't having it and latched on tighter.

"Why are you in here, Santa? And where are your elves?"

"I don't have any elves!" the old man grumbled. He refused to look at the boy, instead went about trying to kick him away.

"Well," Jamal said, hanging onto his knee, "I'm here, and I want to wish you a Merry Christmas! And don't worry, your elves'll be back, because you're Santa Claus! And we all love you!"

This stopped the old-timer cold. He halted his kicking and grumbling, and stared down at the child, a look of extreme puzzlement spread across his face.

"I gotta get my gifts tonight," said Jamal, finally letting go and gazing up dreamily. "We ain't in New Orleans. We're in that motel, 'cross the freeway. No chimney there, but we'll leave milk and cookies out for you."

The old man winced. He looked at Drizzle, shaking his head, as if begging for help. Seeing this, Drizzle just lowered his gaze and sneaked a grin.

"Why are you so sad, Santa? Huh?"

The old man shrugged and sighed. "Christmas isn't my favorite time of year."

"Well," said Jamal, sliding closer and squeezing the old man's hand, "Christ was born this time of year! I bet Jesus forgives you for feelin' sad. Just like He forgave my Pops for the present he didn't get me last year. You know, that Pac-Man game you brought me, a day late? You forgive my Pops too, Santa, dontcha?"

For a long moment, the old man stood frozen, as if his heart had seized up. Nervously he looked over at Drizzle and Jada, their eyes locked with his. Then his eyes seemed to melt, and he bent down and hugged Jamal, curling his arms around the little boy.

"So you coming tonight? Right, Santa?" Jamal asked, trying to coax a smile out of his new friend.

"You're on my schedule," nodded the old man. He stared straight at Drizzle, his cheeks flushed. As the boy gleefully pressed his forehead into the old-timer's hip, the man gave Drizzle a nervous shrug and a smile. And then, to Drizzle's amazement, he winked.

A few minutes later, at precisely 2 P.M., a buzzer rang, ending the visitation hour. Drizzle stood, hugged Jada, then Jamal, kissing the child's soft black hair, his velvety smooth cheeks. Drizzle didn't want to let go. The other visitors began hugging their family members, saying goodbyes, blinking away tears, drifting away to the door in silence. Taking Jamal by the hand, Jada walked mutely toward the exit, the kid looking back at his father in a silent plea.

Drizzle waved goodbye. Then he sat. He stared for a long moment at the door, then slowly dropped his gaze to the table. The room was quiet now.

Drizzle's chest ached. He looked around at the other inmates, watching the men one by one being escorted back to their cells, down the long concrete hallways to B and C Blocks, the old man in the dented Santa hat the last to shuffle out, tapping his cane and looking back over his shoulder one last time at Drizzle.

Drizz stayed in his seat, his throat tight, still feeling the warmth of the child's last fierce embrace. When the guard appeared, telling him it was time to move to his cell, Drizzle hesitated, a funny feeling in the pit of his stomach.

"Say, who is that old white man?" he asked.

The guard squinted at Drizzle, a look of annoyance on his face. He leaned in closer, eyes probing. "Who is he?" he grunted. "Don't you know?"

"Know what?"

The guard leaned his head back. "That's Murphy," he said. "Father Charles Murphy, the old priest, doing fifty-to-life. He's your new cellmate," the guard said, then added, "Don't you know what he's in for?"

CHAPTER ONE

Sarcasm exorcises the darkness of the soul.

FATHER CHARLES MURPHY, 92, AT seven in the evening on his 3,721st day as the lost saint at Folsom State Maximum Security Prison, queued up in line behind the mass murderers and gangbangers for Saturday movie night. Beside Murphy stood his new companion Drizzle, the kid watching the old man nudge inmates out of his way with his cane, the motley pair now on their third day as C Block cellmates.

Ahead of Murphy huddled a procession of tattooed, bulked-up lifers — drug traffickers and cop killers and Aryan brotherhood bikers — hardened men in orange jumpsuits strolling single-file into the community TV room. Murphy hoped tonight's movie was *Lethal Weapon 3* with Mel Gibson, currently #7 on Murphy's all-time list of greatest Hollywood films. Rumor was that the movie would be something less inflammatory, something unlikely to stir up a jailbreak or a riot. Maybe *Sleepless in Seattle*. This made Father Murphy grumpy.

Watching the inmates scatter and peel away from the taps and whacks of Murphy's cane, Drizzle chuckled. Tagging along with Murphy had become his new pastime. During each meal, they engaged in spirited debates, playfully bumping heads over heavyweight topics: What's the greatest gangster movie, *The Godfather* or *Goodfellas*? Is Martin Luther King a greater orator than Winston Churchill? And whether Bruce Lee could beat Mike Tyson. As the line for the movie snaked forward, moving toward their seats, Drizzle tapped the old priest on the shoulder, prodding him to continue their discussion.

"What we gonna kick around next?" he asked.

Father Murphy handed Drizzle his cane, reached for the pack of cigarettes in his pocket, lit one up with a sly laugh. "Our next debate is near and dear to me, Drizz. A real corker."

"Lay it on me, padre."

Murphy exhaled his first drag of smoke. A glint showed in his eyes.

"The all-time greatest white NBA basketball players," he said.

"Greatest white basketball players? Shit, Murphy, there ain't none."

"Don't be an asshole, son," Murphy said, exhaling his second drag, nudging Drizzle to take it. "I could name a hundred."

"Steph Curry and Blake Griffin don't count. They're bi-racial."

"I don't need Griffin and Curry. Hell, I've got Pistol Pete, Larry Bird, Jerry West, Bob Cousy, Havlicek and McHale and Cowens and Big Bill Walton. Not to mention Dirk Nowitzki—there's a guy who could shoot—and Nikola Jokić, Luka Dončić, and..."

Murphy could see Drizzle was giving him that hard stare—the one that told the priest the kid was trolling him. He sighed, snatched back the burning cigarette, then turned his soulful blue eyes on the slow-moving line of convicts.

"Never mind. Here's another: The all-time greatest stand-up comics."

"Man, I got this one!" Drizzle said, plucking Murphy's smoke back. "There's Richard Pryor. Dave Chappelle. Eddie Murphy. Chris Rock. Kevin Hart. Chris Tucker. And put my man Redd Foxx in there, goin' way back."

"Not bad. All black brothers, I see."

"Hell yes. You got a better idea?"

Murphy's eyebrows knit together, bushy strands of white curls whistling in the prison air.

"Richard Pryor, I'm good with that one. When *Live on the Sunset Strip* came out, I laughed so hard I couldn't breathe. But you left out George Carlin, Robin Williams, Jay Leno, Don Rickles, Groucho Marx, Mel Brooks, Rodney Dangerfield—"

"Here we go with the white folks again."

"Quick Rodney Dangerfield joke: *My psychiatrist told me I was crazy. I asked for a second opinion and he said, 'Alright, you're ugly, too.'*"

"Redd Foxx beats that: *I asked my girlfriend, 'Do you smoke after having sex?' She said, 'I don't know, I never looked.'*"

"You want my all-time #1?"

"#1 greatest comedian? Hit me."

"It's God. God is the GOAT."

"You stoned out your mind, Murphy. You trippin'. God is the funniest stand-up comic there ever was?"

"God is the original stand-up comic. Ever see one of His greatest creations, the non-believer, walking around in a T-shirt that says THANK GOD I'M AN ATHEIST? And His skit about Jonah using a whale like it was an Uber is pure genius. God is the GOAT."

"I'm gettin' unpleasant flashbacks to yesterday, when we was lined up for phone calls, and you said the greatest TV sitcom theme was *Gilligan's Island*."

"Don't be an asshole, son."

The line of cons snaked inside. Father Murphy shuffled past a serial pipe bomber named Shrapnel while Drizzle found a pair of vacant chairs, right up front of the big-screen TV, seated between two scary-looking young Idaho skinheads convicted of hate crimes.

Murphy squatted gingerly, then sat, shifting his bony butt around to find a comfortable spot. Using his cupped hand as an ashtray the priest waited for the lights to dim. As soon as it was dark, he lit another cigarette, inhaled blissfully, glancing up through the smoke to see Lee Marvin training a pack of misfit soldiers to wipe out a chateau filled with Nazi generals in World War II.

"*The Dirty Dozen* again? I've already seen it, 23 and a half times."

Murphy's gaze flicked over to Drizzle's face with concern.

"So what, man? You got somethin' better to do?"

Murphy stabbed the cigarette between his lips, dug through his pockets, snatched a tiny spiral notepad, and started scribbling furiously with a pencil, muttering to himself.

"What you doin'?"

"Writing a note to the warden. Twenty-three Saturday nights I've sat through this film. The 24th time I had to leave near the end—you know the part where Jim Brown gets shot while dropping live grenades into the bunker?—to go to the crapper. By the time I got back, they were showing Hulk Hogan in *Mr. Nanny*."

Murphy shook his head, scribbling madly, while he puffed on his smoke. Out of nowhere an overweight old-boy prison guard named Woody came waddling up.

"Father Murphy, you know the rules. No smoking in here."

Murphy sighed, nodded, stubbed the cigarette out on his chair. When Woody left, Murphy plucked another smoke from his pocket, lit a match with his thumbnail, fanned it out and took a deep drag and continued writing.

Drizzle eyed him with fascination, then leaned in, looking deeply troubled.

"Murph, I been thinkin'...I need your spiritual inside."

"You mean *insight*."

"Yeah. Inside. I think I may have insulted Pagliano."

"You mean the vicious organized crime boss they call the Cremator? The West Coast head of the Mafia is not someone you want to piss off. What did you say?"

"Well, I was power-lifting in the yard yesterday, and Pagliano and his crew came boppin' by. On my third rep at 200 pounds, I dropped it—accidentally, of course—and it smashed down on his foot. He yowled and I picked it up and apologized. But then I noticed, and maybe said a little too loud, 'Yo, Cremator, you got a hole in your shoe!' And you know how perfect the dude keeps his hair and them shiny-ass Italian shoes."

"And before something happens to you, you want to know how best to address the situation?"

"Something like that. Maybe God can help."

"God doesn't spend His time on men from the mob. He lets the Feds deal with that. That's why he created the FBI. Besides, He delegates most of His work nowadays."

"Maybe if I go to confession and say a few prayers He'll listen. Provide some inside."

"You mean *insight*."

"Yeah."

"Well, God doesn't always give you the answers you want. He's a little disappointing that way."

"It's worth a try, Murph. Ain't it?"

"So basically you want to *use* God. Hoping He can magically convince Mr. Pagliano, on a subconscious and divinely spiritual level, to not have one of his capos beat the crap out of you for disrespecting him?"

"Damn straight."

"Drizzle, I think even God is fearful of treading on Mr. Pagliano. Did you think of asking him to forgive you and, as an act of contrition, sending the Cremator something?"

"Like what?"

"I hear he likes Cuban cigars."

"Hmm, cigars. He does smoke that shit in the yard."

"What you want is to facilitate Pagliano's innately-human sense of forgiveness."

"What I want is you to put the word in with God and protect my ass from getting a shank in the back next time I take a shower."

Murphy blew out a puff of smoke and smiled. Inhaling the last drag, he stubbed it out with his toe, then curled both fists around his cane and stood, blocking the TV screen. Guys in the back started screaming and yelling.

"Drizz, I'm outta here. If I stay much longer, technically that'll make 24 and a half times. Besides, I need to work on my total rewrite of the Gospels. Matthew's version of the Sermon on the Mount isn't funny enough. I'm adding a few hecklers, and Jesus talking smack to the flock."

Suddenly the cane dropped from Murphy's grasp. He wobbled, eyes whirling, face turning blue, lost his footing and stumbled backward, catching himself by grabbing Drizzle's shoulder.

"Murph! You okay, man? You look like hell!"

"Just a dizzy spell. I'm seeing the prison doc tomorrow. He swears it's my prostate. I think I just have a bony ass. See how it sticks out? Feel."

"I ain't touching your ass, man."

Murphy heard the cons in the back cussing him out again. Hunched over his cane, blasts of World War II explosions booming off the dayroom walls, he plucked another smoke from his pocket, then waved it at the men while gesturing the Sign of the Cross.

"Carry on, my wayward sons."

Drizzle shook his head and chuckled. He squinted at Murphy's frail profile, the orange prison uniform that was several sizes too big for the old man, but showing barely a wrinkle, as if the Almighty Himself ironed it out for Murphy every day.

As the priest turned to exit, Drizzle stayed in his seat and tugged on his pantleg.

"Say Murph, how'd you wind up in here, doing fifty-to-life? A nice old white guy like you?" Drizzle had heard the rumors but refused to believe them.

"You mean a disgraced and convicted Catholic priest?" Murphy sighed, as if seeing it all in his mind again. He breathed mournfully. "It's a long story."

CHAPTER TWO

*In the theater of karma, accountability is the
final act.*

MURPHY'D BEEN HOUSED IN A CELL at Folsom for several years, transferred here from a minimum-secu-
rity prison in Mississippi, nearly a decade after pedophile
pastor Father John Geoghan was murdered at Souza-Bar-
anowski Correctional Center in Shirley, Massachusetts,
strangled by a fellow inmate. It was Murphy's fourth
prison, convicted of sexually molesting six young boys.
He'd been accused of molesting more than fifty boys and
girls over five decades in three different states.

When Murphy came to his first prison, Georgia's Macon
State Penitentiary, he was 82, a shrunken little man with
purple veins in his forehead, wavy silver hair, and a
crooked lump of a nose he'd broken years ago falling off the
church altar, which gave him the look of a broken-down old
prizefighter.

Ten years later, at 92, Murphy'd lost a few pounds since arriving at Folsom after cellmates were no longer unable to sneak him contraband items, such as Popeye's fried chicken and cheesy hash browns from Waffle House and pork rinds he'd fallen in love with at his second prison in Florida.

There, he was able to fly under the radar, a model prisoner. Walking out of the movie at Folsom now, his skin as crumpled as an old paper bag, hunched over on a cane from scoliosis, Murph's the only white guy in the yard, respected as a man of the cloth by the other cons despite his heinous crimes. As a sex offender, he knew he'd be a target here, that he could be punched, stabbed or have his throat slashed at any moment. Yet Father Murphy—maybe because he carried his burdens so heavily in his soul—survived.

∞ ∞ ∞

It was a juicy story, Murphy's scandal. Who would have guessed the kindly old priest—a charismatic figure in his Georgia community, shooting hoops with the troubled teens, chain-smoking in the dugout when he coached youth baseball, counseling the recovering alcoholics and addicts in his parish—was a predator, preying upon innocent children? Who could have known a serial sex offender was lurking underneath that snow-white collar?

It was the summer of 2010 when the first accusations broke. The evidence against Murphy came from boys in Peachtree Corners, a suburb 20 miles outside of Atlanta, where Murphy was in his third year of pastoring at Our Lady of the Miraculous Catholic Church. The community was stunned. How could a beloved priest be a sexual predator?

Then more accusations surfaced.

The Catholic Church, expecting a legal circus, tried to keep the accusations quiet. They suspended Murphy, offered to pay for the three boys' therapy, wrote checks to shut the parents up. Then one of the anguished mothers went public.

The flood gates opened. The next day, three lawsuits were filed. Allegations were televised. Newspaper phone lines lit up with more angry accusers, claiming Murphy sexually assaulted them. The Church panicked; the avalanche of victims seemed barely beginning. How many more were still out there, afraid to speak out? Holding the memories deep? The pain, the trauma keeping them silent?

Arrested and eventually charged with twelve counts of sexually abusing minors, the court set Murphy's bond at $800,000. The Atlanta Prosecutor, licking his chops to punish abusers of children, smelled blood. He convinced the judge to remove the seal on Murphy's case.

As the number of Murphy's victims continued to mount, the Prosecutor used local media, releasing videotape of the victims' testimony, seeking swift justice. Sensing an impossible battle, Murphy's attorney begged him to plead guilty, to avoid a trial; he was a new lawyer for the Diocese and had never defended a sex offender before, much less a disgraced priest, and the State of Georgia let him know they were going for the knockout.

In the end, there was no trial. Murphy pled guilty, avoiding a drawn-out criminal court case that would have disgraced the Church, knowing his plea led to a life sentence. Speedy settlements were arranged. Massive cuts of the money—plus attorney expenses—went straight into the pockets of the two lawyers.

At his sentencing, as the judge banged his gavel, Father Murphy hung his head in shame. Moving pictures and whispering voices of the children he'd abused replayed in his head, even as the guards tugged at his sleeve and slapped him into leg irons.

Murphy expected prison would be a living Hell—and he was right. His spine curling in on itself as he dawdled through the gates at Macon State—an overcrowded maximum security prison—the horror stories he'd been fed in the county lock-up suddenly blew into him, and he began trembling.

A week later, hearing whispers about another convicted priest's murder through the prison grapevine, and hardened thugs calling him a dead-ass white man, anxiety took hold. After a month, he was transferred to the Apalachee Correctional Institution near Chattahoochee, Florida.

It seemed the answer to his prayers.

Nine days after arriving at Apalachee, Murphy was targeted—a 260-pound liquor store robber who'd just been transferred from the county lock-up slammed Murph into a wall, landed an uppercut to the balls, and got him in a chokehold. The facility's 366 surveillance cameras had given Murph confidence that any violent misbehavior would be seen and dealt with, that he'd be safe. Instead he was jumped in the shower, rammed with a pipe to the head and kidneys, his bed urinated on, his food defecated on.

Meanwhile, the guards offered no protection. One jammed his elbow into Murphy's nose, breaking it again. He was marked as a troublesome inmate, all his privileges revoked, even visits to the prison chapel.

The beatings got worse. Body shots to the ribs, rabbit punches to the groin, razor blade nicks to the neck. A broken jaw, a ruptured spleen. They didn't want Murph dead, just punished so bad he'd take his own life. A young Nazi with a shaved head shoved a stainless-steel shiv against his eyeball. "Kill me! I don't care!" Murphy demanded, clutching his cracked ribs.

For his own protection, the warden placed him in solitary confinement.

For the next seven days and nights, Murphy considered suicide. The voices of his victims pierced his nightmares. On the eighth morning, he tried to hang himself from his bunk, forcing the warden's hand.

After a month at Apalachee, diagnosed by the prison doc as suffering from a mental condition, Murphy was transferred again, to Mississippi State Penitentiary at Parchman.

Six months and several beatings later, he was transferred, for the final time. This time out West.

He arrived at Folsom a broken man. There, he was placed with all the crazies, the sickest, the meanest, the most psychotic and brutal offenders. *To hell with it,* Murphy decided, surrendering any chance at surviving prison up to Fate.

Turns out dumb luck—or maybe the Almighty—was on his side. The warden at Folsom was a devout old-school Catholic who, in spite of Murphy's crimes, still thought of him as a priest and a Man of God, and took it upon himself to see Murph remained unharmed under his watch. In his heart, the warden prayed for Father Murphy; in his gut, he knew Murphy was already doomed.

Most of the Folsom cons gave him space anyway. Many feared him for being one step away from God, not realizing how far away Father Murphy was from the Big Guy's graces. And Pagliano, a die-hard Catholic from the Bronx, who loved all the old Church rituals, and was seen to weep through prison Mass, leaned into the priest for advice and absolution, hoping to uncover a secret path into Heaven despite all of his sins. Murphy always replied there was nothing he could do to save him, and the Cremator walked away scowling, gloomier than ever.

Over the years, there were appeals by various organizations faithful to the Church for a lighter sentence, calling his punishment "death by incarceration" and citing the old priest's age, though Murphy himself always rejected any petitions.

Years Seven and Nine, Murphy came up for parole. Each time, he was denied—a denial Murphy felt fitting for a pedophile.

Now Murphy spent his time bullshitting with the bikers in chow line about Fantasy Baseball, or locked in the prison library, reading romance novels, obsessed with *The Bachelorette* reruns and rewriting the New Testament, turning the Books of Matthew, Luke and John into a screwball comedy he knew would never see the light of day. In some ways, he was happy to be locked up, no longer forced to listen to daily confessions of the same sins over and over, nor to those whose temptations a convicted pedophile priest might find appealing. *"Father, I sinned, I masturbated over my sister's girlfriend in the boys' bathroom."*

Prison solitude allowed him time to reflect, to hold himself accountable, to look in the mirror and see the monster who wreaked pain and destruction in the hearts and minds of so many young children. The one thing he prayed for now was a way to reverse the carnage.

His last cellmate, a ponytailed dude from Oregon who flew cocaine into Florida's Port Everglades, and arranged getting Murph's contraband fried hushpuppies flown in from his favorite restaurant down South, had been released. Finished his time and left for a new life in Phoenix. Something died in Murph that day. He saw time running out.

And suddenly being alone—and dying alone—scared Murphy.

And then Drizzle arrived from New Orleans, sweet as a peach and newly born-again in prison. "Man, I'd fight 15 rounds with the Devil, if the Big Man let me," he told Murph with that gleaming smile. Murph watched the kid make the rounds of C Block, guiding drug dealers to pray, radical bombers to come to Jesus, and proposing a prison fellowship ministry to equip inmates to become Christians. It made Murphy wistfully recall his years in the clergy, spreading the Gospel and defending the faith.

Maybe prison had done him some good, Murphy thought, as he left the movie and went outside to light up a cigarette and wait for Drizzle. Softened his relationship with the Big Man, he realized, exhaling a long stream of smoke, the prison air feeling good on his face. Locked inside four walls with no one to face but God, there was nowhere left to hide. Yet the voices and the nightmares continued. He'd be haunted forever by three words: *Don't tell anybody.* Haunted, Murphy knew in his soul, all the way to the grave.

CHAPTER THREE

In the Depths of Darkness, God dwells in the silence.

THE NEXT MORNING MURPHY, STOOPED and limping, entered the cell he shared with Drizzle, his eyes on the floor. He'd spent the morning with the prison doc, and looked exhausted. He found the young black kid seated on the top bunk, hunkered over a dog-eared spiral notepad, scribbling madly with a blue pen.

"I just spoke with Doc Dillard," Murphy said.

Drizzle wasn't listening. *Maybe he hadn't heard,* Murphy thought, too busy doodling words and childish stick figures, eyes fixated on the page and head down, wrapped in a purple do-rag bandanna.

Annoyed, Murphy banged his cane on the floor. Once. Twice. Drizzle ignored him.

Murphy looked at the kid for a long minute, sighed, then drew back his cane and gently tapped it against the bunk frame. *Tap, tap.*

"Man, I'm busy," Drizzle said, and kept scribbling.

Murphy raised his cane and hammered the bunk in frustration. Drizzle didn't react, so Murphy poked him in the ribs with his cane.

"You listening to me?"

Drizzle stopped writing. He flipped the notepad shut. His eyes wandered over to Murphy, then squinted.

"Yo, man, what's all this damn hostility about?"

Murphy didn't answer. His throat felt like it had been sliced with a razor. To the kid, it looked like the old man had been kicked in the stomach.

"What's eating your dumb ass, man?" Drizzle asked.

He looked over. The old man swayed as if in a trance. Murphy's eyes flicked between Drizzle and the floor, then the four concrete walls, then straight back at his cellmate.

"The doc ran some tests. They came back positive."

"Positive for what? That you're an asshole?"

Murphy's face stayed expressionless. "Positive for prostate cancer, stage 3. Sorta fitting for a pedophile, don't you think?"

"Stage 3. Ain't that a bitch?" Drizzle said.

They were walking along the wire fence by the prison basketball courts. Father Murphy watched the cons play, throwing up wild shots, not one of them hitting the backboard, his shoulders hunched, his eyes expressing nothing.

"What you gonna do, Murph?" Drizzle asked. He cast a sidelong glance at the elderly priest, pain and tenderness washing across Drizzle's face.

Murphy allowed himself a small dark chuckle. He rolled up his sleeves. Both forearms were crosshatched with shiny bandages. "They poked and stabbed and stuck me in just about every vein imaginable, including places I'd rather not think about. Doc says they won't prescribe expensive drugs for the pain until the symptoms get worse. Later, they might put me in a special housing unit."

"But the doc can fix it for you, right?"

Murphy stared. "Doc says they can shrink it, but they can't cure it."

Drizzle hung his head. His eyes wandered off to the swirl of inmates running on the court, ripping into each other for a rebound.

"My Pops caught that shit last Christmas," he said. "Only 52. Always eating fried foods, fried chicken, fried onion rings, deep-fried Oreos, fried potato chips and pork rinds and glazed jelly donuts. Last time I saw him the man couldn't piss so much as a trickle, said his balls swollen so big and so bad he could barely walk."

"You ever heard of TMI? I just got diagnosed this morning, Drizz."

"Maybe the doc will let you see a specialist, might give you some inside about experimental drugs."

"You mean *insight*."

"That's what I said."

Murphy smiled. They walked in silence. Murph lit a cigarette, Drizzle cupping his hands for the priest to shield the trembling flame from the wind. Murphy drew on his cigarette, working the butt between his thumb and middle finger, and realized the sun felt surprisingly cold. "Hell, Drizz, who wants to live forever anyway?" he asked.

Drizzle was about to answer. Suddenly Murphy grunted and groaned and bent over. "Ah, God!" he moaned, leaning against his cane to keep from swaying.

"Damn, Murph! You okay?"

"I'm fine," Murphy insisted. He thrust the burning cigarette between his lips, coughed and laughed. "Probably that turkey meatball burrito I ate for breakfast. Death by burrito is the fifth leading cause of fatality in America, you know."

Murphy coughed, lips quivering, arms hanging at his sides. Finally he straightened up, tamping the cigarette out with his toe. Drizzle stared, puzzled.

"Man, I can see you hurt. But cancer can't take you down, only make you cry out to the Lord in your trouble. God got the final say." He placed a hand on Murphy's back, felt the flutter of his heart. "I'm prayin' for you, Murph. The darkness you facing can't diminish the Light of Christ, even when the whole world 'round your ass is crumbling."

Light, my ass, Murphy thought. He squinted against the slanting sunlight. "Well, don't start memorizing the last rites just yet. Doc Dillard said I could have a year, maybe two. I'm hoping the end comes sooner. I'm not adverse to having some disturbed sicko like the Cremator stick a shiv into my heart one night."

"Man, keep quiet with that Cremator shit…"

In the distance they saw the Cremator, hobbling across the prison yard with a limp and a scowl. His goons were there, doing push-ups and wind sprints and pumping iron, boasting about the banks they'd robbed and the men they'd beat up, flexing their muscles, trash-talking each other and butting heads. Murphy noticed the hard stare the Italian mob boss was giving Drizzle.

"What the hell's *that* about?" Murphy asked.

"Dude's still pissed about me droppin' that weight on his foot. Says he's gonna cut my ass."

"You sent him the cigars we talked about? His favorite ones, a gift to ease his anger?"

"Hell yeah, brother."

Murphy pondered and shrugged. "Maybe they weren't Cuban enough."

Watching the goons slamming their shoulders against each other, Drizzle froze for a heartbeat, feeling the Cremator's angry stare scorching his soul.

They kept walking, Drizzle taking long strides, Murphy hobbling unsteadily. Inmates shooting hoops tore up and down the court at the far end of the prison yard. Murphy lit another cigarette and exhaled. He held the butt while Drizzle took a long pull. The kid wiped his mouth with his orange sleeve, a worried look on his face.

"You believe in God, Murph?"

It seemed a long time before Father Murphy found an answer.

"You mean a God who sits back and watches little boys being abused? Who allows monsters like me to prey on innocent children? Who chooses not to intervene in their suffering? Who allows torture and brutality and hatred and murder to be part of His master plan?" Murphy glanced around the prison yard, eyes probing. "I don't see God anywhere in all this pain. And even if there is a God here, He stopped talking to me a long time ago, son."

Drizzle felt a heaviness in his chest. He took another pull from Murphy's cigarette, kept walking and shaking his head.

"When I was a kid," he said, "God was never real to me. Just this invisible thing. Never said one damn word to me. But then, my first night in lock-up, God spoke. 'I want you to build something for me, Drizz,' The Big Man said. Wanted my ass to build Him a seafood shop, 'bout 60 miles outside of New Orleans."

Drizzle stopped, pulled the spiral notepad from his back pocket, flipped through the scribbled pages of notes and building diagrams and cartooned fishermen.

"Thought I was trippin' at first. God want me to go into business? He say, *Yes, Drizz.* Say, *Write this down.* We get catfish straight from Lake D'Arbonne, crawfish and fried alligator, too. Say my Daddy gonna run the place with me. Then when he's old enough, little Jamal take over. Be my last shot for forgiveness from my old man. Set things right with him. And with *Him*." Drizz tucked the notepad in his pocket, pointed his finger at the sky.

Murphy chuckled so hard the kid also had to laugh, then shook his head. "You know what I felt, when I heard the voice of God? Back when I was a young priest? It was the first time in my life I saw my purpose. I felt like I'd been touched by God. But then God abandoned me. Pulled a fast one, and revealed that my purpose was to be a monster, a fiend, a drooling pedophile, a predator, His tool for suffering. That's when I lost faith in God and His purpose."

Hollers erupted from the basketball court, one inmate throwing down a slam dunk. Murphy closed his eyes and leaned forward on his cane, his face brooding. "Problem is, without faith, I have nothing."

Drizzle looked stunned. A chill passed through his body. He stared down at the stooped-over priest, uncomprehending. Suddenly he froze Murphy with a grin.

"Man, I call bullshit."

"Bullshit?"

"I don't see no monster when I see you. I see a old man runnin' fast as his ass can from what he once hoped he could be. I see a man runnin' from his true purpose."

Father Murphy looked up, puzzled, and smiled. He tried not to tell the kid there was no such thing as purpose, as hope. But he turned away, and bit his tongue to keep from screaming.

Wednesday night. 11:50 P.M. Pale moonlight creeping through the cell. Murphy rolled in his bunk, clutching his lower back, his neck twisted into knots, his pulse racing. He held his breath, trying to keep the pain down. He moaned, grunted, and his face contorted.

Drizzle rolled over, heard him yelp, finding it unusual that the old man was awake.

"You okay, Murph?" the kid leaned down and whispered. He was met by two feverish eyes staring back at him.

"Murph! You look like *hell!*"

Murphy cursed, veins bulging in his temples, pain roasting his brain. "I feel like I'm giving birth," he said, stifling a laugh. After several gulps of air, he began to cough and wheeze.

Seeing this, Drizzle swallowed hard.

"Man, listen. Can you hang on 'til the morning headcount?"

Morning headcount? Murphy thought. *For Christ's sake!* Biting his lip then, his eyes slid to Drizzle, and he nodded.

"I hear them bikers smuggle in Oxys," Drizzle whispered. "They trade 'em with the mob guys workin' the prison kitchen for bottles of booze and Dunkin' Donuts. Soon as lockdown's over, I'll go down there, see if they'll trade me some Oxys for a couple packs of your cigarettes."

Yes, nodded Murphy, unable to speak or breathe. Drizzle winked and they slapped palms. Then the kid cupped his hands together, closed his eyes, and in the dark cell started to pray.

"Lord, please, if You can hear me, save Your servant Father Murphy. Give the man Your mercy. Give him healin'. And give him a sign, so he can find his way back to You. Lord, let there be light in this man's life again. Let there be light, Jesus!"

Murphy remained silent, watching his young cellmate fall deeper into prayer, Drizzle's shadow rocking back and forth against the far wall. Rolling in sweat, Murphy smiled, then slowly turned away, so the kid couldn't see his tears.

∞ ∞ ∞

Thursday morning. Murphy startled awake on his bunk, tears of agony on his cheek.

He labored to catch his breath. Sweating, his guts twisted into knots, he awkwardly rose from his mattress, pain sending stabs up to his brain. Finally he stood and scanned the top bunk with a hopeful smile.

No Drizzle. *What the hell? Where was the kid, with those Oxys?*

Murphy waited until 10. Drizzle didn't come. Murphy was in so much pain that he missed breakfast. 11 o'clock and then 12 passed, and Drizzle still hadn't returned. Murphy had the shakes bad. He needed a smoke, but was out— Drizz had taken the last of his packs to barter for pain pills.

Cursing, he remembered the kid liked to watch afternoon cartoons in the dayroom. No Drizzle there, he discovered, only Huckleberry Hound playing to empty chairs. Frowning, he watched lifers filter into C Building for group therapy, newbies in leg shackles marching in from Reception.

Finally he asked one of the armed guards on the third tier, waving his cane as he approached.

"I'm meeting my cellie here. Black kid, Drizzle. You seen him?"

The guard looked up, sort of surprised, hiding a half-chewed cheeseburger and a bag of Cherry Pop Tarts behind his back. He frowned, squinting at Murphy.

"Drizzle your cellmate?"

Murphy, starting to smile, said, "Yeah."

The guard kept staring at Murphy. "You don't know nothin', do you, old-timer? Drizz is dead, Pops. Pagliano murdered him."

CHAPTER FOUR

To fall is human; to rise again is the anthem of the soul.

FOR TWO DAYS, FATHER MURPHY grieved. He lay stiff on the bed in his lonely cell, clutching his blanket, staring up at Drizzle's empty bunk, eyes sunken and lifeless. He refused to eat or sleep. He hobbled alone around the prison yard, chain-smoking cigarettes traded by one of the Aryan bikers for Murphy's extra Jell-O, his heart ridden with guilt, his soul stabbed with anguish, his mind blazing with spasms of inextinguishable rage.

Ah, God, why him? Why the kid? he asked the heavens, staring feverishly at the clouds with red-veined eyes. *Drizzle would have given his life to serve You! Where are You, God, when Your children turn to You for protection? Who will hold Pagliano accountable for murdering Drizzle? You?* He dropped his head and waited for an answer, knowing one would never come—not from God anyway.

Two days passed like this. On the third day, his hands trembling, blind with stinging rage, Murphy went looking for Pagliano.

He approached the Building B shower entrance, his pace quickening. There Murphy found the Cremator and five of his goons in the shower room. The Cremator was stripped of his orange jumpsuit, butt naked, flexing his muscular arms and smiling at his mob, his gel-styled hair glistening with steam. The other big bruisers wore towels wrapped around their waists.

Murphy came lurching furiously out of the shadows. The minute they noticed him, guys stood in his way, staring the old priest down, blocking his path to the Cremator.

"Hey, Pagliano, you scumbag!" Murphy rasped with a menace. His eyes promised violence. Looking down, he saw the Cremator's bare left foot was reddish-purple and swollen, the result of Drizzle's mishap.

Scanning the stooped-over mouse of a man, Pagliano smiled. "Look who's here! Father Short Eyes! How's your boy Drizzle? Still getting your kicks giving blow jobs to young black boys, Father?"

A vein throbbed in Murphy's forehead. He fought back the tears. "Why murder the kid? And not me? *I'm* the monster here!"

Pagliano stared innocently at the elderly priest, then turned away.

"Why couldn't you just *forgive?*" Murphy screamed, waving his cane, whacking goons out of his way. Snatching the Cremator's arm, Murphy's hand hooked around the mobster's wrist, his fingers accidentally grazing Pagliano's nude hip.

Startled, Pagliano flinched and threw himself backward, his eyes bulging with disgust. His upper lip curled in repulsion. "Why you old perv," he hissed. Quickly his eyes flicked to his men, who met the mobster's burning stare.

That did it.

Pagliano's fist smashed into Murphy's jaw. There was a bright flash in Murphy's brain. Then the Cremator slammed Murphy in the belly to make him scream. Murphy's head spun around, and he was hit by first one goon's fist, then another, with so much force that his cane flew across the room.

Soon he was surrounded, gigantic brawny thugs raining punches to the kidneys that dropped Murphy to his knees. Blood dripping from his chin, they hoisted the old priest up by the armpits, then dumped him in a heap under the shower spray, cranking it to HIGH.

Around Murphy the men choked on hysterical laughter. Pagliano strolled over, leaned down with a malevolent glare. Then he spat in Murphy's face. "Pagliano don't forgive. Only God forgives," he said.

∞   ∞   ∞

Murphy was discovered unconscious in the shower room by the guard coming on duty. Three inmates carried the old priest to the prison medical ward. There, Doc Dillard sutured Murphy's face, iced the bruised purple lumps rising over Murphy's left eye and torn ear, also finding a cracked rib and two of the priest's teeth knocked out. The whole time, Murphy's stare was blank. It made Doc Dillard want to cry.

"What happened, Murph?" he asked, poking around Father Murphy's bloody scalp. "Cut near the eye like that, it's damn lucky you didn't go blind. I ought to hospitalize you for brain damage." He swabbed with sterile gauze pads above the eyebrow to stop the blood. "What purpose does it serve trying to hold the Cremator accountable for killing Drizzle, God rest his soul? Might as well try to hold the Pope accountable for putting your ass in here."

The old priest's gaze stayed vacant. Suddenly his expression changed. His jaw slackened, eyes flicking into focus, as if he'd been struck in the face by an insight, an epiphany, a holy vision.

The Doc's right, he realized, feeling a prickle at the back of his neck. *Yes, the Cremator murdered Drizz—but Pagliano's not the only one who should be held accountable.*

But who else is? he pondered, staring quizzically at the ceiling. *God? For allowing the Cremator and his thugs to even exist? For giving vicious men the opportunity, time and again, to brutalize, terrorize, steal and murder, to rain down bloodshed on the weak and the innocent?*

All at once the words sounded familiar, as the faces of Murphy's young victims came charging into his aching skull. *What's the difference between me and the Cremator?*

Cringing at the thought, he winced as the Doc finished stitching up another large gash under his left eye socket. Doc Dillard's words were forming something deep in

Murphy's soul, something he hadn't felt since writing those letters to the Bishop in the seminary years ago. A sense he could, he had to—had a *duty* to—do something. But what?

The final thought came out of nowhere, in the form of another question—the answer so clear Murphy's head shot up, causing Doc Dillard to stab his cheek with the suture.

"Sit still, dammit Murphy!" he grumbled. His words though were distant, as the question exploded in Father Murphy's mind.

What's the difference between the Cremator and the Creator?

Murphy shifted his gaze and looked at Doc Dillard. Suddenly the difference was clear, Murphy wincing twice as the Doc patched his ailing ribs.

The Cremator gives orders. God doesn't. Pagliano instructs his henchmen, telling them who to butcher and how to get the job done. And God? God tells his apostles to "go build Me a church." With no playbook. No instructions. When they asked Him how to construct it, God said, "Follow your heart." When they asked Him how to run it, He said, "Have faith."

God's misplaced faith in men created a man-made church which has committed the worst crimes in human history, a church which indulged rapists and torturers by hiding them in robed majesty—like the priests who trained me then raped me, urging me to say nothing, using religion as their cloak of silence!

Murphy's eyes watered—not from the pain, but from the memories. Memories flooding back about his first crush on a girl. Then painful memories of his first homosexual encounter with another seminarian, at the age of 14. He felt dirty after his superior sought the same from him at 15.

Writing letters to the authorities at 16, eventually he gave up.

What was the use when his appeals for help were never heard, when nothing would be done, nothing would change?

And what about my accountability? Murphy's jaw tightened. *What about me—sending poor Drizz to Pagliano for some Oxys, when I should have seen the danger? I'm just as accountable for Drizz's murder. If only I hadn't been placed here, in Folsom. If only I'd never touched a child. If only I'd been strong enough to ward off the priests who raped me, violated me! If only I'd turned those predators in so someone could stop the abuse!*

The light in Murphy's eyes grew slowly now, as his thoughts raced.

The trouble didn't start with God—it started here, down on Earth. If the Bishops, the Popes I wrote letters to early on, asking them for some sort of counseling—if those pleas were answered, maybe none of this happens. But no, they stuck their heads in the sand, ignored the obvious, shuffled pariahs like myself around from parish to parish, so we could abuse again.

His eyes burned brighter now, like an erupting volcano, overflowing with emotion. Intuitively Murphy knew: This was a moment he couldn't turn back on.

Had I not abused. Not landed here. Would Drizz still be alive? My abuse may have caused Drizzle's death. But I wasn't born a pedophile. The priests, the Pope, the Catholic Church and the Vatican are accountable for that.

Murphy stared up at the gleaming surgical lamp shining in his face. Hypnotized by the light his lips trembled, then curled into a crooked smile.

Somebody needs to hold the Catholic Church accountable. Hold them accountable for the raped and violated children. And that includes me. If God can't stop the abuse, fix it, save the innocent, maybe some earthly justice is what's needed!

Murphy's chortle pierced through the pain, causing the Doc to drop his suture. Both Doc Dillard and the guard raised their eyebrows.

Poor guy must be hallucinating, the Doc ruminated. Then he stared into Murphy's eyes. They stared back, alert, bright, on fire. *And holding some strange mystery,* the Doc thought, as the men stared at each other.

Dillard cleaned up the cuts and stitched them tight. He dropped two pills into Murphy's mouth. Then he turned to the guard. "Take him back to his cell."

The guard helped Murphy to his feet, handed him his cane, guided him toward the door. Twenty minutes later, the same guard returned, scratching his head, a dazed look in his eyes.

"That old guy was talking crazy," he told the Doc. "Said that beating was the answer to his prayers, a sign from God. Laughing his fool ass off, like it was some big joke. Said something you mentioned about the Pope showed him the path, showed him the Light and the way. Plus he said he wants to see the Moose."

"The Moose?" Doc Dillard considered this for a moment.

Mustapha "Moose" Ahmadi, born Maurice Jeffrey Mayweather but converted to Islam in prison, was a loudmouth, take-no-prisoners political radio host, at one time the most successful "shock jock" on West Coast FM radio. Said to be the meanest and the angriest convict in Folsom, he was arrested in Long Beach on a charge of murdering one of his radio guests with a claw hammer. Five cops tried to jump the Moose, but the Moose snatched up his hammer and started bashing skulls and smashing heads. By the time he was in cuffs, two squad cars having been called in from Compton as back-up, four uniformed bodies were piled at his feet.

Word was the Moose, five years into a life sentence, had trained himself to be a jailhouse lawyer during his stretch in Folsom.

"Why the Moose?" the Doc wondered. The guard shrugged, looking stumped.

"Beats me. But that's not the craziest part, Doc. Old guy kept yelling that he's a weapon now. Said it came to him, why he was put here, what his purpose is. 'God's using me as a weapon,' he said, 'a tool, to stop the abuse, to set things right.' Can you believe that? Oh, and God told him to do one more thing."

"What's that?" asked the Doc.

The guard waited, holding his gaze. "Sue the Vatican," the guard said. "God told Murphy to sue the Vatican, for making him a pedophile."

CHAPTER FIVE

To do the impossible, become the impossible.

A T 9 A.M. THE FOLLOWING MORNING, Murphy crawled out of bed, and went hunting for the Moose.

Thirty minutes later he stood hunched in the Moose's doorway, C Block, Cell 71, second tier. Lying in the shadows of the bottom bunk he beheld the angriest-looking man he'd ever seen. A brilliant radical political thinker. A controversial radio host, known for his inflammatory conspiracy theories, harassing his call-in listeners and threatening in-studio guests, the Moose's eyes were those of a madman, a lunatic, and pierced Murphy's soul like the tips of sharpened icepicks.

His shaved head slumped back on his pillow, his goateed chin pointed directly at the priest, the Moose wore expensive red Air Jordan sneakers he'd boosted from an ex-football linebacker in A Block. The name ALLAH was tattooed in the very center of his forehead.

Locking his fingers behind his head, sinking further into the brown-stained pillow, the Moose listened intently.

When Murphy stopped speaking, he rose and strode toward the priest. Inches from Murphy's twisted nose, the Moose snarled.

"You think it's a sign from God? A message from God?"

"Of course."

"Suing the Pope? The Vatican?"

"Yes."

"The entire Catholic Church?"

"Yes."

"You're crazy," the Moose snapped, shaking his head. "You're yanking my chain, old man. Nobody's that stupid." Then he shoved the priest hard enough that the old man's teeth rattled.

Walking back to his cell Murphy remained undeterred.

∞   ∞   ∞

Later that day, Murphy limped, his right leg dragging, his steps unsteady, and again went looking for the Moose. He wheezed to catch his breath, colliding with inmates as he crossed under the guard tower. He peered into the mess hall, into a Substance Recovery meeting. The Moose wasn't anywhere in sight. He asked a guard watching the surveillance footage on four tiny TVs, a fifth one with a spider-webbed cracked screen; the guy frowned then said he was pretty sure since it was Saturday and the Moose was probably at the movies.

His knees buckling, Murph stumbled into the dayroom. Tonight's movie was one of the *Die Hard* flicks, Murphy couldn't tell which one. Fragments of twisted metal and roaring fireballs flew across the TV screen. A throbbing lump at the base of his skull, Murphy scanned the room for the Moose. At last he noticed him seated in a middle row, leaning back with his feet on the chair in front of him. Murphy plowed through the row of seats, waving his cane, inmates cursing and scattering to get out of his way.

The Moose looked up. The sound of men ditching their chairs to escape Murphy's cane broke the movie's spell.

Murphy approached the bald-headed convict and leaned over him. He fixed the Moose with a shining stare.

"Sit the hell down, dammit!" The Moose shouted, trying to shove the old man out of his way. "You're blocking the screen!"

"Moose, I need your help, please!" Murphy gasped, his face almost purple. He leaned down and put his hands on the Moose's shoulders.

In anger the Moose grabbed the priest by the front of his prison jumpsuit, shook him and cursed him, ready to bust him in the head until he saw what he was too angry to see earlier: Murphy's bruised and bashed-in face, coagulated blood stuck to his mangled ear. Murphy's stitched-up lips painting the agonizing portrait of a man running on empty.

"Help? Old timer, what you need is a *gravedigger!*" he grumbled, carefully dropped Murphy from his grip, and had the guards toss the nagging old man from the dayroom.

Two hours later, as the movie ended, the Moose returned to his cell, plopping onto his bottom bunk. He heard a clicking noise from the corridor, then shuffling footsteps. Looking up at the door, he saw the shadowy figure of Father Murphy hovering there, staring in, leaning on his cane.

"Come on, Moose, say you'll help."

"Man, get lost."

"I'm begging you."

"Begging me to what? Sue the Vatican? That's fantasy, old man."

"Do I need to get down on my knees?"

"No."

"Then what's the problem?"

"The problem is the last idiot who tried to help you got a knife in the back."

Murphy sighed. His back and his knees ached from standing. "Okay. I'm sensitive to that."

"And it's nuts. You can't sue the Vatican. You can't blame the Pope for making you a pedophile. No priest has ever done that."

The Moose turned his face away, not wanting to hear any more preposterous ideas. Seeing this, a sense of desperation slithered through Murphy's soul.

"Moose, listen, just hear me out. It's important."

The Moose didn't move or speak.

"If you'll just hear me out, I'll leave. I'll split. *Vamos.* Otherwise, I'll just stay here all night bitching and moaning and whining and getting on your nerves."

The Moose slumped his shoulders and groaned. He rolled his eyes and turned back to the priest, drilling him with a deadly stare.

"Why come to me? You need what? A lawyer?"

"I just need somebody with legal know-how. That's all."

"I don't like priests."

"Me neither."

"I don't like talking with priests."

"I'm not a priest. The Church excommunicated me."

The Moose frowned, fixed Murphy with a squint. Finally, he turned away. "I don't give a crap. Let me sleep."

Murphy's face turned ashen. For a time he didn't move. Then he waddled over and plopped on the edge of the Moose's bed. He poked his cane against the bald con's sneakered feet. *Tap, tap.* The Moose growled but didn't move. *Tap, tap. Tap, tap.* Finally Moose shot up on the mattress.

"Stop that!"

Tap, tap. Tap, tap.

"Son of a bitch!! What *is* your problem? You asking for another beatdown?" His eyes stabbed back at Murphy, shooting him a soul-searing scowl that could cut through ice. "I told you I'm out. I told you this was insane. And even if you find some lawyer to take the case, and win, what then? You're a priest!"

"*Ex*-priest."

"You're a holy man! The Vatican will never allow you back in the Church again! And they'll never forgive this!"

"You still don't get it."

"Get what?"

"It's not their forgiveness I need."

The Moose frowned. He tried to push Murphy off his bed. "Go away, man. I can't help you. Nobody can. No lawyer is stupid enough to get in a fight with the Vatican. It's absurd, and Almighty Allah in the Quran warns us to avoid the absurd." He gave a merciless scowl and kicked the old man's cane off his feet. "The only option you have is to represent yourself."

Murphy stared in disbelief. "How would I do that?"

"By not wasting my time! That frees your ass up to go to the prison library, study the law books there, and review the database of legal cases." Seeing Murphy was about to say something, the Moose cut him off. "You've seen *My Cousin Vinny?*"

"Eleven times. So?"

"So if Joe Pesci can hoodwink an Alabama jury into saving two dumb-ass New Jersey white boys from the electric chair, by some miracle maybe an old geezer like you might be able to beat the Vatican."

CHAPTER SIX

The heart that responds to God's whisper is a vessel carved by lightning.

THE NEXT DAY, MURPHY SHIFTED into high gear. He started at 8 A.M. sharp, waiting for one of the cons to open the Folsom prison library, moved two tables together, grabbed a stack of law books down from the shelves, wiped the dust and mildew from them and got up to speed.

Without time for anger or grief, he cracked open *We The People Legal Primer* and *The Jailhouse Lawyer's Handbook,* and flipped to the instructions on how to file writs, appeals and motions. Shelving those volumes, he pulled down the library collection of Supreme Court rulings on cases involving legal challenges.

Rolling up his sleeves, Murphy ponderously opened Volume One, peeled back pages to the table of contents, focused on church litigation, reading case briefs, studying depositions and trials. *This is no different than studying for seminary,* he told himself.

Quickly he found he had no clue about filing a motion, or entering an appeal, with any degree of competence. For many aching hours, Murphy sat there, alone in the sprawling library labyrinth, wondering what he was doing. And in his heart, as he did on the day Drizzle was murdered, Murphy felt the weight of doom creeping in.

"Intercede for me, Lord," Murphy pleaded, as he dropped exhausted into bed that night, feeling the flutter of anxiety in his chest. "Even though I spent decades turning my back on You, please help me."

As he lay in his bunk, in agony, he tried to muffle the groans and moans of pain stabbing his back, unable to control the spasms in his legs. He felt sick, and then sicker—so sick that even lying about it to Doc Dillard no longer worked.

"What's happening to me, Doc?" Murphy asked the following morning, wheezing mightily as he climbed onto an exam table.

"What's happening is all that jailhouse lawyering is killing you," Dillard said.

"That's pretty severe, don't you think?"

"Maybe. But that beatdown you took from the Cremator sure didn't help."

"This is your diagnosis?"

"This is what your body is screaming at you. You're punching your ticket straight to the grave, Murph. If you don't quit this hallucination, you'll be dead in a month. If you don't get into chemo, you'll be dead sooner."

Murphy shook his head in distaste. They spoke about his options for another hour. The next day, he scheduled an appointment for chemo.

Escorted by two guards, Murphy approached the hospital entrance, his pace slowing with every step. While the uniformed officers stood outside, Murphy, robed in blue, sat reclined in a chemo chair, pale and drawn. He watched the intravenous drip enter his body and felt the world spinning, beads of sweat running down his neck.

"Agh...Aaaaghhh..."

"Which part of your body hurts?" asked the pretty pink-cheeked candy striper, no older than seventeen, as Murphy squeezed her arm.

"It burns in my groin...aaaaaghhh..." he moaned, fear and terror in his eyes.

Two weeks later, Murphy was back for a second round.

"Is something wrong, Father?" the candy striper asked, looking into Murphy's red-veined eyes with concern.

"These drugs, these drugs..." he groaned.

The young girl smiled, tapped the IV drip with the tips of her fingers. "Any side effects?"

"Side effects"? Murphy had to chuckle. "Only nausea. Vomiting. Fatigue. Sometimes I weep in clinical depression. Hair loss. Oh, did I mention my balls are in excruciating knots? And..."

By the time Murphy left his third chemo, hobbling back to his cell, he was in a state of full-blown desperation. He collapsed onto his bunk, burrowed under the moth-eaten prison blanket, his eyes burning.

God, I'm so tired, he thought, *please let me get some sleep.* But he lay awake, scared and staring at the ceiling. He shivered in the darkness, waiting for sunrise. Doc Dillard had said his time was running out. *I've wasted so much time,* Murphy realized, and once again felt betrayed by God.

The next morning, his knees buckled as he climbed out of bed. Standing at his sink, gripping it tight for support, he gazed out of his cell window, pondering.

It was a foggy day in February, the pine trees and clouds outside fuzzy and out of focus. *No more,* he told himself. *I can't do this anymore,* tears filling his eyes. *I need help. But who?*

Turning on the tap, he splashed cold water on his face. He only knew one real, honest-to-goodness heavyweight attorney, he concluded. One lawyer supremely skilled and nervy and daredevil enough to take on anything.

Murphy'd kept tabs on the man over the years, knew where to reach him. *Do people reach out to their antagonist, their opponent, their greatest enemy?* The thought hurt his brain. *They do when it's too late for anything else. They do when they're trapped and cornered, when they can't outrun Death anymore.*

His mouth dry, Murphy focused his eyes carefully on the cracks in the ceiling, seeking a revelation. After what seemed like hours, he looked around the cell for something to write with.

For the entire morning, Murphy sat alone on his bunk, hands quivering as he scribbled and scrawled letter after letter on yellow legal-sized sheets. The writing looked stiff and shaky; each word squeezed Murphy's heart.

Outside the window he could see it was nearly noon; the bright sun hurt his eyes. His wrists aching, Murphy got up, washed his face again with cold water, grabbed another yellow sheet of paper and let out his breath slowly. With a passion igniting behind his eyes, he snatched up his pen, stabbed it at the paper one last time, and began writing.

Dear Attorney Vance,

I have a feeling you remember me, Father Charles Murphy.

I can't thank you enough for the steadfastness and determination you displayed in court, making certain I was found guilty and put away for a long time.

I recall the look on your face when I asked the judge not to forsake me in his sentencing, like God did in allowing the creation of the pedophile and monster you so easily and rightfully pointed out I had become.

I have thought of you often and remained grateful for your efforts in seeing that justice was served.

I am writing because I want to access those efforts to hold the one source that allowed me to continue abusing. The Vatican.

I wasn't born a pedophile, Vincent.

I was groomed and nurtured into becoming one.

I look back and see the father and husband I could have become; my first sexual urges were always for a woman. Something neither you, nor my thick-as-a-brick attorney, brought out at my sentencing. You didn't because I never told you, for fear the Catholic Church would find some way to spin it as a defensive tactic. You see, I wanted to plead guilty from the beginning. Something I'm certain my idiot defense attorney never shared with you.

Now I have come 180-degrees.

In the past, I asked for forgiveness from my victims, not expecting to receive any but rather, I suppose, as a way of soothing my soul as I approach the end of my time. So many of the letters came back, marked RETURN TO SENDER, *that I gave up.*

I know your hatred for me runs deep. Know my disgust with the man—the monster—I became is just as strong.

I also have a sense, through reading how you have defended so many victims, that your desire to put a stop to the insanity also runs deep. Your tireless prosecution of monsters like me is proof enough.

I ask you to look at the bigger picture. Allow me to help you put a stop to the abuse once and for all. Seek justice on a higher level and finally hold those accountable in a way they will never be able to ignore.

I ask you to represent me in suing the Vatican, and finally putting to rest the pedophilia the Vatican has openly allowed to run rampant throughout its institution. Provide solace to the hundreds of thousands of children—now adults—whose lives have been ruined by the Vatican's callous disregard for human life.

I ask you to seek a judgment so great it will tear down what our God has created. Maybe help start it anew with a fresh brand of real priests whose urges can be tempered by marriage and family, and who can give back through a Church that holds no secrets.

Please consider this request not as one from an old man asking for forgiveness, but as a request for all the children whose lives have been traumatized by monsters like me.

Thank you for taking the time to read this, Vincent, and please know all secrets are now truly off the table and open for all to hear.

Sincerely Yours,
Father Charles Murphy

Then Murphy took the sealed letter to the prison mailroom staff and had it stamped, postmarked from Folsom to Memphis.

His throat aching, he returned to the cell, slipped quietly into bed. Finally he slept, dozed for an hour, then woke with a whimper.

The cell was muggy, bright with blinding sunlight. As Murphy lay there, his tortured memory quickly took control.

Soaked in sweat, he thought of Drizzle—Drizzle with his gleaming smile, his spiral notepad of doodles; Drizzle with his mad scheme to build a seafood hut, to cook alligator and boil crawdads in the Big Easy; Drizzle with that self-righteous zeal to plan a future, to redeem his past, to trust in an unknowable God who could wash away all his sins.

Dozing, finally falling into REM sleep, Murphy's dreams revealed grown men and women, sobbing loudly. Fighting back their memories of the rape and torture so many years before. Lost lives revealing lost souls, floating into the abyss.

He awakened to fear, the tears falling.

The cell was shadowy, his skin clammy. He tried to bring something else to mind.

Reaching for the pillow to smother his nightmares, his mind still numb from haunted memories of his young dead cellmate, the faces of his victims now invaded his waking thoughts. Murphy could hear their voices echo through the cell. They whispered in his ears. Letters he'd written years ago. Seeking forgiveness. Some returned unopened with the word *Monster* scrawled across the envelope. Another with *Die in Hell*. One from a mother, containing a picture of her son, days before hanging himself.

Their faces popped in and out of the air. Murphy felt their hands on his face, clawing at his back, pounding him, blood tingling on his flesh. Their voices grew louder and louder. *Unforgivable. What you did is unforgivable, Father. Why? Why us?* Then as Murphy's mind choked off the voices, he heard his own, slamming into him, whispering to his victims, calling to them from his past—

Don't tell anyone.

Never tell.

Never tell.

Never—

Heart pounding, Murphy sat up, tears dripping down his cheeks. The room was empty. Daylight surrounded him. *Did I scream out loud?* he wondered, working himself into a darkened corner of his bunk.

He put his head down and listened; no more voices, only his lungs wheezing painfully. *I'm so sorry!* he wanted to say, his thoughts blubbering, hoping the voices would take pity on him. *I'll make amends! I promise! Just give me more time!*

A new burst of tears exploded from Murphy's eye sockets. And then something snapped inside Murphy.

It hurt his knees to crawl out of bed, but Murphy did.

It took ten minutes for him to limp down to the dayroom, another ten to hobble to the prison chapel.

The church was deserted in the early morning chill. Blundering inside, Murphy dipped his fingertips into the font of holy water, crossed himself, staggered past the plastic potted palms and the stained-glass windows, falling to his knees at the carpeted altar rail. Then he bent forward, clasped his wrinkled and trembling hands together, heart pumping blood faster and faster, beads of sweat dripping from his brow, and with all his soul prayed.

"God, I'm sorry! I thought it was a sign from You. I don't care about You forgiving me. This isn't about me. I just want to protect Your children!"

He tilted his head back, keeping his eyes focused on a statue of Jesus hung crucified on the wall, splashed with morning sunlight. "This is a war. *You* should be waging it, Lord, not me! I want to believe, I desire to believe in this battle, but it's too much for me! It's too—"

Again the voices of his victims surged up inside of him. If they would just be quiet, he'd be fine, he could do this. Murphy took a few deep breaths, his head throbbing, and felt the unforgiving face of God was staring down at him.

What are You waiting for, God? he thought. *To betray me with another sign?* Finally the words he'd been holding back blazed out of him, tears springing from his eyes.

"I'm *sorry*, Lord! *I can't do this!* I *can't!* I'm not the right man for this!" He held his empty hands wide. "I can't hide from what I've done! And I can't fight the Vatican! It's too much! It's over, it's hopeless!!"

He leaned back, grieving for help, arms extended, the statue of Christ glowing. "Please take me, God. Please take me home, Lord!" he shouted and clutched at his bursting heart.

CHAPTER SEVEN

*The hardest part of the journey through trauma
is believing you're worthy of the trip.*

F*ORGIVENESS IS OVERRATED*, ATTORNEY VINCENT Vance
thought, pulling his sunglasses down to the bridge of
his nose and squinting.

Attorney Vance had listened to his client repeat those
three words in his Memphis office an hour ago. Now as he
stood convened with his legal associate and ex-partner Jesus Juice, a/k/a Jay-Jay, at the Shelby County Animal Shelter, on the east side of the Mississippi River from Arkansas,
two o'clock on a Friday in January, those three words replayed endlessly in Vance's brain.

Forgiveness is overrated.

Forgiveness is overrated.

Standing before the two men was Kennel 17, the last
kennel in the shelter's concrete canine shed. Staring up at
them from the pen's floor was the accused, a skinny white

mongrel dog named Fatty. Stamped on the dog's green plastic collar was a single word: BITER.

"This is the dog?" Vance asked. Adjusting his sunglasses he peered down at a red line painted on the floor, two feet outside the kennel—a warning for visitors to keep their safe distance.

"This is the dog," said Jay-Jay.

"This is the fugitive hound from Hell our client, Dr. Oglethorpe, wants to sue for $500,000?"

"Well, he's not actually suing the dog, Vince."

"Since when did we start taking dog bite cases, Jay-Jay?"

"Since we started needing money to chip away at your gambling debts, Counselor."

Vance sighed, plucking the sunglasses from his nose and placing them in his breast pocket. He narrowed his eyes at Fatty. Silently the dog watched them, sitting on its haunches, acting as cool as they come. Vance noticed the mongrel's eyes were pale blue.

Vance rubbed his face and mumbled something. All over the kennel forty other dogs were howling and barking.

"You want to hear the particulars?" Jay-Jay asked. Vance nodded.

"Through my rather lengthy investigation, here's what I found out." Flipping open his notepad, Jay-Jay read. "The accused—that's Fatty here—belongs to Dr. Oglethorpe's neighbor, a Mr. and Mrs. Danny Chablis. The long and the short of it is that last November 9th, at approximately 4 P.M., Fatty was so hot and horny he jumped the fence and did the dirty deed on the Oglethorpe dog, an expensive purebred Black Russian Terrier named Moonbeam. Sixty-three days later out pops a litter of raggedy-ass white pups. So Dr. Oglethorpe, justifiably miffed and suitably enraged, hot-foots it over to the Chablis home, knocks on the door, Fatty here answers and bites him, takes a big chunk out of the good doc's ring finger. Now he's suing the Chablis family and their dog for half a mil."

"Dr. Oglethorpe, he's what? A heart surgeon? A neurosurgeon?"

"He's a podiatrist, boss."

Attorney Vance turned to Jay-Jay, giving him a squint.

"Look, Vince, I know what you're thinking. What moronic, back-country brain-dead redneck Shelby County jury is going to believe a dog bite is worthy of 500 grand? And under normal circumstances, I'd agree. But what the hell, we need the income. We need a client. Even if we are suing for dog bites."

Vance chuckled. "To support my affluent lifestyle," he muttered. He noticed the dog was staring at him now, blue eyes watery and shining.

Vance surveyed the other kennels, arranged in four concrete rows, noticed the three cages nearest to Fatty were empty. At the end of Row 4, a cute little college-girl volunteer held a steel door open for a young couple, and out hopped a fluffy, white-coated Pomeranian, ready for adoption. For a long moment, Vance just stared. Then he turned back to Jay-Jay, trying to analyze the situation.

Jay-Jay—real name Jesus G. Jussio, a third-generation Mexican-American who clawed himself out of a drug-filled ghetto, passing the Tennessee bar at age 22 —stood 5 foot 2 inches tall. The size of a 12-year-old child, he flexed full-sleeve tattoos of Our Savior Jesus Christ fighting a bear and a tiger across both arms under the faded TITAN UP! T-shirt he'd worn since stepping away from his practice two years ago.

Once Jay-Jay'd been a District Attorney in Philadelphia, a master at obtaining death penalty verdicts at high-profile murder trials. He made a bundle but was waging a complex but losing struggle after learning the innocence of one death penalty convictee only hours after the man was denied a pardon and received the needle. For the next few years he wandered the streets mumbling case law to lampposts, still searching for a verdict that might undo the one that broke him.

Later known for filing flimsy and frivolous personal injury lawsuits and getting sub-par awards, Jay-Jay was now a pony-tailed and bearded burn-out of the American legal system, smacking gobs of Dubble Bubble chewing gum.

Vance pivoted his eyes back to the dog. Fatty hadn't moved, just staring up at Vance without a word. "I honestly don't understand why we're even discussing this case," Vance said. "Our specialty is automobile wrecks, personal injury lawsuits, picking up rich clients from overbooked probate lawyers, a couple of divorce cases a year, and the occasional whiplash cheater."

"None of which offer long-term payoffs," said Jay-Jay. "What we need is something with maximum billable hours."

"Although there's nothing wrong with straight cash up-front," Vance said. "Can we cajole Dr. Oglethorpe into a quick settlement?"

"Dude says it's non-negotiable."

Vance snorted. The dog was still watching him, never blinking. "What's the downside?"

"Downside? We get picketed by PETA, the ASPCA, Friends of the Animals and every other animal rights org on the planet. Our street rep, crummy and sub-standard as it already is, plummets to diddly-squat. Or, we take the case, get our butts kicked in court, the Doc sues us for malpractice and we lose the few measly assets we still have."

"Is there *any* upside?"

Jay-Jay shrugged. He watched the young couple cuddle the happy Pomeranian. "The Chablis family got scared, dumped the dog here, hoping to avoid a suit and financial ruin, and praying somebody'd adopt the poor pooch. But look at him..."

Vance's eyes pierced the cage. Fatty's ears were out-spread now, flaring out almost horizontally, floating on both sides of the mutt's head like grungy angel wings, the eyes still focused on Vance, pathetic and pleading.

Jesus, Vance thought, with a grimace.

Jay-Jay flipped his notepad shut, gave the dog a warm, longing smile. Vance scowled, rubbed the back of his neck. *I cannot believe I'm doing this*, he thought miserably.

"What about the case, boss?"

"How much money again? Our end?"

"Our end? You mean supposing the Oglethorpes don't drop it, don't win, they don't settle? Maybe two grand, after we pay the two months' back rent, back IRS taxes, and the 30-percent interest you still owe Freddie the loan shark on that Alabama football wager."

"And how much is currently in the firm's kitty?"

Jay-Jay gave Vance an embarrassed look.

"There must be something in the bank. Right? Personal capital? Business capital?"

"A few grand, chief. And Greasy Grimes, your lovable landlord, has his hands all over that."

The dog kept staring at Vance. As far as he could tell, it hadn't blinked once. All over the shelter stray terriers and pit bulls barked in a frenzy. Jay-Jay cleared his throat. "What about the case?" he asked.

Vance watched as Fatty lowered his head, then lay down, muzzle pressed to the cold concrete, staring at his empty water bowl. Vance felt his neck get hot.

"The *case*, Vince?" Jay-Jay asked again.

"Drop it," Vance said, and took a step over the red line. He hunched down, extended his right hand to the dog, fingertips inserted through the wire cage. The dog paused, looked up, ears laid flat. Finally it rose and came to the wire, pressed its muzzle to Vance, sniffed and then lovingly licked his fingers. Once. Twice.

"And the dog?" Jay-Jay asked. "What about the dog?"

Vance reached in and stroked the scruff of the dog's neck. Gently Fatty raised his head, and nudged Vance's fingers, staring at Vance.

81

"He's scheduled for EU at 5 P.M.," Jay-Jay said, pointing to the dog's chart hanging down from the wire fencing.

"EU?" Vance said.

"You know," said Jay-Jay, and mimed an invisible syringe needle being stabbed into his wrist vein, the plunger going down. "That's if nobody adopts him. Then it's sleepy-time-time, like that song by Cream."

"Nobody's going to adopt this dog," sighed Vance, rubbing the mutt's plastic collar. "He's a biter."

Both men continued staring at the dog, in perfect unison. Immediately Vance regretted coming here. Was it because the poor dog had been abandoned, with nobody left in his life to come up to bat for him?

He patted the dog's chin and saw that Fatty was missing one of his front teeth. Heaving a sigh, Vance's eyes held the dog's for a moment, feeling some sort of connection. Was it pity? Maybe. Or maybe it was guilt that the little fellow was locked in a cage. *Who knows if he's really a biter,* he thought. *Maybe he just had a bad day, a moment of foolhardiness, one bad decision. Maybe he just needs a second chance...*

Finally Vance stood, looked away, and strolled back behind the red line, putting his sunglasses on to hide his eyes. He looked over Jay-Jay's right shoulder at the Memphis sun going down. *Forgiveness is overrated,* he reminded himself. *Hell, Vance, life is all about the luck of the draw anyway. If it wasn't for bad luck, you'd have no luck at all...*

"How long we gonna stare at this dog?" Jay-Jay asked.

"You're staring, too."

"Maybe you need a therapy dog, help you with all your stress, instead of more extra-strength Prozac."

The dog rubbed its ear then took up its position again, sitting back on its haunches, head raised and blue eyes staring up at Vance through the wire mesh, not even blinking. Vance's throat closed up and his insides went dry. Then his heart melted.

"Alright, buddy," he said. "You win."

∞ ∞ ∞

Ten minutes before closing time they walked out, Vance carrying the dog through the animal shelter gates to his beat-up little 2005 Honda CRV with a dinged fender, cracked sunroof and dented door, Jay-Jay bitching about money.

"How much was the adoption fee?"

"250," Vance said.

"Which we can't afford."

"I put it on the maxed-out Discover card. I'll cover it tonight," he said, knowing he'd have to raid his secret, shrinking cash stash at home.

Looking down at his feet, Jay-Jay just shook his head.

Approaching the Honda, Fatty slobbering wet kisses all over Vance's face, the attorney grimaced and handed the dog to his former partner. "I'm late," he said, climbing in the vehicle and fishing for the keys in his pocket.

Jay-Jay clumsily put out his hands, took the wiggling dog. "Another disciplinary hearing?" Vance slammed the keys into the ignition. "You don't want to walk? It's only four blocks to the Bar Coalition."

"No," said Vance and rolled the dirty window down. "Meet me in an hour at Teasers."

Jay-Jay thought for a moment, listened to Vance crank the tiny engine, then threw a look at Vance, his eyebrows coming together sternly. Teasers lay on the rough side of town, an ill-lit high-crime area that tourists avoided, its peeling walls holding a strip club with wall-to-wall sports betting.

"What's the matter?" said Vance.

"No more screw-ups, right Vince?"

Vance didn't answer, just kept grinding the motor. Jay-Jay held tight to Fatty's collar, to keep the dog from leaping into the car. "You want me to take the pooch back to your place? Get him cleaned up?"

"Are we sure he doesn't have a problem with bladder control?" Vance pictured the mutt left alone in his house. "Maybe we should cut off his direct access to water?"

"The truth?"

"Please."

"Fatty already lost control twice." Jay-Jay shook his head, and a tiny smile curled on his lips as the dog licked him.

Vance had to squeeze hard on the gearshift to put it in reverse. The little Honda jerked drastically into gear, Vance backing up in a zigzag, leaving Jay-Jay and Fatty in the parking lot, the dog barking and wagging its tail, both of them choking on the exhaust. They watched it make a right turn at the corner.

A few seconds later, zooming back up the street was the Honda, Vance skidding to a stop in front of them. Swinging the dented driver's door open he pointed his finger at Fatty. "Hand me the dog please," he said. "No one deserves to die without a second chance."

Jay-Jay handed him the dog. Vance placed Fatty on the passenger seat. Vance's eyes bore into the dog's. He lifted Fatty's face to his, and sighed, "Forgiveness is not over-rated, buddy."

∞　∞　∞

Driving past four bars, three pawn shops, Papa Kay-Joe's Southern BBQ and Miss Girlee's Soul Food, Vance parked in the lot behind Slymm's Gym. Slymm's was already jammed with cars, parked three deep, thirty minutes before the rush hour.

Vance was part of a boxing club at Slymm's. Sixty minutes of therapy three times a week for stressed-out paralegals and cops, lawyers and probation officers and insurance adjusters to forget their caseload, forget their back pain and unpaid bills, their screaming kids and over-inflated mortgage payments. For Vance, pushing 60 years old, it was physical therapy on steroids.

Slymm's was a safe place to hit the speed bag, to throw jabs at his anxieties, to take out his aggressions on some overworked Soulsville accountant in the ring, to punch through his addictions and all the sins of the past slithering through his brain since fleeing Atlanta.

Fleeing from his ambitions. From the trauma permanently etched in each victim's face. Their stories of abuse haunted his soul.

Then there was the face of the pedophile priest he tormented on the stand. Daily. Remembering the words of entrapment he used to victimize each child. "I told the children, it was 'our little secret,' that God was listening."

Vance knew it all too well.

While the Murphy verdict earned him a nice payday and a place in attorney heaven, just thinking of the $50,000 loss on the Braves shipwreck of a World Series was a metaphor for his life. The loss shook his core.

There were missed AA meetings. Broken relationships. The need for one last drink.

He couldn't outrun his nightmares—but he tried. Tried to forgive—himself, others. All he felt he was the craving: to get blinding drunk. To place a bet that could keep him alive. Secretly hoping a loss would justify his self-imposed isolation, from everything and anyone.

He knew he needed a change. The sandstorm in his head kept how at a distance.

Today had to be different. Shutting it out, a priority. Vance wouldn't be hitting the gym. Instead, he flashed his perfect teeth at the lot security guard, tossed him the keys to the Honda, and disappeared down the sidewalk toting Fatty under his arm to the Memphis Bar Coalition, a dingy one-story brick building on the narrowest street in the city.

The hearing was already underway when he blew in the room.

Everything stopped abruptly as the broken latch on his briefcase unexpectedly popped open, sheets of paper and rubber-banded index cards falling out and scattering across the floor. The five attorneys on the disciplinary panel watched him snatch them into a pile, fumble to find his seat at a desk, clapping his hands to get Fatty's attention away from peeing on the wall.

The dog came and sat under Vance's chair, nuzzling his leg gently.

"Thank you for showing up, Counselor," muttered one of the attorneys, introducing himself as Booker Harris, a pompous-looking bankruptcy lawyer in a pinstripe suit.

Vance smiled, re-knotted his tie, adjusted the microphone on the desk and cleared his throat. He noted the heavy eyelids on the faces of the four other lawyers. As the charges against him were read he hung his head, having heard it all before in a previous disciplinary hearing. This was his second violation of Rule 9, an investigation into grounds for suspension or disbarment.

Vance knew in Tennessee that three strikes could mean he was out. Loss of license. End of career. Thank you, and goodnight, Irene.

"The council has made a few inquiries into your case history, Counselor," Attorney Harris grumbled into his mike with a wicked smile. Vance pulled out a legal pad, pretending to take notes, while Harris read him the riot act. "While you were a living legend in Atlanta, sir, a gifted litigator who excelled in trial work—a fighter for justice, a defender of the innocent, hell, a *crusader,* some would say— here in Memphis you don't seem governed by the same ethical and moral standards every member of this panel strives to uphold."

Beneath the desk, Vance heard Fatty growl. He placed his hand over the mike and gently shushed the dog.

"The truth, Counselor, paints an ugly picture. And the truth has come home to roost today." Harris turned to the others, face fixed in a frown, then read from his itemized notes. "Our investigation revealed the following facts: an ex-wife with an unpaid divorce settlement, pending litigation for credit card fraud, illegal Social Security loopholes for seniors, loan shark debts and nuisance suits and allegations of ambulance chasing and..." he droned on and on and on.

"But let's get to the real meat of the problem, sir." Harris rose from his seat, looking down at Vance, and spat into the microphone. "You are an *addict.* You are addicted to booze and gambling. You are out of conformity with Rule 9 of the Board of Professional Responsibility of the Supreme Court of Tennessee." Harris sat and hissed fiercely. "Which brings us to today. What sham, deceit, false pretense or fairy-tale fabrication can you possibly offer this council that would persuade us to not rubber-stamp your disbarment pronto?"

Fuming inside from the pompous arrogance spewed in his direction, Vance was about to counter in an even more bombastic voice when he caught Fatty's eyes boring in on him. Head tilted, the dog's probing eyes stopped Vance dead on. His new companion of less than three hours seemed to sooth his soul. Understand his fears. Penetrate his anger.

Turning slowly toward Harris, Vance calmly uttered, "I'm getting the drinking under control. I'm in AA. I have a sponsor, sir. The gambling, I'm working on and will beat it. Everything else will fall into place when I do."

Loudly clearing his throat, Vance continued. "If I'm given 90 days, sir, the proof will be evident. That, I promise you Mr. Harris."

For a fleeting moment, Vance almost believed his own words.

∞ ∞ ∞

"Probation," Vance scowled.

"You lied, didn't you? You son-of-a-bitch!" Jay-Jay chortled.

There was Vance, Jay-Jay, Ted the taco truck owner from East Memphis, and Easy Money Cecil an hour later at Teasers, the sports bar and strip club Vance frequented on the corner of Beale Street and Rufus Thomas Boulevard. Vance was on his third bottle of Viva Las Lager beer, his head buzzing, Jay-Jay drinking watered-down Diet Cokes, Fatty munching a $7 hot dog, everybody sitting in the glow of Vance's triumph in keeping his law license.

"I can't believe you pulled this off!" Jay-Jay hollered.

Vance slapped Jay-Jay's hand, glanced at all the guys in the bar, watching as two girls stripped to Van Halen's "Hot For Teacher" in the next room, blonde hair flying.

"Dance, baby, dance!" Jay-Jay wailed. Vance looked at his ex-partner, eyes spinning. *Life is good, bro,* he almost said out loud. Okay, maybe his credit was crap; pretty soon even the bartender and the strippers at Teasers would figure that out. But in the eyes of all the chemical-dependent bozos and losers and regulars at Teasers, he was a local hero, a guy who despite his setbacks continued to beat the system—and one who needed more than a few ice-cold Vegas Lagers as congratulations.

Eyeing the Memphis Grizzlies game on the big-screen TV gave Vance an idea.

Pulling out his cellphone, he clicked on the screen, scrolled quickly through the miniature icons, pressing his thumb on an app for sports betting. He scrolled past Fantasy Football and Fantasy Baseball then clicked on the NCAA college basketball schedule and the Gonzaga vs. Alabama game, tip-off in 5 minutes. The money line was on Gonzaga at +135. For a split second, Vance hesitated. Less than three hours since boasting he could become a model citizen, the bet was just too appealing. Besides, celebration was in order. Even Jay-Jay was soaking it all in.

Vance was a compulsive gambler. He'd taken all the high-profile sexual abuse cases because he was an adrenaline junkie, addicted to the thrill of winning, the rush of outwitting his opponent, the spellbinding drama that transported him from being a nobody to a legendary king of the courtroom and stroked his ego. He was also $3,200 in the hole to a shark on Austin Peay Highway for Game 1 of the

World Series, when the Braves star closer choked and gave up 5 runs to the Red Sox.

It's your day, Vance, he told himself, floating with booze. *Fate, Karma, Lady Luck—they're all riding on your shoulders tonight, big guy. Let's rock.*

Feeling hope and destiny surge through him like a runaway freight train, he placed a $200 bet on Gonzaga. Then he put the phone back in his pocket, watched the strippers grinding and bobbing their wild blonde heads to Van Halen, ordered another hot dog for Fatty and signaled the bartender for his best bottle of Heaven's Door Tennessee bourbon.

Three shots of Heaven's Door trickled down, and now Vance felt better. No, not just better, *immortal. Invincible.* In an hour he would win a $470 payout. His fingers began itching for another bet, so he thumbed open the app to the NHL hockey screen and placed a $200 bet on the Nashville Predators game.

Jay-Jay had gone home, taking Fatty back to Vance's place, Vance telling him he'd be there in an hour. Half the bottle gone, Vance was starting to feel bodiless. The lights felt too bright.

Rather than pass out, Vance wandered around the bar, every now and then remembering to check the scores on the big screen, then teetered down a filthy hallway toward the men's room. He stood dizzily in front of the gleaming toilet, unzipping his pants. Urinating, he stood there a long time, arms hanging limp at his sides, spending the money he'd win tonight in his head.

He continued urinating, his thoughts swirling happily, swaying drunkenly. He wiped his mouth with his sleeve. There was something weird about the lights; the fluorescent bulbs in the men's room seemed to rotate, a gleaming and revolving triangle of brilliant reds and yellows, spinning so fast Vance couldn't look at them. He heard somebody coming up behind him, though he hadn't heard the door open.

That's when Easy Money Cecil slapped him on the back. And the next moment he heard Ted's voice shout: "Hey, somebody get a mop! Vance is pissin' on the jukebox again!"

∞ ∞ ∞

Minutes later Vance was sitting on the curb outside, staring hypnotically at the buzzing neon Teasers sign, trying not to throw up into the gutter. His hair was wet and plastered against his skull, beads of sweat dripping from his brow.

Over his shoulder he heard the music booming "Round and Round" by Ratt, the slashing guitars and slamming drums making his stomach lurch. The city lights of Memphis shining above him were too bright, giving him a migraine, and the cold January wind surging over the Mississippi River blew trash everywhere.

I don't understand it, Vance thought, keeping his head down. Sure, he'd been drunker than usual, pissed himself and gotten kicked out. The worst part was Gonzaga and the Preds losing their damn games, and Vance's $400. Those were sure bets! He let his thumb roll over the edge of his cellphone, its dark screen telling him the battery was dead.

Vance closed his eyes and felt humiliated. Now he'd have to atone for the lost money by getting a case somewhere, begging Jay-Jay to bag him something. Anything.

Cold winter wind howled around Vance's ears. Though his nausea hadn't passed, he staggered up, standing shakily on his feet, and walked along the cracked and lonesome street of bars and tattoo parlors to his car. He thought of hitting Slymm's; it was open 24-7. Instead, he climbed in the Honda, wiped his mouth with the back of his hand, and drove around looking for an open liquor store.

Thirty minutes later, with a squeal of tires and a slamming of brakes, Vance arrived at his home. The little house was bleak, the windows dark, the whole neighborhood depressing. He got through the front door, heading straight for the kitchen and a beer.

Vance, you need to eat something, brother, his dizzy mind warned him. He finished two beers and a bucket of leftover Popeye's chicken, found Fatty asleep on the couch with a note from Jay-Jay: THOUGHT YOU SAID AN HOUR, BOSS. Smiling, Vance stroked the dog's head, plugged in his cellphone, hit the voicemail button. And his smile vanished.

Eleven missed messages. *Christ.*

The first was from Vance's son, Jordan. "Hey Dad. It's me, Jordy. Remember? Your son? The one who got married last weekend? I'm calling to make sure you're alive. You didn't make it to our wedding, and Beth and I are worried you've fallen off the wagon again. I really thought you'd be flying down...you said you would. But I'm used to you bailing out at the last minute when it comes to family things. Okay, well, that's it, hope you're okay. Over and out, Pops."

"Shit," Vance sighed. His fragile peace of mind crumbled. *As if I didn't try to be a good father. Hell, maybe I was gone a lot. I suppose the fact that Jordan called and said he was concerned shows I was at least present in his life. Don't know where I got that from, considering my old man was emotionally absent 99% of the time. Cheated on my mother. Abused her. And then the asshole never missed a Sunday Mass! How many times can a man ask for forgiveness for doing the same shit?* He winced, felt a twinge to call his son back, then let it go and deleted the message.

The second message was from Vance's ex-wife. "Vince? It's Marsha. I can't get by on the alimony you're sending. Plus you were a week late with the last payment. I'm going back to court this week to petition for an increase in — "

Vince deleted that message as well, then the next eight. Four were from his sister, which he deleted without listening. Three were robocalls. The last message was from Jay-Jay, sent at 11:12 P.M.

"Bad news, Chief. That sexual abuse case you turned down, must be a year ago? The 17-year-old kid, Frankie Moran, who was raped by his high school football coach? Just heard the kid committed suicide. Hung himself in the closet." There was a long pause, the phone line crackling. "Oh, plus there's a letter at the office from Folsom Prison. Thought I better open it. That priest, Father Murphy, the old pedo you put away? That crazy psycho wants you to sue the Vatican."

94

Vance shook his head. He tossed the beer can aside, went to the refrigerator and pulled out two more beers, then returned to the couch and deleted Jay-Jay's message. There was a long stretch of silence.

For a while Vance sat on the battered and lumpy sofa, trying to erase the message about Moran and Murphy by shutting his eyes.

Finally, feeling the urge and picking up one of cold Buds, he dug his thumb with savage force into the beer can and trembled with anger at himself for not taking the kid's case. And now Murphy. Coming back to haunt him.

Damn you, Murphy. I put away a scumbag—a serial sex molester—for a lifetime of crimes committed against innocent children, and now you've come back? And not just back, but blaming others, blaming the Catholic Church? Probably blaming the court, the whole system, and my ass too, Vance thought, sagging back and taking a deep breath. He couldn't get his head around Murphy's request. *Sue the Vatican?*

He lurched up and walked with heavy and lifeless feet around the room, replaying the voicemail in his head. He felt triggered, mocked, brimming with hatred, wishing the old priest had simply stayed a bad memory, buried in the past, a tragedy that time had slowly faded, instead of a reminder of who Vance once was.

VANCE THE SAVIOR. He'd read that somewhere in a Georgia newspaper, or maybe seen it on TV. ATLANTA DA TAKES DOWN PEDOPHILE PRIEST. Back then he was Attorney-At-Law Vincent Vance, one of the South's best and brightest. He'd turned down joining his father's law firm, struck out on his own as a crusader against abusers in the state's largest county. He'd fooled the voters, the judges, fooled everybody—especially himself. Until the day he crumbled and fled. And why? No matter how hard he tried, Vance couldn't pretend he didn't know the answer, the secret truth he kept trapped behind a mental door. *The truth that turned you into an old pissed-off drunk guy phishing for clients on the Internet, the kind of weak, scum-sucking lawyer your father would have been disgusted by.*

Why can't you forgive yourself? What's your excuse now?

Vance lay back on the couch with the dog, letting Fatty lick his face. He pictured Father Murphy floating above him, the elderly predator watching and mocking his every move, still craving to fondle young boys. Murphy had been out of his life for more than a decade now. Why couldn't he just stay there, locked away in the prison of Vance's mind?

And now this kid, Frankie Moran. *I said I'd have nothing to do with sexual abuse cases after Murphy. Never go near them. And now the kid hangs himself, when I know I could have brought some semblance of peace. Get a conviction to ease the pain.*

Now who's the scum-sucking lawyer?

As the lights dimmed, Fatty's head melting into his lap, Vance knew sleep would only bring the monster he'd become.

CHAPTER EIGHT

To seek forgiveness is to walk barefoot over a field of thorns.

WHEN THE PHONE RANG, VANCE had been asleep on the couch for hours. It was after 11 A.M. He rubbed his burning eyes, blinked at snoring Fatty through the stinging sweat, then answered the call.

It was his sister, Janice.

"Hey Sis, listen," Vance said, his tongue still swollen with booze, "I'm really busy right now, can I call you back tomorrow, I'm—"

"Have you talked to Mom?"

Vance couldn't believe it. *Talked to Mom?* "Not a word. Why?"

"Vince, I've been calling you for days! Haven't you heard?"

"Haven't I heard *what?*" There was a pause on the line. Vance waited, sensing a cold draft in the house.

"It's Dad."

"What about Dad?"

"Dad had a heart attack. He's at Methodist University Hospital. In intensive care."

∞ ∞ ∞

Vance sat in the Intensive Care unit with his mother and sister, waiting for his father to wake. Both women's eyes were weepy and red. In his hand Vance held a bunch of flowers. Beyond them his father lay in a hospital bed, doped up, hooked to beeping monitors, stiff and rigid on his back, hands clasped to his chest, eyes closed as if the old man was lying in a casket.

"You okay, Mom?" Vance asked. His mother made no reply. He could see the events had caused her face to sag, her shoulders to slump. He checked his father's chart, flipping through pages, scanning the blood pressure readings, the list of painkillers and antibiotics.

"What are you looking for?" His sister was giving him strange looks.

"I don't know. Any fever, mental deterioration, brain damage."

"Since when did you become a doctor? You haven't seen the man in five years."

"Do you mind if I check?"

Suddenly his father grunted. He roused and opened his eyes. Vance bent forward in his chair. "Hey, Dad. How are you doing? It's me, Vince."

His father squinted, blinked, then stared over at Vance. He said nothing. His eyes were bloodshot, surrounded by purple bruises. Finally he turned to Vance's mother with a scowl. "What the hell's *he* doing here?"

Everything went silent. Vance was met by six eyes, staring at him. For a moment, it was as if he sat naked before his aging parents. Then he leaned down, brushed his father's hair with his fingers, and uttered a gentle, "Dad, I'm here. I care about you."

His father grunted. Fists clenched, he ignored Vance's hopeful smile.

"You *care?* You didn't care about my feelings when you ran your career into the ground. Or when you couldn't hold onto that bitch of a wife you married, or—" he paused, wheezing and coughing, trying to catch his breath, then continued. "Instead, you became a drunken jackass, a self-pitying crybaby—not to mention the time you tried to slit your wrists. You were 14 years old!"

He coughed again, a gagging cough, like he wasn't getting any air. Veins bulged in his face. Finally the old man controlled his breathing, then sank back in his bed, staring Vance down.

"Wow, Dad, *really?* This is how you talk to me, the first time in half a decade?" Vance watched his mother dry her tears on a handkerchief.

"You were accomplishing great things," his father jumped back in. "Until something happened and you threw it all away."

"Holy hell! Can't we get past this, Dad?"

"Don't use the H-word to your father!" His mother dabbed at her tears.

"Maybe Dad doesn't *want* to get past this," his sister interrupted.

Vance looked back over his shoulder at his sister. He sighed, dropped his chin to his knees, in shock.

This is what he needed right now? A lecture from his parents? From his three-time divorced sister? Was it too much to ask that they not eternally judge a guy for the sins of his past? *Aren't they ever going to forgive me?* He'd held the tears in all these years, the disappointment, disapproval and rejection. Now their knives were out, and they were carving him up for bait.

Suddenly his father rolled away from him, to the other side of his bed, grunting and reaching around for something. "I need to use the toilet. Where's the damn toilet?" he roared.

"Here's your bedpan, dear."

His mother handed it to him, propped the pillow behind his head. She turned to face Vance, placed a hand on his shoulder, eyebrows lifted in fake innocence.

"Are you drunk, son?" she whispered. "Are you drinking again?"

"I'm not drunk!"

"You know how you get when you're drunk. Have you been going to AA, like you promised? Have you been gambling, Vince?"

Vance felt a cold anger pierce his heart. He watched his mother take a comb from the bedside, neatly and carefully combing his father's hair.

Silently Vance rose, placed the flowers on the bed. He told his sister he'd call later to check on Dad. His sister said not to bother. Then he walked out of the room, left his mother and sister weeping. As he rounded the corner and entered the hallway, he willed his own tears to come.

∞   ∞   ∞

Spasms of rage exploded out of Vance. He ran to the bathroom. Jumped into a stall to loudly sob away his shame. Going through half a roll of toilet paper, the rage mounted. Finally calming himself, he realized his only solace was a violent workout.

He drove to the gym, wrapped his hands, then cleared his mind of the stinging regrets by ripping mercilessly into the heavy bag, slamming it with left hooks then right hooks until his entire body broke into a sweat. Then he pounded the bag with combinations, beating it nonstop until his hands throbbed with pain and his legs gave out.

By the time Vance got home, stopping first to buy a bottle of tequila, his brain felt fried. He drove with his fists clenched on the wheel, anger bubbling inside of him. The moment he walked in the door and Fatty saw him, the dog rolled over on its back and smiled.

"Not today, fella," Vance said.

"What?" Vance asked. He wondered if he was the kind of drunk knucklehead who'd talk to a dog. *Go on, Vince, say something stupid.*

"I bet you forgave your family, for dumping you in that kennel. Didn't you?" The dog raised its eyes, looked up at him thoughtfully. Vance bent down to pet the dog, then broke into a twisted half-grin. "I bet you'd even have forgiven me, if I'd left you there."

Fatty licked Vance's hand, peering up at him. Vance sat on the sofa, resting the tequila in his lap. He closed his eyes and was submerged in thoughts of his family.

"To hell with 'em," Vance muttered to himself, opening a bottle and taking a sip. "To hell with all those shitheads," he told Fatty. He wiped his lips, took a chug of tequila, rolling it around on his tongue. Instantly he felt the pain in his head going away, the sharp edges blurring.

He'd hoped seeing his family would have a cathartic effect. Instead, it was a stark reminder to Vance of all he wasn't, all he'd lost.

Slowly he fell into a deep dark sleep.

His dreams melted one into another, an endless tunnel of memories. Images and faces rushed through his brain, nothing at all making sense. There was the Reggie Jackson outfielder's mitt his father had given him on his 7th[h] birthday. There was the Big Wheel his mom bought when he was 8. There was the bully he punched in the 4th grade and little girl in 5th grade who liked him, what was her name? And little Vince scrunched up in the back seat of their '69 Chrysler as his parents drove him on the first day of being an altar boy. The smell of the priest's after-shave making him want to vomit. And then there was the kid, young Frankie Moran, the rape case he'd turned down. All those years wasted in law school studying his balls off to protect and save the innocent, and the reality was he couldn't protect anybody.

The dreams pounded through him, flooding Vance's mind. All that wasted bravado, all those lies opened wide, all that pain eating him alive.

Running away was not the solution. But Father Murphy's original trial, that had taken just too much out of him. Wasted him like he never thought possible.

What he thought would be the trial to end all trials — would put him in the driver's seat, maybe even see him make attorney general — did just the opposite. Drove a wedge between himself and everything, everyone, he loved. He didn't know why. And he just couldn't forgive himself for the fuckup he'd become.

Forgiveness was almost an impossible dream. His father was right. He was not worth anyone's time.

Vance lurched sharply awake at three-thirty, with a blinding hangover. It was dark in the house, and the air was suffocating. Fatty lay tucked beside him, snoring in his sleep. Vance hugged the dog, clutching it to his chest. He took a few deep breaths, tried to get his bearings.

He wanted to do something; did he have enough gas in the Honda to get there and back? All he had in his wallet was a $20 bill and three maxed-out credit cards. Not much money at all. *Christ.*

He thought of the stash of cash he'd hidden away, money he'd committed to never touch again, after paying off Freddie the loan shark and the IRS. The commitment, a self-imposed punishment for his years of indiscretions.

His head was spinning.

A passing headlight flashed through the house, fracturing the silence.

You need to do something, Vince.

Every instinct in him recoiled at what had to be done, but the need for forgiveness screamed louder than reason.

"I'll be right back," he told Fatty, while the dog pressed its warm nose against his arm. "And no, you can't come."

He gave Fatty a forced grin as he patted the dog's head. Then he grabbed his keys and a bottle of Rolling Rock and went to his car, spinning out on the neighbor's knee-high grass as he steered into a U-turn.

The ride wasn't a long one. The kid's parents lived in Lakeland, a suburb, 18 miles from Memphis down Interstate 40, then another two miles past the Cracker Barrel.

Vance drove drunk. He slurped down the beer, tossed the empty on the floorboards, let it rattle around. Halfway to Lakeland he started wishing he could roll the clock back an hour and cancel this insane quest. Maybe seeking forgiveness from somebody would provide him with a good feeling, even if it was a stranger; maybe not. As his phone's GPS led him closer, he decided to ignore his fears. *I can do this. I'm strong. Hell, I'm Vance the Savior.*

As Vance rolled into the neighborhood, he scanned the house numbers for 427. A Volvo station wagon was parked in the driveway. Under the moonlight the lawn looked green and sculpted, just like every other lawn on the block.

He parked quietly behind the Volvo, climbed out of his vehicle without a sound. It seemed like a long walk to the front door. He hesitated a moment, certain everybody in the house was fast asleep, then raised his right hand to knock, his mind ready to be confronted.

For three minutes Vance stood there, his fist raised, his body swaying. He sucked in a breath and straightened up, but couldn't knock. He imagined the family on the other side of the door. The parents answering half-awake in their robes, their pajamas, surprised to see some drunk guy standing on their porch, while heaped behind them stood neat stacks of sympathy cards and flowers from the neighbors.

Hello, sorry to bother you folks, I'm the asshole lawyer who rejected helping your son and drove him straight to the grave, a voice whispered inside Vance.

His heartbeat slammed into his temples. *What are you doing here? You think the parents give a damn about you telling them you're sorry, sorry their kid had to die, sorry you didn't take the case, begging and pleading for forgiveness? What are you hoping for? Apology accepted? Guilt wiped out?*

Thinking of the boy, Frankie Moran, he wondered what would have happened if he'd just swallowed his fears and pursued litigation. *You feel guilty because you knew the kid needed help,* his mind blubbered. *You feel guilty because you didn't save him,* and it stabbed something in his heart.

"Walk away," he muttered desperately to himself. "Just walk away."

Lowering his fist from the door, Vance started his legs moving. Abruptly his eyes went from the porch to a bedroom window. There was a light on, burning.

There, under the shiny wash of the moon, a beam of light radiated from a downstairs window, its ray strung across the lawn. Vance snuck over, elbowing aside bushes, creeping through the shadowy flower beds, squeezing through the shrubbery.

It looked like a kid's bedroom. A teenage boy's. Vance stared at the walls, scanning hazy photographs of friends, snapshots of family, posters of rappers, an Xbox controller on a vinyl gaming chair, football helmet and pads on a dresser, Polaroids of a cheerleader girlfriend with a beautiful smile taped all over a mirror. Beyond the bed he could see a connected room, a bathroom, with another mirror, in which Vance spied his own tortured reflection. Then he saw the door to the bedroom closet—

I'm not ready, he thought in a mental scream. *I'm not ready to do this. I—*

Suddenly, there was a man in the window. A man in the shadows, standing in his bathrobe, staring back.

The man silently observed Vance, his eyes penetrating and puzzled. Reflected in his blazing pupils Vance saw anger. Blame. Shame.

As Vance watched, the man reached down and plucked a shiny object—a cellphone—from his pocket, his fingers stabbing three numbers then putting the phone to his lips and speaking.

Vance didn't wait. He got up and left the window, not quite running.

∞ ∞ ∞

Five minutes later Vance stumbled into an all-night convenience store. He staggered into the restroom, and splashed cold water on his face, trying to wash all that guilt down the drain.

He drove home, grabbed Fatty, drove to his office and let himself in with the spare key Jay-Jay kept hidden inside a brass statue of Buddha for when Vance wasn't sober.

Unlocking his desk Vance grabbed the bottle of rum from his file cabinet. Nearly empty, he chugged what was left.

By 3:10, he hit rock bottom, started screaming and using a tire iron out of the Honda to pry open the bottom desk drawer where he kept his emergency bottle and a .38 revolver.

That's when a knocking sound caused Vance to jump. He whirled, craned his head, to see Jay-Jay hunched in the doorway, rubbing his hand over his jaw.

"You're hammered, aren't you, Vance?"

"Did you bring anything to drink? 'Cuz I'm out." Vance woozily raised the empty pint to Jay-Jay.

"What happened to the dog?" Jay-Jay pointed. Vance noticed Fatty was passed out on his desktop, drooling and snoring on his back.

"Looks like he couldn't handle his liquor," Vance slurred.

Jay-Jay stepped inside, eyes wide and mouth agape as he gazed around the room. The office was trashed, desk drawers upended, trash strewn everywhere, as if the building had been slammed by a tornado.

"Christ, look at this place!" He wandered around, uprighting Vance's torn leather chair, kicking empty bottles and cans out of his way. "Wow," he said, waving away the stench of liquor. "I wish I didn't have to do this, Vince. I really do. But, oh Jesus…"

Vince let out a burp. He felt a need to explain but his head was too thick with booze.

"You're killing yourself, you're killing both of us, and for what?" Jay-Jay crossed the room and leaned his face into Vance's. "You have a darker side, Vince. But you won't let me in. You won't let *anybody* in. And then you throw away a golden opportunity like this Murphy thing that could pull us out of the poorhouse, that could be our way out of debt!" He let out a sad breath, fixed Vance with his gaze. "I'm quittin', Chief."

"You're going to leave me?"

"I've been covering for your ass and jumping on live grenades for years. No more, brother."

"My family has left me. This dog will probably leave me. Everybody hates me."

"Not me," Jay-Jay said. "I love you, you asshole. But I'm not gonna hang around anymore and watch you get sucked into a bottle of Scotch," he said, plucking a bottle from the office floor.

"That, sir, is rum."

Jay-Jay gave Vance a long look. Then he smiled. "I wish you luck, partner," he said, and walked out.

Vance blinked at the empty doorway through the sweat in his eyes. He shrugged, not surprised Jay-Jay had abandoned him.

He rubbed a hand through his sweaty hair, scratched the stubble on his jawline. *To hell with Jay-Jay, too. What you have to do now,* he told himself, *is get your mind off everybody else's problems. Maybe go to Teasers. Find somebody who'd take a bet on whether the Lakers can beat Golden State by double digits.*

Shaking his head, Vance wandered around the desk, rummaging the floor for his keys. He dug into the office trash and came out with a stack of bills and junk mail, at the top of which was Father Murphy's letter, postmarked from Folsom.

Vance froze. *Perfect,* he thought to himself, *just perfect,* eyes swimming with contempt, as he dropped into a chair. Vance stared at the envelope, one eyebrow cocked, his brain freezing up.

And in that moment, he felt himself starting to crack.

Fists trembling, sweat drenching his clothes, he ripped the letter from the envelope, eyes dissecting it with a feverish intensity. With each word, that monster he'd locked behind bars peered back at him. Haunting him. Laughing at him. Slamming a wrecking ball to his fragile sanity.

The old desire to lunge at Father Murphy, squeeze his throat in his hand and snap his neck, returned.

Murphy must be 100 years old by now! What's he trying to prove? He'd taken the fall and now he wants to blame somebody else and cut a deal?

Vance bared his teeth. He wanted to laugh, wanted to laugh until tears exploded from his eyes. The more he sat and thought, the more his hangover turned his sanity to sludge, and the more Murphy's letter picked at his brain.

His bloodshot eyes rolled back to Murphy's letter. He swatted aside the garbage can, sending up a flurry of paper. He lunged back to the desk, slapped the letter on top of it, cradled the sleeping dog to the office sofa, rifled the drawers for a legal pad. Then he sat at his desk in a swivel chair, scratching out rage-filled words —

Murphy,

I cannot bring myself to refer to you as "Father," since I certainly do not consider you deserving of the moniker that was created to represent the one all-loving God you profess to represent, nor refer to you as "Mr." since that title was derived from the word "master," and the only thing you were and still are is a master of abusing innocence.

Quite frankly, sir, your letter has disgusted me.

I put you away for a good reason. So that the children you abused would never have to hear your name again. Knowing justice had finally been served.

You weren't "born" a pedophile?

How can you honestly say that, when you abused nearly two dozen children—not to mention the dozens of others who were so traumatized by your abuse that they were incapable of coming forward with their stories of how you raped them, molested them, over and over again. Some for years!

And those who committed suicide? Because of you!

You weren't "born" a pedophile?

That comment alone is beyond repulsive!

At the end of your trial you confessed that you knew what you were doing.

You rationalized your behavior by saying the children should have known. Their parents should have protected them.

When a man murders another for sleeping with his wife, he may claim it was justified. However, he had other options. One of those was to listen to his soul and behave in the manner it was guiding him. The soul is the only reliable and honest source we can turn to that will always challenge our behavior—and always be truthful.

You choose not to listen to yours, sir.

You choose to create your own warped and deviated truth.

I am certain your soul gave you a way out. I'm certain that before every child you abused, it spoke to you, telling you not only was this wrong, but you had options.

Masturbation, leave the priesthood, meet a woman and settle down, even insist the Church provide courses on how to handle the sexual urges young men and single adult males naturally have who decide to become clergy members and remain celibate.

You could have organized a protest against the Church for its repeated handling of priests like yourself.

You could have sought the very change you now seek, just like Father Timothy Coyle did.

So much you could have, but chose not to do. Instead you chose the easy way out, by simply abusing the youngest and most vulnerable of our society.

And now you ask me to sue the Vatican for making you a pedophile, because you were too weak to choose an option your soul was crying out for you to embrace?

You ask for forgiveness?

How dare you!!!

I have seen the anguish in each of your victims' eyes. I have experienced their pain. The lives that were changed the moment you decided to desecrate their innocence when you insisted they keep your "little secret."

These are the emotional scars you left behind, Murphy.

So no, I most certainly will not represent you!

Write a book if you like, about how you were wronged. And, if you do, I can assure you I will write one in response, detailing the monster you were and will always be.

Signed, Vincent Vance

Attorney-At-Law

The letter took twenty minutes to write, yet it didn't suppress Vance's anger. By the time he finished, he felt the hate burrowing deeper into his brain, and his mind begged for a drink.

Second-guessing the letter made him feel even more sorry for himself. Something crumbled in his chest as his anger disintegrated. He needed to erase and extinguish

Father Murphy from his memory. A letter to the monster who ruined so many innocent lives was not the way.

He headed for the bathroom. He dropped into a squat, ripped Murphy's letter into tiny shreds, flung them into the porcelain bowl. Then he did the same with his own scribbled letter, flushing them both down, watching the little shredded pieces swirl round and round in circles.

Slowly Vance felt the need for a drink pass out of him. He remained still, staring into the water. For a moment he wanted to reach down, and pull the words back out of the sewer, and his own life with them.

In that moment, the threat of Murphy left his body, replaced by…what?

Vance tilted his head, listening to the voice of his ex-partner. *Opportunity. A way out.* Vance put his head down, a smile breaking across his face, and started laughing.

What am I doing?

All at once his anger evaporated, as if writing the letter had purged it. He rubbed the back of his neck.

Jay-Jay's right! This could be my big shot. My way out. Now he chuckled like he was having a drugged seizure. *The Vatican won't want this case in the media. They'll be stupid, and offer to settle. A big fat ridiculous settlement, a third of it going straight into my pocket!*

Vance laughed until the tears poured down his cheeks. And then he stopped. He could hear his own breath now, shallow and slow.

An hour before, he'd never been more terrified in his life. And now...he caught himself dreaming, and began laughing louder.

You're a gambler, aren't you? What are the odds this thing ever goes to trial? Even Vegas wouldn't take that bet! And as he thought this, and the happy tears oozed from his eyes, Vance felt a sense of things falling perfectly into place.

Plucking out his cellphone he googled for the Folsom Prison inmate roster. Seeing Murphy's mugshot, his flesh tingled.

Vance removed his hand from the phone, stood up, wavering with a drunken grin. *You're looking at a ton of money,* he told himself. *More money than you could ever blow on booze and bad bets. This case is impossible to win. And this is your way out,* he realized, and touched Murphy's digitized face with his fingertip.

He wanted to stop laughing and cry for joy. Instead, he plopped back on the lumpy sofa with the dog, lying there with his eyes wide open, staring at the ceiling. He saw the two of them, he and Fatty, crawling out of a hole, fleeing from the burning and fiery gates of Hell. Then he fell into a deep sleep, seeing only dollar signs.

CHAPTER NINE

A monster isn't always a monster.

IT WAS 4 P.M. ON A THURSDAY when Vance arrived at the gates of Folsom. Joints aching from the three-hour plane ride, he was led to the prison Visitation Room, still on a natural high, dollar signs with eight figures rotating in his eyes. The repulsive thought of seeing Murphy was replaced with a *cha-ching* only he could hear.

He'd laid off the booze for a week, sobered up, dried out. The case became his new addiction. The past, a fading flicker.

He felt hesitant and unexpectedly tense about meeting Murphy, but reminded himself *I'm about to win the lottery,* as he passed through the metal detector and was patted-down by the guards. *Hell, maybe we'll sue the Vatican for a million. Ten million. Settle for a third of that. I'll take the case, file the papers, wait for the phone to ring from the Pope, and that'll be all she wrote, brother. They'll be scared to death of going to trial,*

Murphy sharing his sordid story in open court, facing the media, having another sick pedophile priest connected to the Catholic Church exposed on ABC, NBC, CNN, Fox News, the Today Show...

Thinking about the money, Vance could hardly keep it together. He'd struck paydirt with Murphy, was feeling good—hell, better than good, a spring in his step.

His financial worries and gambling debts would soon be over. Memories of the trial that gripped the nation became a distant blur, his subconscious horrors buried, at least for the moment.

In a fever he nearly dashed to the Visitation Room, toting his valise. The greasy paper bag full of fried hushpuppies was still in the car, a gift for the old padre he secretly knew he could not bestow.

Now it's my turn to use him, Vance thought.

He waited almost an hour, while the guards went to fetch Murphy from the prison med unit. *What was the old fart doing in there?* Vance wondered. Finally, shortly after 5 o'clock, with less than twenty visitation minutes on the clock, the steel door slid open, and in hobbled Father Charles Murphy.

Vance raised a hand, forced himself to smile, trying not to hate the man he dismantled on the witness stand so long ago.

As he did, his eyebrows rose in surprise, his smile froze. The dollar signs, spinning in his mind, evaporating.

White hair flying atop his skull, Murphy limped through the door, raising a cane with a bone handle to knock bystanders out of his way. His skin was sickly pale, almost albino white, as if he lived in total darkness. Two soulless eyes ringed with scar tissue hung from his lumpy face. There were ugly scabs on his cheekbones, another scar above his right eye, as if he'd been in a brawl.

As the old priest limped closer, a crinkled bag of Lay's potato chips bulging from his wrinkled left pocket, Vance's anxiety returned.

After putting a small fortune on a new credit card to fly out here, buying a new suit and renting a car, he was repping a guy who looked like satanic grinning Death itself, the personification of ancient evil. A limping and lunging version of all Vance hated and despised and feared—and all he'd locked away.

No judge or jury in their right minds would buy into this convicted fiend as a victim, and award him the big bucks.

Seeing Vance, Father Murphy smiled and waved his arms expansively. He lurched over, short of breath, and sat on the other side of the visitor's table. Vance tightened his lips and squinted.

On closer inspection, seeing Murphy up close—his skeletal neck and spindly white legs flopping out of his orange jumpsuit—Vance was even more shocked. *Jesus Christ*, he thought, *what happened to this guy?*

"Thank you for coming, Vince," Murphy grinned. "And sorry for the wait. Mother Nature calls at inopportune times," Murphy chortled.

Vance didn't answer, stared straight ahead.

There was a silence. Vance couldn't help but stare.

117

He'd had all these questions about the case; he thought about where to begin and his mind blurred. *I must be drunk,* he thought. *I feel like I'm drunk.*

Usually he'd be on his second or third bottle by this time of the day, and starting to see hallucinations like this.

And Father Murphy...what was *with* the old guy?

A decade in prison, Vance expected that hardcore thousand-yard penitentiary stare, that psycho killer glare. Yet Murphy's whole demeanor radiated a gentle peace, a shining serenity that spooked Vance. His entire mood seemed changed from the day he was marched out of a Georgia courtroom in handcuffs.

But it was Murphy's eyes that gave his transformation away; no longer emotionally detached, the eyes were shining with...*what? Love?* And for some weird reason Vance couldn't figure, the old guy looked stoned.

Murphy coughed, groaned, then sat forward, leaning on his cane. He pondered something, and stroked his beard. "You remember the first time we ever spoke, Vince? Long before that day in court?"

Vance had to stop and think. The million questions that no longer mattered raced wildly through his mind.

"It was 1973. You were 9 years old, and your mom and dad asked me to make you an altar boy. We talked about movies, *The Satanic Rites of Dracula* with Christopher Lee. Or was it *Taste the Blood of Dracula*?"

Their eyes met, and Vance froze in his seat. Murphy smiled, then he reached down and patted Vance's right knee.

In that moment, everything went silent around Vance. He looked down at the priest's wrinkled hand, leaned back in his chair. Then his mind took him back to the trial—

Throughout Murphy's trial and sentencing, the old priest said little. The defense attorney the Vatican assigned to Murphy, Puddin, was no match for a skilled, cut-throat prosecutor like Vance.

With the Vatican's head attorney, Roland Simmons, busy representing a Bishop in Boston for allowing pedophile priests to be transferred into his Diocese, without informing parishioners, Vance was able to go after the old priest with a vengeance. His hatred for people like Murphy made it easy for him.

Finally, at the sentencing hearing, Murphy asked to make a statement.

"Your Honor," he said, "I don't deserve leniency just because I'm a priest. God has forsaken me; I ask the justice system not to. Give me the maximum sentence under the law."

The judge didn't disappoint. And yet, as Vance watched Father Murphy being marched by Federal marshals to prison, rather than the rush of a courtroom victory that usually surged through him, Vance felt his hands begin to quiver and shake.

Ten years later, after he'd finished writing his venom-filled letter to Murphy, Vance's hands trembled in that same way.

Suppressed memories bubbled up.

He saw himself as one of five first-year altar boys at Murphy's parish, St. Joseph's Catholic Church on the south side of Mobile, Alabama. Young Vance loved donning the holy cassock, collecting towels after Murphy washed his congregation's feet on Maundy Thursday, kneeling before the Blessed Sacrament and swinging the brass incense burner at the elevation of the Host.

Father Murphy was a counselor and a molder of young men, motivating Vance to try out for his school's Peewee football team by portraying him as the next Dick Butkus, the most brutal beast to ever play linebacker.

Over the years, Vance wondered what had happened to those other boys; had they become any of Murphy's silent victims, too ashamed as adults to come forward during his trial? And if they had suffered and remained silent, Vance wondered what emotional torture those tormented boys had to go through?

Vance felt a lump in his throat. Murphy kept talking and yakkety-yakking away, like Vance wasn't there.

"Something wrong, Vince?" Murphy finally grunted. "You still here?"

Vance shook himself, realized he'd been staring into space, then closed his eyes tight. Beads of sweat trickled down his neck as the priest eyed him.

"I catch you at a bad time?"

Vance's eyes snapped open.

The sounds of the prison returned. He ignored the padre's question, watched him dig through the bag of Lay's, placing a handful between his wrinkled old lips, his blue eyes sending messages to Vance's screaming subconscious while the old man bullshitted about movies and blood-sucking vampires...*How's the family? How's Memphis? Had he been to Graceland, seen The King? Still a terror in the court-room, huh Vance? Why'd you buzz out of Atlanta, hope it wasn't something about my case...*

"Holy shit these chips are *divine*," Murphy gushed.

Vance took a few deep breaths, trying to relax himself. *I thought I could face this. I thought the old terror had gone away. I thought this would give me closure.* Now all he wanted was to be out of this room.

As if on cue, everything around Vance seemed to stop. He looked up, noticed the old fellow had stopped eating, and was eyeing him strangely.

"Why did you choose to come here, Vince?" Murphy asked. "It wasn't about the case, was it?"

Vance hesitated. He watched the two guards come closer.

"I...I'm not certain now..." he murmured.

He looked at his watch. His time was almost up, other visitors gathering up their things, saying goodbyes, getting ready to leave.

"It's okay, Vince," Murphy sighed. "Just try to find the answer."

Standing up, between choking coughs, Murphy gently looked at Vance. "Know this Vince. I'm not the only one to blame. The Vatican has its claws deep in this."

Vance gave Murphy a half-smile. "I have to get going," he said, grabbing his valise, quick to rise.

He stood and buttoned his vest. Then he pushed the chair back, and slid it under the table. "That's all for now," he said, wanting to say more but no words seemed right. Out of habit he reached to shake Murphy's hand. Then something stopped him, and Vance shoved the hand deep in his pocket, turned in the direction of the door, and fled.

∞ ∞ ∞

It was after 8 P.M., and dark, when Vance returned to his motel room. He showered and tried to sleep. Rolling over and over in bed did no good, so he turned on the TV to a *Hogan's Heroes* rerun, then *Diff'rent Strokes*, Vance watching one insipid brain-numbing sitcom after another. *I came 2,000 miles for this? For ten minutes in a Visitor's Room? To be confronted by the face of absolute incarnate evil?*

He leaned forward, elbows on his knees, his face in his hands. He closed his eyes and asked himself, *What am I doing here? What was I thinking? A convicted sex offender suing the Vatican? Blaming the Pope, the Catholic Church, for his crimes? Let's not even start debating the ethics!*

The ridiculousness of it made Vance retreat into a spasm of useless self-righteousness.

The Atlanta court had given Murphy exactly what he deserved. Let him rot in a cell! Yet the amount of money Vance could clear by settling the case out of court kept gnawing at him. He could spellbind the Vatican into a big lump sum with the threat of going to trial, facing a jury. *But what if you do, Vance? That won't be the end of it. You think the Vatican won't come after you with a hard-on? Dig around for something in your past you don't want exposed? Bug your home, your office, your cellphone? Comb through your tax returns, interrogate your estranged son, grill your ex-wife? Or worse, firebomb your damn home, burn it down?*

And what if he went through all this pain, only to have a judge dismiss the case?

Vance considered this through a red fog, reached under the bed and found the bottle of Kentucky Gentleman he'd bought from a bottom-shelf liquor store. One shot and he was done. He fell asleep and woke the next morning, his guts churning. Voices hummed from the next motel room. Vance winced and squeezed the screw-off bottle of Pepto-Bismol he'd grabbed from the medicine cabinet. Battling it for a hit to relieve the pain.

What was driving him to this level of insanity, this pain? He wasn't interested in sifting through the garbage in Murphy's head, all that poison spilling out. What lurid despair was motivating him to see if he was strong enough to even be in the man's presence again, without reaching over to smother him breathless?

Face it, schmuck. The money's screaming at you to go back there, one more time, and face the man, confront the past. So you can move forward.

And maybe the case had merit.

No priest had ever sued the Vatican. Maybe now it was time. *I can show the pain the faces of Murphy's victims showed, the pain I so often saw in other victims' faces, make the Vatican feel dirty, make them feel somehow to blame.*

What he'd need to do is take the case, and win.

Do it for the big payout, not let his anger and disgust for Murphy get in the way.

Vance stared into the mirror for what seemed like an hour. Then he staggered to his bed, fired up his laptop, and started taking notes, fingers slamming the keyboard as fast as he could type.

∞　∞　∞

The next morning, Vance watched the sun climb in the sky. He packed up his notes, his laptop and his suitcase, bought a Sacramento newspaper at the front desk, walked to his rented Chevy Malibu savoring the crisp early March air. Then he drove to Folsom for his second visit.

Clocks ticked and the air conditioning hissed as Vance weaved his way through the prison's maze of corridors, stairways, and thick steel doors.

For five minutes he waited outside the Visitor's Room, flexing his fingers nervously around his leather valise handle, two armed guards chattering about bass fishing, guns, and how the brake drum on some fool's '94 Nissan Pathfinder broke and caught fire, a line of inmates' friends and family meanwhile gathering.

Finally, at 10 A.M. sharp, the door clanked open, the guards moved aside, and Vance was admitted entrance.

This time, Father Murphy was waiting for him. Flushed with excitement, Vance quickly crossed the floor, sat, pulled out a lined legal pad, started scratching notes. Murphy stared straight ahead, silent, face drawn.

The padre's probably wondering why you want to speak with him again, Vance thought to himself, smiling.

"So...let's talk about the case," Vance said. "I'm taking it."

"Sweet," Murphy replied, without expression.

"We may not need to worry about your testimony," Vance leaned his body forward conspiratorially, "any depositions, or taking the stand. We'll file the motion and get you a major settlement without even going to trial."

Murphy's stare was blank.

"Now let's talk settlements. The Church will probably start at half a million. Maybe less. We'll ask for ten million. They'll bristle at ten, we'll ask for fifteen. They'll offer some kind of structured annuity, somewhere in the range of a million. We'll come back with a demand of twenty million, one lump sum, and..."

Vance glanced over, noticed Murphy looked numb.

"Or maybe *you* pick a number," Vance continued. "Thirty mil, fifty mil. A million for every month you've been locked up. I've got all these numbers burned into my brain—"

"I don't want a settlement, Vince."

Father Murphy managed a gentle smile. Vance sat immobile, eyes staring wide.

"I don't want any money. I have prostate cancer, Stage 4." His voice was hoarse, a whisper. Vance stared at him, staggered. "Doc has me on Metastron for bone pain. Blurs my vision. That's why I seemed so dopey yesterday." Murphy smiled, and suddenly his eyes sparkled.

Vance didn't seem to be listening. He suddenly felt sick. Not for Murphy's diagnosis. He could die tomorrow and dancing on his grave was not out of the question.

No. All he could see were dollar signs melting away. All his dreams going up in flames. Murphy leaned forward, reached across the table, pressing a hand on top of Vance's. Vance not even noticing.

"I don't want a settlement. I want to go to trial. I want to take the Pope, the Church, all those sons of bitches into a courtroom. To expose the lies, the cover-ups. I want justice, Vince. Not money. They can keep their money. Do you still want the case?"

CHAPTER TEN

*When the tears flow and the bourbon goes sour,
the whispers of truth become screams.*

A FTER A SIXTY-SECOND PANIC ATTACK, thoughts of suicide and visions of squeezing Murphy's scrawny throat between his hands, Vance agreed to take the case.

Though he hated the fact he wouldn't be getting a settlement, something deeper reacted. Saying *yes* in the moment came from somewhere he was not used to hearing from. Yet it was there. Shouting! Screaming! *"It's not about the money, Vince."*

Walking out of the Visitor's Room, his head pounding, the voice continued. *"Children come into this world with their innocence intact. They should remain that way.* With the image of Frankie Moran, hanging from his bedroom door, burned into his brain.

Children need to be protected from future monsters like Murphy," the voice continued. *"This case can make a difference.*

And still make you a bundle, Vince. Maybe through new clients who want to fight the system. More abuse cases. Maybe even a win and a big judgment. I'll ask for an impossible $100 billion to repay abuse victims worldwide. Ask the jury for a judgment so great it will tear down the Church. Start it anew, without the abuse.

As Vince's dreams spun out of control, his determination seemed to grow with every unrealistic vision. Always getting back to Frankie Moran.

He couldn't let that happen again.

Vince left the prison telling himself, *I took the case, but I don't want it. Suing the Vatican for making him a pedophile? It just doesn't seem enough to hit the jackpot. There has to be more.*

Watching two kids shoot hoops as he sped back to the motel, Vance pulled over. Skidding to a stop, the thought hit him.

File two complaints.

Murphy's, and one that sues the Vatican for covering up years of abuse. For transferring priests from one parish to another, knowing they would abuse children again. Without telling parishioners there was a pedophile in their midst.

Hell, sue the Vatican for crimes against humanity. Maybe get the International Criminal Court in the Hague to recognize the judgment.

Sitting back watching the kids practice layups, his mind shifted. He still couldn't shake Murphy placing his hand on his. The victims those hands touched. The lives shattered by what those hands did.

Their trauma became his. Their sense of hopelessness his. Their depression engulfed his once driven mind.

Could he handle absorbing all this?

Actors embrace, becoming one with a character.

Attorneys. We're supposed to keep an emotional distance, Vince thought. Why did he have to care so much?

It was the bleeding-heart side his father despised. The part of him he could never bury, no matter how hard he tried.

The great attorneys, they never let this happen. And he was once great.

I thought I could handle anything, Vince thought.

But this.

Frankie Moran. Hanging himself.

All because of me!

Vince's mind kept racing.

I could have extended his life with some sense of justice. The settlement the Church would propose would have given Frankie a break from his memories.

Money has a way of extending a sense of worthiness, but only for a while. Those memories. The trauma they embrace. They always emerge from the subconscious with a knockout punch.

Suddenly, out of nowhere, the tears flew. Nothing could shut them up. Not thinking of all the money he could make from the trial. The notoriety of being back in the news. And certainly not his father's acceptance.

In fact, his body screamed, *let the tears fly. Stop trying to shut me up.*

Vince didn't fight back.

The weight that had been holding him down for so long dissipated with every sob, every spasm of his hands clawing through his hair.

Twenty minutes felt like a year. When the rain stopped and the rivers dried up, Vince looked in the rearview mirror. Face puffy and red, he laughed. A nearly hysterical, guttural, wrenching laugh that brought joy.

"Fuck!" Vince yelled. "Fuck! Fuck! Fuck!" his stomach exhaling. "Yes!

I have no idea if I'm back, Vince thought, *but shit it feels good.*

Feeling a glow now, Vance watched one of the kids miss a layup badly. He chuckled remembering the year he failed to make the basketball team, but found wrestling an easy sport.

Suddenly the taste in his mouth went sour.

How would he fund the case? If he took the case pro bono, he'd be out expenses. Where to get the money?

There was still a few thousand bucks left on a credit card he'd paid down from his secret stash cash, but even that was dwindling. Maybe one last bet. A smart one, if there ever was such a thing. Maybe the Man Upstairs will intervene.

Now Vance felt the rush of adrenaline, his pulse racing, his gut warming. Another risky move; that was what his soul needed. Hell, what the case needed.

You're not screwed yet, he thought.

Driving back to the motel he noticed a tiny church. He went inside, sat alone in a front pew, and said a prayer, something he hadn't done in a long time.

Later, when he reached his motel, he sat on the edge of the bed, flipped on the TV, scrolled past the porn channel to an old episode of Dr. Phil, "My Dad's 25-Year-Old Fiancée Is A Gold Digger."

He decided to call Jay-Jay. Maybe ask him to come on board one last time. Maybe broach the subject of a settlement with Murphy.

Jay-Jay in his prime had bulldozed Memphis's biggest insurance companies into enormous malpractice payoffs. Calling their bluff was Jay-Jay's specialty.

Vance phoned, listened to the number ring, braced himself for yelling, cursing. But the call went to a recorded message: the number's voicemail box was full.

Hanging up, Vance decided to call and check on Fatty at the neighbor's. "You doing okay, Fatty?" The neighbor held the phone up to Fatty's ear. "You taking good care of yourself?" Fatty didn't say anything. For a second Vance felt like he might cry.

His neighbor, Peggy, was a former jazz and blues singer he'd represented in a domestic violence and divorce case the year before, Vance refusing to accept any payment knowing she'd have to sell her entire collection of rare Big Bill Broonzy records.

"How's it going, Vince? Was your new client everything he was cracked up to be?" Peggy's voice sounded upbeat. She'd gotten back into singing with a jazz band, Daddy's Trio, and at the age of 63, was experiencing a rebirth.

"More than I expected, Peg." Vance wanted to say more, but knew Peggy's heart always took on everyone's burden, and he was glad to hear her vibrant voice. "But that's a good thing, Peg." *Why was lying so easy?* Vince thought. "I'll be back to take Fatty off your hands sooner than later. Keep singing, young lady. Fatty's a good listener."

Hanging up, he felt more than just alone. Reminding himself to place one last bet—to erase that feeling. The possibility of winning at something, anything, was his go-to mindset whenever depression began to set in. Now there was a cause involved. One bigger than his own tender ego.

Opening his phone, he scrolled the rows of NBA games and NASCAR races until he found what he was looking for: the Rey Vargas vs. O'Shaquie Foster title fight at the Alamodome. Of all the sports, he knew boxing. Foster was +150 at Caesars. Perfect. At those odds a $2000 bet, nearly everything he had, would net him nearly $3,700. Not big odds, but it was bet he could get behind. One that would give him seed money to take on the case, not to mention feed the adrenaline fix he needed and give him a sign that Murphy's case was a go.

If he never risked he would never win. Thinking of the case, he placed what he hoped would be his last bet.

Pressing the BET NOW icon, Vance sat back on the bed, then pulled out his laptop. There was one last thing he needed to do before filing the complaints.

The Vatican would call up their best hired gun, a little pitbull of a lawyer down in Texas with a hair-trigger temper, and an occasional stutter when things didn't go his way. This same Texas hotshot had once called Vance a loose cannon. This was the man he'd be opposing, and wanted to give him the courtesy—call it a heads-up from an old warrior—of hearing it from him first.

> *TO: roland.simmons@simmonslaw.com*
>
> *SUBJECT: Suing The Vatican*
>
> *Dear Roland,*
>
> *Hope life is treating you well, as I hear you've moved to Houston and are enjoying the experience of Texas living.*
>
> *I'm writing as a professional courtesy to let you know I will be filing a complaint against the Vatican, on behalf of Father Charles Murphy.*
>
> *Yes, that Charles Murphy. The one we both agreed was the worst of the worst among the pedophile priests put behind bars.*
>
> *I can assume you'll soon receive a call from the Vatican to defend the suit, since you are often their go-to legal eagle in such matters.*
>
> *As always, I will provide you with any evidence we present at trial, and do my best not to offer any surprises in court. I trust you will provide the same courtesy.*
>
> *Please be well, Roland. I am heartened to hear you are finally taking time away from the courtroom to work on that golf game you always expressed improving. May the Big Man Upstairs be your caddy, may all your drives reach the putting green. And may the best fighter win, sir.*
>
> *Yours Truly,*
>
> *Vincent Vance*
>
> *Attorney-At-Law*

Satisfied, Vance pressed SEND. He sat in front of his computer, staring at the screen. Then unshaven and hollow-eyed he fell into bed with his arms wrapped around a bed pillow, imagining it was Fatty. Before he closed his eyes his phone chimed. Looking briefly, sleep came easy to Vance that night. Foster won.

CHAPTER ELEVEN

Let there be light.

ACHUBBY LITTLE PRISON GUARD LED Murphy through a set of steel doors, up a cracked marble staircase, and down a corridor back to his cell, Murphy telling the guard more than the guy ever wanted to know about the male prostate.

They passed the med ward then turned a corner, then another, finally running into a repairman trying to fix the air conditioning, the ceiling dripping water.

"What's the problem this time?" Murphy asked.

"Beats me," shrugged the repair tech, slamming the massive unit a couple of times with his monkey wrench. "Shit's always fucked up around here."

His neck beaded with perspiration, Murphy chuckled, then entered his cell. The air was dead and thick. He hobbled to the sink and splashed cold water on his face, slicked back his thinning white hair with a plastic comb, then sat on the edge of his bunk, head bent over his knees.

Okay, Murphy, what's bothering you? he asked himself. His stomach felt tight.

Up and down the cellblock he heard the howls of enraged inmates bitching about the A/C. Murphy listened, the screaming so loud he couldn't think, resting his cheek on the knob of his cane. He was exhausted, and wanted to sleep, but it was too early in the day. Instead he leaned back, trying to block out the noise, and drilled his sad blue eyes at the gray granite wall in an unblinking stare.

For the next ten minutes he didn't move or speak, letting his thoughts roam to Vincent Vance, recapping the last strange seconds of their meeting, and the look in Vance's eyes. Murphy groped to understand what the look meant. *Deep intestinal pangs from a bad salad on the plane? Or maybe the guy's back in detox, drying out from the booze?* Then it came to Murphy: *Intense outrage,* his mind spat back, and he brushed it away.

Vance seemed stunned when I told him about the money, didn't even try to conceal it.

In Vance's face he could still see the sensitive little boy who'd once come to Murphy, begging to be an altar boy, pissed-off at his father for withholding any sense of appreciation for the sensitive yet highly-intelligent kid he'd become. As he told Murphy, only his mother seemed to feel his pain. Murphy breathed out a sigh.

Louder and louder the shrieks and howls in the cellblock grew. Whatever passed between Vance and

Murphy in that final second troubled the priest; he felt burdened by something he couldn't express to anyone, not Doc Dillard, not a therapist, not the prison chaplain. He no longer had a best friend to confide in, with Drizzle gone. Who then?

Maybe God.

Maybe God would listen.

"Bullshit," Murphy mumbled with a grimace, staring at the wall with lonely eyes. Talking to God wouldn't provide him with hope or any answers. That kind of benevolent, all-loving God was a fabrication, a fantasy created for other people; Murphy's Almighty dealt only in terrible judgment and fear.

Still, he couldn't help thinking of Drizzle, his goofy sidekick. *I wonder if the kid forgives me for putting him on a collision course with the Cremator?*

Murphy tilted his chin up, toward the ceiling. He imagined Drizz in his purple do-rag smiling down at him from the Pearly Gates, waving as if to say *Have a nice day, Murph!* not even a little pissed-off, even as Murphy watched the blood leak out of the nine gaping holes the Cremator had carved in Drizzle's throat and chest.

"Yeah, yeah, I know, son," Murphy answered, waving back and smiling. "You, of all the crazy assholes on Earth, *would* forgive me."

He saw a flash of Drizzle's orange jumpsuit as the kid waved again and slowly faded into the wall. Then a thought wiped the smile off Murphy's face. He lowered his head, and whispered.

"And what about You, God? Is there no room for forgiveness between us, Big Guy?"

Murphy shifted his gaze back to the ceiling. *Dammit, Murphy,* he thought, *do we really have to go there?* He climbed off the bunk and got down on his knees, half-wheezing, half-groaning with the effort.

"You there, God?" he muttered. The words left his lips in a dry chuckle. "Remember me? Father Charles Murphy?"

Murphy stopped, listened for an answer. None came. *Typical,* he thought with contempt. He placed his hands around his cane to rise. One more thing was nagging at him, so he stayed on his knees.

"Listen, while I'm here, I want to say a prayer for Vince Vance, my attorney. You and I have put him in a bad spot. Hell yes, I said *You and I,* God. Maybe You could find some way to let him off the hook. You put your spiritual meathooks into him when Vance was a kid, filled with inexhaustible faith in Your promises of eternal forgiveness and unconditional love. Maybe You could pick up the check one more time, and free him from any guilt if he chose to drop the case." Murphy shifted his weight uneasily.

"Anyway, I hope You're still open for business 24-7. This is Father Charles Murphy, signing off..." he stopped, feeling a little nervous, pressed his hands together in a position of prayer, then added "...And get him off the booze, too, while You're at it. Amen."

Murphy paused, listening to the silence. For at least an hour he waited, hoped, thirsted, ached for an answer. None came.

"What happened to You, Mr. Almighty? You used to hear me in my younger days," Murphy said, leaning forward on his cane.

Rocking back and forth, Murphy smiled. "Hell, Boss," he nodded. "I remember the days, long before You became my 'go-to-guy' for all things invisible…"

When Murphy was a boy, being in the priesthood and having a direct line to speaking with the Almighty had been the furthest thing from his mind. His father had been a boxer, a journeyman heavyweight whom greedy promoters used to pad the records of their more-promising fighters, knowing Joseph Murphy was a brawler and a bleeder with a glass jaw, an easy knockout.

He quit the ring at age 30, a record of four wins and twenty-one losses, after sustaining a serious eye injury. Having never made big money in the fight game, and never smart enough with the little money he did make, he went to work collecting garbage, and sedated himself with Olde English malt liquor for the next forty years.

Murphy's relationship with his father was a love/hate one. He longed for his approval as a child, yet as he became older, Murphy could see his father was broken, and became sympathetic towards the way the old man lived his life.

He often wrote letters to his father, asking how he was doing, hoping the old man—then a berserk and frightening alcoholic, working odd construction jobs around the neighborhood of their Bronx home—would write back and build a relationship.

Murphy never received a response to any of these letters, causing him intense pain. When his father died of liver failure at age 72, other than his wife and only son, no one came to his funeral.

Fortunately, Murphy was close to his mother.

Maureen Murphy worked as a seamstress, was well-read and intelligent, with a great sense of humor. Before meeting Joseph Murphy she'd studied at the Brooklyn Academy of Music, with dreams of playing cello with the New York Philharmonic Orchestra—dreams that were squashed upon marrying. Still, the music of Bach and Vivaldi always filled the Murphy home, and his mother's cello sat inside a locked closet in their rented brownstone.

She'd been told by doctors she'd never have children; thus young Charles's birth was a pleasant surprise. He became her golden child, and the only reason she stayed together with Joe Murphy, who used her as a punching bag, the helpless recipient of his terrible anger.

Thinking of his parents now slowed Father Murphy's heartbeat, his head aching slightly. With his father, there had always been a distance he longed to correct.

My father wanted a son who wasn't afraid, wasn't a sissy, Murphy remembered. *So I fought the bullies like he instructed, limping home bruised and beaten day after day. Dad would meet me at the door, sigh deeply and walk away. Only Mom saw my pain.* Murphy cast a dark look at the wall, and swallowed hard. *The pain became intense when the old man laughed at my efforts to fight back.*

Murphy fell silent, scrutinizing some invisible scene from his past. *Seeing my father laughing at my futile efforts to hold my ground against the bullies was bad. But when Marilyn Johnson laughed too, I'd had enough.*

Marilyn was his first budding fantasy, although she didn't know it. She was 14, two years older than Murphy, who at 12 suddenly felt the rage of hormones begin to rear their ugly heads. His first wet dream was in honor of the pretty teen with the larger-than-life breasts.

Whenever he was in Marilyn Johnson's presence, he did his best to entertain her, to make her laugh and smile, all the while keeping his fantasies to himself.

On Tuesday nights Marilyn came for dinner at the Murphy house. Both of their mothers worked late on Tuesdays—Marilyn's as a literacy mentor at the Bronx Library—so Murphy's father invited the pretty neighbor girl over and made an Irish feast of corned beef. Something Murph always thought was creepy.

During the night, Murphy's dad was unusually attentive to her, asking about her lipstick, her latest hairstyle, her miniskirts. Joking with Marilyn, teasing her, making her laugh—often at another's expense. When it was young Charles's turn to be the butt of jokes, his father told Marilyn how the boy tried to stand up to a thug named Ralphie on the schoolyard—but returned home with cuts lashed across his face and bruises down his back. Hearing his father portray him as a weakling and a wimp, young Murphy stumbled upstairs to his bedroom, crying whimpering tears.

141

Dad laughed, Murphy remembered. *And then Marilyn laughed too.*

She laughed until there were tears streaming from her eyes.

Young Murphy never finished dinner that night, seeking the comfort of his pillow seconds after his father told that story, the moment tattooed forever in his brain.

It was also the moment he made the decision.

For weeks, Father Sullivan of Our Lady of Mercy in the Bronx had been recruiting boys to enter the priesthood. With Murphy's newfound hormonal urges, he had never considered the Church; girls had become his focus, his obsession, his light of salvation in the darkness, replacing the sadness he felt from an absent father.

Obsessing over girls put him in a dreamy state, giddy and lightheaded, where his fantasies could be concealed in the unreachable places of his mind. These fantasies gave him hope that he was worthy of being loved, being wanted, that Charles Murphy wouldn't have to become a broken-down prizefighter who took too many blows to the head like his old man, that he could become something more than the neighborhood embarrassment.

Until he'd heard Marilyn Johnson laugh.

The next morning, Father Sullivan welcomed his decision to enter the seminary.

When the priest spoke to the young boy's parents, it was the first time Murphy had seen his father eye him with any degree of respect. In that moment, the thousand times his father had called him a coward vanished. The old Charles was gone. And the new Charles found a home in the Catholic Church.

In the seminary, as Murphy's body grew and his hormones surged, the need for a release became more urgent. When he satisfied that need—masturbating in the bathroom in private—every cell in his body told Murphy it was wrong. That it was a sin—even though he knew it was a natural human urge. Every urge became a mind-numbing moment of betrayal. An embarrassment to him—and to the One he'd promised his life to, the Almighty Him.

A sense of shame crept over me with every release, Murphy recalled. *And I knew God was watching. Judging. Yet, I persisted. The urges were too strong. The tools to deal with them were never made available.*

While he'd often think of Marilyn during those moments, Murphy realized he was not alone with these urges. Other seminarians, boys his own age, feeling the same desire, began to replace her. Soon, those in charge of the seminary, the priests and the assistant priests, took part. "Do this, or God won't love you," the boys were told. "And don't tell anybody."

Seeking their acceptance, their approval, the love of his superiors and mentors, Murphy was forced to become their sex partner, and they to become his role models.

Is it any wonder when I was given my first parish assignment I modeled their behavior? Murphy grumbled, slipping down against his cane.

Even before my first sexual encounter I asked Father Morse, the head of the seminary, about courses to teach us how to curb or better deal with our sexual urges. I suppose my soul was older than I'd given it credit for, because looking back, I don't know where the courage to speak up came from. But Father Morse calmly explained to me such courses were frowned upon by the higher-ups in the Church.

Had I known the monster I would become, I may have pushed harder, Murphy sighed, *although I now know such courses weren't part of the process in creating a priest. By the time I was ordained, at the age of 34, I was fully vested in that process.*

After glowing recommendations from my superiors, I received my first assignment to St. Michael's, a small parish on the out-skirts of Cleveland. Its congregation was a devout one, always fill-ing the pews on Sundays. Filling the donation plates as if an extra ten dollars would forgive their infidelity and other sins over the prior week. It was at St. Michael's when the urges became more difficult to control.

I was alone. No longer were there other seminarians to satisfy my urges.

Research says men think of sex at least twenty times daily. With me, it was more. Much more.

I'd never felt the touch of a woman, experienced the smell of her perfume up close, enjoyed the intimate conversation they both bring. I was more than a priest but no one wanted to see that. They saw a man who was supposed to be the image of Christ Himself, as if Christ had no human desires. An unrealistic depiction of every priest, everywhere.

While the images of Marilyn had faded, the desires for a woman crept in with every marriage counseling session. Every romantic comedy I watched. Every time I listened to a man or woman confess their infidelity.

Knowing I could never be with a woman, the desires created a state of anxiety no counseling could ever hope to eliminate. Like every suppressed human desire, it had to be replaced with something.

Georgie Peterson was my first altar boy, and my first victim. He reminded me of myself when I was 12. Slight of build. Curly hair. Giving off a sense of uncertainty. Walking with his head down as if that would ward off the bullies.

During his first Mass, Georgie dropped his Bible. Nearly in tears as the other two altar boys laughed, my heart went out to him. After Mass, in the sacristy, I talked with him. Made him feel better about himself. Hugged him.

Later that day his single mother, whose perfume when administering communion always made it difficult to focus, called asking I provide guidance for her son. Math was his poorest subject. I agreed to see him at the rectory twice a week. She was euphoric.

He eventually began accompanying me to conferences, and camping trips, his mother so proud I was taking an interest in her boy. As if she didn't know his hotel bed and sleeping bag were also mine.

Georgie is the first face I see in my dreams, tears running down his face after each weekend together.

I reminded him that God was watching and was proud of him. That only God's love could save him, and this was our "little secret."

He took our secret to his grave, after committing suicide on his 16th birthday.

You'd think that would have been lesson enough to stop. Instead, it was the beginning of wondering just who was really guiding me. God or just plain ol' human nature.

No God would have allowed me to harm another, especially a child. But this God did, and so I fell into the trap. If it's okay with You, God, it's okay with me, and I quickly moved on from Georgie's death.

Albert, Patrick and Ginny were my next victims at St. Michael's. Each was roughly the same age as Georgie. Albert, a short chubby boy, came with a lisp the other children made fun of. Patrick was the manager of the boys' basketball team. Too skinny and meek to play the game, he handed out towels and water to those who could hit clutch free throws, throw elbows and rebound, or cover the fast break. Ginny was my Marilyn — with dazzling budding breasts — for the few short months before her parents moved out of state.

They all kept our secret. Some just not as good as others.

Patrick began to act out at home, especially after returning from our private tutoring sessions. When his parents became suspicious and complained to the Bishop's office, it was the first time I was transferred.

By the time I'd arrived at my second parish, St. Leo's in Cincinnati, I had my grooming techniques down to a science. Find the most vulnerable ones who needed male guidance, a father figure, and the rest was easy.

My stint at St. Leo's went much like at St. Michael's, as did St. Patrick's, St. Cecelia's, Notre Dame, St. Matthew's, St. Francis Xavier and Holy Trinity Church. From Ohio I was transferred to Rhode Island, then to Louisiana, Georgia, Maryland, Texas and

Mississippi. No one ever seemed to have heard the rumors about me. At some, besides my priestly duties, I was asked to be a guidance counselor for children at the school associated with the Church.

In my quiet times, God continued to amaze me with His ruthless disregard for my prayers for guidance, as He gave me more opportunities to do damage to so many innocent children.

The final one was Timothy. A more confident, athletic boy than I usually sought out, whose acting out in class often caused him to be sent to the guidance counselor's office.

By the time Timothy's parents coerced their son to tell them why he was acting out after our tutoring sessions at Holy Trinity, I'd become quietly known among my superiors as a problem they seemed to enjoy moving around.

My arrest made headlines. "Longtime, Well-Respected Priest, Father Charles Murphy, Accused of Sexual Abuse Against Minors."

I'd seen that headline in my head for a decade. It was almost a relief to learn God finally heard my prayers.

Why it took HIM so long to stop the monster he created was anybody's guess. Was it His inability to admit a mistake? A stubbornness that would question His perfection? Maybe He is more like us than we care to admit.

After all, "we are made in His image and likeness" was a theme in every Catechism class. My journey, and his hesitation to protect the most innocent among us, should be proof enough to question his infallibility.

It took years before I could bring myself to write to my victims. Several years to write a therapeutic letter to my since-deceased mother. Not blaming her for allowing my father's emotional abuse to put me here, but asking her forgiveness for my weakness in the face of my dad and for the shame I brought upon future generations of our family.

I will always be known as Father Charles Murphy, the disgraced priest, the convicted pedophile, the serial rapist who abused innocent children, and the only member of the Murphy clan who spat in the face of God.

As the memories swirled, blood rushed to Murphy's skull. He clamped his eyes tight, shutting out the clanging cell doors and the screaming voices of Folsom.

When he opened his eyes again, a few hours had passed. The room was scorching hot, the A/C still on the blink.

Breaking out of the dream, staring at the wall, he mopped the stinging sweat from his forehead with the back of his hand, remembering what it felt like to talk to God, the need to confess, to plead for forgiveness from his Creator, to pray.

What did God think of him suing the Church? Would the Big Guy damn him for all time? *Hell,* he groaned, *who knows, it's probably too late to worry about being damned anyway for what I became, a convicted child molester locked in a cage with a building full of screaming psychos.*

Murphy hung his head, cleared his throat. He still had one final question for God. The gut instinct to ask his Creator was puzzling to him, yet he couldn't contain it.

"Should I press ahead with the lawsuit, Big Guy? Hold the Church accountable?" He looked up and imagined he saw Drizzle waving down at him again. Feeling a sadness,

Murphy thought of Drizz's little boy, who'd hugged him at Christmas. "For Your children, God?"

Murphy kept silent, and waited. And waited. He heard no movement and no sound except irate inmates arguing to his right, and the prison repairman muttering *"C'mon, bitch, work!"* to the A/C unit down the corridor.

Murphy shifted his eyes to the floor, and then he laughed.

"Look, if You can't answer me directly, just give me a sign. You gave John the Baptist a sign. You gave Peter a sign. Give me a sign."

Suddenly the lights in Murphy's cell flickered, went out. In the darkness, the air conditioning kicked on. A breeze swept through the cell, cold air flooding down from the vent, hitting Murphy in an icy blast.

Murphy slumped back against the wall, freezing and shivering, surrounded by the shrieks of joy from the other inmates.

Was this his sign? This icy room? In his face was a look of confusion. The roar of convicts in his ears became deafening.

Then the voices stopped. The breeze vanished. Goosebumps rising on his arms, Murphy glanced at the floor, the walls, then the light bulb in the ceiling. It hummed, seemed to vibrate, and flickered. Then it blazed on, illuminating the darkness, burning brightly.

It must be the sign! "Let there be light indeed," Murphy chuckled, and started sobbing uncontrollably.

And then in the light, knowing he was now an instrument of the Man Upstairs, he felt God's rage. Punishment for Murph's years of abuse, he felt a hot knife enter his bowels. Pain slicing through his lower intestines. He flinched in shock. The pain surged lower, burning down toward his genitals.

Murphy gaped down, forced his eyes to focus.

Trickling slowly beneath his groin, from the seat of his pants, staining the bunk where he sat, he saw the crimson rivulet, the river of blood.

CHAPTER TWELVE

Arrogance is a mask for the secrets of the soul.

A T 11:20 P.M. IN DOWNTOWN NEW ORLEANS, the Vatican's American legal team of three defense lawyers stepped out of the Smoothie King Arena, bleary-eyed after attending the Pelicans vs. Lakers playoff game. Heading to their luxury rental car, the attorney from Chicago they called Porkchop turned to the others as they marched through the darkened parking lot, three men in Cerruti and Armani suits, neckties undone, shirttails out, bumping into and trying to outrun Pelicans fans exiting the arena after Zion Williamson threw down 35 but blew a point-blank layup that would have won the game, Porkchop moaning and bitching.

"$19 for a beer. $21 for nachos," he whined. "Can you believe that?"

"You believe those hot cheerleaders?" said Sacko, a mustached lawyer from Baltimore. "It's still early. Maybe we should go bar-hopping in the French Quarter. We've got a whole week here in the Big Easy, before the prelims." He stood gaping around the immense parking lot, as if he was lost.

"We're meeting the Pallbearer at seven in the morning to go over the case. You want to face the consecrated one with a hangover?"

The men went quiet, unnerved, staring at each other. Roland Simmons, A.K.A. the Pallbearer, the Vatican's head defense counsel in nearly every major Church scandal, was graced with a killer instinct to win-at-all-costs. A trait only an institution like the Vatican could appreciate.

"Listen, we better talk about the case," Feral said, his voice sounding panicked. "Simmons is gonna want to know what we've come up with."

"Tell him we talked about the cheerleader with massive...."

Feral cut Sacko off. "He's pressing hard to get Murphy's mouthpiece to settle. Or to get a judge to throw the lawsuit out."

The attorney named Porkchop rolled his eyes.

"Jesus, do they even *have* a case? How do they plan to prove this Father Murphy was groomed by other priests?"

"I bet they've got nothing. It's all threats."

"We seized his personal medical records from Folsom."

"And?"

"He's being treated for cancer. Prostate. Doc's notes say it's progressed to Stage 4. The man is terminal."

"Probably serving as someone's bitch in the joint. Serves him right."

Climbing inside their car, Porkchop kept the discussion going, Feral and Sacko fighting over the front seat. Porkchop drove toward the gate, honked at an old gent in a Lakers hat, his Oldsmobile blocking them, as their car approached a trio of blonde girls in tan jackets and shoulder bags trying to find their keys.

"Listen, roll down the window, so I can talk to these girls…" whispered Sacko. Porkchop ignored him.

"You talk to the guy again?" Porkchop asked.

"What guy?" replied Feral.

"What guy do you think? The idiot who filed the suit, Vance."

"No. Son of a bitch called me in the middle of the third quarter, right when the Lakers were making a run."

"And?"

"What do you think? I hung up."

"Maybe he's calling to see if there's more money on the table."

"I say we blitz him. Bury him with paper."

"The Pallbearer tried that. Seven boxes, the size of trunks. Vance sent it all back with a note. Said something like, 'Nice try. Already saw these docs two months ago.'"

Feral sighed, dragged out his laptop, went to his case notes. "Why'd the Holy See wait so long?"

"Evidently that was the strategy. The longer we wait, the better chances that (A.) Murphy croaks, or (B.) he gets a screwdriver in the back from some psycho. Finally they had to stop waiting for A and B to happen, caved in and called the Pallbearer."

"Should have called him in four months ago."

"Hey, there's Bourbon Street!" said Sacko. "I hear there are more diseases a man can catch there than anyplace on the planet."

It became easier and easier for Porkchop to ignore the man's stupidity.

"This guy Vance will settle. He has to."

"He's outgunned."

"He's scared."

"He's a boozehound."

"You can't win this case in a courtroom. A convicted pedophile priest?"

"The Pallbearer's never lost a Vatican case. The last legal eagle who tried to beat him kicked the bucket, two days before going to trial."

"Hey, we go to trial, who's gonna sit next to Simmons?"

There was no reply, no movement.

"Not me," said Feral.

"Hell, me neither!" piped in Sacko. "Simmons scares *me!* And I'm on his side!"

"We're just show horses. Paid to look good," mocked Porkchop.

"To sit there and never, ever interrupt or question the Pallbearer," quipped Feral.

"We meet tomorrow. Go over the strategy. After that Simmons will not want to hear from us. Just sit there and look bad-ass."

"I was at a deposition and saw the man in action," said Porkchop. "His tactics, the ones everyone talks about. The stuttering, breaking down in front of the victims, acting like a germaphobe. He'd question abuse victims and with all his antics, *boom*, they'd begin to feel sorry for the man. The plaintiffs ended up settling for far less than the Diocese expected. That's the reason the Vatican called the Pallbearer in for this case."

"So we'll be good little show horses and clam up."

"How about if Simmons drops dead in front of the jury?"

"I'd wait fifteen minutes, before saying anything," as they all laughed. "Just watch, enjoy the performance, and the generous payday, boys."

∞ ∞ ∞

At midnight, seated alone in his 17th-floor hotel room before the flickering rays of a big-screen TV, sunken-cheeked attorney Roland Simmons watched Mr. Spock, Captain Kirk and the crew of the Starship Enterprise on a late-night rerun. Thinking about Spock made Attorney Simmons grin; he upped the volume on the remote control whenever the pointy-eared character spoke.

Simmons worshipped Spock, the emotionless half-human, half-Vulcan science officer with razor-edged intelligence and steely logic.

An hour earlier Simmons had pressed PAUSE on the episode and strode down to the lobby in his black silk trousers to complain to the hotel manager about three curly pubic hairs he'd found on the floor of his suite.

Simmons didn't want to call the desk. Didn't want to hold the hotel phone close to his mouth, not knowing what slobbery politician or sex-starved celebrity might have contaminated the plastic instrument with his germs.

After sticking his head in the manager's office—the only time he'd left his room in three days—he'd rushed back to his 17th-floor suite to shower. It was Simmons' fifth shower of the day.

Afterward, Simmons sat with his eyes on the glowing screen in the dark of his luxury suite. He'd brought a suitcase of individually-wrapped organic foods on his flight from Dallas, carefully preserved in airtight canisters, not trusting in room service.

As a child, his mother had lovingly reminded him there were few things dirtier than the bathrooms or food handlers in hotels. Even the silverware contained noroviruses. "And there's nothing germier than the toilet seats," snapped his mother. "Dirty, dirty, dirty," she hissed, striking little Simmons if he didn't nod back.

But as an adult he learned to hide his phobias well.

He'd learned to become a "win-at all costs" attorney in spite of his OCD tendencies. Refusing to seek treatment, hiding behind his fake bravado, only served to increase stress with every passing trial. Not to mention increasing his stutter. Nevertheless, he'd been able to use it to his advantage in court, always seeking sympathy from the jury.

In his personal life that strategy backfired, with an ex-wife and son he'd never been able to connect with. A shame that quietly haunted him during his moments alone. Friendships, even from childhood, were few and far between.

Captain Kirk and Dr. McCoy came on the screen. Simmons hit the remote's MUTE button, and ran through the Father Murphy case in his mind. He was having trouble gauging why the Vatican had seemed so panicked — and yet they flew him to New Orleans in coach, instead of the first-class seat he always requested.

Seated in 31D, next to the bathroom, he grumbled to himself. *What happened? Budget cutbacks?* He'd seen the Church's financials. An extra $700 upgrade wasn't a big deal. Not if they wanted to win this case.

Anger drummed through Simmons's head. *What a bunch of arrogant fools. In some bizarre way they probably prayed Murphy's case would go to trial, give the Pope, all those Cardinals and Archbishops a chance to show up in their fanciest clergy garb, all that shiny gold and pointy hats. And the Pope's ring for the jury to kiss.*

What worried him wasn't the Vatican; even the dozens of Catholic dioceses who'd been sued and had to file bankruptcy from the thousands of lawsuits over sexual abuse claims didn't faze him. It was the opposing counsel, Vincent Vance. *Vance is a madman. Always going for the throat, the stiffest sentence, the toughest conviction.*

I hear he's washed-up now; maybe he thinks he can milk the Holy See for more money by pretending to hold out. I wonder what his real game is? Doesn't Vance realize if we go all the way to trial I will fry his ass?

Simmons shook his head, and chuckled. He recalled the desperate late-night call from the Vatican City. *"Attorney Simmons, we have a situation requiring your assistance. An unusual case has been filed against the Church, one that is highly concerning. The Holy See requests you bring your A-game..."* Simmons scoffed. *Bring your A-game? What was the man with the big hat so worried about? I'll get them off the hook.*

Vance is a nobody now. He's a clown. A loser.

No matter how many over-inflated stories Simmons heard in the past about Vance the Savior, Vance with his unbroken record of winning sexual abuse cases back in Georgia, something had spooked him. He'd had to hide out in Memphis, hire his deadbeat partner to do the dirty work, keep Vance pinned down and off the alcohol.

Make a note of that, Simmons told himself. *Send the guy a case of 15-year-old Kentucky Scotch in the morning,* he thought and grinned.

That will be Vance's downfall, he told himself. *He'll screw this case up and lose by not fathoming the depth of dirty tricks I'll resort to. Witnesses suddenly gone missing, misplaced files, threats to jurors—hell, bust a few kneecaps, if we have to. It'll be a nasty trial, if it goes that far.*

Vance was trying to redeem himself for something Simmons couldn't quite put his finger on. The man seemed resigned to self-destructing. *That makes it almost too easy for a shark like me to move in for the kill,* thought Simmons, as he clicked off the TV, stretched his legs out, and imagined he was in a steaming hot shower, washing all of the world's ugly germs and contaminants away.

He could still hear his father's voice, thick with condescension. "You're washing away all the good stuff, kid. Stuff that makes you human. That the body needs to protect itself. May as well live in a fucking bubble," were Dad's favorite comebacks when Mom insisted he take another shower, after an afternoon of sandlot ball.

Not known for his warmth, his old man, an often laid-off construction worker, never understood his tendencies. Never realizing how those tendencies made his kid feel so fearful, different, and alone.

Never having attended his funeral, it was moments like this he wished his father could see him now. The best cars, homes in three time zones and enough money to buy the old man a construction company of his own. Although he'd probably get laid off from that as well.

He misjudged me, Simmons thought, *and so will Vance,* turning his thoughts back to the trial.

Just like my old man, Vance made an error in judgment, knowing I would be his adversary. And writing as a professional courtesy, letting me know in advance? Who does that?

Simmons learned a long time ago about keeping things close to the vest, evaluating the opponent before stepping in the ring. Surprises, frivolous motions, failing to produce discovery documents, scorched-earth litigation tactics followed by an insincere apology to the judge went a long way to winning a case in the halls of justice.

But that's Vance. Always playing by the book. What a stiff! He's got a few skeletons in the closet somewhere. I'll dig them out. And if he follows the book here, I'll bury him.

Hearing his cellphone buzz in the bedroom Simmons clenched his teeth and grunted. Walking over, he saw the caller ID said CARDINAL LOPEZ. He glared at the phone a moment, then answered.

"What is it now, Cardinal?" Simmons hissed, white-knuckling the phone. "Yes, that was my pre-trial bill. Your client has billions of dollars, I'm sure they can sell a few Da Vinci paintings from the secret archives if they need to make payment."

What a bunch of cheap ass-kissers! he thought. *God, I hate priests!* Then he paused, realized his angry tone, took a deep breath. "My apologies. No sleep on the flight and I'm a little jet-lagged…" *From sitting in coach, you asshole.*

"Cardinal, it's late, I'm due in court in the morning. I expect Vance to offer a settlement proposal. Then this will all be over, and your secretary can book my flight back to Dallas. And this time," he said, a knot of anger clawing its way through his throat, "this time, book my damn flight first class." And Simmons punched the END CALL button, and hung up.

CHAPTER THIRTEEN

Grace is born of suffering.

A T 6:31 A.M., STRIPPED TO HIS boxing trunks and 10-ounce leather fighting gloves, Vance slammed the 100-pound hanging bag at Slymm's Gym, drilling and attacking the equipment in a crazed fury.

Stay focused, Vance, he told himself, pounding his gloved fists into it again and again, weaving and punching, punching and sticking, sticking and moving. He wiped his lips with the back of his glove then tucked his chin down and charged at the bag with a series of left hooks, hitting it so ferociously that each shattering shot made his teeth rattle, and took his breath away.

Slymm's was still dark this time of the morning. There were only two other fighters in the gym, hulking Hispanics getting laced up to climb in the ring and spar.

Vance had driven downtown before sunrise, Fatty in the passenger seat, after awakening that morning to find his hands clutching the bedsheets in unexplained terror.

Desperate to drive the fear from his brain, he and the dog stopped to grab coffee from a hipster street barista, a pale white kid with braided dreadlocks blasting a Memphis rap station from his pawn shop boombox. Buying a sprinkled donut for Fatty, Vance scooped the hound up, hustled inside the gym, ducked into the locker room and laced up, pretending to touch fists with an imaginary opponent as he strode to the heavy bag, smashing it with his fists and talking to himself the entire time.

Come at me, you son of a bitch. Come at me.

Fatty sat in a corner of the gym, ears laid flat, gnawing at his donut with monstrous ferocity and guarding Vance and his water bottle. Fatty was a permanent fixture at Slymm's. Anytime one of the fighters rolled up to pet the dog—"How ya doin', boy?"—Fatty snapped his jaws and bared his little teeth, eyes popped wide and glaring out from his furry brow. Waving their arms the boxers fled, and Fatty went back to guarding his master.

In the morning, Vance thought, as he climbed into the ring, *I'll be flying out to New Orleans.*

Four months ago, Vance had filed Murphy's paperwork with the Orleans Parish courts—Orleans Parish being the place where Murphy had first been sexually abused as a boy in the seminary.

He also filed a motion with the Criminal Court in the Hague, hoping the court would recognize any New Orleans judgment against the Vatican as Crimes Against Humanity. It was a longshot, but one Vance felt worth taking.

Once Vance had filed the papers, he felt much better, soothed but thankfully surprised that they took the case. *How could they not?* he thought. He requested the case be fast-tracked, fully expecting the Vatican to object to a speedy trial, their strategy being a long-drawn-out, pitched battle for an out-of-court settlement.

It was with this expectation that he set up a meeting with Judge Delbert T. Berger, an old-school Southern liberal who'd once run for governor, a hardline defender of victims' rights and lost causes. Vance drove on a Wednesday to Louisiana, poked his head into the judge's chambers. Judge Berger was sitting alone in the darkness, dressed in a New Orleans Saints zip hoodie tracksuit, his bare feet up on the desktop, hearing aid turned off, eating from a bag of boiled peanuts while he stared out his window at the Superdome.

Noticing Vance's shadow entering the room, Berger swung around.

"So you know about their hired gun," the judge sighed, after he'd turned on his hearing aid and learned the name of the man who'd be opposing Vance. "And how will you rebut the Church's argument?"

"Well," said Vance, "the Defense has already asked the court to dismiss the case, based upon the Sovereign State Immunity Act—"

"—which places limitations on whether foreign nations can be sued and made responsible for the acts of its citizens," nodded Judge Berger, popping a peanut in his mouth. "And?"

"And the court refused to dismiss the case. There is also the possibility of a common-sense defense."

"Meaning no nation on Earth can be held responsible for the acts of its citizens, employees, or those acting in its behalf," said the judge, plucking the errant shells off his lap. "Which is rather weak, as I see it...Peanut?" He held out the paper bag.

"No, thank you."

"And you think your client, a 92-year-old convicted pedophile diagnosed with Stage 4 cancer, can hold up to the pressure of a trial?"

"All we want is an opportunity to present the facts, and a jury's fair and honest verdict, your Honor."

"You are one crazy sumbitch, son. I like that," said Berger, grinning like a co-conspirator, then turning his hearing aid off again and rotating his eyes back to the Superdome.

Vance instantly felt his worry going away. He felt like he'd won the opening shot and left, dazed at his good fortune.

Misfortune was waiting for him right around the corner, however.

A week later it snowed in Memphis. Vance's home wi-fi and internet had gone out, as had everybody's in the neighborhood.

Driving through a blizzard to the office, Vance trudged across the snowy sidewalk to the door, only to find his key no longer worked. He squinted at the lock, then at the key, then tried again — *No dice, what gives?* — coming to the nasty conclusion that somebody had changed the lock.

Angry, he marched around back to the alley, found a hunk of concrete, broke a window, crawled inside. The office was dark and freezing. *Heat and electricity must be off,* he grumbled, remembering that he'd actually paid the bill this time. Going to the office phone, there was no dial tone. Vance's face reddened. He punched in his office number with his cellphone, waited until a recorded message from customer service told him the line had been disconnected. Vance's eyes got big. *These fellas don't mess around,* he thought, the corner of his mouth twitching as he held back his explosive anger. Then he tilted back in his office chair and gave the room a long hard look.

The death threats, emails promising we're coming after you, were becoming all too common, he mumbled. *And now this.* He knew he was going to have to get used to it.

For a good number of Catholics, sympathy for the victims was something hard to attain, he thought.

One day Vance awoke to find 194 hostile emails and voicemails filling his in-box. The next morning an anonymous letter arrived, enormous unhinged words scrawled on the page in blood-red permanent marker —

STOP NOW.
OR YOU & THE FATHER
WILL BE KILLED
VERY SLOWLY.

Vance was stunned.

In the past, he'd developed a thick skin, an armor plating against attorney dirty tricks. In his heart he knew the Vatican's team of expensive lawyers were screwing with him, intimidating him, sending threats, hacking into his computer, uncovering his unpaid gambling debts, digging into his checking account. It only proved Vance's gut feeling: Murphy's case was a dangerous one, and these guys weren't playing.

It was during the second month after filing the suit that boxes and bulging manila envelopes of legal documents marked STATE OF GEORGIA VS. CHARLES MURPHY, APRIL 2012 seemed to disappear from Vance's office.

Great, just great, he thought, trying not to panic. He scoured the office, searching everywhere—desk drawers, bookcases, his trash cans, under the couch, behind the toilet. Nothing. And nothing else looked disturbed. "Has Jay-Jay been here, hiding things, moving my crap around?" he asked Fatty.

He went out the back door, hunting and digging and plowing through the dumpster, until he was soaked with sweat.

Fumbling to grasp what had happened, he asked his Jamaican landlady, who owned the building and ran the dance studio next door, if she'd noticed any strangers, any visitors. Her answer knocked the breath out of him.

"Don't see any particular people. Just summa dem young skinheads."

"Skinheads? How many?"

"Oh, five, maybe six. Say they got a business for you. Come at night. They have key. Take stuff. Say you ask dem to burn it. Say they come back, visit another time too."

Duly noted, Vance frowned. Still, Vance was convinced he would nail the Church if he could get in front of a jury.

The key is to get depositions, he thought. Statements from well-known psychiatrists, pedophilia experts, and Murphy's victims. It was a dangerous strategy, one Vance knew could backfire. Murphy's victims might not want to go public again. Hell, Vance couldn't blame them. Digging up unspoken episodes of sexual abuse would trigger buried memories that had lain silent for years. Vance knew he couldn't force the victims to testify; what reason could they have for wanting to exonerate the man who'd robbed them of their childhood, stolen their innocence?

What depth of forgiveness could keep those old rages from churning when asked to defend the deviant behavior of a serial pedophile?

And even if some of them were agreeable, how to gather their testimony? Interviewing victims in person was more effective.

Murphy's victims were spread all over America. Beating the bushes and getting all the principles together would be impossibly expensive; Vance's bankroll didn't afford the opportunity to crisscross the country either, hunting up witnesses.

Solicitation of funds was a technique Jay-Jay had mastered as senior partner in a big firm who specialized in hustling insurance companies. Jay-Jay had always solved

Vance's funding problems. But no amount of pleading or gentle coaxing could bring Jay-Jay back into the fold now — even for a noble cause such as Murphy's.

Realizing the odds stacked against him, Vance resented Roland Simmons and the unlimited budget at his disposal even more deeply. Then one day while watching the street coffee barista using Facetime to video-call his girlfriend in Montana, it dawned on Vance: *Why go broke traveling? Sure it's better to reach out in person in cases like this but Good Lord, you can contact half of the damn universe for free on your laptop.* An energetic smile broke across his face.

A decade ago, he'd met with each victim in person, paid for by the Georgia state's expense account. Now he could reach them through the Internet, record their depositions simultaneously without anybody ever being in the same zip code.

Trying to find victims, willing to tell their stories to the world, was not a thought he embraced. The idea of cold calling victims brought back haunting memories from Murphy's first trial.

It's what he bought into though when taking the case.

The next morning, he dug down deep and at 9 A.M. sharp began dialing.

Most victims recoiled at the thought of making a case for their sexual abuser. Several broke down sobbing, others slammed the phone. Two threatened harassment charges if he ever called back.

For a few Vince was able to convince, spewing the trauma Murphy caused them, for years, was enticing enough to get them on board.

Within five days Vance had organized a Zoom meeting to record three victims' depositions, plus those of two experts: Father Timothy Coyle and Dr. Bertram Adler. He sat at his kitchen table, wearing his faded basketball jersey with MEMPHIS GRIZZLIES embroidered across the chest, he pressed a button on his computer desktop.

Slow down, take a deep breath, he told himself. *You've got this.* Then breathing in big gulps, he leaned forward and clicked the START MEETING button.

"Folks, thank you all for joining this Zoom conference as we prepare for Father Charles Murphy's trial. Let me first thank you all for agreeing to testify in this case…

"I understand, Mr. Parker, that you'd rather not be here. To be frank, sir, I'd rather not be here either, but Father Murphy has a right to have his truth told in court, and as his attorney I've vowed to uphold that right. It's also an opportunity, sir, to help others who are not able to display the courage you three have shown, in agreeing to tell your story. To hold the Vatican accountable for grooming Father Murphy to become the abuser of not just you three, but countless others he assaulted."

Looking at the victims' faces streaming before him, their eyes sunken and beaten down, Vance paused. *These poor, pitiful souls. How much torture they've already gone through!* Keeping his head up and remaining strong required a special effort, so Vance smiled sympathetically.

"As victims," he continued," I understand how each of you feel. But for this case to move forward, and for justice to be served, we truly need you on board. You all are doing something very heroic. I asked you to join me today so I can explain how we are going to proceed in court, and what you can expect.

"For the purposes of this call I'll proceed first with the victims.

"You have chosen to record your statements which will be played in open court. Once your recording is public, you will likely be contacted by members of the media. It is your choice to respond or not. And if you choose not to, I have prepared a letter, signed by me, for each of you to send to the media requesting they cease and desist contacting you.

"As for Dr. Adler—" Vance saw the doctor's eyes narrow at him, "you, sir, can expect to be hit hard by the Defense. As a renowned psychiatrist and author who's written about sexual abuse, you will be addressing the specific point of pedophilia development outlined in Father Murphy's complaint. Be prepared for the Defense to accuse you of outright lies and bush-league fabrications in their legal maneuverings."

Dr. Adler started to say something, but Vance caught the look in his eyes and deftly interrupted.

"Finally, there's Father Coyle. We have also privately gone over the history lesson you will share with the court, related to the continual sexual abuse that's run rampart in the Catholic Church for centuries and the limp efforts to subdue it. So integrating yours, Dr. Alder's, and the victims' testimonies, along with the Cardinals, Bishops and ex-Popes I intend to question directly on the stand, should give us a solid prosecuting strategy."

Five faces nodded, the victims seeming comforted by Vance's words. Vance relaxed, hands shaking as if he'd just crawled through a minefield.

"Now, if there are no questions," he said, "I will begin recording your depositions…"

∞ ∞ ∞

Late that night, after concealing multiple copies of the recording on cloud storage sites and using third-party encryption apps, Vance shut down his computer. Now he felt better.

And he still had one hidden card up his sleeve: a star witness named Tyrell Thorne, an African-American ex-priest from Philadelphia who had been sexually molested in the seminary. Thorne claimed it was the Church — A.K.A. the Vatican — playing an active role in developing these characteristics in the young men they recruited, his fellow students coerced into lives of porn and pedophilia. Thorne maintained it was the Church's insistence on young men remaining celibate that forced them to act out their urges on others, and was ready to speak out on the subject, in court, much to Vance's shock and glee.

"When am I due to testify?" Thorne asked over the phone.

"In about a month," Vance said, trying to hold back a smile. "However, sir, let me forewarn you. If you testify, things will get hot."

"Bring it *onnn*," Thorne grunted, and this time Vance didn't hold back his smile.

As soon as Vance got off the line with Tyrell Thorne, his cellphone rang again. He picked it up.

"Vance, this is Booker Harris, of the Memphis Bar Coalition...." Vance squeezed his eyes tight. *Dammit, it's that fat-bellied dirtbag who tried to disbar my ass, what the hell does he want?* "Word is," Harris continued, "you're representing Father Charles Murphy, the convicted pedophile?"

"That's right," Vance said, thinking, *And what the hell business is that of yours, sir?*

"Well, Vance, I just wanted to give you a heads-up."

"A heads-up?" *Jesus, what now?* Vance leaned back in his chair.

"Seems we have new reports of public intoxication involving you," Harris drawled. "A former client of yours describing you as high as a kite on cocaine, crashing your car outside the gates of Graceland, and soliciting topless dancers. Thought you'd like to know the Bar Coalition will be moving forward with disciplinary actions, including an evaluation into your mental incapacity, expedited suspension, and further investigations into revoking your license, as soon as we can get the paperwork filed."

What an ass, Vince thought. Then the words just flew out of him.

"I have to ask you, Counselor, are you a devout Catholic?"

"I am. And proud to be a follower of Christ!"

"Would Christ approve of his priests, his representatives, abusing young children?" With every word, Vance's voice seemed to increase an octave.

"You don't have to answer that Mr. Harris," he continued. "The answer is clear. In closing, Counselor, should you go forward with this disciplinary action, without allowing me to finish this trial, and prove to you, and the board, where my head is at now, well, I think the public will be the ones to judge you. Good day, sir."

Booker Harris paused, and Vance felt the flutter of heart palpitations. "Good day to *you*, Counselor," said Harris, letting the sarcasm sink in.

Vance hung up, lowered his head, a crazy look in his eyes. "Well, shit," he muttered out loud. *High on coke and crashing into Graceland?* Now he was furious; the Vatican was pulling out every stop to make certain he didn't have a prayer of winning at trial. The audacity stuck in his throat.

For weeks he'd managed to stay sober, avoiding old bad habits, keeping out of places like Teasers, not hanging out with drinking buddies like Ted and Easy Money Cecil even though it made him irritable and cranky and triggered his gambling addiction, his hands getting clammy every time he scrolled over his betting app.

As he drove home with Fatty in tow, the thought of having just one drink—just one—pacified him greatly.

"Hell, it's the weekend," he told Fatty, "and I'm thirsty," stopping the car at a mid-city liquor outlet to buy a fifth of Scotch, asking the clerk to wrap it in paper, he slipped the bottle into his filthy jacket, so Fatty wouldn't notice.

Arriving home, he snuck the bottle behind boxes of Cap'n Crunch in the cupboard, washed the dirty breakfast dishes in the sink, and chicken-fried a steak. He wolfed down a jumbo bag of potato chips, waiting for the dog to eat his supper and fall asleep, so he could knock back a few. But Fatty refused to sleep.

"Man, I thought you and me were buddies," Vance scolded the dog. Finally, he took the jacket-swaddled bottle and a glass into the bathroom and sipped his booze quietly. The liquor went down strong, stinging his gut. Vance wanted more. Two more hits was all he needed.

No surprise, it made him feel better. Throttled his confidence.

The old aura of the fearless Atlanta prosecutor returned.

He wanted to drink until his eyes lit with a beastly glow and the room swam each time he lifted his head.

He wanted—no, he *needed*—to convince himself he'd done some of his best legal work on a bender. That he was a better attorney drunk and loosened up. He began to believe it—until he noticed Fatty in the doorway, eyeing him.

Vance gazed at the dog blearily. He rocked back in his seat. "Fatty, go find your chew toy," he scolded, waving the dog away.

Fatty didn't move, just kept staring up, eyes narrowed in silence.

"Look," Vance said, "I appreciate what you're doing. Really I do, boy. But I'm busy here. Go away." Fatty didn't move, gazed up at Vance, eyes pained, wounded.

Vance hunched over, teeth clamped together in anger, seized with indignation. Finally he let his breath out slowly, and said in an apologetic voice, "Sorry, pal. Can I explain?" The little mutt stared at him, as if waiting in the silence for a confession. "I messed up, Fatty. Didn't I? It's never just one drink, is it boy?" Hearing the words come out of his mouth, Vance's face went pale.

Seeing this, Fatty waddled over, and licked Vance's hand. Vance leaned back, cocked his head, his mouth half-open. Every time he took a breath, something stabbed at him. He wiped his face on his sleeve, then locked eyes with the dog, who seemed to pity him.

Trembling with guilt, his thoughts went back to that day at the Memphis kill shelter, and then to Jay-Jay, his long-time partner. Where was Jay-Jay now? Would Jay-Jay, that smooth operator, have been a better fit for a case like this? Pressure like this? Jay-Jay would have protected him, wouldn't have let him get shit-faced and careless and reckless like this.

Plucking Fatty off the floor, Vance hugged the dog. "I love you Fatty," he said. As he did, loneliness exploded through him. *Dear God, I'm petrified. And weak. The demons just won't let go. I can't escape them.* "What can I do?" he whispered in the dog's ear, a wave of dizziness slamming into him.

Then he collapsed.

∞ ∞ ∞

Waking to a snoring dog laying within inches of his right ear, Vance forced himself into a cold shower to rattle his brain into consciousness.

An hour and two coffees later, Vance found himself at Slymm's, viciously hitting the heavy bag. Wanting to sweat out the booze and get his mind straight. Remembering Alcoholics Anonymous' adage, "Once an alcoholic, always an alcoholic," a moto he desperately didn't want to believe in. Knowing he could beat the addiction on his own.

Suddenly the ringside bell rang, forcing Vance out of his trance. He looked up; more fighters had entered the gym now, trainers on the ropes yelling at boxers, a southpaw sparring partner suffering a knockdown, another raising his fists in victory. The winner was a local kid with a spotless record. Twelve fights. Ten by knockout. Considered a contender for a spot on the Olympic Team.

Perspiration dripped from Vance's face, puddling on the floor. He cast his eyes down, his jaw going slack, remembering every boozy day and blitzed night.

The past few months disgusted him. He blamed himself for taking Murphy's case, when he wasn't ready, should have been in detox, straightening out his life. He had a son, Jordan, whose entire adult life he'd missed out on, who probably hated him, rejected him as a father, and Vance needed to push all that pain on somebody, on something, on—

That's when he heard the trainer call his name. "Vance, the kid needs a sparring partner. You up for it?"

Vance looked at Fatty, asleep in the corner, head leaned against the wall. He tied his leash to a hook where a dozen jackets and dirty gym bags hung, jammed against each other. *Hell yeah,* he thought. *Why not give the kid a chance to kick my ass? A beat down I probably need.*

Banging his gloves together, Vance nodded.

Leaning through the ropes he got a close-up of the kid. *He must have thirty pounds on me,* he thought, *not to mention thirty years.*

The bell rang...and suddenly the kid's face became Murphy's. Vance took a few stinging left jabs, followed by a vicious uppercut. One that had floored the kid's previous sparring partner. Vance didn't feel a thing.

Seeing Murphy's face, he felt a rage that had his adrenaline working overtime. He began throwing haymakers that missed as his opponent bobbed and weaved.

Until he couldn't.

Vance had the kid in the corner throwing body shots and uppercuts that would have knocked the heavy bag off its chains. There was nowhere for the kid to run.

I have you cornered, Murphy. And this time you're going down for the count. It's all or nothing, Mr. Pedophile. One shot for every kid you destroyed.

Vance didn't hear the bell ring as the kid lay crumbled in the corner, the trainer stepping between his fighter and the wild-eyed attorney twice the kid's age, yelling for Vance to stop.

Out of the corner of his eye Vance saw Wally jump in the ring, arms wrapping around Vance. 'What the hell, man?" Fatty barked feverishly trying to pull the hook off the wall and save his master from Wally's grips.

Vance looked at Wally, tears in his eyes, staring into nothingness.

"Go home Vince!" Wally shouted. "You're done for the day. And get your shit together, man!"

In the locker room Vance's shower was plagued by visions of a bloody Murph, cuts over both eyes, bleeding from the mouth. *You deserved it worse than you got, old man,* the voice in his head screamed.

His thoughts of Murphy were interrupted by a familiar voice. Wally, a 6'4" behemoth of a man at 75 who once fought Kenny Norton, stood outside the shower stall.

Vance and Wally had been close ever since he moved to Memphis and he helped him settle a lawsuit that allowed Wally to keep the gym and avoid bankruptcy.

"Vince, I know you're going through shit right now with this trial, but please take that rage into the courtroom, not here."

"You're right. Just all the pressure with..." Vance paused, then asked, "How's the kid?"

"His ego's a little shot after getting a beat down by an old man, but he'll be fine."

Walking away, Wally grinned. "If lawyering ain't your style anymore, looks like you got a place in the ring. Imagine the headlines: 'Old man fights for the heavyweight championship of the world.' Every AARP senior will pay to see that one."

Vance chuckled, apologizing again as Wally waved him off.

Shit, Vance thought as he slid into his $125 Walmart suit, straightened his second-hand shop tie and looked in the mirror then at Fatty.

Maybe I am still a drunk. Addicted to a lousy bet. But I just gave a contender a beatdown he'll always remember. If you can beat the kid, shit, maybe you can beat the Vatican.

As he gazed down at Fatty it flashed into his mind all at once. *Beating the kid is one thing. Wining a case like this, in a courtroom? It has to be in the name of something greater than saving a pedophile's soul.*

Hell, maybe winning isn't about forcing the Church to pay damages, getting a shitload of money, enough to buy a hundred homes, a thousand hot babes and a million bottles of booze. Maybe a win will be the beginning of healing the souls of the innocent, Vance thought.

In his soul, he knew this should be his true purpose.

It was the first honest conversation he'd had with himself in months. Then just as quickly his spirits sank. *But I'm not Vance the Savior anymore. I'm a broken-down drunk, a lush, an addict, a loser and a lunatic.* He stopped in the middle of mind-rant, found Fatty looking up at him, ears dropped down, eyes burning with sadness, the glint of adoration for his master vanished.

Vance slumped back. *Christ, I really do need a drink. A drink will fix everything. A drink will save me.*

Thinking of that, he slipped into a trance, imagining himself standing on a Memphis sidewalk, looking in the window of Teasers, his face like that of a man who's starving, deprived, ravenous. *I'll quit the case. I'll call Murphy and quit. Tell him I'm finished, I need to pull out. Or beg him to settle. Then I can celebrate with a drink I want but don't need. I can let go of my insane convictions.* Vance looked over his shoulder at the dog, who stared back, his droopy eyes blinking twice before closing completely.

The damn dog can read my thoughts, Vance thought.

Even he's disgusted with all this back and forth. Drink. No drink. Drink. No drink.

Make a decision, dammit, Vince!

And then the deeper truth hit him, and he straightened to his full height. *But I can beat this. Sure, the game is rigged. It's rigged against our side, against the victims. But gambling is something I understand.*

Suddenly Vance felt embarrassed for not seeing this before. The stakes were high because he was gambling with a man's soul. That was the burden that was trying to crush him. But he'd bet on the horses, on the races, on the ballers and the brawlers. He'd bet on who could piss the longest and the farthest with Easy Money Cecil.

So what if the stakes were high. He was a gambler. Gambling was his compulsion. If he could gamble on a long shot in the feature at Belmont, he could gamble on a more righteous purpose, healing the tortured souls of the victims.

He was always at his best when something was on the line. *Why not bet on myself for once?* Vance thought. *The odds makers give me 500-1 to make the Vatican pay.*

"Fatty, let's go," he said to the dog, drenching his face with water and grabbing a towel out of his gym bag. "I need to wrap this hand. And I need to make a few calls."

Raising his head. Cocking it to the left. Fatty eagerly followed.

Hobbling out of the dressing room, Vance plopped down on a wooden bench. Brought up his MGM app and laid down $1,000 on the case.

Then, using one numb finger, he dialed the Orleans Parish courthouse, where the padre had been transferred to under the shadow of the impending trial.

As the phone rang he waited, rubbing his swollen hand, his brain blazing with images of winning the case, the jury swayed by his masterful summation, Judge Berger in awe of his performance, his legal calculations, his star witness, the defense fulminating, wicked Roland Simmons ripping his hair out. Receiving an automated voice service, he was routed to the courthouse jail, then held the line waiting for Murphy to come on. The voice he heard was Murphy's, but sounded tired, wooden, expressionless.

"Guess you heard the news," said Murphy.

"News?" Vance shifted in his seat, his heartbeat thumping.

"No shit? You haven't heard?" Murphy hesitated, concern in his voice. "Looks like the Big Guy's dealt me the joker card. You know He loves surprises."

Vance's jaw stiffened. *You're making me nervous now,* he thought. Quickly he set his mind back on winning the case, dragging the towel across his face.

"Can you be more specific?" he asked.

Murphy chuckled. "Story I have from the Doc is I only have a few months left to live. Said I should expect increased pain, fatigue, loss of appetite, confusion, maybe even delirium and hallucinations as I near the end stage."

Suddenly Vance's head buzzed with the drone of panic. He leaned over his phone, eyes closed, realizing they were always headed this way, toward a violent meeting with Fate. He set his jaw, trying not to let the sob rising inside of him escape. *This can't be happening, God.*

"You call for something in particular, Vince?" Murphy asked.

Vance forced his eyes open, stared at the glowing phone screen, didn't answer. He felt Fatty's warm tongue on the back of his leg, licking his ankle. His hands gripped the phone tighter. He opened his mouth to say the words, to answer, but something inside of him broke.

"Just called to see if you needed anything," he said, a choking sound in his throat. "And to pray for you, old-timer."

Hanging up his body shook.

Why did he care? Why the hell did he say he'd pray for him? For God's sake, the man tortured far too many to deserve prayers!

The emotion struck him far harder than any in his 64 years on this planet. So deep-seated it rankled his senses.

Almost like a bodily shift. From outrage to...what? Compassion?

Forgive the man, his inner voice echoed, *and move on. Let Karma take its course.*

Hell, maybe that's what this trial is all about, Karma and balancing the scales of justice.

CHAPTER FOURTEEN

Chicanery can ignite a blaze of determination.

VANCE PARKED HIS TINY HONDA in front of Walk-On's Sports Bistreaux on South Rampart Street, three blocks southeast of the New Orleans Civil District Courthouse.

He'd wakened in the Economy Inn on Chef Menteur Highway at 6 A.M. with Fatty beside him and his heart thumping in his throat. A quick shower and breakfast at Big Ed's, a 50s-style diner less than one hundred yards from the Inn, and Vance was back sitting on the bed, head sweating, arms shaking, knowing he was going into a battle he hadn't faced in ten years.

Damn, 8 o'clock already. Can't put this off any longer.

"Be back in a jiffy," he whispered to the still-snoozing mutt, leaving the little guy cuddled in the unmade, still-warm motel bed, having begged one of the soft-hearted maids to peek in on Fatty during the day.

As he'd chugged the battered Honda toward the court-house, spewing blue exhaust fumes, Vance decided to stop first at a corner Seven-Eleven. He bought a couple of candy bars, needing a sugar high.

On his return to the car he paused on the sidewalk to try Jay-Jay's number one more time, feeling a desperate need to speak to his old partner, their break-up still hanging over Vance's head.

The call rang twice, three times then went straight to voice-mail. "Jay-Jay, it's me, listen, I…" *Jesus, why is this so hard?* "…I was a jerk, and I…aw, shit, brother, I love you. Call me back." Vance's voice broke, and he hung up the call, dripping sweat from the Louisiana heat. *Oh hell, he probably thinks I'm drunk.*

His mind full of unspoken words, Vance walked with his head down toward the Honda, stopping when he noticed the business he'd parked by was Sip's Lounge, a cocktail bar.

Vance's heart beat faster. He felt his sobriety falling away, suddenly wanting, needing, to get roaring drunk, to go on a bender. *The hell am I thinking?* he realized. *I could get the trial dismissed, if I go on a bender!* Faith in his once-imposing courtroom skills was skidding quickly downhill. And all night long, the court bailiff's office had been calling him, leaving messages, prompting the Prosecution team to be on time for court.

What the hell's everybody so worried about?

Vance's head began to ache. He looked down at the candy bars in his fist, a king-sized Baby Ruth and a

Butterfinger, squeezing them. Then he turned on his heels and climbed into his car.

When he sat behind the wheel, sinking down in his seat and devouring the Baby Ruth, chocolate melting across his face, he felt better, more in control. He slipped the Butterfinger in his coat pocket, flipped the radio on and started the engine, ramming his foot down on the gas as he drove with WWOZ 99.7 blasting Big Joe Williams the final two miles through the neon and traffic of Basin Street to the courthouse.

By the time he parked and stepped onto Poydras Street, stooped over under the weight of his briefcase stuffed with trial documents, Vance was out of breath. A hot, gusty wind whistled down the sidewalk. Rounding the corner, he looked at the colossal glass-fronted courthouse and froze in terror.

The building was surrounded by TV trucks and police cars. The wind howled and roared around a mob of screaming protestors. It looked like a riot, Vance thought, a cross between a riot and a three-ring circus.

Vance heard the shriek of police sirens behind him, nervously shoved his hands in his pockets and kept walking. The street was blocked off with yellow tape, lines of police dogs on leather leashes barking. More cop cruisers slammed around the corner of Loyola Avenue, lights flashing.

Standing at the bottom of the courthouse steps Vance saw a crowd of demonstrators, chanting slogans in a deafening chorus, the mob surging toward him. Some had ripped up the courthouse foliage, tossing trash cans and splashing graffiti on the glass walls. As Vance got closer, he noticed a fenced-in area had been erected for the media, cameras zooming in on him, reporters waving their cell-phones dashing across the street, all yelling his name.

Vince! Vince Vance! Hey, it's Vance!

Vance ducked down, elbowed through the mics and the cameras being thrust in his face, shielding himself with his briefcase. "Move it! Get the hell out of my way!" he shouted. New Orleans PD officers pushed the media and the protes-tors back, TV lights flashing in his eyes. Squaring his shoul-ders, Vance veered left, shoving through the crowd, batting away the protest signs—HANDS OFF OUR CHILDREN! JUSTICE FOR THE VICTIMS OF THE CHURCH—preparing himself to get cracked on the skull and beaten to death.

Vance dodged and weaved away from the screaming crowd and the blinding lights, fists clamped tight around his briefcase, swinging it like a club, fingers and hands claw-ing at him, wondering if it was all a bad dream. He batted at the crowd of reporters and they drew back. He plowed forward, seeing a path open, two mustached cops in riot gear blocking the bottom of the steps.

The first cop, the shorter of the two, held up a hand. "Who the hell're *you?*"

Vance stared at him, nerves shot, for a moment racking his brain. "I'm the Prosecution attorney!"

The officers looked at Vance and grimaced. Another barrage of screams and shouts roared behind him.

Reporters swarmed forward—*"Vance! Over here! Give us a statement!"*—microphones thrust at the sky. Hands clawed in a blur at his neck and throat, ready to pounce.

"Listen, I need to get in there!" Vance pointed.

The two cops stood there, staring Vance down, disgusted. Vance held up a finger to say something. As he opened his mouth, the smaller policeman grabbed him by the lapel, hollering in a hysterical voice, looking at Vance as if he'd gone crazy. *"Suing the Church? You oughta be ashamed!"* he bellowed, loosening his fingers and thrusting Vance halfway up the stairs, the attorney rolling onto his back.

Getting to his feet, Vance quickly mounted the staircase, panting now, risking one final glance at the crowd of reporters and protestors, ripping and clawing after him. Then he fled.

∞   ∞   ∞

Inside the courthouse, after Vance had been frisked and searched and escorted through the metal detector and handed off to an armed guard, his stomach was bubbling. He raced off to the men's room and heaved his guts out into the toilet. *Feeling better now?* he sighed. Then he got up, tightened the knot in his tie, the paisley one his son Jordan had gifted him ten birthdays ago, and staggered back into the lobby.

He reached the curved staircase going down, stopped to tighten his grip on his briefcase and massage his temples, and looked around. There was a long line of spectators crowding into Courtroom B. Avoiding their eyes, Vance turned to face the other direction.

Suddenly an icy chill spread through him—studying him from across the lobby was Defense counsel Simmons and his hotshot lawyer team, camped outside the judge's chambers. Vance stiffened, his throat going dry, seeing the beady black eyes of Roland Simmons go small and then smaller for a moment, as if reducing Vance to nothingness. Then Simmons grinned, pivoted, showing Vance his back as he and his team headed into court.

Vance sighed, hair matted against his temples. Jittery and exhausted, he glanced at his watch, fumbled with his briefcase, hunched his shoulders forward, then headed downstairs to visit his client.

The courthouse jail was in the basement, a deep and dark subterranean place with marble floors and cold gray walls. Father Murphy was waiting for Vance in his cell. As he entered, the old man rose from his metal bunk, his hand outstretched.

Not wanting to shake a pedophile's hand, he deadpanned, with a sly smile, "Help an old altar boy out, fadduh"? quoting an old movie line from *The Exorcist*.

He was doing his best to show compassion for the dying old man, when every cell still wanted to choke the man unconscious.

I'm here for the greater good, Vance kept reminding himself.

Murphy's response faded into an abyss, as Vance stared like a deer caught in high beams, his first look at Murphy a shocker.

His mane of silvery white hair was gone now, the hairline receding, a grizzled five-day beard cut jaggedly. One blue eye was half-shut, the lid hanging down, as if somebody'd tried to blind him with a hot poker. His wrinkled flesh was stripped of color, bruises rising on both arms — probably from the chemo, Vance decided. One hand was clapped over a worn-out old Bible. Papers, with notes scribbled illegibly, bulging from its hundreds of pages.

"Just got through re-writing the crucifixion scene. Made the Roman henchmen seem less like assholes," chirped Murphy, as he struggled to take his seat next to Vance.

Vance wasn't listening. Frozen, his entire body screamed to turn and run. Logic assaulted him. *You locked this monster up; now you're freeing him?*

Snatched from the silence with the crowd filtering from the courtroom upstairs, Vance's inner voice spoke an octave louder. *The man is trying to make a difference. Give him empathy.*

The first time they'd met, Murphy's benevolent smile stunned him. Now when Murphy smiled, that same goodhearted smile, it was the old man's sunken eyes that gave away his sickness. The irises floating, they looked exhausted, deathly ill. *Poor guy looks like he's swimming underwater,* Vance thought, *drowning and running out of time fast, as* they sat together on a bench, both men slouched against the metal cell cage.

190

Seeing Vance, Murphy's eyes glittered. "I missed you, Vince."

Vance gave him a quizzical look. *Missed me?* For a second, he wondered if Murphy was kidding him. He felt a nervous need to ask, to say something, to inquire about the old man's health, the cancer, anything personal. It burned his mouth not to say something. But he swallowed against it, and said nothing. Finally Murphy shrugged it off, sighed and looked up at the ceiling.

"You want me to go over the case files with you?" Vance asked.

Murphy kept staring at the ceiling, not saying anything. At last he flicked his eyes over to Vance, and his blue eyes glittered.

"You ever drop acid, Counselor?" he asked.

Vance raised an eyebrow. "Acid?"

"Psychedelics." A glint showed in Murphy's eyes. "Today's Top Five list is a dilly. My all-time top sports achievements while flying on psychedelics. There's Doc Ellis' 1970 no-hitter for the Pirates while under the influence of LSD. Mike Tyson soaring on magic mushrooms when he bit Evander Holyfield's ear off. Not to forget Aaron Rodgers ingesting ayahuasca—a psychedelic drink—during his MPV season in 2020…"

Vance relaxed, his face softening. A second later he heard the guard coming over, rattling his keys, rapping his knuckles on the cage. "It's time, Counselor."

Vance sat silent, hypnotized by the priest's nutty spiel. Murphy's last words broke the spell. "Ready for the trial of the century, Vince?"

Clearing the knot in his throat, Vance asked, "You sure you want to do this? Go through with this?"

Murphy's eyes met Vance's again. A dreamy smile came over his face. "Don't be an asshole, son," he said.

The guard rapped on the cage again. "Well, guess I'll see you upstairs," said Vance, rising to exit. For a split second he wanted to tell the old man they were going to win; clients always liked the sound of that. *Would it make things any better? Probably not.* Instead he gulped down the words, picked up his briefcase, turned to exit, his head down. Then he stopped in the doorway, hearing Murphy's voice.

"It's a sin to hate, you know. I don't hate the Church. I just want them to be held accountable."

Vance looked back at him. Murphy smiled. Feeling the guard take his arm, Vance retreated back up the stairs to the courtroom.

∞ ∞ ∞

The rumble of spectators massing at the doors to Courtroom B shattered Vance's angst.

As he joined them, plowing forward, armed court officers squeezing everybody through the entrance shoulder to shoulder, he felt...what? A surge of peace and relief? *I feel back home,* he realized.

In two big strides he jostled past the spectators, strode into the court, approached the Prosecution table, plopped his briefcase on one of the mahogany seats, leaving the second seat empty for his client. This is the place where he had all the moves, the slick tricks, the cunning it took to outfox his opponent. He smiled and nodded, buttoned his vest and his jacket, took in the whole courtroom, the gallery of onlookers, the platoon of court officers, the clerk's desk and the witness stand and turned to his right —

And froze.

Ten feet away the Defense team was staring at him. Four highly-polished, thousand-dollar-an-hour attorneys, faces blank, eyes sharp, watching. *And waiting,* Vance realized, *but for what?* A couple of them turned to whisper in another's ear, but kept staring at Vance. Roland Simmons, at the center, silk suit, silk shirt and pearl-studded tie clip, stared too, his glare scalding.

Vance didn't flinch. *Keep staring, asshole.*

Yet something about the way they all stared, their sly and crafty expressions, disturbed Vance, and made the hairs on his arm stand on end. He took his seat, and as he sat the craving for alcohol became a roaring volcano.

C'mon, Vance. Just breathe. Get through the next minute.

There was a loud clank, and Vance's heart leaped inside his chest. He whirled, spied Father Murphy entering through a side door, in manacles, escorted by four guards. His entrance produced an explosion of gasps in the courtroom, whispers, angry chatter, gossip.

For a long minute, Vance sat completely still, watching Murphy slowly cross the room, hands clasped, his legs barely keeping him up, one of the guards holding him steady. As he approached Vance, he grinned. He paused at the desk, held up his hands, watched as the manacles were removed. Taking his seat, he leaned in and whispered in Vance's ear.

"It's showtime, brother. Now the real surprises begin."

Vance narrowed his eyes, uncomprehending, but didn't say anything. *Surprises? What surprises?* Then a chamber door opened, the court bailiff bellowed, "All rise!" Heads whirled, eyes cut toward the bench, the gossip and chatter stopped, and what Vance saw knocked the wind out of him.

As the courtroom silenced, striding in huge loud steps toward the bench marched His Honor Finn Conor O'Grady, a gargantuan red-bearded, red-headed Irishman, a powerhouse Louisiana judge who wore his Catholic faith like a mantle of righteousness.

Vance knew the big face and enormous hands from O'Grady's political ads on billboards stretching from the Texas line across to Biloxi, up and down Interstate 10. Born to a family of moonshiners, baptized in the backwoods and too smart to stay there, he'd served as Chief Justice of the Louisiana Supreme Court until 2015; now frightened attorneys called his district court "the Valley of Death."

Vance stared, bewildered, the hairs on his neck prickling. He shook his head...*Whoa, wait, what's going on here? What the hell happened to Judge Berger?* Everything seemed to be happening in slow motion.

He stared at O'Grady, whipped his eyes to the Defense table, at Roland Simmons; the man was staring right back at Vance, a goofy grin on his face, smirking and smugly laughing. *You didn't expect to win, did you?* that look said. But the grin was the worst part, the grin of a man who'd just spat in Vance's face.

Vance gaped at Simmons and felt his jaw drop. *Smooth, you are too smooth.* He hunched over, face almost touching the desktop, numb even with the loud buzz of the court-room. *Vance you dummy,* he whispered to himself, *you choked. This is a set-up, and you didn't see it coming.* He stared at the judge, mortified, humiliated. Suddenly his head throbbed, from lack of sleep, lack of preparation, lack of al-cohol. Now he realized what all those missed calls from the court bailiff were. His shoulders slumped. First minute in court, first minute of the trial, and Simmons had already sucker-punched him.

BOOMBOOMBOOM—

Judge O'Grady banged and slammed down his gavel and got quickly to the point. "Judge Berger has suffered a terrible injustice this morning. A horrible pain in his chest." Vance felt eyes in the courtroom move on him, his hands going clammy. "I'm in charge of this shit-show now. Every-body take your seats. Bailiff, bring in the jury. Counselor Vance, be a good boy and enthrall us please with the Prose-cution's opening statement."

The lawyers sat. So did the spectators, and Father Mur-phy. Vance sank down in his chair. His eye roved over the jury box, the witness stand, then to the Defense table, eyeing it with hostility.

Across the aisle Roland Simmons stared back at him, dark eye sockets burning, a smug twist to his lips, Vance watching his rival with an agonized expression, until Judge O'Grady's harsh voice broke into his consciousness.

"…Counselor Vance? Counselor?" Vance noticed the judge was hunched forward, snapping his fingers, as if trying to waken him. "You ready, sir? Or did you just drop by my court to shoot the breeze with us?" he glared, then defiantly rocked back in his chair.

Vance's eyes opened wide. Startled, his thoughts a million miles away, he bent over, staring at the yellow legal pad of notes on his desktop, his face locked in a grimace, his mouth open for words that would not come. Beneath the Prosecution table his knees wobbled. Thinking about winning the case seemed insane now—yet the thought of losing filled him with fire.

Bring it on, you hotshots, he thought, nodding to himself, gritting his teeth, as he and Simmons stared hatefully at each other. Then kicking back his chair, pulling in his stomach, and drawing a deep breath, Vance rose and strode to the jury, surveying the court as he gave his opening statement.

The Trial

CHAPTER FIFTEEN

"**L**ADIES AND GENTLEMEN OF THE JURY," said Vance, leaning on the wall of the jury box, his adrenaline pumping as he scanned the twelve faces, "and my esteemed brothers and sisters!" he added, waving his arms to acknowledge the courtroom of spectators, the bailiff and guards, the reporters hastily scribbling notes. "Sexual abuse—whether verbal, emotional or physical—and rape are crimes, heinous crimes against humanity.

"Those are not my words. Those are sentiments expressed by the United Nations and its Human Rights Council through the International United Nations' Committee Against Torture (CAT) and through International Human Rights Law.

"In fact, CAT specifically stated if the abuse is systemic, it may qualify as torture, especially if the state is complicit or negligent in its prevention.

"Further, Article 2 and 16 of the United Nations Convention Against Torture require states to prevent acts of torture and other cruel treatment by public officials or with their acquiescence. Failure to prevent or punish sexual abuse in institutional settings, especially involving state or church complicity, can be prosecuted on the international level under CAT.

"In addition, ladies and gentlemen, the International Tribunal also wrote that rape and systemic sexual abuse are *torture*, a crime under international law — and a crime we intend to prove the Vatican is guilty of, and should be prosecuted for on the international stage under CAT."

Taking a beat, Vance said in a firm voice, "I remind you folks," nodding as he turned to Judge O'Grady, "that in its annual human rights report Amnesty International cited the Vatican for widespread evidence of childhood sexual abuse by members of its clergy, which the organization described as being the Vatican's agents and representatives across the globe, lasting for decades. *Decades!* Amnesty International cited 'an enduring failure' by the Vatican to seek redress for its crimes.

"In fact, several of these representatives, right here in this great city of New Orleans, have been accused of sexually abusing numerous children, over and over again. The archdiocese' very own records show the Vatican had known of these crimes of torture for decades. What was done? Priests were moved to other parishes, without telling parishioners there was a pedophile leading their congregation. And did those priests abuse more children? Unfortunately, the answer is a very big *Yes*. Is the Vatican complicit in this New Orleans case? Absolutely. It is one of hundreds of thousands of cases, for decades, the Vatican has been complicit in."

Casting his eyes to Father Murphy, who sat ramrod straight at the Prosecution table, Vance pointed to his client.

"Ladies and gentlemen of the Jury, and Your Honor, I represent Father Charles Murphy. A man who was sentenced to prison for the remainder of his life, for unspeakable, wicked crimes. A man I prosecuted and put away myself. A man who has admitted to sexually abusing young boys, not just once or twice, mind you, but for years...for *decades*."

Every eye in the courtroom swept over to Murphy. He raised his eyebrows at Vance. Vance stroked his chin and turned back to the jury.

"Now Father Murphy insists he was not born a pedophile. The first time I heard him declare this I became angry. How dare he make such a statement after abusing so many innocent children! Anger may be an understatement, if I am to be honest. But then I listened. I listened to him explain that his first desires, at the impressionable age of 13, were to have a girlfriend. That he was targeted by the Church at an age when his hormonal urges were just kicking in. That his pedophilia was induced and ignited not by exposure to pornography, not solely by his own urges, but by becoming a victim of the very institution he worked for—the Vatican!"

Murphy stared at Vance, didn't move a muscle.

"I listened to the fact he begged for classes that would teach young seminarians how to deal with their sexual urges. Yet he was denied this, time and again by the Vatican.

"Brothers and sisters, we intend to prove the Vatican is guilty of crimes against humanity—guilty by methodically, meticulously and knowingly orchestrating the systemic sexual abuse, rape and torture of hundreds of thousands of children across the globe, through its institutional policy of celibacy.

"We intend to prove that the Vatican *made* Father Murphy a pedophile," Vance announced emphatically, scanning the hushed courtroom and giving Judge O'Grady a challenging stare.

"We also intend to prove that the Vatican, through its policies of moving pedophile priests from one parish to another, knowing they would sexually abuse children again, is guilty of crimes against humanity—and should be prosecuted as such!

"In closing, ladies and gentlemen, it is crucial to emphasize that The International Criminal Court at The Hague is observing this trial with unwavering focus. They have formally agreed to recognize this court's judgment as equivalent to their own—binding, final, and enforceable. It falls upon you to deliver justice long denied—to ensure that the hundreds of thousands of men and women, who have carried the scars of childhood betrayal for decades, may at last know peace, and see their suffering honored not with silence, but with truth, accountability, and rightful redress." Taking a pause, Vance stepped back. "Thank you."

Vance could feel the heat of O'Grady's seething glare trailing him to the Prosecution table, his fury stoked by the revelation that another court had fixed its gaze on the unfolding trial.

Sinking heavily into his seat, Vance looked to Roland Simmons for a reaction. Strangely, he found the entire Defense team was smiling. Vance turned away, staggered.

∞　∞　∞

"Will the Defense please make its opening statement?" Judge O'Grady said in a deadly, flat tone, leaning back and folding his hands in his lap.

Roland Simmons rose. Elegant in his double-breasted and tailored gray Gucci suit he strode confidently up to the jury, focusing his attention calmly on the foreman, a short bald-headed man with black, heavy eyeglasses.

"Ladies and gentlemen...The Prosecution just told you they intend to prove the Vatican is guilty of a crime. A heinous, abominable crime, an unspeakable crime. A crime for which an entire nation is guilty, they claim. This is an extremely dangerous path to walk down," Simmons nodded, pacing slowly down the jury box, as if loving every eye focused square on him, "for no nation in history has ever been found guilty of any crime committed by its citizens, nor any of its representatives. Such a finding would establish precedent you don't want to set," he said turning to the judge, "for if you do—if *we*, ladies and gentlemen, do—every government, every township, every neighborhood across the globe whose citizens commit any sort of crime will be held responsible. And *that*, ladies and gentlemen, will be the end of all government, all community, and all respect for the rule of law and order as you and I know it.

"You see," Simmons said, showing his fury as he slapped his hands down firmly on the jury box and leaned forward, "it is *men*, not institutions, who are guilty of these crimes! *Men* who raped. *Men* who molested and abused children. *Men* like Father Charles Murphy," he scowled and pointed, "who after taking an oath to God, to uphold His eternal laws, went behind His back, as if the Almighty couldn't see, and sexually abused and preyed upon hundreds of thousands of innocent boys and girls! Children just like your own!" he snapped at a wide-eyed woman in the front row, who stared in steely silence.

"Men like Father Murphy are predators. They were made predators by their own *choice*, their own *weakness* — they were not made nor produced by any government, any religious institution. There is no doubt it is these *men*, these fiendish *monsters*, who are to be prosecuted. And prosecuted they must be!" And Simmons threw his hands in the air.

"But *not* the Vatican," he said, turning his gaze over to Murphy. "Not the nation they reported to. Not the nation that passed laws to prevent their disgusting and deviant behavior, laws to protect our innocent children from the depraved."

Pacing back to the foreman, Simmons spoke the next words slowly, quietly. "Just men. Heinous, abhorrent pedophiles. Prosecute *them*. Not the Vatican. Thank you."

Simmons dipped his chin, remained silent a moment. Then the Pallbearer strolled back to the Defense table, never once looking over at Vance.

Across the aisle, Vance took a deep breath, his face flushed. The seconds ticked by in silence.

"Counselor Vance, sir, we'll hear your first witness."

Vance didn't seem to hear. He blinked and looked away and seemed uncomfortable, in deep concentration. Seeing the judge staring at him he straightened up.

"Counselor Vance?"

"The Prosecution calls Father Timothy Coyle to the stand," Vance said.

Clearing his throat, leaning forward, Vance rose and began the first witness's testimony.

"Father Coyle, please state your credentials, sir."

"I have been a priest for 50 years. I served as a canon lawyer in the 1980s at the Vatican embassy in Washington. I have five Master's Degrees, and a doctorate in Canon Law. I assisted in the report *How the Vatican Declined to Defrock a U.S. Priest Who Abused Deaf Boys.* I have reviewed over 1,000 sex abuse cases all over the world, from the United States, Ireland, England, Australia and Canada to New Zealand, Belgium and Brazil." He looked at Vance coolly and paused. Vance's eyebrows rose gently.

"Go on, sir."

"And I lost my collar and my calling because I pursued the issue of sexual abuse in the Church, and the cover-up by the Vatican."

"When did you first realize how widespread the sexual abuse problem was in the Catholic Church, Father Coyle?"

"In the 1980s. I presented a report, *The Problem of Sexual Molestation by Roman Catholic Clergy*."

"And upon presenting this report, you were told…?"

"I was told the Vatican knew all about the flaws, and had a policy to deal with them."

"What was the Vatican's policy?"

In the witness chair, Father Coyle squirmed. "When I asked about the policy, I was told nothing was actually written down."

"I see. What else were you told?"

"I was told that if I wanted to continue a career in the Church, I'd need to put this 'abuse stuff' behind me. I didn't, and was soon let go of my job at the Vatican embassy, and have been an inactive priest ever since."

"I'm sorry that happened, sir." Vance turned away to see Simmons smirk at him. *You smug bastard,* Vance thought, shaking his head, struggling to keep his focus on the witness.

"Father Coyle," he said, looking down at his shoes, "do you believe in the concept of forgiveness?

"Of course. Christ teaches us that."

"And yet as a forgiving man, you still lay blame. Whom do you blame for the abuse of these children?"

"The Bishops and Cardinals who tried to conceal and lie about the issue for decades. But ultimately, the blame was and is the Vatican's."

"Why the Vatican's?"

"Because in trying to deal with it, they've moved deeper into dishonesty. Lying. Covering it up. Making it more systemic."

"Can you be more specific?"

"The system creates pedophile priests. The system produces these predators, these hungry beasts in collars who prey on innocence." Coyle shook his head and let it hang a moment. He locked eyes with Father Murphy. *Go on, go on,* Vance's mind screamed. *Stop staring and tell the jury your story!* "The boys they preyed on are yearning for fatherly affection. Seeing this, the priest grooms them. Shows a special interest in them. The relationship becomes intimate. The child is seduced by the priest's attention. They have a bond, a secret—to the child, it's like having a secret with God Himself. The priest then isolates the child. Quickly their secret relationship becomes a sexual imprisonment. The child is trapped, a captive in a cage, abused over and over in a torture chamber. Eventually he succumbs to the priest's desires, and becomes the priest's pet. This abuse doesn't start with the priest. It trickles down, from the Vatican's chain of command. From the Pope down."

"You're saying that instead of fixing the problem, the Pope becomes the ultimate keeper of secrets."

"It's like having Hitler fix the problem of anti-Semitism among the SS. There is no 'will' to fix it. The only 'will' there has been is to collectively and methodically cover it up, to protect the image of the institution."

"Can you expound on that?"

"Say the victim goes to the police. The Church dismisses the molestation claims. The allegations get swept under the rug. While the Church hides it, priests go on raping and abusing and preying on kids. After too many molestation claims, these priests are moved to another parish, then another, and another. Their victims are too scared and ashamed by what they've done to ever come forward. The Vatican and its leadership have been aware of the sexual abuse issue for the entire duration of the Church's existence.

"In my 2006 book, *Sex, Priests and Secret Codes: The Catholic Church's 200 Year Paper Trail of Sexual Abuse,* I traced the history of clergy sexual abuse of children to 98 A.D., the same century the Church was founded. But it became a bigger problem once celibacy was mandated."

"Why did celibacy make it worse?"

"As I said, the problem is systemic. The Church recruited young boys into the priesthood. Many of these young boys are awkward, introverted, with few friends, rejected by their classmates, without a father figure. They yearn to belong to something. So when the priests—holy men who are admired and revered in the Church—approach these young boys to join, many of them jump at the chance to be respected and looked up to. Even today, with young men joining the priesthood at an older age, many of them have the same issues of belonging and fraternity lacking in their lives.

"The bottom line is that the recruitment system of the Church does not embrace a motto like the Marines, *Be All*

That You Can Be, but rather, a motto something akin to *Fade Into the Fold.*"

Vance nodded, turned to face the jury. "Father Coyle, you're the expert. Tell us, sir, about the history of celibacy."

Coyle relaxed. "Celibacy was created, in part, out of greed. It became a practice in the 11th Century. Prior to then, priests could marry, have children and live normal lives. The problem was the Church was losing property to divorce, and through the Last Wills that handed the priests' property over to their children. That was the main reason celibacy was implemented at that time, and one reason it exists today—to protect the Vatican's assets—assets estimated to be more than $15 billion, not including priceless art, land, gold and investments across the globe."

"Would you say, sir, that the Vatican recruited young, impressionable boys into the priesthood at an age where they were just discovering their manhood?"

"In many cases, yes."

"I have no more questions, your Honor." With a trace of a smile Vance turned to the Defense table. "Your witness."

Attorney Simmons rose, advanced toward Father Coyle, his lips set grimly. "Mr. Coyle," he said, staring straight down his long, sharp nose, "isn't it true that you've been a thorn in the Vatican's side for many years?"

Father Coyle looked at Vance and then back at Simmons. "Well, I wouldn't describe it as—"

"And isn't it true that you have a disdain for those in authority? That you sought to abandon efforts to influence Church decision-making, which some describe as nothing more than surrendering the Church, its parishes, and its ministries to what you refer to as 'the evils of clericalism and hierarchical power'?"

"That's not exactly—"

Simmons jumped in. "In a letter to you, dated January 29, 2008 from the *Voice of the Faithful,* they urged you to reconsider your stance against the Church. Haven't you always felt a disdain for the very institution that has provided you with a good living because they reduced you to inactive status?"

"That is not the reason—"

Simmons lurched toward him, hands gripping the witness box. "Do you really expect this court to believe that you have no malice whatsoever towards the institution that demoted you, stripped you of your ability to be the one thing you always dreamed of being, an active priest? You are *human*, sir, and it is only human nature that you harbor resentment for the Vatican, for what they did to you!"

Coyle sat stiffly in the witness chair, hands folded tight in his lap. The attorney smoothed the front of his suit with one hand, his eyes locked on Coyle. He took a few measured steps forward before speaking.

"Let me ask you something, sir," he began calmly. "Suppose you held a significant position at an aircraft manufacturing plant. A place where precision means lives. A place where one mistake—one screw turned wrong—could bring down an entire jetliner."

Coyle's eyes shifted uneasily.

"And suppose one day," the attorney continued, his tone darkening, "you began to notice a pattern. Shoddy workmanship. Dangerous shortcuts. Decisions that prioritized profit over safety. And so, you did what a decent man would do—you spoke up. You warned them." He paused.

"But instead of thanking you, they demoted you. Silenced you. And when that didn't work, they fired you. For telling the truth."

The courtroom held its breath.

"Would you be angry?" the attorney asked, his voice low. "Would you harbor resentment toward that company?"

Coyle swallowed hard. "Of course I would. I mean... as you said, I'm only human." He looked down at his hands. "But this situation is... different. It involves—"

"How is it different?" the attorney snapped.

Coyle blinked. "Because this involves the abuse of children," he said, trying to steady his voice. "That makes it more urgent."

Simmons spun around. Eyes scanning the jury.

"More *urgent*?" he echoed, his tone incredulous. "More urgent than planes falling from the sky? Than hundreds of innocent people—men, women, children—dying in flames because someone decided to cut corners?" His voice rang through the courtroom now, echoing off the marble walls. "No, sir. It is exactly the same!"

Coyle sat frozen.

The attorney took a step closer, voice turning cold and deliberate.

"And if a plane *did* crash, and we learned that the employees responsible had knowingly ignored safety protocols—and that their manager had known, and let it happen—should those employees, and that manager, be fired by the CEO of that company?"

"Yes," Coyle whispered. "Of course. But this—"

"This is different?" Simmons said, cutting him off. "Tell me, Mr. Coyle, how is it different?"

Coyle opened his mouth, but nothing came out.

Simmons leaned in slightly, eyes unblinking.

"The foreman who turns a blind eye, the workers who carry out the harm—they are accountable. Just as bishops who shield abusers, and priests who commit the abuse, are accountable." He paused. "It is the men in charge, and those they protect, who must answer for it—not the Vatican."

Coyle's head dropped. He gave a small, almost imperceptible nod.

Simmons straightened, his voice trembling with rage, "I-I-I've seen those c-c-children," he said, eyes dark. "I've held the p-photographs. R-Read their letters. I've heard the recordings their parents made—asking for h-help, for mercy, for someone to l-*listen*." He pointed at Coyle with the weight of every broken voice behind him.

"And now you take their suffering and twist it into a weapon to attack an entire faith. To attack an institution, a nation state—because it's easier than holding individual monsters accountable?" He shook his head. "You haven't just failed them, Mr. Coyle. You've betrayed them!

"I'm done with this witness, Your Honor," Roland Simmons spat out, storming back to the Defense table, then collapsed into his chair, fists still trembling, staring daggers at the floor.

A low murmur swelled through the courtroom.

Seeing Simmons tremble like a man haunted Vance wondered: *How many of these trials can a man take before something in him finally shatters?*

His gaze drifted toward Father Coyle, who had just begun to step down from the witness stand.

"Your Honor—please," Vance's words seemed clipped and urgent, "I'd like to redirect."

Even before O'Grady could nod his approval, Vance wheeled towards his witness.

"Father Coyle," he began, pacing slightly before pivoting to the jury, "the Defense's poetic metaphor left out one crucial truth."

He paused, letting silence dig in.

"Tell me, sir—are you familiar with the term *vicarious liability?*"

Coyle shrugged.

"I didn't think so," Vance said. He pivoted again to the jury, voice rising with momentum. "It's also called *imputed liability*. It means when an employer is held responsible for what its employees do—on its behalf, under its watch."

He stepped forward.

"Major companies pay for that every day. Some bleed quietly with settlements. Others? Others collapse under the weight of justice."

His voice grew thunderous.

"JK Harris & Company? Sued for the lies of its employees. Bankrupt. Gone. Celadon Group? Accounting fraud. Forty-two million in penalties. Bankrupt. Shuttered. The largest truckload carrier to cease operations in the U.S at the time, all because its employees committed accounting fraud."

He flung his arms wide, eyes flashing. "So yes. *Yes*, the Vatican is absolutely responsible for the sins of the men it empowered, protected, and allowed to keep harming!"

As he made his way back to the Prosecution table, Vance's eyes flicked toward Simmons—still trembling, barely composed.

Something had changed, Vance thought. The air was different now. Electric. Charged.

Awake.

A sense of conviction hung over him.

Struggling to steady his breath, Vance stared down as Father Coyle passed him, then squinted up at the judge, clinging to hope that a recess might be called, granting him a sliver of silence before the next storm."

O'Grady banged his gavel, then tossed it aside. "Counselor, call the next witness."

With a heavy breath, Vance stood.

"We call Dr. Bertram Adler."

∞　∞　∞

Adler walked to the witness stand and was sworn in. Vance took a deep breath and approached.

"Please state your credentials for the court, Dr. Adler."

Adler transferred his attention to the judge. "I am a certified clinical therapist with a Masters of Psychology from Stanford University, and a PH.D in Human Sexuality from the California Institute of Integral Studies, with a specialty in health and mental health factors that influence sexual behavior. I am also a journalist and author of several books on the topic."

"You made some interesting remarks about celibacy in the Church, Dr. Adler. Particularly at the recent National Association of Sexual Educators Conference, as well as last year's Sexual Matters National Conference, where you spoke on such topics as *How the Vatican Needs to Respond to Clergy Sexual Abuse,* and *The Truth the Vatican Has Hidden From Us.*"

"My remarks were prompted by the Australian Catholic Church's Truth, Justice and Healing Council that examined a link between celibacy and sexual abuse by Vatican members. The council found that sexual abuse against children should not be considered, and I quote, 'moral failings of clerics to observe celibacy.' In fact, that same report cited the failure of Church leaders to recognize sexual abuse of minors as a crime. The Royal Commission that worked alongside the council found 'no casual connection between sexual abuse against children and celibacy.' It was also suggested, that 'the Holy See consider voluntary celibacy for diocesan clergy.'"

"When was this report written?"

"Over six years ago."

"And you saw a problem with the report?"

"I did. First of all, the Holy See—the Vatican—has never considered celibacy to be 'voluntary.' Secondly, to say there is just a casual connection between celibacy and sexual abuse against children is ludicrous."

"You say 'ludicrous.' Why is that, sir?"

"As a trained therapist whose entire life has been spent studying, writing and counseling on sexual behavior, to not provide any form of counseling to young men entering celibacy on how to deal with their sexual urges is more than inhumane. It is *criminal.*"

"Do you believe the Vatican has been criminal in allowing this sexual abuse against children to continue over the years?"

"Absolutely. Any organization that institutes a mandatory policy for its members, knowing full well the problems caused by its policy, but does nothing to stop it? That knows the power the elder seminary priests have over their victims, to keep this abuse secret? That organization's failure to act is not only criminal, but ultimately responsible for enabling this abuse. This is especially true where that policy results in physical and emotional harm to its members and non-members, yet that organization does nothing to deter the behavior, and in fact perpetrates it by moving priests around, knowing they will prey upon children and abuse them again and again." Adler's eyes gleamed with indignation. "Yes, Counselor, they should be held responsible."

"Should that organization—and I'm not talking about the men running the organization but the organization itself—should it be prosecuted?"

"The men *and* the organization. Especially if they were instrumental in allowing the known criminal behavior to continue. As Father Coyle just stated it has, for centuries."

Hearing the rumble of murmurs from the gallery, Vance pursed his lips together, pleased. He stepped closer to the witness stand.

"Sir, my client is suing the Vatican for making him a pedophile. Father Murphy has stated they recruited him at a very young and vulnerable age, just when his hormones were kicking in. Gave him no training on how to deal with those powerful adolescent urges. Turned a blind eye to the homosexuality within the seminary as boys, who were becoming men, needed to satisfy those urges and then—again with no training on how to deal with celibacy in a world filled with temptation—sent him, sir, to a parish where he no longer had other seminarians to express his urges to, resulting in my client turning those urges toward the young and vulnerable in the Church he now oversaw. Wouldn't you consider that a recipe for creating pedophilia in a person?"

Suddenly Simmons leaped to his feet. "Your Honor, I object!"

"You're objecting, Counselor? To what?"

"To you, sir, leading the witness!"

"I am *not* leading the witness!"

"Thank you, Mr. Simmons," Judge O'Grady intervened, with a nod to both attorneys, "but I am going to allow Mr. Vance his question."

Simmons nodded back. Vance blinked at the judge, continued. "Thank you, Your Honor. Dr. Adler, please proceed, sir."

"The fact that young, vulnerable and impressionable boys are recruited into any organization without the proper training to deal with what lies ahead in life—especially when it comes to sexual urges and the behavior that can result—yes, that should be considered a crime. And someone or something should be held accountable."

"Thank you, Doctor. No more questions. Counselor, your witness."

With military precision Roland Simmons rose and marched straight to the witness chair.

"Dr. Adler, regarding that same report you referenced: Didn't the Vatican concede its vow of celibacy could have led to the abuse of children at the hands of clergy members?"

"Only vaguely. Its solutions involving psychosexual development are unclear."

"Nevertheless, the report is a step in the right direction, is it not?"

Adler scoffed. "If you think such a first-time report, after over 1,000 years of sexual abuse to hundreds of thousands of children, some estimate well over a million, clears the Vatican of its responsibility, then we are living in two different worlds, Counselor. Because the report also stated that some of its own leaders did not understand that the abuse of a child was a crime. If you believe that, then, as they say, 'I have some swampland in Florida I would like to sell you.'"

Simmons turned to take in the chuckle from the spectators. The irritation in his eyes deepened and blazed. Before he could turn back to Adler, the witness spoke:

"Do you think abusing a child is a crime, Counselor?"

Simmons looked back over his shoulder and squinted. "I am *not* the one on trial here!" he bellowed. The irritation in his face was gone now, turned to anger as he wiped the sweat from his upper lip. "Of course, abusing a child is a crime, and one that should be prosecuted! But a government did not commit that crime—a man, excuse me, *men* did! And the court needs an answer, Doctor. Was, in your clinical opinion, the report an attempt to remedy the problem? A simple yes or no will suffice."

"Yes. But…"

"Since the answer is 'yes,' then shouldn't we be blaming the priests? This is a large institution, and just like any large institution there is a culture, and within that culture there are always some bad apples working within it who take advantage of the weakest links. As a trained therapist, I'm certain you will agree with that. Do you agree with that, Doctor?"

Now Adler was the one sweating. "Yes, I do, but…"

"How many patients have you seen who have been sexually abused by clergy members?"

"Many," Adler said, darting his eyes over to Father Murphy." Certainly in the hundreds."

"And during these sessions, do these patients blame the clergy member? Or do they blame the Vatican?"

"Of *course* they blame the clergy member."

"But *not* the Vatican? Tell me, how many of your patients have blamed the Vatican, Doctor?"

"Well, honestly…"

"Yes?"

"I can't think of any that have."

"Just as I thought," Simmons said, and started marching stiff-backed to the Defense table. "No further questions, Your Honor."

"But the pain they feel is *very* real!" Dr. Adler begged. Vance's head spun from Simmons to the witness. He noticed Adler's eyes were teary and filled with compassion, his lips trembling, begging to ask the next question. "Have you ever been sexually abused, Counselor?"

Simmons took a sharp breath. "Have I *what?!*"

"Have *you* ever been the victim of a predator who knows he can do whatever he wants to you, whenever he wants, over and over, because he will not be punished?"

In shock Simmons gaped at the judge then back at Adler. "H-H-How *dare* you a-a-ask—" he stammered.

"Because if you *had* been abused, over and over, then surely you know the only reason that predator was allowed to be so free with his pedophilia is because it is condoned and accepted by the very organization you speak of—and that is a crime that organization should be prosecuted for!"

"A...A-A-A *crime?*" Simmons leaned back, eyes wide, as if he was losing his mind. Two members of his Defense team, Porkchop and Feral, shot half out of their chairs, then sat down when Simmons glared their way.

"Y-Y-You s-s-*said,*" he continued to Dr. Adler, stammering, "the report stated some of the Church's leaders didn't consider abuse of a child a crime. Tell me: Wh-Wh-*Who* were these leaders?"

Dr. Adler smiled. "The report did not name names, for confidentiality purposes. I'm sure you understand why it would keep them secret."

A befuddled look flashed across Simmons' face. "I DO NOT understand!" he shouted. "We are talking about men abusing children! In what world is that not a crime? The world above? One below? Or the one we are stuck in right now?"

"I'm sorry, Counselor, but I can't answer. Confidentiality doesn't permit me to reveal who those men are."

"Can't, Doctor? *Or won't?*"

Adler shrugged and held up his hands. "The report doesn't name names."

"Of *course* it doesn't! Because those people, if they even existed, were low-level managers within the Church!" Simmons shook his fist angrily.

Adler made no reply, let his silence stretch out, seeing the Defense attorney was flustered. "Counselor, why are you so angry? Did I hit a nerve? If so, I am truly sorry. But I have to ask. When you speak of priests, the tension in your voice rises. If you were abused, that certainly plays a role in your representing the Vatican. *Were* you ever sexually abused?"

"*I-I-I* am not the one on t-t-trial here, Dr. Adler!" Simmons almost shrieked. "And, I…" his eyes whirled to Judge O'Grady, "I r-r-resent this witness trying to t-t-twist my words!"

"If you had been sexually abused and the organization, the company, knew about your abuse but promoted your abuser anyway while also putting him or her in another situation so they could abuse you or another innocent person again, wouldn't you resent that? Wouldn't you say that company was to blame, Counselor? Of *course* you would! And you'd want recourse. You should be ashamed of yourself for defending this institution."

"How *d-d-dare* you embarrass this court w-w-with your outburst! How *d-d-dare* you insinuate I was—"

"I can see I've struck a chord. Although I do not know the circumstances, my heart goes out to you." With a compassionate smile, Dr. Adler rose from the chair. "I'm a volunteer witness here. I'm done answering any more questions." He straightened and exited the witness stand, elbowing past the enraged and red-faced Defense attorney as Simmons clawed at him.

"You will *not* leave this stand until I say so! You were paid by the court as an expert witness! This is ludicrous, a farce, wild conjecture, Your Honor!" But Simmons couldn't stop the witness from ramming past him, and when he turned back to Judge O'Grady, the judge sucked in a deep breath and slumped back in his chair with a sigh.

Simmons stared around, incredulous. Finally his arms dropped to his sides.

"My apologies, Your Honor. I...I overreacted. I have no more questions."

Vance looked over at Simmons, aghast as the attorney blundered unsteadily back to the Defense table, then collapsed into his seat. Simmons ran a limp hand through his sweaty hair, fixed his widened eyes on a spot on the wall. One of the Defense attorneys patted Simmons on the back; instantly Simmons pushed away, in horror. He leaned back against his chair, taking long breaths and letting them out. And for a moment, Vance felt a surge of tenderness toward his adversary.

"Maybe we're in luck," Vance whispered in Father Murphy's ear. "The guy's off his game."

"I don't buy it," Murphy whispered back.

For a moment the words didn't register. Then Vance met Murphy's gaze. "Why not?"

"Because I've seen enough bullshit in my life to recognize a bullshitter."

Stunned, Vance watched Simmons closely. If he was bullshitting, acting, pretending, Vance thought, the man was brilliant at it, spellbinding, a master. *But I'll still beat him,* Vance told himself, galvanized by the sound of the words, as he announced to the judge his next witness.

∞   ∞   ∞

"The Prosecution calls Cardinal Benecio Cupak to the stand."

Leafing through his notes as Cardinal Cupak was sworn in, Vance studied the twelve jurors' faces. He took a swift look at Simmons then strolled with calm confidence to the witness box.

"Mr. Cupak," he began, "at the recent Papal Summit you insisted that Church leaders must acknowledge decades of their own cover-up and secrecy. Furthermore, you acknowledged that the Vatican, for decades, had given Bishops—who had moved pedophile priests around from parish to parish to cover those abuses up—a free pass. Did you not, sir?"

"I did," stated Cupak, then added, his cheeks puffed out, "and it's *Cardinal* Cupak."

"You also called for a new culture of accountability in the Catholic Church to punish priests. Does that imply the old culture was not accountable, *Mr.* Cupak?"

Cupak grunted. "To a degree."

"You also stated that new legal procedures were needed, did you not?"

"I did."

"And why would you do that, when it has already been established that Canon Law 1395 exists for that very purpose?"

"We need new laws to not just punish priests under Canon Law 1395, but to prosecute those who are covering up the abuse, who use the power of their position as clergy to pressure victims to keep it secret."

"I see," Vance said, and strolled back to his notes. "Let me read what Canon Law 1395 specifically says." He plucked his reading glasses off the table, flipping through a large stack of papers until he found what he was looking for. "A cleric who by force, threats or abuse of his authority commits an offense against the sixth commandment of the Decalogue," he read, then lowered his glasses to the bridge of his nose," — in other words, sir, the Ten Commandments — 'forces someone to perform or submit to sexual acts is to be punished.' The penalties are very specific, by the way — 'not excluding dismissal from the clerical state.'"

Removing his spectacles Vance averted the suspicious gaze of the judge. "So the natural question, Mr. Cupak, after reading this, is: Why is another law needed? You have a law that clearly says violating it will result in punishment, with specific penalties laid out by the Vatican. Yet pedophiles in the Vatican are not punished. Can you honestly say that the Vatican is *not* turning a blind eye to the abuse?"

Cupak squirmed. "I suppose."

"You suppose? May I ask if you feel you should change your answer to 'Yes, the Vatican has been complicit' by the mere fact that Pope Benedictus, whom we will hear from later in this trial, has testified that he feels the Vatican *has* been complicit in this abusive culture?"

Cupak sighed. "I guess so."

"You *guess* so? Sir, I vehemently suggest — "

"Objection!"

Vance's eyes widened, as he whirled to see Simmons suddenly alert, rising from his chair.

"Your Honor, once again this esteemed counsel is badgering his own witness!"

224

"On the contrary, sir, I am—"

"You are to proceed with caution, Mr. Vance," warned Judge O'Grady with a squint.

Vance stared Simmons down. His gall was astounding! He rolled his eyes, shook his head and sighed. "Yes, Your Honor, I will," he nodded, plucked two sheets of yellow legal paper from his table and returned to question Cupak, looking him square in the face.

"Sir, your answer is unbelievable. It is a good indication that far too many of the hierarchy in the Vatican are reluctant to indict what is obvious. In fact," he said, waving the yellow sheets, "you have been Bishop of the Diocese of Chicago since 2014. You insisted the Vatican acknowledge their cover-up, yet in December of 2018 the Illinois Attorney General issued a scathing report accusing your Diocese, sir, of failing victims of sexual abuse, by neglecting to investigate their allegations, and in the 2023 final report from the Illinois Attorney General, Kwame Raoul's office stated that: 'The Catholic Church failed to support survivors, investigate claims, or remove abusive clergy from ministry for decades.' It specifically detailed that the Archdiocese of Chicago, despite reforms in recent years, failed for decades to respond adequately to abuse complaints.

"So, Mr. Cupak, on the one hand, you insist the Vatican should acknowledge its cover-up, yet you withheld the names of hundreds of priests who were accused of sexually abusing minors—in your own Diocese! How is anyone supposed to believe you are serious, when you are knowingly complicit in contributing to this worldwide cover-up of sexual abuse against hundreds of thousands of children? How, sir?"

Cardinal Cupak sat without a word, not even blinking his eyes.

"Your silence says it all," glared Vance. "No further questions. Your witness, Counselor."

He stalked off, rubbing the back of his neck, then half-way to the Prosecution table he stopped. "My apologies, Your Honor. I *do* have one more question...Mr. Cupak, do you always wear your Cardinal cassock, cross and Biretta hat wherever you go?"

Cupak seemed confused. "Of course. I'm a Cardinal."

Vance stared at him and smiled. "Of course you are. Your witness, Counselor."

As he sat, Murphy patted Vance on the back and said, "Nice move. It is a great hat though," with the perfect smirk.

By the time Vance took his seat Simmons had already launched into his cross-examination.

"Cardinal Cupak: Aren't you in fact trying to make a difference in the Church?"

The Cardinal puffed out his chest. "I am."

"Why is that?"

"This abuse has been going on far too long."

"Do you feel you are part of the problem? People like yourself refusing to release the names of pedophile priests? People like you admitting to the problem, after the fact? Men like yourself who make the decisions to let pedophiles run rampant under your watch?"

For a moment, Cupak sank down in his seat, letting out a deep breath. "It was a mistake, one I regret."

"One nevertheless *you* made. Can you admit you are part of the problem?"

"I serve at the behest of the Vatican. The Holy See."

"Yet it was *you* who made the decision to withhold those names, did you not? It was *your* decision. *Not* the Vatican's! Do you agree, Cardinal? Yes or no?" Simmons leaned forward and stared.

"Yes."

"Good. But why, sir, would you possibly *do* that? Why would you allow men—*pedophiles!*—to continue to sexually abuse children?"

"The culture needs to change. I admit that."

"Don't play politician! Own up to your responsibility! You are responsible for children being abused! Now answer the question!" Simmons shouted.

Silently the Cardinal glared, hunched over, one hand trembling in his lap; he seemed near tears, unnerved by the accusation, yet unmoved to answer.

"You refuse to answer? I'll say something then! The problem isn't with the Vatican. The problem is *men!*" Simmons bellowed, his voice rumbling. "*M-M-M-Men* like you, protecting pedophile priests! *M-M-M-Men* like you, covering up decades of abuse. *T-T-That* is the problem, sir! *Men!*" he stammered to get the last word out.

There were murmurs and loud gasps from the courtroom. Even the court reporter held his breath. Again and again Judge O'Grady brought his gavel down. "Mr. Simmons! Mr. Simmons!!"

"No more questions, Your Honor!"

"This is a damn court of law, not the monkey cage at the zoo!" the judge growled, his teeth clenched.

Seething with anger, his face blazing red, Simmons moved to take his seat. All around the court, spectators whispered unintelligibly.

Vance sat, puzzled. He looked at the silent group of Defense lawyers and his anxiety mounted. Yet seeing Simmons' loss of control, becoming a prison to his emotions, filled him with a strange excitement.

Triumphantly he stood and called for his next witness.

∞ ∞ ∞

"We call Cardinal Bruno Darnatelo."

A sardonic smile tugged at Vance's lips as the Cardinal approached the stand, cloaked in the pomp of his own self-ordained significance.

"Mr. Darnatelo I shall be brief. You were Chairman of the 2019 Bishops Conference to confront sexual abuse against children by priests, were you not?"

Cardinal Darnatelo just looked at the attorney and remained silent.

"Can you at least nod your head 'yes' or 'no, sir?" Darnatelo remained silent then slowly nodded.

"I see. Thank you. And you were also the Bishop, head of the Diocese for the Dallas, Texas area in the United States, were you not?"

Again Darnatelo slowly nodded. *What's his game?* wondered Vance, deciding his best tactic was not to bully the witness.

"Very good. Now you were accused of mishandling charges of sexual abuse against children within that Diocese. How many charges of sexual abuse against children by priests were filed that you ignored?"

Still Darnatelo remained silent, his lips tight. Sensing the concern among the jurors, Vance leaned in.

"Mr. Darnatelo, did you hear me? You need to answer, sir, you're under oath. Were there charges filed in your Diocese that were not investigated?"

"Do you realize," said Darnatelo finally, with a glare of menace, "you are talking with a high-level priest, Counselor? A representative of God Himself?"

Vance smiled. *Gotcha.* "I do. And God is waiting for your answer, sir."

"I don't recall."

"You don't recall. How convenient. In that case, I am going to ask you a question fit for a child, befitting one of God's chosen children. It's not a trick question. Yes or no will do. Were any of the aforementioned charges looked into?" Darnatelo turned to the jury, reacting as if he didn't hear Vance. "Yes or no, sir!"

"They were looked into."

"Now we're getting somewhere. Do you have paperwork that shows you, anyone from your staff or anyone you hired, looked into these charges? Do you have any cancelled checks that show an outside source was hired to investigate these charges?"

"No."

"What happened to those priests, in your Diocese, who were accused of abusing children? And please remember, sir, you are under oath."

"They were sent out for treatment and later reassigned as pastors in the Diocese of Beaumont, Texas."

Turning to face the jury, Vance continued. "You moved priests, who were accused of sexual abuse, to other parishes?"

"Yes."

"I see. And did you tell anyone at the other parishes about the charges against these priests?"

Darnatelo, silent, shook his head.

"You're shaking your head 'no.' Are you embarrassed to say the word 'no,' sir?"

"I am not."

"Why didn't you notify the other parishes?"

"I didn't feel it was pertinent."

"You didn't feel it was pertinent? Priests were abusing children! And you didn't feel that was important to tell those at the parishes you were transferring them to? Did those priests you transferred abuse other children after you placed them in another parish?"

Darnatelo remained silent.

"Again sir, a simple yes or no answer."

"Object, badgering the witness!" yelled Simmons.

"Sustained!" howled the judge.

Darnatelo stared at Vance, his eyes penetrating, then silently nodded.

"Another nod because the witness is too cowardly to answer," Vance told the jury then swiveled his gaze back to the Cardinal.

"Isn't it true, sir, you transferred other pedophile priests, didn't invoke Canon Law 1395 when you found out about the abuse they were inflicting on children, had them transferred to other parishes, then neglected to tell those parishioners? And sure enough, those pedophiles abused more children?"

"That's not pertinent."

"Not *pertinent*, you say, sir! You didn't think it was pertinent to tell the parishioners at the new parishes that their children were potential prey to the ravenous wolves in their midst? At which number of sexual abuse charges, by any of those priests, would you feel it was 'pertinent' to tell the other parishes? Speak up, sir! Two? Five? Fifteen?"

"Object! Object! Object!"

"Sustained! Sustained! Sustained!"

"When did it feel important enough to say something? Or are you such a despicable, self-righteous man of God that even knowing about the rape and abuse of innocent children would not loosen your tongue?"

"Enough!" roared the judge.

The Cardinal shot out of his chair. "How dare you insult the Catholic Church and its hierarchy!" he snarled. "How *dare* you!"

Striding forward, Vance poked his finger in the witness's chest, shoving him back. "You self-righteous coward!"

"You're *way* out of line, Counselor!" cautioned the judge, pointing his gavel.

"You hide behind an image you created in your mind," Vance continued, on a roll, "where you are one rung below God Himself. Most certainly He is ashamed of you!"

For a moment Vance stepped away from the witness stand, brushing his hair back from his face to compose himself. *Should I keep pressing him? See if he'll fold? Hell yes,* he decided. Nodding vigorously, he whirled back to the Cardinal.

"So let me get this straight. You allow all this abuse to continue because you felt it wasn't pertinent—and now the Pope, your friend and another child of God, positions you as President of the 2019 Bishops Conference, a conference whose sole purpose is to deal with the mishandling of charges brought against priests for sexually abusing children. Can you see how that may look like this government, this institution known as the Vatican, is giving the keys to the henhouse to the wolf?"

"I was chosen because of my experience."

"In that case, you have some resumé, my child," Vance said and looked up at Judge O'Grady. "Your Honor. I would like to play a short video at this time."

"Proceed."

As the lights in the courtroom dimmed, the recorded deposition of Ruben Sanchez appeared on a video monitor. The jurors watched, silent, spellbound.

"I met Father Alfonso when I was in school. I…I think I was twelve," said Sanchez on the recording. "I wanted to be like him. He was bigger than life. Everyone admired him. When he took an interest in me, I felt like I was part of something. The abuse lasted for two years. For two years—"

Sanchez paused, head down, began to cry. The spectators gazed, everyone mesmerized, the room hushed. Vance looked back over his shoulder at Father Murphy. His head hung, Murphy wiped away tears. Suddenly, Vance's heart cried out with compassion for both men.

"He talked about God the Father," Ruben Sanchez continued, looking back into the camera lens. "I needed a father. A strong yet affectionate male presence in my life. I couldn't tell anyone about the abuse, not for years. It caused two divorces and my kids—" For a moment Sanchez stopped, his shoulders trembling as he sobbed, "— my kids felt the worst of my anger. I learned Father Alfonso abused other kids at other churches. He ruined their lives as well."

The video recording stopped. Lights were flicked on. Vance scanned the rows of spectators, the jurors, the judge. He studied the room then slowly approached Cardinal Darnatelo.

"Mr. Darnatelo, you saw the video. We all heard Ruben Sanchez's testimony. Yet here's what Mr. Sanchez *didn't* say: The priest who abused him, Father Alfonso, was transferred *by you*, within your Diocese. You knew Father

Alfonso was a pedophile, yet you transferred him to church after church, with no warning to the parishioners, to their children, to the police, to anyone. How does it make you feel when you hear that? Do you feel any responsibility for what happened, sir?"

"I was doing my job to the best of my ability."

"I see." Vance rubbed his chin, turned and stepped away from the witness, then stopped. "One last question. Do you think you will get into Heaven?"

"Will I get into Heaven? What kind of question is that? Of course!"

"So God will forgive you?"

Darnatelo smirked. "God forgives us all. The Almighty always does."

"Somehow I doubt that…I'm finished with this witness, Your Honor."

Roland Simmons was already strutting to the witness box by the time Vance reached his chair.

"Cardinal Darnatelo, would you say that another way to look at it is that you learned from your experience? And because of that, you were the ideal person to organize such a conference?"

"I would indeed."

"And since that conference you orchestrated, has the Catholic Church made efforts—taken strides—to fix the problem of sexual abuse? To make a difference?"

"Indeed we have."

"Then doesn't it bother you, sir, that the Vatican is the one on trial here?"

The Cardinal's face turned scarlet. "Excuse me?"

"Shouldn't *men* be tried for these crimes? Aren't *men* to blame? Men like Father Murphy, who raped and abused innocent children?"

"I...I'm not—"

"Wasn't it *men* who committed these heinous acts? *Men* who betrayed their sacred calling? How can you sit there and defend the actions of these *men*, sir?"

"I...I *don't!*" Darnatelo cried out, horrified.

"Then *say* it, Cardinal Darnatelo! *Say* what you know! Who is to blame here? Men? Or the Vatican?"

Darnatelo pursed his lips, mopped the sweat from his brow. The words seemed to take forever in coming. "Men are to blame," he said, enunciating each word slowly to make it perfectly clear. "*Men.* Not the Church."

"No further questions, Your Honor."

"Fine," O'Grady said, rapping his gavel as he rose. "Then let's end today here. We'll pick up with the Prosecution again tomorrow."

The gallery stood. Vance watched the judge exit the courtroom, visibly annoyed.

Suddenly Vance had a bad feeling. He saw Simmons scribble a note, fold it, then hand the folded note to a spectator, a scruffy young man in a Kid Rock T-shirt and Converse hi-tops. *What is that scoundrel up to now?* Vance wondered.

"You're killing 'em, Vince," Father Murphy said at his back.

Confused, Vance whirled around. The words stopped him, threw him off-balance. He turned to see the smiling old man being handcuffed, two muscled courtroom guards taking him by the elbow, leading him back to his cell.

For a moment, the thought of what an awful thing it must be to know you're going to die in prison popped into Vance's dark brain. Then Murphy looked directly back at him, asked, "Hey, you think we've got this case in the bag or what?" with a twinkle in his eyes that nearly blinded Vance.

Vance shrugged. His chest tightened, the familiar tension rising, struggling to balance his emotions between hate and a sense of forgiveness for the man. A quiet battle he fought alone, nearly daily.

He was trying. Trying hard to forgive. Not for Murphy's sake, but for his own. Holding on to the hate was exhausting. Some days, forgiveness felt like the only way to keep breathing.

Vance shrugged, "Don't ask me, Murphy," he said, rubbing his neck, eyes drifting past the man's face. "I haven't a clue."

Chapter Sixteen

IN SILENCE VANCE DROVE HIS HONDA back down Basin Street, through Iberville and into heavy traffic to his motel room. On the seat beside him sat the *USA Today* with the headline screaming, *TRIAL OF THE CENTURY IN LOUISIANA*, as well *The Times-Picayune* newspaper with a front-page headline about the deteriorating mental health of Baton Rouge resident Dexter Bechet, one of Murphy's Louisiana victims.

Another Simmons leak to the media, Vance reasoned. *That's how the big boys carve us up, how they win, going balls-to-the-wall with fear*, he grumbled, switching on the radio to hear WWOZ 99.7 and the blues.

Digesting the day in court discouraged him. The Vatican would do whatever it took to blow his case to pieces. *Just let 'em try, though*, as his partner Jay-Jay would say.

The thought of Jay-Jay made Vance nostalgic. Without warning he whipped out his phone, punched the button for Jay-Jay's number. There was no answer. *Seriously?* Vance scolded himself, hanging up. *He's not going to answer. The man's still shitting on you, holding a grudge. Whatever happened to forgiveness in Jay-Jay's world?*

Still gripping the phone, he dialed up his neighbor Peggy to check on Fatty.

"Little fellow's eating," Peggy said, with a chuckle. "Been eating since the moment you left him."

Vince could hear the dog barking, sensing it was his master.

"Thanks," Vance said. Before hanging up Peggy hit him with, "Been followin' the coverage on CNN and Fox. Looks like the whole world is watchin' you get your ass kicked, Mr. Vance. Memphis bookies have the chance of you beating the Vatican now at 500 to 1."

"Take the bet," Vince said. "You'll be able to play slots for years after you win."

"I'm a gambler Mr. Vance, not an idiot. Gotta go, before Fatty pulls the phone out of my hand. I'll give the pup a hug for you."

Shit, Vance thought, *just when I feel the anxiety draining from my body, knowing Fatty's okay, Peggy reminds me the whole world is watching and tightens the noose.*

To hell with it, I'm ready for tomorrow, he told himself, cranking up Fats Domino again. As The Fat Man played, he got a feeling he'd never experienced before. *Funny. But I don't know how this case will turn out.* Then the realization hit Vance, hard and swift, and his anxiety mounted again.

Like hell you don't. You know.

∞ ∞ ∞

"The Prosecution calls Archbishop Cyrus Siklona to the stand," announced the bailiff to the packed courtroom, as Day Two of Father Murphy's trial began.

A nurse had come earlier to check on Murphy's blood pressure. She jotted down numbers, asked the proper questions, then sat in a chair to the side.

Seeing Murphy's uneasy smile, Vance felt his own chest tighten. He wanted to ask the old priest how he was feeling, but decided to wait until the first recess. Pity was not an emotion he could afford right now.

"Mr. Siklona," Vance began. "You were the sexual abuse prosecutor, officially referred to by the Vatican as the 'promoter of justice.' I believe you wanted to take a hard line on prosecuting these abuse cases, did you not?"

"I felt there needed to be a hard line on such cases, yes."

"Is it safe to say you didn't make many friends in the Vatican for this approach?"

"There were some who felt I was overstepping."

"Overstepping? After attempting to employ a hard-line approach on prosecuting pedophile priests, the Vatican transferred you to Malta, as a coadjutor. Is that correct?"

"Yes, for a while."

"Why do you think that is?"

"It was a promotion."

Vance's eyes twinkled. "A *promotion?* You consider becoming an Assistant Bishop in the country of Malta, which has just over 500,000 citizens, to be a promotion over being named Head Prosecutor for the largest, most vile scandal the Vatican has ever had?"

"That's what I was told. And they were *not* the most vile, Counselor."

"*Not* the most vile? Good Lord, sir! What other scandals could the Catholic Church have been a part of, that could possibly be worse than the repeated and systemic rape and torture of children?"

"I didn't mean to demean the actions of those priests."

"Yet you did. I ask again, what scandals could, in your mind, be worse?"

"I just meant the Church has been involved in many scandals over the centuries, scandals that would compete with the—"

"Do you consider this a competition, Mr. Siklona?"

"No! All I meant was—"

"Pardon me for interrupting, but I asked that question because I also know you are somewhat of a historian of the Church. That being said, what in your mind has been a historical equal in vileness, in perversion, in utter unspeakable depravity to this scandal?"

"Well, uhhh," stammered Siklona, turning his head to meet the eyes of the jury, "there *have* been other sexual abuse scandals throughout the Church's history."

"So this current scandal—and by current I mean *over the last seventy years*—is nothing new in the Catholic Church?"

"No! The current scandal is similar to a series of crises in the Church since the Middle Ages, as far back as the 11th Century."

Vance's eyes narrowed. "Forgive me if I'm not the idealist you are, sir. But isn't this current scandal *exactly* the same? Back then, Church leaders were also complacent about their priests' sexual abuse. In fact, as a historian of the Church, wasn't it true that Bishops, during that period, used their august authority over the clergy to compel priests into performing acts of sodomy?"

"I—"

"But let's not stop there! Didn't a very famous Cardinal during that period, nearly 1,000 years ago, a Cardinal Peter Damian, warn two Popes, Pope Leo IX and Pope Nicholas II, about all the sexual abuse against children taking place at the time? And yet both Popes decided to remain silent, covering up the sins of its Bishops and priests, in order to avoid a scandal? You don't need to answer that because they are *facts*, sir! So all this sexual abuse in the Catholic Church has been going on for many, many centuries—and still the Church, the Vatican, has done *nothing!* Why?"

Vance waited for an answer.

Leaning forward he fixed a hard stare on Siklona. "Knowing this history, Mr. Siklona, and putting yourself in the shoes of that hard-line sexual abuse prosecutor you were originally hired to be, would you say the Vatican is the central figure that has allowed this centuries-old abuse to continue? Just nod your head if you agree, sir."

Siklona looked in surprise at the judge, then turned his head to Vance and nodded.

"Thank you. And knowing all this, can you understand why it looks suspect when a prosecutor, such as yourself, one who becomes a bit too vocal for the Vatican's taste, is suddenly and unexpectedly given a different assignment?"

"As I said, I was told it was a promotion."

"Did you really believe that?"

"I don't question the Vatican and its motives."

"So it was Pope Benedictus who gave the order? Excuse me, gave you the 'promotion'?"

"Yes. Pope Benedictus transferred me."

"Would you have liked to stay on the job as prosecutor, on a full-time basis? Do you feel you could have saved children from being preyed upon, from being molested, tortured and abused?"

"Yes and yes."

"No further questions, Your Honor."

Attorney Simmons raised his eyebrows as Vance strode away to brood at the Prosecution table. With a smile, Simmons pushed back his chair and approached the witness.

"Archbishop Siklona, didn't you manage to have hundreds of priests removed from ministry during your time as Head Prosecutor?"

"I did. And I'm proud of that."

"So would you describe the Vatican today as trying to make a difference? Trying to put a stop to all this abuse?"

"They're trying, is all I should say."

"No more questions, Your Honor." Simmons saw Vance's head go up as he returned to the Defense team. Simmons stopped midway, took a sterile handkerchief from his pocket, patted his upper lip, smoothed out his jacket cuffs, then turned with a nod back to O'Grady.

"Your Honor, I have one further question for the witness, if I may?"

O'Grady smiled smugly at Vance and Father Murphy. He leaned back in his seat. "Proceed."

"Would you say all decisions, such as transfers of priests from one parish to another, is something the Vatican is fully aware of?"

"It is not."

"Thank you. No further questions."

No further questions? Vance stared at the retreating attorney, worried, paranoid that Simmons could have pursued Siklona in so many directions. He gritted his teeth and anxiously scanned the Defense team, trying to understand the pattern in the opposition's questions. And now Roland Simmons, that son-of-a-bitch, was smiling at him! The hostility floating through Vance's head flared and exploded. *You're letting him get away with murder,* he told himself, picking up a pen to distract himself by scribbling notes as fast as he could, digging through reams of handwritten documents.

Breathe, Vance reminded his thumping heart, *just breathe*. He peered over his shoulder to see a crowd of observers hunched together, waiting for the trial to continue, Father Murphy sitting silently, not paying attention, though every eye in the courtroom was on him.

Looking over at Vance, Murphy smiled, his eyes twinkling, and this calmed the attorney as Vance called Cardinal Ronaldo Santos Lopez to the stand.

∞ ∞ ∞

"Mr. Lopez," Vance said, putting down his pen and rising from his paperwork, "in a 2018 speech at the Pope's summit to confront sex abuse in the Church, you warned the 190 Bishops in attendance that they could face imprisonment for a cover-up of sexual abuse by clergy members if they failed to properly deal with allegations. Why did you make that statement?"

Cardinal Lopez frowned. "I was disenchanted with the way Rome was handling the issue."

"So you agree that the Vatican was and is complicit in creating an environment that allows priests to continue to rape innocent children?"

"To a degree."

"What do you mean, sir?"

"Well," Lopez hesitated, "there is Canon Law."

"Canon 1395, you mean? The Sixth Commandment of the Decalogue.

"So the Vatican does not enforce its own laws, laws it created to protect children from rape by priests?"

"Correct."

Vance froze the Cardinal with a look of bewilderment. He walked back to the Prosecution table and stopped. "Let me ask you Mr. Lopez, at what age did you enter the seminary? Was it 13?"

The Cardinal nodded.

"What were you like before you entered the seminary? What was your father like?"

The Cardinal's manner grew furtive. He turned to the judge for support. "Your Honor, I shouldn't have to answer this! What relevance does it have here?"

O'Grady arched an eyebrow at Vance. "Counselor, what—"

"Your Honor, please have the witness answer the question! I will prove its relevance."

O'Grady started to balk, then waved his hand. "Proceed."

"Thank you. Mr. Lopez, shall I repeat the question, sir?"

"No need," said Lopez, his eyebrows knit in deep thought. Vance waited, holding Lopez's gaze. *Come on, come on, answer!*

"I was a quiet boy. A shy boy. Timid. I didn't have a lot of friends. Kept to myself most of the time. No father figure. I...My family was...I suppose you could say it was dysfunctional."

"Go on."

"My father—the few times he was around—the man liked to yell a lot, put me down, say I'd never amount to anything. And my mother, she was in denial of dad's womanizing. So I spent a lot of time alone. Feeling rejected, unwanted, unloved. I just wanted to get away."

"And when you entered the priesthood, you felt you belonged? You felt accepted, embraced, loved?"

"It was a level of love I'd never experienced. I still feel that to this day, but in a different way."

"How so?"

"There is a bit of shame. For some of the men I once admired."

"Please explain."

"The way they handled their..." he paused, clearing his throat, "...their urges."

Staring down Lopez, to let the jury take it all in, Vance continued.

"What sort of education did you receive in the seminary—regarding celibacy, I mean?"

"None. I tried talking to several of the older priests about celibacy, but none wanted to discuss it. They always said it was God's Will."

"When was the first time you had sex?"

Lopez froze. He drilled Vance with an unblinking stare. "That first year in seminary," he murmured, his face becoming ashen. "With one of the older priests."

"Was it one of your counselors?"

"Yes. I..." Lopez paused, shook his head, then fell silent. "It did make me feel like I was loved. Even though I didn't like it. If I'd been stronger, I may have left."

"Left the room you were being abused in? Or left the priesthood?"

"Both."

"No more questions, Your Honor. Your witness."

Vance heard Simmons before he saw him. The Defense attorney had his eyes closed, squeezing them tight. Head bent to the Defense table, he was whimpering and swaying as if he had a hangover, lips curled in an angry pucker and whispering to himself the strangest words Vance had ever heard: *It's okay Roland, it's okay you little bitch you little…*

What is happening? Is Simmons having a nervous break-down? Vance wondered, just as Simmons' second chair leaned over to pat the trembling Defense attorney on the back, as Simmons brushed him off.

"Counselor? I said, your witness."

Instantly Simmons sat up, in shock. He seemed deeply distressed. His hair wet, he stutter-walked to the witness stand, wiping the sweat off his upper lip.

"Are you okay, Counselor? You appear ill, sir," Vance asked.

"I…I'm fine…" Simmons muttered. "Ca-Ca-Cardinal Lopez…"

"Mr. Simmons," Judge O'Grady interrupted, leaning forward in his chair, "do you need a recess? A break?"

Simmons stared at the judge with his eyebrows raised.

"N-No, Your Honor, I don't need a break, thank you. Allow me to continue, please." He lifted his trembling gaze to the witness and stood up straight. "Cardinal Lopez…y-you warned those 190 Bishops at the Papal Summit that they 'could' be p-put in prison if they didn't do something to protect ch-ch-children from abuse. Would you agree that the Vatican has been trying to d-do something, and that the Papal Summit is an example of th-that?"

"Yes."

"Thank you. No questions, Your Honor." Simmons re-treated to the Defense table. Suddenly he stopped. "Wait. I d-*do* have one last question. How did you feel when you were being a-a-abused, Cardinal Lopez?"

"How did I feel?"

"So you *were* abused!"

"Yes. I mean no!" Lopez said, shifting uncomfortably in his seat. "It was more consensual. We had no outlet for our urges," he said, hands beginning to tremble. "We're just human, Counselor."

"Yes you are. And it is humans who are responsible for this rampant abuse in the church. Not the Vatican." His gaze locked onto the jury. "Now, I'll ask again. How did you feel, sir?"

A distasteful look fell over the Cardinal's face. "Ashamed. Violated."

"Yet you stayed. Do you b-blame the Vatican for making you stay?"

"I never thought of it like that."

"Think of it C-Cardinal Lopez. Think l-long and h-hard. Do you blame the Vatican for making you stay after you were violated? You could have l-left, yet you stayed. It was your choice to stay…

"So I ask again sir, do you b-blame the Vatican? Or was it your own w-weakness that prevented you from l-leaving?"

Cardinal Lopez remained silent, hands in his lap, head down.

"Of *course* you didn't b-blame the Vatican! Just like you cannot blame the Vatican for making Mr. Murphy a pedophile!"

Regaining his composure, his lips became lopsided. "No more questions, Your Honor. And I…" Turning back to Cardinal Lopez, Simmons suddenly looked scared. "I…I-I'm sorry, sir…I'm sorry you had to go through that."

Vance tilted his head sympathetically as the trembling Simmons moved past him. "I need to sit down," the attorney whispered to the other members of his team, waving them away by flapping his arms. "Take your hands off me!" he snapped, his eyes focusing and un-focusing as he crumpled into a chair.

The man looks faint, Vance told himself. *He must be ill.* He watched the other lawyers, looks of concern etched in their faces. *Maybe he's ashamed of his emotions, his outburst. Clamping his eyes shut as if he only feels safe, at peace, alone in the darkness.*

In pity, Vance gave Simmons a final glance, then said to O'Grady, "Your Honor, perhaps a short recess is in order."

"Denied."

"Excuse me?"

"Denied, Mr. Vance," the judge said, with an arrogant look.

Denied? Vance felt a sudden lurch in his chest. "Your Honor, it's not for me. It's for—"Vance glanced to his left, and saw Simmons staring at him. He cleared his throat, plowed ahead, switching gears. "It's for my client, Your Honor. My client, Father Murphy," he said, turning his gaze to the old priest at his back, "needs his medications, Your Honor."

"Denied," O'Grady snapped, folding his hands together. "Motion denied. Any other motions you'd like me to deny, Counselor?"

Vance stood astounded, expressionless, his heart pounding. He looked desperately to Simmons; Simmons gave him a hateful sneer. Fists clenched then, Vance took the only recourse open to him.

"Your Honor, the Prosecution calls Cardinal Thaddeus McCarroll to the stand."

∞ ∞ ∞

As Cardinal McCarroll was sworn in, Vance studied him. McCarroll scowled at Vance as he took the witness stand. Behind Vance, the gallery murmured. Vance buttoned his vest and stepped forward.

"Mr. McCarroll…"

McCarroll's eyebrows shot up. "That's *Father* McCarroll."

"*Mr.* McCarroll," Vance repeated. "When I was in Catholic school, I was taught that each of us is made in God's image and likeness. Do you believe that?"

"Yes. We all are."

"So if *you* are made in His image, then God must be a pedophile," said Vance, squinting down at the witness. "God must be a child molester, an abuser. You abused seminarians for years. If A = B and B = C, then A = C. Isn't that correct?"

McCarroll's shoulders jerked in shock. "How *dare* you imply God is a pedophile!" he barked. "God is *forgiving*. God is *perfect*. I do not question God's plan!"

"Do you question His motives? Because if there *is* a God—and that's a big *if* knowing He positioned men like yourself to lead His flock—are you saying that no matter what you do, including the rape and torture of all the children you've abused in your life, all you need to do is say 'I'm sorry' on your deathbed and Heaven will open wide its Pearly Gates?"

"That is what the Bible says."

"The Bible also says homosexuality is a sin, yet you have committed that offense, that mortal sin, at least according to the supposed 'Holy Book.'"

"It does. And it is."

"Well, if what you say is true—because, remember, it was men who made all this up, who wrote the words in the Bible—and you concede that no matter what evil and atrocious thing you do in life, at the very end if you say those two magic words, 'I'm sorry,' God forgives you and lets you into His Heaven—another man-made creation—then, sir, I say to you that is a Heaven I have no interest in being in, and a God I have no interest in knowing nor seeking forgiveness from!"

Vance stalked to the jury box and paused. Out of the corner of his eye he saw the Defense attorneys taking notes. He turned back to the witness.

"What I am interested in knowing, Mr. McCarroll, is this: Is it true that you were one step away from the Pope in the hierarchy pecking order at the Vatican?"

McCarroll swallowed. "Yes. Well, I mean, I *was*. For quite some time."

"And you are no longer? Explain to the court why you are no longer second in line to the Pope."

McCarroll remained silent.

"No comment? I'll ask again, sir, why are you—"

"I heard you the first time. I resigned."

"Why did you resign?"

McCarroll stared at Vance.

"No comment? Perhaps, sir, a better question would be in the form of an honest answer: A laicization decree was issued on January 11, 2019, finding you, Mr. McCarroll, guilty of soliciting sex in the confessional, committing sexual abuse against children, and having sex with seminarians—for *decades*. Is that accurate, Mr. McCarroll?"

McCarroll acted surprised but said nothing.

"Very well, sir. Stay silent if you wish. That *is* a fact, sir. And your silence speaks the truth." Vance turned to the judge. "Your Honor, with your permission I would like to play a short video for the court, showing the comments of Mr. McCarroll at the City Club in Cleveland in the year 2002."

Judge O'Grady nodded.

Again the lights dimmed, the courtroom video player hummed, the room igniting with a taped recording of

Cardinal McCarroll at a podium, before a packed room of Ohio onlookers.

"It is clear now," McCarroll's video-self said, grinning from ear to ear, "that we know what we have to do. It is unfortunate that it took us so long to figure out what we have to do. But in doing that, we were reflecting the societal understanding of the time. Not to excuse—*never* to excuse!" McCarroll paused, placing his hands together on the podium. "What I want to do is say, 'I'm sorry,' in my own name, for anything that any of us have ever done. Because this is so hurtful to young people, so hurtful to the family, and ultimately so hurtful to the Church. We are anxious to make sure that not just these notorious people are thrown out, but that anyone who would do this to a child is thrown out. There is no place in the Church for a priest who would harm children!"

The video ended. On the stand, McCarroll had his head down, looking perplexed.

"Mr. McCarroll," Vance continued, "this video contains excerpts taken from your talk in 2002. Long after your sexual abuse of children began. Those are quotes you made, long before you also were accused of sexual abuse. Long before you were defrocked and disgraced. You made those remarks all the while knowing that you were a notorious sexual abuser. The Pope's right hand man. How does that make you feel, sir?"

McCarroll sighed. "Those were trying times in the Church. Everyone seemed to be trying to save face. The

Pope knew of the allegations against me for many years, but did nothing. We were friends."

"And friends defend each other. And you're speaking of Pope Francisco, of course. Who is now a Saint. McCarroll nodded. "We were close, for so long."

"In fact, Mr. McCarroll, isn't it true that Archbishop Carlos Biganò testified that a network in the Vatican's hierarchy, including Pope Francisco, had knowledge of your abuse yet took no action? And that friendship, that bond you spoke so reverently of, resulted in Pope Francisco ignoring all that evidence of abuse against so many children and young men. Is that a fair assessment to make?"

McCarroll nodded.

"Good. I see we agree on something," said Vance, shifting his eyes to the jury. "Still, there's one thing I don't understand. As a former Cardinal, you needed to be well versed in all the goings-on within the Vatican and among its highest-ranking officials, including among all the other Cardinals and Archbishops. Would you say that's true?"

"For the most part. We were all a close group."

"Then surely you know the answer to this: How many Bishops in the Catholic Church have been accused of sexual crimes against children?"

"How many? I'm not certain."

"Not certain? Sir, by the very nature of your position, as you indicated, you would most assuredly be certain! The answer is: More than 100 Bishops. Each one of those reporting to the Pope, one of your best friends. Let me ask you another question. I know you were found guilty of sexually abusing seminarians, but were any of these sexual encounters consensual? And please, sir, don't pull another hypocritical act and lie to the court. Answer yes or no."

"Yes. It was something that was rampant throughout the seminary."

"And why was that?"

A chill seemed to pass through McCarroll's body. "I don't have to spell it out to you. Human nature is human nature. We all have those urges."

"We know there were no classes on proper sexual behavior as a celibate member of the clergy, yet while you were advancing to different positions in the Church, did you or anyone else suggest offering such courses?"

"No, that was never discussed. We didn't want to bring attention to the topic. Having such classes might have caused the younger recruits to leave the priesthood in favor of a normal sexual life."

"Meaning marrying and having a family."

"Yes."

"Instead, you favored the grooming of innocent young children into a tormented purgatory of sexual slavery." Vance looked over at the jury then back at the witness. Seeing McCarroll looking wounded, he kept hammering.

"Robert Sipian, whom I believe you know as a former Benedictine Monk, psychotherapist and author of six books about Catholicism, conducted a 25-year ethnographic study published in 1991 about the sexual behavior of supposed celibates, in which he found that 6% of Catholic clergy were involved in sexual relationships with minors.

As of 2022 there were 407,730 clergy members worldwide, which means 24,463 Catholic clergy have sexually abused minors.

"That is the behavior your mandate of priest celibacy has willingly created! And the Vatican *knew* this for years—actually decades—truth be told *centuries!* They aided and abetted this aberrant behavior, which was satisfying a simple human need, yet they did nothing to stop it. Offered no classes to teach ways to temper this behavior. Offered no counseling. Nothing! All this, while knowing seminarians would take this deviant behavior and carry it into the general population—and after centuries of seeing that behavior result in rape, torture and sexual abuse of children, the Church continued to offer no solution to those seminarians who were simply acting out a very human need. The Vatican knew of all this, yet did *nothing!*"

"*Objection!*" shouted Simmons, leaping out of his chair.

"*Sustained!*" boomed Judge O'Grady as he banged his gavel. "Mr. Vance! You will not harass this witness with your sleazy insinuations! Do you hear me, Vance?"

"Yes, Your Honor! My apologies to the court. And now I will get to my question...Mr. McCarroll, as you know, an unprecedented Vatican internal investigation found that the Pope knew about and overlooked sexual misconduct allegations about you for two decades. Yet in that video we just saw—recorded more than twenty years ago—you say it is 'unfortunate it has taken this long to do something.' Yet, after more than twenty years since you made that remark, still nothing has been done, has it?"

"You must understand. This was a process. It was complicated. Each person has been guilty, at some time or another of sexual abuse. A fair number of seminarians, that is. It is just something that was never acknowledged."

"Are you saying the Pope is guilty of sexually abusing children?" McCarroll's lips remained shut. "Sir, I am not a mind reader! *Answer the question!*"

"I never said any such thing about the Pope!"

"I see. One last question, Mr. McCarroll. Did you ever record videos of young seminarians? Use them as blackmail to keep them in the seminary?"

"Not videos," answered McCarroll, casting his eyes down. "There were other means to keep them in."

"And those means were?"

McCarroll paused. "I can't recall."

"Can't or won't? Or does it burn to see your depraved little secrets dragged into the open?" Taking a deep sigh, eyes shifted to the jury foreman, Vance continued.

"Robert Sipian also wrote about 'a pattern of institutional secrecy' within the hierarchy of the Vatican. Would you describe this as accurate?"

"Old habits. Some never die."

"Old habits." Vance grunted and studied McCarroll. *The bastard seems ready to take me on. So be it.*

"Your Honor, if I might, I would like to play another short video for the court."

"Proceed."

Vance returned to the Prosecution table. He stood beside Father Murphy, leaning on his palms as the bailiff pressed PLAY on the recorded deposition of victim Robert Ciolek.

"I was in my early twenties," testified Ciolek, lifting his head to face the camera, "and a young seminarian, when this brilliant, charismatic Bishop in Newark, New Jersey, Father McCarroll, told me I was a rising star in the Church. We began going on overnight trips together. He'd reserve one room and make certain there was one bed. At first it was just requests for me to rub his shoulders. I felt unable to say no, partly because I was abused by a teacher in a Catholic high school." Ciolek paused his testimony, began to cry.

"I shared that with Bishop McCarroll," he continued, wiping away tears. "I trusted him, admired him, confided in him. That trauma has never left. It has adversely affected everyone I meet. How he continued to do that while rising to such heights in the Church is, is…unconscionable."

When the video finished, Vance strode up to McCarroll.

"How does that video make you feel, sir? Dirty? Disgusted? Does it make you feel proud?" He watched the Cardinal's eyes wander. "Is it painful to watch this man relive one of the many crimes you are guilty of?" McCarroll stared back silently, with a malevolent glint. "Your Honor, please instruct the witness to answer my questions!"

Judge O'Grady sighed, examined the witness thoughtfully. "How 'bout it, Cardinal?"

McCarroll remained silent.

"Mr. McCarroll?" Vance repeated, leaning on the witness box. "I'm waiting, sir."

The Cardinal's shoulders shook. He sat quietly for a moment, then answered. "It *is* painful."

Feeling a rush of excitement Vance whirled over to the jury. "Finally, sir, are you familiar with Cardinal Jorge Pellion? The former Vatican Treasurer who was acquitted of charges of sexually abusing altar boys in the 1990s by the Australian Supreme Court in April of 2020? Pellion was convicted by a jury, saw an appeals court reject his motion to vacate that conviction, then saw the Supreme Court acquit him on a technicality. Do you feel he was guilty?"

Cardinal McCarroll made no reply.

"You refuse to answer?...Your Honor, I instruct the witness to answer the question, or be held in contempt of court!"

"Just answer the Counselor's question, sir."

"Well, McCarroll? This court is waiting." McCarroll made no reply, refused to look at Vance, didn't move a muscle.

"Sir, you disgust me. I expect Your Honor will be fining this witness for his contempt. And Mr. McCarroll, sir, I'm certain God holds you in His contempt as well. I have no more questions."

The judge waited for McCarroll to collect himself, then motioned to the Defense table. Attorney Simmons got up, smiling, slowly crossed the room to the witness box.

"Cardinal McCarroll," he began, "it was mentioned that Pope Benedictus thrust you into a life of prayer. Did *your* prayers and penance help you deal with the abuses the Prosecutor mentioned?"

"Yes, very much so."

"So while some people believe in therapy with a live human being, your therapy is praying to your ultimate boss. To God. To your Almighty Father. And your faith tells you God the Father has forgiven men like you."

McCarroll heaved a sigh of relief. "Without question."

"Do you feel the Catholic Church is trying its best to deal with the abuse issue?"

"Absolutely."

"Has the Church made positive strides in dealing with it?"

"The Church has made enormous strides."

Glancing to the jury, his mouth twisted into a smile, Simmons nodded. "Finally, let me ask: Were you ever instructed, by any of your superiors, to sexually abuse children? To have sex with seminarians? Did anyone in the Vatican ever instruct you to do this?"

"No."

"So it was *your* decision—as a man—and not the Vatican's?"

"Yes."

Simmons smiled. "No more questions, Your Honor."

The spectators stirred. Simmons turned and strutted back to the Defense table. To Vance's bewilderment, he sat and methodically started cleaning his fingernails.

Vance wiped his lips and looked around the courtroom. Strategically he knew he'd made a strong case; he was sweeping the floor with Simmons, if the reaction from the jurors told him anything. Realizing this, an exhilarating feeling swept through him. He tried not to look at Simmons, but just couldn't help himself. He'd expected fiery orations, turbulent sermonizing from his opponent, not simple calm questions. Things were looking hopeful; the New Orleans sun shone in through the courtroom windows, and outside the sky was blue and cloudless. Yet even without the court-room drama and theatrics he expected, something in the back of Vance's mind was screaming.

He's good, he thought. *He's very, very good. Always doing the exact opposite of what I expect. No wonder they call him the Pallbearer! Guy'll do whatever it takes to bury us. Was his break-down an act?*

Vance watched the Defense attorney seated quietly at his table, cleaning his perfect fingernails as if he didn't have a care in the world. Vance stared with perspiration begin-ning to bead on his face, worried to death, worried about something he couldn't put a finger on, couldn't even name.

Vance then called his next witness—Robert Ciolek, the young victim whose videotaped testimony had been intro-duced earlier. Ciolek had agreed to testify in person on Fa-ther Murphy's behalf. Escorted into court by two guards, he walked through the silent courtroom, took the oath and sat at the witness stand, fidgeting and rubbing his hands, and pulling at his shirt collar like a scared schoolboy.

"Mr. Ciolek, you testified to being sexually molested by Cardinal Thaddeus McCarroll while in seminary school, did you not?"

Ciolek gazed at Vance out of the corner of his eye. There was a long pause.

"I did not," he said in a low voice.

Suddenly Vance felt the hairs rise on the back of his neck. *What did he say?*

"Mr. Ciolek—Robert, if I may," he blurted out, "let me ask you again: Were you a victim of rape and assault by Cardinal McCarroll?"

"You asked me that already," Ciolek stated, his eyes looking puffy from lack of sleep. "And I answered. I was *not*."

Vance's heart was beating wildly now. *Vance, be brave,* he reminded himself. *Stay calm. Stay cool.* "Mr. Ciolek, you agreed to come to court, did you not? To testify in this trial. To affirm and attest in-person to the facts you presented in that videotaped testimony."

"That testimony was made under duress," Ciolek said, and took a deep sigh. "I was pressured into the things you made me say."

Vance stepped back, looked behind him at Father Murphy. Murphy shook his head. *Surely this isn't happening!* Vance paused, attempted a smile at Ciolek, hoping to clear his head.

"Mr. Ciolek, remember, sir, you are on the witness stand. You are under oath. Perhaps you need a moment to think."

Robert Ciolek swallowed, ducked his head. *Answer me, please,* Vance thought. He heard Ciolek's breath, fast and shallow. Outraged, Judge O'Grady waved Vance away.

"Counselor, the witness has answered your question!" he scowled. "If there are no questions from the Defense," and his eyes darted to Ciolek, "the witness may be excused."

Ciolek gazed down at the chair, his face red. Vance gave the judge a scalded look, then turned it on Ciolek.

"Where is your dignity, sir?" Out of the corner of his vision, he saw Simmons, and the entire Defense team. Vance could swear they were chuckling; Simmons himself had a tight little smile on his face.

Pacing back to the Prosecution table, Vance rubbed the back of his neck with his clammy hands as he watched the witness exit.

Shit, Vance muttered to himself, *I'm dying here. How stupid can you get, Vance?* He suddenly wanted to beg to be excused from the case and hide. He bumped into Father Murphy as the old man slowly rose and placed a hand on Vance's trembling back.

"Easy there, amigo. Don't get paranoid. Just stick to the game plan," Murphy smiled, reaching down and touching Vance's hand. "Go home, make a few karmic adjustments, defrost a pizza, catch a few Z's, crank up *The Best of Marvin Gaye,* and—"

"Hey, Father!"

Across the courtroom, there boomed a voice, rising from the gallery. Vance stood and stared, trying to make out who it was, where it was coming from. Even the guards whirled around, hands flying to their firearms, unable to see who'd shouted.

"Hands off our children! Kill the priest!" The voice was high-pitched, deranged and angry. *"Make him pay!"*

There was a buzz of panic as the guards identified a short, stout, bearded man wearing a black t-shirt with the Holy See Coat of Arms scribbled across the front. Still shouting, they swiftly escorted him from the courtroom.

Vance straightened, and surveyed the room. The Defense team had their heads in their notes, scribbling memos. Judge O'Grady was checking his phone, holding a ballpoint pen to his lips, acting like nothing happened. *Why doesn't he say something?*

Vance was speechless. He felt somebody poke a finger in his back, turned to see it was Father Murphy, trying to guide Vance back to his seat.

"Didn't mean to scare ya," Murphy chuckled, gently patting Vance's shoulder, eyes scanning the gallery as if to locate the nutcase. "Some hombre out there's got a fragile hold on reality. But it's the assholes in the mega-stretch limos we need to worry 'bout," he winked, eyes pointed directly at Simmons.

Vance looked at him, groaned, then dropped back into his chair. He said nothing, just gazed across the aisle at the Defense table, dumbfounded.

Is this another one of Simmons' tricks? he wondered. *Another scumbag lawyer ploy, pressuring Ciolek to reverse his testimony?* The blood in his head pounded. Thank God he still had his star witness, Tyrell Thorne, in his back pocket. Consulting his watch, Vance reminded himself to call the hotel to check on Thorne's arrival in the city. Thorne's testimony would wrap this case up. Without it, they were sunk. He was putting all his chips on this one witness.

Suddenly Judge O'Grady slammed his gavel down. Vance flinched.

"Counselor!" the judge thundered, his eyes popped wide, "it's getting late. Call your next witness!"

"Yes, Your Honor." Vance cleared his throat, looked toward Murphy, took a deep breath, then nodding to the bailiff he stood and called Stephan Parker to the stand.

∞ ∞ ∞

"Mr. Parker," Vance began, approaching the last witness for the day. Seeing the man's eyes were foggy and frightened, he stopped a few feet short, acknowledging him with a warm tone. "Steph, that is. You were a victim of sexual abuse by Father Charles Murphy, were you not?"

Vance smiled encouragement as he watched Parker adjust himself in the chair. *Take your time, there's no rush.* He waited, wiping the corners of his mouth. He was unprepared for what came next.

"I prefer not to be here today," Stephan Parker said, shrugging belligerently.

"No, of course not. None of us do. But—"

"And I prefer not to answer that."

Vance looked the witness up and down, suddenly thrown a curveball. "But we discussed this earlier, did we not?"

"I don't recall discussing it."

"Wait a second...what?" Vance stood in silence for a second. "You don't recall? You recorded a deposition, a video statement we're about to play for the court."

"You paid me to make that statement."

Vance straightened, his face going crimson. "I paid you...?" he blurted, almost swaying, as his mind whispered *It's okay, it's okay, don't panic, it's okay.*

"Yes."

Vance held up a hand, paused, tried to smile. *What the hell is going on here?* "Are you refuting your video statement?"

"That's right."

"And you're accusing me of bribing you. Paying you for that statement."

"$100."

Vance straightened, closed his eyes, bit his tongue. He forced himself to breathe. "Do you know the penalty for lying to the court like this, son?"

The judge thrust his face down toward Vance's and snarled.

"How *dare* you pressure your own witness, Counselor! Have you no shame? Coercing victims to bend their testimony? All to save a convicted child molester!"

"Your Honor, I beg your pardon, I don't know exactly what's happening here!"

"You are badgering your own witness, that's what's happening! And if you have no further questions, I suggest you hand this poor soul over to the Defense for cross-examination, before I hold you in contempt of court!"

Vance felt himself losing control. "No questions, Your Honor. Your witness."

Grudgingly, Vance stepped away, gave the floor to Roland Simmons. "Mr. Parker," Simmons began, his greeting warm, "or may I call you Steph? Steph, why did you record that video?"

"Mr. Vance blackmailed me." Parker's fingers tugged at his shirt collar. "Said he had a video of me blowing a guy."

Vance stood up, slammed his hand down on the Prosecution table. Files and paperwork flew across the floor. "Your Honor, this is *ridiculous!*"

"Mr. Vance, sit down!" roared the judge.

"The witness is obviously lying!"

"Sit down, I said!"

"Your Honor," Simmons at the bench interrupted, "I have no more questions. This witness can be excused."

"But Your Honor!" Vance demanded. *Fuckin' Simmons. He's got his hand in this.* "Something's not right! If it please the court, I need a minute…"

"Denied."

"Just one minute please, Your Honor…"

BANG! went O'Grady's gavel. "I said denied! Now—"

Just then a chant erupted from the gallery. *"Kill the priest! Kill the priest!"* Vance blinked around through the sweat in his eyes. A line of court officers stepped forward, peering into the crowd. Vance sat down, in a panic, leaning his head back and staring dizzily at the ceiling. He couldn't accept it, all this legal chicanery, all this betrayal, this chaos. *I'm not crazy. This isn't happening,* he told himself. He turned around in his chair, looked over at Father Murphy, who shrugged. Suddenly he saw Murphy's eyebrows arch. And then Vance heard the scream.

"KILL HIM!!!"

The man in the Kid Rock T-shirt burst through the crowd, hoisted himself up over the rail and leaped at Murphy. *"KILL HIM!!!"* he howled, spit shooting from his mouth. Hefting a clenched fist he swung it down, and slammed it solidly into Murphy's face. Then he curled his fist into a ball and slammed him again. And again.

With a thud the old priest hit the floor. In a mad fury, the man was instantly upon him. He pulled Father Murphy up by the collar and punched him in the throat.

That got Vance moving. He dragged the scruffy attacker to his feet and slammed his nose with a right uppercut. Before the kid hit the floor, four court officers converged on him, pinning him down on the carpet and cuffing him.

Hearing a cough Vance looked behind him.

"Murphy!" he shouted, bending over his client. "Murphy, you okay?" He dropped to the floor, his hands bloody, fists propped on his knees.

His head wobbling, Murphy nodded. Limp as a rag doll, blood smearing his mouth, he let Vance cradle him to his feet. His eyelids drooped as he and Vance held each other's gaze. Then Murphy gave him a feeble smile, tears streaming from his love-filled eyes. Before he could say anything, Judge O'Grady's voice screamed down from the bench.

"Bailiff, get him out of here! Guards, arrest that man! And somebody call 911! This court is adjourned!"

CHAPTER SEVENTEEN

L OSING HIS CLIENT WAS NOT an option, Vance thought, wondering if redemption had a place in his life, as he stumbled down the corridor to the Emergency Room, one hand shoving nurses and doctors and patients out of the way, the other cradling a plastic shopping bag.

After making one stop at Rouse supermarket, out of guilt, he'd arrived to find four police vans parked outside, a local news crew broadcasting the story of Father Murphy's assault at the courthouse.

Murphy was already in a private room on the third floor. *Christ, so he's not dead,* Vance thought, relieved. Posted outside was a pair of armed patrolmen. To his shock and surprise, when Vance arrived, the old priest was already sitting up in bed.

"Vince, it's you," said Murphy with a smile, clicking the TV remote to see if he was being featured on the WEUV news.

Vance did a double take, expecting a comatose, bandaged Murphy on life support. Instead he stood stone-faced, watching a punch-drunk old ex-priest flipping channels, searching for his fifteen minutes of fame. "Who were you expecting?" Vance asked.

"I heard Lady Gaga's in town. Mind if I check myself out on the news? I'm waiting for them to finish the 3:00 movie, Charles Bronson in *Death Wish V.*"

Vance rolled his eyes, melting his stony expression. He noticed Murphy's face was padded with gauze, one ear bandaged. Even sedated, the priest looked like a younger man now, his voice lighter, blue eyes brighter.

Nothing seems to kill the guy. The Keith Richards of the priesthood, Vance thought, with an inner smile, wondering if the old man's sense of humor was rubbing off.

Murphy noticed Vance staring at him. He wiggled a bandaged right fist.

"What happened to your hand?" asked Vance.

"I got in a sucker punch to that kid," Murphy said, knitting his eyebrows mischievously. "It doesn't hurt. Really." He flexed the five swollen fingers and winced.

Across from the bed stood an ECG monitor which showed Murphy had normal heart activity. Realizing the priest was okay, Vance's eyes began to moisten, wondering why, after everything that has happened, he gave two shits for the guy, outside of need for this case.

He set the mysterious shopping bag in Murphy's lap, pulled up a chair, and sat at the old man's bedside.

"I wanted to kill that kid," Vance muttered, glaring at the wall with black eyes. "I've been thinking about the ten—no, fifteen—unpleasant ways I could murder him."

Murphy looked sympathetic. "Don't," he said.

Vance met his gaze in silence.

"Is that for me?" Murphy opened the plastic bag, pulled out a box of Kellogg's Froot Loops, which Vance had heard was his favorite. Part of his media manipulation to redeem what has been one hell of a polluted reputation for far too long.

Murphy gave the box an inquiring look, then dug in, munching on the dry cereal as excited as a nine-year-old.

"Don't?" Vance asked, confused.

"Don't be hateful, Vince."

"The kid was thrown in the slammer. You know Simmons set that up."

"Forgiveness is a virtue, Vince. Let's practice it. Listen, I don't want that kid in jail. You know what those places do to people."

Vance stared, without the vaguest understanding of Murphy's lack of turmoil or outrage. Munching on Froot Loops, the old man groaned with joy, his bandaged face all light, transformed.

"You and me, Vince, we're not the kind of people who hate. We're the kind of people who forgive." Murphy held out a handful of cereal, beckoning Vance to take it. "Best thing to do is to forgive the kid, and forgive whoever set him up to do it."

Struggling to embrace a smile, Vance said, "Representing you is making me crazy."

"Hearing the truth is what's making you crazy. Don't be a slave to hate, son. The Vatican needs to pay. And the bastards will," he smiled, "when you win the case."

The two men looked at each other. Finally Vance shook his head, a ghost of a smile spreading across his face.

"Listen," Murphy said, "while we're on the subject of forgiveness, I forgive you for your decision—a wise one, granted, albeit one I wasn't crazy about—to keep me from testifying on my own behalf. Now that we're deep in the game, we're behind and it's fourth and long and we're running out of options, I want you to put me in, Coach."

"Put you in?"

"Let me testify."

"Oh, come on."

"No, I mean it."

Vance squinted. "Sorry, no way," he said. Murphy started to reply, but Vance cut him short. "No attorney in their right mind would let a convicted sex offender take the stand, in their own defense. That's suicide."

Murphy's blue eyes stared at him blankly. Vance reached into the cereal box, took one more fistful, stood to exit, strode to the door then slowly turned back around.

"Besides, I don't need you. I've got a Hail Mary. One last play left on the play sheet."

"And that is?"

"Tyrell Thorne. My star witness." Vance smiled. "And no one's going to see that fucker until he steps into the witness chair tomorrow."

∞ ∞ ∞

In the back row of the Saengerm Theater, the Vatican's legal Defense team sat. Down below, on the glowing 100-foot screen, Spider-Man was facing off with Doc Octopus. Mid-row the attorney named Feral had a king-size Sprite and Twizzlers resting in his lap. Sacko chewed on a pack of Gummy Bears while Porkchop rubbed his eyes at the screen and yawned.

"The Pallbearer annihilated 'em today," whispered Feral.

"Pallbearer was brilliant," agreed Sacko, turning a Gummy Bear sideways to watch the movie through it.

"Wonder what his breaking down was all about?" questioned Feral.

"The man's done some weird shit to win a case. Consider this another of the Pallbearer's amazing strategies to annihilate anyone in his way. Just watch and learn, my friend. The only chance they have now is through prayer," chuckled Sacko.

"Even prayer won't help Vance. The case is in the bag."

"I wouldn't sleep on that guy. He used to be good."

"Even Perry Mason couldn't beat the Pallbearer with this case. Trust me."

Feral saw Sacko glance his way. Beside them Porkchop yawned as Doc Oc's four mechanical arms engulfed Mary Jane, who was praying for another Spidey rescue.

"Man, I'm lost," Sacko admitted. "What do you know that we don't?"

"I know what the Pallbearer knows. That Vance has a witness he's holding out."

"No…Really? Who told you?"

"Like I said, the Pallbearer. Witness is coming in on the red eye tonight. Only he's not."

For a moment, Sacko didn't dare look at Feral directly. "You mean like the witness from Cleveland last year?"

"Let's just say the Vatican has ways of making people disappear."

The two attorneys looked at each other in the dark and shook their heads. For a moment, no one spoke. Then Feral raised his Twizzlers and saluted.

"To the Pallbearer."

"Pallbearer's the man," said Sacko raising a Gummy Bear. "The law sure is a funny thing."

Feral slipped a Twizzler in his mouth, watching Spider-Man come to the rescue. "There's a reason they call it the criminal justice system, baby."

CHAPTER EIGHTEEN

A WEEK PASSED BEFORE DAY THREE of the trial began. Thursday morning, a minute past nine, Judge O'Grady's gavel banged down.

"Mr. Vance," he said, cutting a glance at the Prosecution attorney, "call your next witness."

Out of the corner of his eye Vance looked over at Father Murphy. The old priest's face was still swollen and bruised, but free of bandages. Murphy glanced at Vance and smiled—it was that smile, Vance realized, that was making him crazy.

Vance had come into court half-asleep, parked four blocks away because the streets were full of TV trucks. As he strode to the courthouse he locked eyes with a kid leaning against a street pole, selling T-shirts bearing the Pope's face and the words HEAD OF THE BIGGEST PEDOPHILE RING IN HISTORY, the kid flashing Vance a pitying glance. Instantly Vance wanted to stop, turn around and go home. The night before, in his hotel room, he'd been as weak as he'd ever felt, his willpower to stay away from the booze tugging at his brain.

It's not the booze, he later realized over coffee. *It's Roland Simmons. The fucker is killing me. He's doing whatever it takes to win this case—even if it means beating up a priest in court! That's the way these guys work. And you have no answer for that.*

Rising in court now, it hit Vance that he'd reached the point where the end was inevitable. He sucked in a deep breath, waited until the whispers and gossip in the gallery had subsided, then stepped forward and faced the judge.

"Your Honor," he said, "I'm in a bit of a bind."

"A bind?"

"Yes, Your Honor. I'm missing my key witness." Vance sucked in a breath. "I've called his phone, checked his hotel room, but he seems to have disappeared."

Over at the Defense table, Roland Simmons began to smile. *Of course he's smiling,* Vance told himself. *Not even trying to hide it, either! Because he knows there's not a damn thing I can do about it.*

Judge O'Grady raised his gavel and brought it down. "Mr. Vance," he snapped, and Vance straightened. "It appears to this court that you've put yourself in hot water by relying on a cheap lawyering stunt, a star witness. And though this court might empathize with your despair at this moment, sir, your shoddy tactics were always on a collision course for the shit to hit the fan at some point. Proceed with your next witness," O'Grady said, and sat back.

"Your Honor—"

"Proceed!"

Vance's shoulders slumped, as he eyed the crucifix dangling from the judge's bulging neck veins.

Seeing he'd made a mistake, Vance realized it was time to move on. "The Prosecution calls Former Pope Benedictus XVI to the stand."

∞   ∞   ∞

Striding to the chair came the first of three Popes on Vance's witness list, a dark little man with a bored gaze.

"Mr. Benedictus," Vance began, "Cardinal Lewis Taggart recently told a gathering of Bishops they were negligent to the suffering of the young boys and girls who were abused. Do you agree with that?"

The Pope nodded. "Yes."

"And is it true that you ventured out of retirement to write an article for the German Monthly *Klerusblatt*, the Catholic News Agency, and other media outlets blaming the Church laws for protecting priests?"

"I did."

"And why did you do that?"

"Pretty simply, son, my conscience."

"But isn't it true that in 2011, the Center for Constitutional Rights—CCR—on behalf of the Survivor's Network for those Abused by Priests, filed a formal complaint with the International Criminal Court in the Hague, to investigate and prosecute high-level Vatican officials, including yourself, for covering up sexual abuse crimes by Catholic priests, and for failing to prevent or punish perpetrators of rape and sexual violence against children, *and* for engaging in a systemic and widespread practice of concealing sexual crimes around the world?"

"It wasn't quite that simple."

"Actually, it couldn't *be* any simpler, Mr. Benedictus. Facts are *facts*, sir.

And isn't it true that Amnesty International's and the Child Rights International Network's human rights report concluded that the Holy See had failed to comply with its obligations under international human rights law to protect children from sexual abuse and to ensure accountability for perpetrators?

"And before you answer that, remember Mr. Benedictus the UN Committee on the Rights of the Child, the Human Rights Watch as well as national commissions like Ireland's Ryan Report had made strong statements about clerical abuse alongside Amnesty's report that there was widespread evidence of child sexual abuse by members of the clergy over decades, and that the Vatican was responsible for, and I paraphrase, 'an enduring failure of the Catholic Church to address crimes committed by its clergy and further that the responsibility is assigned to the institution of the Vatican as a state.'"

"Those allegations were against the Vatican, not me."

"So you admit these were crimes against humanity — not by you, but by the Vatican."

"Exactly."

"Do you now admit the Vatican repeatedly and systematically refused to prosecute the thousands of priests and Bishops and Cardinals who sexually abused and raped hundreds of thousands of children across the globe, for these crimes against humanity, for decades?"

The Pope glared at Vance with icy clarity. "It appears that is the case, sir."

"Yet you wrote that article, blaming the Church for protecting these priests. Explain what the article stated."

"It says this whole thing started in the 1960s with sex in movies and the formation of homosexual cliques in seminaries. It was around then that the Church laws gave accused priests undue protection and that during the 1980s and 1990s the right to a defense for priests was so broad as to make a conviction nearly impossible."

"It started in the 1960s? The court has shown this abuse and rape dates back nearly 1,000 years, sir. Do you acknowledge that?"

"I do."

"Then why did you say it started in the '60s?"

"That's when it became more prevalent."

"More prevalent than the systemic rape and torture of women and children in the years 1100, 1200, 1300 and so on?"

"It is what it is, sir."

"Do you know Cardinal Bernard Law?"

Benedictus whipped his eyes over to the Defense table. He saw that Simmons was watching him intently. "I do," he answered.

"As you know, he was the Cardinal in Boston who turned his head to all the pedophile priests who were abusing young boys for many years. Yet in spite of this proven cover-up by the Church Cardinal Law was brought back to Rome by Pope John Paul II and given the cushy job as Archpriest of the Basilica di Santa Maria Maggiore. A position you allowed him to stay in for six years. A job described as having only ceremonial duties. Some saw this as an attempt to shield Cardinal Law from potential criminal prosecution, as his new position conveyed citizenship in Vatican City. Do you agree with that assessment? That he was given that job to shield him from criminal prosecution?"

"I know how it looks. But Cardinal Law was a friend."

"Answer the question. Yes or no."

Benedictus swallowed. "Yes."

"No more questions. Your witness."

Vance stepped back, looking uneasily at Roland Simmons as they passed. Halfway to the witness chair Simmons paused, turned back to face the Defense table, seeming uneasy with this line of questioning.

"Pope Benedictus, didn't you pass laws to make it easier to remove priests for sexual abuse?"

"I did."

"And wouldn't you say that the Vatican has tried to rectify its handling of pedophile priests since then?"

"It has made some strides."

"*Some* strides?" Simmons snorted. "Shouldn't greater strides have been made?"

"I suppose."

Simmons' eyes bulged, as if he wanted to scream.

"Y-Y-You s-s-*suppose*??" he blurted out. At the Prosecution table, Vance's face blanched. *Why is Simmons suddenly stuttering?* "Then sh-sh-shouldn't we put the blame," Simmons continued, "that greater strides haven't been made *not* on the Vatican, but on leaders such as yourself? On *men*? On the *men* who were responsible for overseeing the abuse, the r-r-rape and t-t-torture of innocent children, and not on an entire nation state?"

"How *dare* you attack men such as myself!" Benedictus shouted. "Of course we make mistakes, wrong decisions. But we are following the revealed Word of the Almighty! Are you trying to destroy everyone's belief in the Holy Word, in the Catholic Church, in God? In the religious principles great leaders—*holy men,* like myself—conceived and constructed over the centuries?"

Simmons seemed suddenly to shrink. He stared, stricken, threw a malevolent look at the witness and retreated. "T-T-T-Thank you, P-P-Pope Benedictus. N-N-No more questions, Your Honor."

Like a shot Sacko leaped out of his chair to suggest more questioning. One look from Simmons simply froze the man, as he crumbled back to his seat.

Vance jumped up quickly. "Your Honor, if it please the court, I have another question for Mr. Benedictus."

"Proceed."

"Sir," said Vance, barely able to control his disgust for the witness, "in 2019 Pope Francisco held a summit to deal with this sexual abuse issue. The Bishops and Cardinals at the summit implemented some reporting rules for Bishops to deal with pedophile priests—the same Bishops who have been covering up all the abuse. Wouldn't you say this put in jeopardy hundreds of thousands of innocent Catholic children—children whose lives would be forever corrupted, perverted and defiled by these depraved priests?"

"I suppose it could be described as that."

"Do you recall Richard Sipian, the former Benedictine Monk, publishing an open letter to you on the Internet in 2008?" Benedictus nodded.

"You do. Good. The letter was titled: *Statement for Pope Benedictus XVI About the Pattern of the Sexual Abuse Crisis in the United States.* In it, Mr. Sipian states, and I quote, 'Sexual aberration in the Catholic Church was not generated from the bottom up...' He used the handling of Cardinal McCarroll as an example of the systemic problem in the Vatican. Why wasn't a thorough investigation completed of McCarroll? Invoke Canon Law 1395.

"The Boston Globe research team had exposed Cardinal Bernard Law in 2002 for a mass sexual abuse cover-up. Was the Vatican directly complicit in covering up Cardinal McCarroll's sexual abuse?"

Vance waited patiently for an answer. None came.

"You have nothing to say? Can you see how the Vatican has fostered a culture of sexual abuse against children by its priests, Bishops and Cardinals?"

"I wouldn't call it that. And I didn't—"

"Please don't insult the court with your denials, Mr. Benedictus! On another topic, in 2002 the Vatican ratified the *UN Convention Against Torture and Other Cruel and Inhuman or Degrading Treatment or Punishment,* did it not?"

"Yes," the Pope grunted.

"And because of this ratification, the United Nations Committee Against Torture and International Human Rights Law instituted an inquisition, in 2014, of the Vatican. Was it the Vatican's stance that the treaty you ratified in 2002 only applied to sexual crimes that took place within the walls of the Vatican, which is only 110 acres and has only 800 residents?"

"We argued that, but the ruling was not to our liking."

"Not to your liking. In fact, the UN Committee on both Torture and International Law handed down their decision that the responsibility of the Vatican does *not* end at its physical borders. Its responsibility extends beyond those borders to wherever your agents, acting on behalf of the Vatican—which includes every Catholic priest, Bishop and Cardinal and in fact every clergy member who committed or turned a blind eye to unspeakable crimes against children. The Vatican's responsibility, they ruled, knows no borders."

Vance turned to the jury, announcing his next question to the witness without looking at him. "Are you familiar with Australia's 2017 report by the Royal Commission into Institutional Responses to Child Sexual Abuse?"

"I am."

"Why do you suppose the commission found the Vatican has created an institutional culture that permitted abuse and silenced victims?"

"Because it is true."

"The commission also found for decades the Vatican responded to sexual abuse allegations with pleas of ignorance, denial, minimization and inertia, even colluding to protect abusers. Is that also true?"

The Pope silently nodded.

"Thank you. So your opinion is the Vatican is ultimately responsible for the sexual abuse of hundreds of thousand children, sir."

"I didn't say—"

"You just acknowledged it."

"Objection!" Simmons cried out, sweeping forward to the bench.

"Objection?"

"Mr. Vance is putting words in the witness's mouth!"

"Counselor, I am *not* putting words in the witness's mouth! I am simply—"

With a scowl Judge O'Grady slammed down his gavel. "Mr. Vance! You *are!*" he roared.

Vance looked into the judge's face and caught his breath. "Yes, Your Honor. My apologies. I'll continue with the witness."

He slunk back to Pope Benedictus, gazing up at the top of the Pontiff's ornate hat. "On another note, Mr. Benedictus, did you know that priests, even defrocked priests, who abused and raped children, were given glowing references when they applied for jobs in the 'real world'? Like Father Jonathan McMurray, who was kicked out for repeatedly raping children, meanwhile was given a glowing reference by your office when he applied for a job at the Shed Aquarium in Chicago, where he was applying for a job as a tour guide—where he had direct access to children!

"Did you know that attorneys, like Rebecca Purdel in Kansas City, who represented hundreds of abuse victims, received death threats during a trial against the Church? Or do you even care, sir?

"Did you know one woman in Africa was told by a priest that he would beat her if she didn't have sex with him? That complaint was sent to your office, and you did *nothing.* Do you even care?"

"Of *course* I care! But that is the culture. It's been around for centuries. What can I do?"

"What can you do? What can you *do???* To even ask that question, as the former head of this nation called the Vatican, is an insult to every parishioner who has ever knelt in your pews, or sought you out for confession! It's a disgrace to every child who ever dropped money in the baskets you pass at your Sunday masses!" Vance roared angrily, grasping the rail of the witness box. "No, sir, it's not 'what can I do?' It's what can *we* do!

"Objection! Objection!" Simmons shot out of his chair.

"Disband the damn Vatican and start over!" bellowed Vance, over the banging of the judge's gavel.

There was an unpleasant silence. Vance looked over at Father Murphy, then back at the witness. "Let me ask you, Mr. Benedictus. Do you consider yourself lucky that the International Criminal Court, because it was formed in 2002 and its jurisdiction is limited to crimes committed after that date, that Vatican dodged a bullet?"

"The Vatican did. Not me."

"But now the court has allowed us to go forward with this trial because they finally agreed with International Criminal Court that these crimes are, and I quote, 'the most serious crimes of concern to the international community as a whole, specifically, crimes against humanity.'"

"It is what it is."

"Yes, it is. And finally, those hundreds of thousands, some even say more than one million, of abused children may get justice!

"Your Honor, I have no more questions."

The echo of Vance's voice faded as he returned glumly to his seat. Across the aisle, Simmons stared at the floor, his face puckered. He seemed stunned as he rose out of his chair.

Startling the court, an agitated O'Grady said, "Counselor? Do wish to redirect?"

Simmons didn't move. His face showed indecision, as if his brain was still preparing the words. Trying his best to appear composed, his fidgeting fingers adjusted his cuffs. Nodding, he paced skittishly to the witness stand and began to blurt out.

"Y-Y-Your Holiness," he said, lapsing into stuttering again. "You said the Vatican dodged a b-b-bullet, not you. Is it fair to s-say, that as h-head of the Vatican, you were in charge of thousands of priests, Bishops and Cardinals? Just like the CEO of any large company oversees their employees?"

"It's not the same thing. It's—"

"O-O-Of course it's the same thing! The Vatican is an organization, under the heading of a nation. The words *nation, organization,* they r-r-really are i-i-interchangeable for the purposes of the argument before this court. And as head of that nation, that organization, it is your r-responsibility to make certain all your *employees* play by the rules. If they break those rules they get fired. Not t-t-transferred to another part of the organization."

He took a few steps away and stopped. "Let me ask you, sir. In any organization, w-who is responsible when employees break the rules, are not fired, and allowed to continue breaking those rules?"

Pope Benedictus remained silent.

"Y-Y-Your Honor, please instruct the w-witness to answer the question!"

"Answer the question," the judge said thickly.

The Pope placed both hands in his lap. For a moment he appeared to mutter to himself. "The people in charge of course, but it is not the same thing. It—"

"H-How is it different? You—*men*—created Rule 1395 that s-specifically was written to punish, even fire, employees—excuse me, priests, Bishops and Cardinals and even Popes—who break that rule. Yet, you and all the other people in charge did not enforce it. Who is responsible? The Vatican? Of course not. Y-Y-*You!* M-*Men* like yourself, Your Holiness, and t-t-those other *men* who work for you are responsible. Not the nation known as the Vatican!"

"We're men. We make mistakes."

"For once you're correct. Y-You are just a man, y-y-your Holiness." Simmons gave the witness a long penetrating stare. "N-No more questions, Your Honor."

As Pope Benedictus departed the witness stand, Simmons remained standing, eyes glazed. Before Vance had time to call his next witness, Simmons with a weak wave of his arms interrupted.

"Your Honor, a few hours ago I learned my expert witness, who had trouble getting here due to cancelled flights, has arrived. May I call him to the stand now?"

Judge O'Grady sat back in his chair. "You may."

"Thank you. The Defense calls Mr. Henry Camper to the stand."

The arrival of his witness taking the oath and the chair shook Simmons out of his meditation. His tension lifted, he approached.

"Mr. Camper. Will you please tell the court your occupation?"

"I am an attorney specializing in the Foreign Sovereign Immunities Act. My firm defends foreign entities who are sued here in the United States."

"You specialize in Sovereign Immunity. Can you define Sovereign Immunity for the court?"

"It's the principle that countries have special protection in both their own courts and the courts of their sister and brother countries across the globe."

"And what is the Foreign Sovereign Immunities Act?"

"It is a law, passed in 1976, that creates limitations on suing a foreign sovereign nation, its agencies or instrumentalities. Under the act, foreign states have immunity from litigation. It is customary international law that one foreign state is immune from the jurisdiction of the courts of another foreign state."

"In the case before this court, does Sovereign Immunity apply?"

"Most certainly."

"And in the case before this court, does this 1976 law apply?"

"Absolutely."

"And why is that?"

"Because the Vatican is a foreign nation, and under the law, it cannot be sued."

"So should this case be dismissed?"

"Objection, Your Honor!" Vance shouted furiously. "Counsel is asking the witness for an opinion only the court can determine!"

"I'll withdraw the question, your Honor. And no more questions, Mr. Camper. You may step down."

Vance slammed his fist down on the tabletop. "Hold on now! Your Honor, I would like to question the witness!"

"Why?" asked Simmons breathlessly.

"Excuse me?"

"He already stated the case should not be allowed to move forward because—"

"I know what he said, Counselor. However, I have a right to cross-examine this witness."

"Fine. Go ahead. Waste your time."

Vance strode to the witness with a look of determination on his face. "Mr. Camper, is it not true that there are exceptions to Sovereign Immunity?"

"Well, yes, but those are rare…"

"Are you familiar, sir, with Section 1605(a)(5) of the Act you refer to?"

"Not off the top of my head."

"You're *not* familiar with it? Just a moment ago you said, and I quote, you 'specialize in the Foreign Sovereign Immunities Act.' As a 'supposed expert' on this Act, shouldn't you be familiar with this Section? In fact, with *every* Section, since you yourself said you 'specialize' in it?"

"Well *yes*, but I shouldn't be expected to—"

"Of course you should! You're supposed to be an expert in this matter!"

"Your Honor," Simmons interrupted, "what is the point counsel is trying to make? To embarrass the witness because he isn't God and doesn't know everything?"

"Your Honor, please bear with me. I will make my point with the next question."

"Make sure you do, Mr. Vance," the judge said, squinting one eye down.

"Thank you…Mr. Camper, since you can't recall what Section 1605(a)(5) of the Sovereign Immunity Act is, let me read it to you."

Plucking a thick legal book from his table, Vance flipped to a marked page and read. 'States lose their immunity under Section 1605(a)(5) in cases where plaintiffs seek damages for personal injury or death, or damage to or loss of property, occurring in the United States and caused by the tortuous act of any official or employee of that foreign state while acting within the scope of his office or employment.'"

Closing the book Vance leaned forward.

"Now since the International Tribunal has already stated that the sexual abuse of children is an act of torture, and that an Amnesty International study shows the Vatican has a systemic problem that allows its representatives in the field—that being its clergy members—to repeatedly sexually abuse—excuse me, *torture*—children, and since there is a mound of evidence that the Vatican has provided that support these torturous acts, isn't it evident the state known as the Vatican has lost their Sovereign Immunity under Section 1605A(5) and 1605A?"

"Well, yes, I suppose you could look at it that way."

"Mr. Camper, that is the *only* way to look at it! The Vatican does not get a free pass this time. The Act that you so callously said you specialize in specifically excludes the Vatican from any such immunity in this case. And if you need a copy of the Act to refresh your memory, sir, just ask. No more questions, Your Honor."

Game and set, Vance thought, strolling back to a smiling Murphy, as panicked whispers from the defense team echoed through the courtroom.

With a grunt Judge O'Grady dismissed the witness. Vance returned to his table, whispered something to Murphy, then thumbed through his notes. With his back to the jury, facing the Defense table, he called his next witness.

"The Prosecution calls Pope Francisco to the stand."

∞ ∞ ∞

The second Pope on Vance's list approached and sat with an aggressiveness. Vance turned his eyes to the jury.

"Jorge Mario Bergoglio…that is your birth name if I am not mistaken, sir, is it not?"

Pope Francisco muttered, under his breath, "It is."

"Mario, why did you create the Papal Conference at the end of 2018?"

"I felt there was a need to deal with the rampant allegations of abuse."

"Yet similar approaches have been used by Popes over the years, correct, sir? Over the *centuries*, actually, and with no results. Still the abuse continues. What made you feel you could do anything different?"

"We needed to try."

"You needed to try? Isn't it true that part of the original mandates that came out of this conference was an acknowledgment to prosecute citizens of the Vatican who abused children?"

Jerking his lips into an unnatural position, the Pope nodded.

"You're nodding your head with a smile, as if that was some sort of grand accomplishment. Yet isn't it true this was all window dressing, Mario?"

The Pope folded his arms, remained silent.

"No reply? Let me restate my question. Isn't it true that you insisted that prosecution mandate apply to only the 800 people who actually live within the Vatican walls? Isn't it true, sir, even though Amnesty International had already stated the citizens of the Vatican included its representative members all across the globe—meaning *all* clergy members of the Catholic Church—that you still attempted to maintain that restriction, keeping it to just the 800 citizens within the Vatican?"

"We did at first but—"

"But it was just window dressing! Just like the time you refused, sir, to acknowledge the abuse of thousands of Chilean children—refused until evidence, which you already knew about, was revealed. Wasn't it?"

The Pope grunted, remained silent.

"Another no reply. Yet facts are facts. Your intention, Mario was to protect the Vatican! To protect the priests, Bishops and Cardinals you call friends! To provide window dressing, just as so many Popes and Church leaders have done for years! Just as Archbishop Viganò alleged that you lifted sanctions and embraced Cardinal McCarroll, your friend, when the evidence was clear he abused seminarians and children, in his own confessional. Even presented with indisputable proof, you played the role of politician—just as McCarroll himself did in the video we saw! What do you say to that, sir?"

Pope Francisco scowled, turned his head away.

"Your Honor, again I ask you to instruct the witness to answer my question."

Grinding his teeth, annoyed, O'Grady spat out, "The witness will answer."

"Thank you...Well, sir?"

"I did what I thought was right, at the time."

"I see...I have no more questions, Your Honor. Your witness."

Simmons half rose out of his chair, thought of declining to ask questions, then appeared to have a change of heart. He approached the witness and addressed him, his eyes narrowing.

"Pope Francisco, I have just one question. We all know that historically efforts to change situations move slowly. Would you say that the Papal Summit made positive strides in dealing with—and hopefully ending—the abuse we have been discussing?"

"Yes. The summit was revealing, and we made strides to deal with the problem."

"Do you believe the Vatican should be punished for the acts of its members?"

"That is not my decision—although I will add, it is *men* who run institutions, and we are trying to weed out those *men* who have made poor decisions on behalf of our organization."

"I see." As Simmons swung around sharply to the jury, his stuttering returned. "S-So it is your assertion, P-Pope Francisco, that *men* run institutions. M-*Men* run governments. M-*Men* in places of leadership make these rules, these decisions, and government shouldn't be held responsible. M-*Men* should."

"Yes."

"Thank you, P-Pope Francisco. That is all we need to know. N-No more questions, Your Honor."

"Your Honor," Vance interrupted, conferring with Father Murphy then rising out of his chair, "some information was just brought to my attention that would bring cause to ask this witness one last question."

O'Grady stared at Vance, skeptical. "I will allow that, Counselor."

"Thank you. Mario, are you familiar with Gabrese Martinel?"

The Pope stared Vance down, as if he were an idiot.

"Sir, I can see from the look on your face you are well familiar with him. Mr. Martinel was your altar boy. He was one of a dozen or so altar boys at the St. Pius X youth seminary on the Vatican grounds who assisted you serving Mass.

"Let me state a couple of facts for the court." Turning to the jury, Vance's gaze scanned the twelve faces. "Fact: At the age of 15, in 2013, Martinel was given the unusual power, by the rector of the seminary Reverend Emilio Radacious, to hand out Papal assignments. Assignments that would determine which boys would get to serve Mass with the Pope. Martinel was seen as the gatekeeper to the Pope.

"Fact: in 2013 you, and several Cardinals, received a letter stating Martinel was sexually abusing other younger boys at that youth seminary."

The Pope's face was burning now. Vance paused a moment, pacing the jury box, then continued.

"Fact: Martinel participated in your first Mass in the Sistine Chapel. Fact: By the end of 2013, more complaints about the sexual abuse perpetrated by this young man had come across your desk numerous times, as well as across a number of Cardinals' desks. Fact: You and those Cardinals did nothing. No investigation. Nothing.

"Fact: In 2014, the third-ranking Vatican official wrote a letter that referenced these allegations and that stated you — and I quote—'know the case well.' Final Fact: In 2017, you ordained Gabriele Martinel. You let this sexual predator become a priest.

"You, Mario, sent this person into the world of the Church, knowing full well he was a pedophile and would abuse young boys—*yet you did nothing!*

"Finally, last year, at the age of 28, Martinel and Emile Radicious were put on trial for sexual abuse." Vance paced to the farthest end of the jury box and stopped. He tilted his head back toward Pope Francisco. "Oh, one more final fact. All this can be confirmed through police reports, witness statements, and transcripts of conversations from Martinel's own phone, after one victim—who was 13 at the time—related how this 'gatekeeper,' this well-groomed young sexual predator, would crawl into bed with him and force him to have oral sex. Hundreds of times Martinel did this, Mario. Yet you knew about this and did nothing. You let it continue."

He stalked back to the witness, disgusted and furious. "And my bet is when I ask you why, you'll say nothing again. But I'll try. Why did you allow this to happen?"

The Pope stared across the room at the Defense table, said nothing, his jaw tight.

"Silence. As expected. Can't you see through your arrogance, sir, that there is no better example that the cover-up in the Catholic Church goes exactly to the top of the food chain at the Vatican? That the so-called leader of the Church, across the globe, is okay with sexual abuse taking place among its rank and file? The question has to be raised. Were you a pedophile, Mario? Did you remain silent because you were having sex with this altar boy?"

The Pope's jaw went tighter.

"Again, silence. Do you really think that is your best defense at this point, sir?"

"Your H-H-Honor!" screamed Simmons from behind. "This is b-b-badgering the witness! Counsel has made his point. There is no need—"

"I agree, Counselor," Judge O'Grady shot back, thrusting his neck forward and glaring at Vance. "There is no need for this, sir!"

Vance hurled himself back to the Prosecution table. "My apologies to the court, Your Honor. No more questions for this arrogant, disgusting example of a human being!"

Plunking himself down into his chair, Vance clenched the muscles of his jaw, swept his notes aside, looked at Simmons and saw the man purse his lips into a grin. Seeing this, he clenched his fists.

Judge O'Grady broke the silence with a strident, "Counselor, are you ready to call your next witness? Or are you hoping the Defense crumbles under your Jedi mind trick?"

A smattering of chuckles rippled through the courtroom.

Slumping his shoulders, Vance turned to the judge. "We call our final witness. Pope Galileo."

∞ ∞ ∞

A stir rippled through the gallery as the recently elected pontiff approached the witness stand. Dressed in papal white, his ring gave off a symbol of something far heavier than authority. He took the oath with a steady hand. Then, without a word, he eased into the witness chair.

Vance gripped the edge of the stand. His jaw tightened, breath shallow. He wanted to tear into the man—but not yet. Not before the jury heard every word.

"Mr. Galileo," he began, measured, "after your election to the papacy, two major organizations representing those who have been sexually abused by members of the Vatican—SNAP and SCSA—spoke out immediately. They expressed grave concern regarding you being chosen to lead the Vatican. They also said it was an insult to every child who had been sexually abused by members of the Vatican's clergy. Do you know why sir?"

Galileo met his eyes with unnerving calm. "I suspect you already know, Counselor. And that you intend to tell us."

Vance blinked. *So that's how this would go.*

"Very well," he said. "Let me explain."

He turned slightly toward the jury, his tone shifting.

"Survivor advocacy organizations have criticized your handling of abuse allegations in the Chicago area as part of a broader pattern of institutional inaction. Specifically on the placement of Father James Ray, a priest under restricted ministry due to credible abuse allegations, at St. John Stone Friary, located near a Catholic elementary school. The proximity of a known accused abuser to a school was not disclosed to the school or nearby residents.

"Why would you ever allow that? Placing a known pedophile near an elementary school? And never notify anyone? Did you sign off on that sir?"

Galileo didn't answer.

"A nod will suffice," Vance said.

Nothing.

"Do you deny that?"

Galileo's chin tilted ever so slightly upward, eyes narrowed in cold amusement, as though Vance's very presence were an inconvenience.

"Your Honor," Vance pleaded.

Judge O'Grady exhaled. "Pope Galileo. Please answer the question."

Galileo finally spoke. "Yes. That happened."

Vance pressed on. "In Peru, while you were bishop there, three women accused two of your priests of abusing them as minors. You later claimed there wasn't enough evidence to take action. Is that still your position?"

"We did our best to respond."

Vance raised a brow. "SNAP filed a formal complaint against you, under the Church's own abuse accountability laws. They also argued that you failed to conduct a thorough canonical investigation, adequately support the accusers, or ensure the accused was kept from public ministry.

"All this, yet that didn't stop your rise to the papacy. Why do you think that is?"

"I was elected by my peers. On my merits."

Vance's voice grew colder. "And you think your record—your handling of abuse—was the most acceptable among all the Cardinals?"

Simmons shot to his feet. "Objection! Counselor is asking the witness for an opinion."

"Withdrawn," Vance said. He turned to Simmons. "Satisfied?"

Simmons grinned smugly. Vance pivoted back to Galileo.

"BishopAccountability.org, an organization that maintains information on priests and other clergy members charged with abuse, reported you never released a list of known abusers under your supervision. Why?"

Galileo didn't flinch. "I didn't believe it was relevant."

Vance stepped forward, "Not relevant."

He paused, letting the words land.

"One of the survivors from Peru, Ana María Quispe, said this: *They always told us the Church is our mother. But a mother protects.*"

"The truth is," Vance said, stepping into the Pope's space, "the Vatican buries its children to protect its secrets."

He let the silence breathe, then turned to the jury. His voice cracked—not with weakness, but fury held back by discipline.

"You taught us to confess—so here is mine: the Vatican is shattered. Broken beyond repair. Men like yourself, in fact all leaders of the Vatican, at every level, need to be removed immediately. Replaced with an institution that will protect the innocent. Not try to protect the mothership."

Murmurs spread throughout the courtroom, as Vance headed for his seat and spat, "No further questions, Your Honor. Your witness, Counselor."

Simmons stood, smooth and smiling.

"Thank you for your time, Your Holiness. I'm sure your schedule is demanding."

He moved in quickly, voice casual, almost soft. "You were asked by these organizations, SNAP and SCSA, to implement a zero-tolerance policy regarding sexual abuse among its members?"

"Yes," Galileo said.

"And will you?"

"We are giving it serious consideration."

"And to clarify—none of these allegations accuse *you* personally of any form of abuse."

"Correct."

Simmons turned to the jury.

"So this decision—this turning point for the Church— will be made not by the Vatican as a sovereign entity. Not by some abstract institution. But by *men*."

He looked back at Galileo, then turned to the jury, slowly letting the words sink in. "Just *men*."

Galileo nodded.

Simmons gave a small bow of his head. "No further questions, Your Honor," he said, flashing a smirk to the judge.

O'Grady sat back, nodding: *Checkmate.*

Seeing this, Vance felt mentally spent.

Why had he ever taken this case, he wondered. He was never going to get a fair shake. There had been a dream, long ago, of resurrecting his career. But now he was trapped, the opportunity squandered, everything stacked against him. He was out of options, and he was receiving divine messages from the Defense and now the judge, that no savior was coming.

It doesn't matter anymore. At least you didn't quit. You put your heart into it, but you lost. Even if your star witness had showed, they would have come up with something to screw you, to screw the case, he admitted, and felt deflated.

Then a voice in the courtroom made Vance look up. It was the bailiff.

"Would the gentleman in the back in the TITAN UP! shirt please stop smacking his chewing gum?"

Vance's head snapped up sharply. He whirled around, eyes scanning the court. And there in the back, seated beside the courtroom nurse, his pony-tailed head and full-sleeve arm tattoos of Jesus bobbing around, sat his ex-partner Jay-Jay. He had that same wildman look, the same bushy beard, the same wad of pink Dubble Bubble clamped between his teeth.

No, it can't be, it must be a mirage, someone else, Vance thought. Then he almost burst into tears.

Jay-Jay, you sweet asshole. And here I gave up on you! With the back of his hand Vance wiped his eyes. And in that moment, something in his psyche turned, and his mindset changed. It was absurd to think he was out of options. Jay-Jay would never let him believe that. Jay-jay would beg him to fight, to brawl, to get in the ring and grapple. To use every option and every weapon available. To—

Vance sat up in his chair. A strange new light glistened in his eyes. He leaned over, touched Father Murphy's shoulder, gently. When the priest looked over, Vance smiled.

"It's fourth and long," he said, bringing his gaze to a point. "Okay?"

They exchanged glances. Suddenly Murphy's face gleamed. He looked up at the witness stand, at the jury, and a chill went through him. "Okay," he nodded, and beamed at Vance with a grateful smile.

Feeling a flutter in his heart, Vance rose, unbuttoned his jacket, hooked his thumbs in his belt. "Your Honor," he announced, pausing a split second to let his eyes move over the room, until they rested on Jay-Jay. "The Prosecution calls one more witness to the stand. Our final witness. We call Father Charles Murphy."

CHAPTER NINETEEN

"FATHER MURPHY," SAID VANCE, AS he greeted his client in the witness chair, "you are suing the Vatican for making you a pedophile. Tell me, sir, how long have you been a member of the clergy in the Catholic Church?"

"More than forty years."

"And during this time, how many parishes were you in charge of?"

Murphy looked over to see the Defense team taking notes. "Eight, I believe."

"Actually, it was *nine*, sir. You abused your victims at eight of those nine. The one parish at which you did not abuse children, you were removed within a month, when a parishioner found out about your pedophilia tendencies. Isn't that true?"

"Yes."

"Thank you." Vance pulled away and approached the bench. "Your Honor, at this time the Prosecution would like to play a short video for the court."

The video player began, showing Stephan Parker's recorded testimony. After letting it play for a moment, Vance stepped in front of the monitor, leaving the image of Parker in freeze-frame.

"Your Honor, if I may, I'd like to stop the video right there. Mr. Murphy, do you recognize this man?"

Murphy squinted, stared. "I do not."

"No? Allow me to refresh your memory. His name is Stephan Parker." Vance took a few steps away and stopped. "Stephan Parker was 10, the first time you sexually abused him, at St. Patrick's Parish. I will now play the video, as every pedophile needs to see the damage they've done to their victims."

The bailiff clicked a button, and the recording of Stephan Parker resumed.

"I...I was an altar boy the first time it happened," Parker testified. "I was 12 years old. Father Murphy was the pastor at St. Patrick's Cathedral in Rochester, Minnesota. H-He was always so friendly, and smiling. Sometimes he'd buy me little presents after Mass. My parents used to invite him over for dinner...They had no idea he—" Parker paused, caught his breath, leaned forward in his chair. "I-I-I wanted it to stop, but didn't know what to do. I-I couldn't tell my parents. They wouldn't believe me. It went on for over t-two years."

Again Parker paused, crying now, his whole body shaking, then continued.

"It was three years later, when I moved to Indiana for college, that I-I learned Father Murphy was a pastor at St.

Ignatius Parish in Indianapolis. I-I-I had to drop out of college after that. It brought back so many memories and— "

In the middle of Parker's breakdown, Vance stopped the recording. He turned back to Murphy in the witness chair.

"Mr. Murphy, did you know the trauma and torment you caused Mr. Parker? He could never hold a job. He was in and out of relationships. Even years of intense therapy couldn't heal him. You traumatized his entire life, sir. How does that make you feel?"

Murphy's eyes wandered back to the video screen.

"I'm waiting, Murphy. Surely your lips aren't glued shut. What is your answer?"

Murphy turned from the monitor and faced Vance. "In the seminary, we weren't given classes about sex. The urges, the lust, the temptation...it was something no one ever talked about. We couldn't be with a woman but—"

"But you wanted to."

"The urges never stopped. They never went away. We were told it was God's Will to be celibate."

"God's Will. I'll get to that in a moment. First, let's get something straight. Did you masturbate?"

"Yes. But it wasn't enough."

"Did you have sex with other seminarians?"

"Yes. We *all* did. Well, *most* of us."

"And when you graduated from the seminary, you were given a position at a parish where there were no other seminarians?"

"Yes," Murphy muttered, dropping his head to rub away his tears.

"Please, sir, there's no need to show us your emotions. No one is feeling sorry for you. Let's continue. How old were you when you went into the seminary?"

"I was 13."

"Were many seminarians recruited in their early teens?"

"Yes."

"And you wanted to be like the priests? The men you so admired?"

"Yes. We were all so vulnerable."

"Explain what you mean, sir, that you were 'vulnerable'?"

"I was an awkward child. I just wanted to be liked. To have friends. To be accepted. To be part of something."

"And would you say that many of the other seminarians you spent time with were also like that? Vulnerable? Yearning for acceptance? To belong?"

"All children yearn to be accepted. To belong."

"Would you say then that it is pathetic that the Vatican put you and so many thousands of priests in this position for close to 1,000 years? Pressured you to obey an impossible mandate? To contain uncontrollable urges?"

"We were pressured by the Catholic Church...Pressured to remain celibate. Yet the urge...the sexual temptation each of us faced...it was *intense*. And it was...it was..."

Murphy broke down, sobbing. Vance leaned into the witness stand.

"I understand your tears, sir. My question triggers so many emotions you've hidden away. Yet it begs another question: Why do you hate God so deeply? In your letters to me, from prison, you confessed to hating God. Why?"

"I blamed God for making me what I became. What I *am*. I blamed Him for His plan. His Will. But I don't anymore."

"You don't? Please explain, I'm sure the court wants to hear this."

Murphy nodded, his head down. "There was a girl."

"A girl. You were interested in a girl? Coming from an admitted pedophile who victimized young boys, you have my attention."

"I was a normal teenage boy when the urges first came. Experiencing normal hormonal urges a boy gets, for the opposite sex. Her name was Marilyn. I recently read of her passing."

"You read her obituary and suddenly you had an awakening that God was not to blame for the monster you became?"

"Yes. I had no attraction to other teenage boys before entering the seminary."

"So you believe that being forced to remain celibate beginning in your early teen years, without any guidance on how to handle the normal hormonal urges young men get, made you a pedophile?"

"We were told celibacy was God's Will. That being with a member of the opposite sex would never happen. Just to accept it."

"God's Will. Again you call it that. Where did that belief come from?"

"Objection!" Attorney Simmons leaped out of his chair again.

"Objection, Counselor? Your Honor, the Defense is challenging this line of questioning regarding celibacy! Yet it is at the foundation of my case!"

Vance stared, gripping the rail of the witness box, waiting, worried. Finally, Judge O'Grady grunted, "I will allow it."

Relieved, Vance felt a rush of adrenaline surge through him. "Thank you, Your Honor...Father Murphy?"

"I don't know where the belief came from. We were told over and over it was a tenet of the Church. When you hear something over and over, for years, you just accept it."

"Mr. Murphy, the idea of celibacy wasn't something God ever wanted, was it? The concept of celibacy was the creation of *men*. Men created it as a Church tradition, and it became a matter of practice beginning in the 11th Century — precisely when this era of sexual abuse in the Catholic Church began.

Let me be even more clear on this point: Celibacy is *not* a God construct. Fallible men in charge of a religious organization—one you worked for, sir—created this tradition centuries ago, eventually making it part of Canon Law in 1917. Yet when the Vatican made celibacy a law in 1917, they did so with the full knowledge that for over 900 years, prior to it being established as a law of Catholic Church, celibate priests had been sexually abusing and raping women, men and especially young boys and girls! What is your response to all this, Mr. Murphy?"

"We were told celibacy helped priests perform better in their religious service, and that we were following in the steps of Jesus."

"Following in the steps of Jesus?!" Vance shouted savagely. "Nowhere in the Gospels nor in the New Testament does it say Jesus was celibate! Nowhere, sir! Men—the leaders of the Catholic Church, the organization *you* worked for—made all this up! They created this fantasy, this deception, to control their members, leading to a thousand years of torture and torment and trauma! And—and—"

Seeing Simmons about to rise, Vance slammed his hand on the witness box.

"*Yes*, Counselor, I already hear your objection! Your Honor, I have no more questions. I turn this witness over to the Defense."

In the gallery there were shocked whispers, angry murmurs. Even the court bailiff seemed agitated. Sensing the commotion, Simmons lurched out of his chair.

"Y-Y-Your Honor! Please! We must have o-o-order!" he stuttered. "The Prosecution is turning this courtroom into a farce!" Still stricken Simmons fixed his eyes on the old priest, his gaze smoldering.

"F-Father Murphy...Hmph. Let me get this straight. A teenage girl made you realize you weren't a pedophile? Seriously? L-Let's leave the world of fantasy behind." He returned to the Defense table and waved around two handwritten documents. "I-I-I want to bring to your attention now two letters I have in my possession. Letters from v-victims of yours, telling about the a-abuse they suffered. The first letter reads, and I quote: 'F-Father Murphy, I read about you suing the Vatican for making you a p-pedophile, and it made me sick. Is it a last-ditch effort to get into H-Heaven? Because that sh-ship sailed many years ago...'

"'You may not remember me, since you a-abused so many children, but my name is Robert Cane. I... I-I was 11 the f-first time you invited me back to the rectory to help me with my math. You had just finished giving a lecture to our fifth-grade class about 'faith,' and when you asked every-one what studies they struggled with, I raised my hand and said, 'Math.' Everyone l-laughed at me, because I-I was con-sidered the dumbest kid in the room back then—those were tough days, being labeled th-that—but you pulled me aside after class and offered to help...'"

Simmons held the document up for the jurors to read, looked to Father Murphy for his reaction, hands in his lap, head down, tears spilling down his cheeks,

Simmons continued reading, his voice shaking.

"'I-I still remember that first session, and your arms around me...a-a-arms around me a-a-as you s-s-showed me the correct way to address my math problem. I still smell your cologne. I-I shiver, just thinking about it. You didn't waste much time before getting to what you w-wanted, tell-ing me what a h-handsome boy I was, rubbing your hands through my hair then down my arms to my...m-m-my gen-itals. I felt dirty then, and feel the s-same just thinking about it now. How many afternoons you'd call me out of class to your office, knowing that, as principal, you could call me in anytime, shut the door and tell me you *and* God loved me, while you were u-unzipping my pants. The thought of you f-fondling me,...p-performing oral...'"

Simmons voice cracked. He stopped, staring at the words that trembled in his hands. Slowly, he reached into his pocket, pulled out a perfectly-folded handkerchief, and dabbed the corners of his eyes. When he finally spoke, continuing to read, it was barely a whisper.

"'T-This has prevented me from having any semblance of an intimate relationship...'"

At the Prosecution table, Vance leaned back in his chair, cocked an eyebrow at Jay-Jay. Both men shook their heads. *We're dead now,* Vance realized.

Simmons gripped the edge of the jury box, fingers whitening. When he finally raised his eyes, his voice had changed—not louder, but sharper.

"'I-I attempted suicide twice while in college. I have been homeless several times. I-I have failed at most I try in life, whether it be marriage, jobs, even being a d-decent father to my own children—all because I c-can't stop seeing your face, no matter how many therapists I see. Even today, at the age of 55. My mind tells me I should be able to r-rid myself of you and just m-move on, but the horror plays over and o-over in my head, no matter how much medication I take. You were a monster th-then—and once a monster, a-always one...'

"'Looking you up online through bishop-accountability.org, I see just how many young boys you have a-abused, as you were moved from one church to the next. There is no

God that would f-f-forgive a monster as horrible as yourself. May you rot in Hell, F-Father Murphy, for your sins.'"

Shaking his head emphatically Simmons scanned the gallery. "The letter is signed, *Robert Cane.*

"This next letter," he said, his voice growing more urgent, "is from the grieving mother of one of your victims...'Father Murphy, I read about your lawsuit against the Vatican and had to write this to the man who stole my son's innocence. Miles Canyon was his name. You a-abused Miles many years ago at St. Peter and Paul Church here in Louisiana. I only found out about the sexual abuse from a friend of his in a SNAP support group for people who had been a-abused by priests—and only after my son's s-suicide ... a-a-at the age of 48.'

"'His friend told me of the years Miles suffered at the hands of a priest his family thought was p-pious, and beyond r-reproach. You may not remember the Sunday afternoons we had you over for dinner, and how you boasted about the wonderful son we had. Remember how you took him on Catholic conferences with you in the name of education? Miles never was able to confess to us how you abused him on those trips, sleeping in the same bed. N-N-Nor was he able to t-t-tell us of the abuse he suffered as an altar boy...'

"'You would r-rape him after...a-a-after M-M-Mass—all within feet of where you raised the chalice in the name of the body and blood of C-Christ! I partly blame myself for this, and have suffered two mental breakdowns since Miles's death. My husband left after finding out. We should have seen through your scheme. We should have paid more attention to our beautiful boy. I have tried to f-forgive you, Father, but you took our son from us. You robbed us of our family. And now you want to blame someone else, the Vatican, when you and you alone were responsible for being the Devil in a white collar—a demon that you were and still are! Knowing where you are headed, after this world, is still not good enough for you. Signed, Martha Canyon.'"

For a moment, Simmons fixed an insolent gaze on the two letters. Jaw thrust forward, his fists shaking, he flashed a gleam of anger at the old priest.

"F-F-Father Murphy…l-l-let's get back to the Prosecutor's question. Why do you hate God so deeply? With such venom? Is it because even the Almighty Father couldn't stop you from abusing and r-raping children? Is it because God, with all His mighty powers, refused to save these children, or to save you?"

"You're right." Murphy's eyes shimmered with tears, a raw reflection of his deep distress. "I *was* angry at God. I blamed God for abandoning me, for deserting me as a child, allowing me to become innocent prey for predators, and then a predator myself. I blamed Him for my own weakness, for the loss of my innocence, and for my lost faith."

The muscles in Murphy's face stiffened, then relaxed. When he looked up suddenly there was a gleam in his eyes.

"Yet in prison, in the isolation and solitude of my own dark cell, God showed me the Light of the truth. He restored my lost faith. He restored my belief by granting me mercy. Now I've forgiven my abusers—both the priests who

315

abused me, and the Vatican. I've forgiven God, as He has forgiven me. And I see that God had a plan all along."

"A *plan?*" Simmons almost laughed. "To make you a p-pedophile? That's outrageous! What do you mean, sir?"

"What I mean is this: I no longer need the verdict of this court to restore my faith in God. I've surrendered my sins over to God. In surrendering them, to the Almighty, and acknowledging that I'd become an instrument of wickedness and evil, God showed me that He had a purpose for my torment, a purpose that would redeem my atrocious acts."

"And just what is this 'purpose'?"

"God can use my life now for healing others. To hold accountable those who knowingly allowed the abuse to continue, as an instrument of justice. God also showed me that I could forgive my abusers—the Vatican, and the priests who raped and sexually assaulted me. Because of this forgiveness, I am at peace. I no longer question God, or His plan." Murphy's blue eyes softened, then lifted to Simmons. "His plan, after all, is what brought you and I together."

Simmons turned white. "B-B-Brought *us* t-together?! Are you *insane?* F-Father Murphy, stop evading the truth. Answer this court. Did the seminary hold you hostage?"

Murphy gazed silently at Simmons. Simmons bent down and put his mouth closer to Murphy's.

"You seem puzzled. Let me ask again. D-D-Did those in charge of the s-seminary hold you hostage? Could you have left the Church at a-a-any time?"

The old priest gazed silently.

"Well, c-*could* you?" Simmons demanded, trembling. He leaned backward, eyes wide. "Of c-course, you could! But you didn't. You stayed! The amazing thing, Father Murphy, is that we as h-human beings have something called 'free will. 'F-Free will' is not a man-made construct. It is granted by God—the gift of choice. Yet now the Prosecution is trying to blame a government organization for the rape and sexual abuse you and deviants like you committed— simply because *y-you* chose to stay and become p-pedophiles! That was *your* choice, F-Father Murphy! *Not* the Catholic Church's! And I assure you that your choice had diabolical consequences, which twisted and warped and destroyed the lives of countless young men!"

Carrying the two letters back to his team, Simmons slapped them down on the table. "No more questions, Your Honor! I'm finished!"

"I couldn't leave," Murphy muttered, staring down.

Simmons was still grinding his teeth when he heard the priest's reply. "Couldn't? What do you mean?"

"They had pictures. Photographs. Of me. In, in...positions."

"P-P-Pictures of...of...? W-W-*Who* had pictures, Father Murphy? The Church? And w-why...."

"They needed priests. They threatened to show the pictures to my parents. And—and I was only 13," Murphy murmured, his head tilted down to hide his tears. "They blackmailed us in so many ways. Threatening to lose our academic records. Defame us in our diocese and community. They gaslighted us. It was psychological crucifixion."

317

His shoulders trembled beneath the weight of the memories, each tear pulling him further inward.

Seeing this, Simmons shuddered. "S-S-Stop crying, sir!" he shouted out, in a quivering voice. Murphy leaned forward, his head in his lap. "Th-Th-This is outrageous, Your Honor! Who is this mysterious *they*, Father Murphy? S-S-Speak up!"

"The head of the seminary. The older priests. The ones who groomed me. The threats never stopped."

"Your superiors blackmailed you? Is that what you're saying?"

"Yes."

Simmons reddened furiously. "Th-Th-This is *p-p-preposterous!* These were *men*, F-Father Murphy! *M-Men* blackmailed you. R-Raped you. Groomed you. Turned you into a p-pedophile. Not the Vatican! *Men*, moreover, who were failing in their sacred duty to find enough recruits to man their churches, if what you say is true. Not a nation, but *m-men!* And still, you refuse to accept this simple concept: *F-Free will!* Something Y-YOU choose not to even c-consider, sir. You could have l-left! You could have w-walked away! You could have s-saved hundreds of innocent children from lives of torment! I...Your Honor...I-I-I'm done with this witness! Bailiff, take him away!"

"But my testimony's not done," Murphy interrupted, lifting his head slowly, tears streaking down his cheeks. His body trembled, but his voice held. He turned to Judge O'Grady, eyes burning. "Your Honor, please, allow me to continue."

The judge looked at Simmons, scrutinizing the Defense attorney, then slowly nodded.

Murphy raised his eyes back to Simmons. "You see, Counselor, when the Prosecution accepted my case, I knew it would be you, defending the Vatican."

"Y-Y-You *whaaat*...?"

"And I knew it would be you, cross-examining me. I knew this would give me the opportunity I had long yearned for, in prison. Just as I knew I remembered you from so long ago..."

"L-L-Long ago? W-W-Whatever do you m-m-mean?"

"You have always represented the Church in pedophile cases against them. I never understood why...Then I realized your father was an attorney for the Vatican and you, an admirer of your father, followed in his footsteps. Longing for your father's approval, for the affection he never gave you. That longing overshadowed what happened to you. You pushed the events down, secretly hating priests yet making a good living off representing them. Keeping our secret for so many years."

Hearing murmurs from the courtroom, Murphy paused. Slowly he lifted his eyebrows at Simmons.

"You see, Counselor, I was the priest at the parish your family attended, when you were a small boy. When you were an altar boy. It was me who took you under my wing, the summer your parents divorced, the year your father left home and never returned. And the year you needed someone, an older man, a father figure, to talk to. Someone who'd understand your pain, your confusion...

"I was the priest, Counselor, who sexually abused and raped you, that summer. Who abused you for the next year. I told you it was our 'little secret.' That you should never tell anyone. You listened, and kept that secret. Now I am giving you my permission to tell that secret to the world."

For a moment, Simmons remained meekly silent. Murphy cast him a confident look of peace.

"Let it go, Counselor. From what I can see, you have made a success of your life, in spite of me—unlike so many other victims whom I will never be able to set free. You're free to reveal that secret, so it will no longer weigh heavy on your soul. And this is my opportunity to make amends for the harm I've caused you, and so many others."

Simmons stared like a frightened child. "Y-Y-You...I...I...I d-d-don't recall...?" He whipped his head around to see his team frozen, caught between the shock of the revelation and the uncertainty of whether to raise an objection—or to let the silence resonate.

"I know you don't recall. Maybe you've chosen to block it out, as so many do. And I don't blame you for that. But please accept my heartfelt apology. Please forgive me. I'm sorry, for the awful and disgusting crimes I committed against you."

"Y-Y-*You*...I...I...*I*...?!" Simmons reeled backward, throwing a wild and desperate look at the judge. "I-I-I have n-n-no f-f-further questions, Y-Y-Your H-H-Honor...I need a recess, time to think..."

Immediately Vance was on his feet.

"Your Honor, I must beg permission to continue—though my heart cries out to Counselor Simmons! Even in a courtroom, we are first and foremost compassionate human beings. However, if what Father Murphy says is true, you must allow me to redirect the witness!"

Judge O'Grady looked to Roland Simmons, saw the humiliation on his face, then nodded to Vance.

"Thank you, Your Honor."

Vance made his way to the witness stand, ready to press his point. "Mr. Murphy, if it's true that you were blackmailed by the head of the seminary, do you know if this was a widespread practice throughout the Church? Is it something seminary heads did as a matter of practice?"

"To my knowledge, it was."

"And sir, was it an edict the Vatican instructed to each of its seminaries? To cover up and suppress the truth about this practice?"

"Not to my knowledge. It was our job as priests to conceal it. Nowadays, I think it's called 'a dirty little secret.'"

"Thank you. No more questions, Your Honor," Vance said as Murphy, head lowered, eyes glistening, hobbled back to the Prosecution table and slumped into his seat.

Vance scanned the gallery, his eyes locking on Jay-Jay. Both stared with pained regret. For a moment, Vance felt a twinge of compassion for Roland Simmons. Then the feeling passed, and he took his seat.

At the Defense table, Simmons sat hunched. Not a single member of his team cast a cursory glance his way. Simmons put his hands on the table, leaned forward, then spoke in a hollow voice.

"Y-Y-Y...Y-Y-Your Honor...I-I-If it pleases the court. I would like to call one more w-w-witness." He paused. "M-Myself."

"Your Honor!" Vance shouted, his eyebrows raised. "The Defense Counselor wants to put *himself* on the stand? I object! Counsel is not on the witness list!"

"Y-Y-Your Honor, if you'll please in-indulge me. I insist my testimony will bring light to this case."

At the Defense table, Feral jumped up, grabbing and snatching at Simmons' sleeve—only to be thrown back into his chair, as the other team members looked on in shock.

For a moment Judge O'Grady just stared, a bewildered look on his face. He rubbed his chin then nodded to Simmons.

"Th-Thank you, Your Honor."

O'Grady rapped his gavel, nodded to the bailiff. The bailiff hesitated then bellowed out to the courtroom:

"The court calls Defense Counsel Roland Simmons!"

His body hunched over, Simmons slowly rose and took the witness stand. He removed a silk handkerchief from his pocket, almost strangling it in his fingers. Lifting his head he scanned the courtroom.

"Y-Your Honor...and l-ladies and gentlemen of the Jury," he began. "The p-plaintiff in this case, Father Murphy, *is* telling the truth. H-He...He was the priest, the m-m-man who first molested me."

322

The gallery erupted with gasps. Vance looked over at Murphy. Turning his gaze to Simmons, he watched the attorney begin to shake.

"I-It was 1977," Simmons said, in a quivering voice. "I was 12 years old. My parents…my family attended St. Louis Bertrand Catholic Church in Texas. We l-loved and w-worshipped this m-man. Had him over for Sunday dinner. He a-a-bused me for over a year. And I h-h-*hate* him for it."

He slumped forward slightly, and stared Murphy down. "For many years, not a day went by when I didn't want to end this m-man's life! Then, a-apparently that a-anger became s-suppressed. M-My way of allowing myself to become r-resilient enough to move on with my life. B-Because of this, I h-harbor a d-deep hatred for *all* priests. For *all* clergy. A-And for the Catholic Church itself."

Objection!" Both Feral and Sacko jumped to their feet and screamed.

"Sustained!" shouted the judge.

Simmons, ignoring the court's plea, continued. "F-For years, through my teens and early twenties, I struggled—g-*grappled!*—with…"

"Stop immediately, Counselor!" yelled the judge.

Turning to him, Simmons angrily replied, "Your Honor, it is *my* testimony. I have every right to speak my truth. This is a court of law and above all else, that is what we seek," he insisted, as Judge O'Grady, looking confused, could only sigh resignedly nod.

Simmons continued. "Hearing Father Murphy's words, those memories began flooding back. Fiercely knocking down any walls I'd built for so many years. I struggled with the inability to forgive myself!" he whispered hoarsely, clinging tenaciously to control his emotions. *"B-But I overcame it!* P-Put it behind me, and chose to lead a f-fruitful and successful life! I-I m-made my p-peace with it, as just being part of some of the h-h-horrible things people do to each other! U-Until today."

Abruptly Simmons stopped. He mopped his face with the handkerchief. All over the courtroom he heard people stirring in their seats and whispering. Simmons sat forward, turning pale.

"But to say...to claim the V-Vatican—the Catholic Church itself—had anything whatsoever to do with it—your Honor, th-this...this is *outrageous!* These *m-men* are the ones who r-raped me! Not a nation. Not an organization. Not the Vatican. *Men!"*

There was a long silence. Simmons wiped his trembling mouth with the handkerchief. "I...I have nothing more to add, Your Honor. Thank you."

His face rigid, Simmons slowly put the handkerchief back in his pocket, rose to exit.

Vance whirled quickly.

"For God's sake, Your Honor, please do not allow this witness to leave the stand! I wish to cross-examine him!"

There was a buzz in the courtroom.

Simmons froze, eyeing Vance with hatred, wanting to run and hide from his memories. He sat a broken man. "No more, please!" he pleaded softly.

O'Grady paused, took a deep breath, then nodded to Vance to continue.

"Thank you, Your Honor!" Vance came and took his place before the witness.

"Counselor Simmons, in 1969 the Plaintiff, my client—Father Charles Murphy, whom you allege as having molested you—this man, sir, was a pastor at St. Gervais school in Washington Falls, GA. Did you know that?"

Simmons stared up helplessly, not saying a word.

"I see, Counselor, by the look of confusion on your face, that you did not. Charles Murphy was also the principal of St. Gervais School in Washington Falls, Georgia in 1969, where he sexually molested a young 16-year-old boy, nearly a decade before molesting you."

Simmons looked desperately to the judge, then back at Vance. "Y-Y-You must s-s-stop this. P-P-*Please*. You can't go there."

"A year after violating this young boy, Charles Murphy was sent away to Rome, 'on assignment' from the Vatican, so as not to face charges…"

"Y-Y-Your Honor, *please!*" Simmons pleaded. "You c-c-can't—"

"Let me ask you something," Vance interrupted, watching Simmons sink down in his chair. "Counselor Simmons: Do you believe in God?"

"D-D-Do I…?"

"Do you hate God? Do you blame God?"

"B-B-Blame God? Of *course!* Any G-G-God who would allow p-p-predators into His house, His institution, is not a

Supreme Being I want to p-p-pay my money to at Sunday services!"

"You sound bitter. You sound like you haven't overcome the trauma this man put you through."

"I hate *all* priests! F-F-For the a-a-abuse I suffered!"

"The truth is, Counselor, you still feel the pain from those memories. You still can see this man before you—in your mind you see Father Murphy raping you, shaming you, disgracing you, humiliating you, molesting you! Don't you?"

"Y-Y-Your Honor! I d-d-don't see *how*..."

"The fact is, sir, you never really believed you were the only one this man raped. Isn't that true, Counselor—and remember, sir, you are under oath!"

"I-I-I said I...I-I..."

The gavel cracked like thunder, barely masking Judge O'Grady's fury. "Mr. Vance, that is enough!"

Softening his tone, Vance nodded. "My heartfelt apologies, Your Honor. You're right," Vance said, and turned back to Simmons.

"You knew in your heart that you were not alone. And while those abused often abstain from sharing their stories with others, they sometimes share it with the people in their immediate families—because they have to get it out." Vance paused, his head down, a mournful look on his face as he murmured, "I know I did."

"W-W-Waaaait..." Simmons said, his mouth distorted in confusion. "Y-Y-*You* did? B-B-But how...?"

Vance looked back through the crowd to Jay-Jay, then edged closer to the witness.

"I never truly believed in God, Counselor, until this very moment. Of all the times I have heard the saying, 'God works in strange ways,' I never really believed it. This, Counselor, is the first time I *do* believe it. I say that because of the hundreds of thousands of young men and women who were raped by the thousands of priests across the globe, over the last nine centuries, He brought two men together, in this very courtroom, who were raped by the same man. What are the odds of that?"

"Wh-Wh-What are you *s-s-saying??*"

"Counselor Simmons," Vance admitted, "I am that boy. I am that 16-year-old who was raped by Charles Murphy, in 1969. Nearly a decade before he sexually assaulted and raped you. And had the Vatican not covered up *my* rape and sexual abuse by Father Murphy, you would never have been abused. Nor would so many other innocent children."

Vance looked around the room, then turned to face the jury. "You see, Mr. Murphy was right. God had a plan. God brought us here to end this. To make certain this never happens again—to *any* child. By keeping the crime committed against me silent, by covering it up, this institution known as the Vatican later sent a known pedophile to the Church you were raised in, to violate and abuse and molest *you*. The Vatican knew this man was a child molester! They knew of Father Murphy's crimes! And yet *they let this happen!*"

His eyes focused on each of the jurors, Vance raised one hand, thrusting his finger upwards.

"But He—God Almighty—saw what the Vatican tried to cover up. He had a plan. He brought us here. Today, we are God's instruments. He is using us for a purpose, Counselor. He is using our confessions, our most deviant and perverse revelations, as His swords of justice. And while I took on this case in the hopes of being able to forgive my client, not believing I would be capable of doing so, I now feel closer to reaching that level of compassion—because for the first time, the very first time, I believe there *is* a God. A God of mercy. A God who gave us free will. And it was that free will that has gotten us in so much trouble! Yet I can see now. He—God—always finds a way to right any wrong the gift of free will has caused."

Backing away from the jurors, Vance returned to his seat.

In the witness chair, Roland Simmons slumped, exhausted. Tears streaked his face. "I...You...I-I-I...I d-d-don't..." he mumbled.

"It's all right," Judge O'Grady said, "it's all right, Counselor Simmons. You may step down now."

Simmons groaned, leaned forward, his mouth hung open. He seemed to be wrestling with something deep inside, going limp. He hung there a moment longer, then raised his face.

"Y-Y-You are right, sir. F-F-Father Murphy..." He slumped on the edge of his chair. "He i-i-isn't to blame. The Catholic Church...The Va...The Vati..." Finally he broke down, his arms hanging over the witness stand, looking blindly at the floor as the words exploded out of him. "The

Vatican...Murphy....t-t-the Church. Raising his head in torment to Murphy, he screamed out, "Christ, you raped me!"

CHAPTER TWENTY

THE FOLLOWING MORNING, AS THE streets in New Orleans filled with police cars, American and international TV trucks, screaming protestors and curious spectators, closing arguments in the trial of Father Charles Murphy vs. The Vatican began.

Inside Courtroom B, Vincent Vance squirmed. As court ended the day before, and Roland Simmons broke down in tears, death threats were emailed to the Times Picayune, the largest daily newspaper in the New Orleans, to AT5, the BBC and CNN, threatening the lives of Vance, Murphy and now even Simmons, should the Vatican be found guilty. Although he thought such threats laughable, Judge O'Grady immediately sequestered the jury.

Now as the courtroom clock ticked over to 9 A.M., and Father Murphy in shackles was escorted in, O'Grady addressed his opening to the Defense team.

"Mr. Simmons, if you're ready, you may now make your closing statement."

Roland Simmons sat in silence for several seconds, his eyes bored into the far wall. Around him his team sat hunched over their legal pads, confused, still believing the prior day's breakdown was a strategic act.

Vance waited impatiently. *Come on, come on,* Vance grumbled at Simmons. *What are you waiting for?* Then Judge O'Grady banged his gavel, breaking the thick silence, and Simmons looked up in astonishment.

"Thank you, Your Honor," he muttered, rising to the jury and clearing his throat. Behind his eyelids his pupils looked raw and red.

"L-L-Ladies and gentlemen of the jury..." he stammered, his hair damp, stuck to his forehead. Vance glanced across at the Defense lawyers, his eyes wide. He realized Simmons was forcing himself to slow down and speak clearly.

"My client...that is, th-the Vatican...This client, this institution which has been charged with these immoral and depraved acts...with these c-c-crimes..."

Simmons' mouth suddenly went dry. His hands shook.

"...*Heinous* crimes...*S-S-Sick* crimes...*S-Secret* crimes... This institution, ladies and gentlemen, my c-client, the V-Vatican, is..." he stammered, caught in a storm of uncertainty, eyes glassy, "...it's men , n-not a-a nation state..." Simmons grasped the rail of the jury box, lowering his head to his chest, and began trembling violently.

Vance stared over at Father Murphy, in shock. *Good God, what's happening?* In the gallery the spectators sat hushed, transfixed as Simmons bowed his head, his silk shirt drenched with perspiration as he looked up at O'Grady.

"Your Honor, I...I-I-I'm sorry...I..." Spittle on his lips, Simmons turned to the jury. "L-L-Ladies and g-gentlemen, hear me out. Having heard the evidence...the testimony...How, I ask, do we forgive these crimes? How do we forgive such a-a-atrocities?"

Inhaling, slow and deep, his breath trembling with something unspoken, he continued. "How...?" The word came out fragile, almost broken. He exhaled slowly, his body stilling as something deep within him shifted.

The fog of confusion was exorcised, leaving nothing but clarity in its wake. Simmons just stared. Five seconds. Ten. Fifteen.

With a rumble of the gavel Judge O'Grady's roar broke the silence. "Counselor, you may proceed whenever your staring act is over.

Another deep sigh and the tremors in his hands suddenly stilled, as if Simmons' body had finally surrendered to the weight of clarity. Simmons lifted his head, his breath slowed, measured—his mind sharpening. With a deliberate exhale, he drew the silk handkerchief from his breast pocket, pressing it against the remaining tears as if grounding himself. His gaze locked onto the jury with a revelation too heavy to ignore—an unshakable certainty, the first stirrings of words that demanded to be spoken had now formed.

Clearing his throat, he started again. "Ladies and gentlemen, I represent the Vatican. A nation of men. Horrible, arrogant and self-righteous men who were responsible for my rape at the hands of this man," he said, turning to Murphy with a sense of both disdain and pity. "This man blames the Vatican. While at this moment, I cannot forgive Charles Murphy, it is easy to understand why forgiveness allows us to move forward, and that I shall.

"Like many victims, I have pushed down these traumatic events for too long. That being said, I have an ethical responsibility to represent my client, the Vatican, as best as humanly possible. I also know there is a moral responsibility that is built into this same code of ethics I must abide by. So, which is it?

"The Vatican's policies of recruiting children at such a vulnerable age, while refusing to provide them with the necessary education that could have helped so many future priests deal with their human desires, is criminal. To knowingly transfer its pedophile priests from one parish to another, knowing they will abuse again, is beyond criminal.

"While men made these decisions, and should be prosecuted for their crimes, they did so under the protection of the Vatican, an institution that could have saved hundreds of thousands of children from the trauma they encountered, had they simply adhered to their own laws, by prosecuting pedophile priests—which they refused to do.

"With that said, I leave it to you," he said, scanning each jury member with an air of certainty, "to find your moral compass, to embrace the fortitude needed to make the right decision. Men or the Vatican? It is that simple. And the decision rests in your hands.

"The Defense rests, Your Honor."

Making his way back to the Defense table, the weight of his past came charging down on Simmons, his face becoming white as he grasped onto a chair, barely holding himself up.

As chaos broke out in the courtroom, his Defense team sprang to its feet, in unison shouting "Objection! Objection! Objection!" with Pork Chop bellowing "Your Honor, *please!* Mr. Simmons is not well! We beg the court to instruct the jury to disregard his closing argument. He has lost his—"

Judge O'Grady slammed his gavel down. "Denied, denied, denied!" he bellowed, the mood in the courtroom growing more chaotic. "The Defense says it rests. Now sit your asses down."

Vance made eye contact with Simmons, who shook his head in disbelief. As he did, Simmons appeared to fall violently ill. He gasped out, swooned and clawed at the air, let go of the chair then collapsed.

Before he hit the floor, Vance leapt up and grabbed him.

"Counselor?..." Hugging and embracing him, Vance wiped the tears from Simmons' face. "It's going to be okay, Counselor. It's over. There's no reason to hide your tears any longer. Bailiff, will you help me lead Counsel back to his seat?"

Vance, the bailiff and two courtroom guards lifted the frazzled attorney, steering him back to the Defense table, as Simmons' team sat frozen in disbelief. The gallery remained in disarray, spectators on their feet, swarming and gossiping, some whispering that Simmons had suffered a heart attack.

Judge O'Grady banged his gavel, surprised by the outburst.

"Mr. Simmons! I take it the Defense rests. Correct, sir?"

Simmons lifted his head, weakly nodded, as his team vigorously objected. As they did, O'Grady smashed his gavel again and again. "Enough! Enough! The Defense already said it rests! Will the Prosecution please, *please* make its closing statement?"

Gripping Murphy's hand tight, Vance rose, and with calm authority approached the jury.

"Ladies and gentlemen, this…" He paused, hands clasped together, glancing at the judge, the Defense lawyers, the roomful of spectators. "…this has been a truly unusual trial. A trial which reaches down into our darkest places, and touches each of us, as humble and broken human beings. Even the best of us seem capable of immoral things, depraved acts, and perversities against the most vulnerable of us all: Our own children."

Returning to his stack of notes, Vance waved a fistful of documents in the air.

"We have given you evidence showing that the Vatican systematically, methodically and knowingly orchestrated the crime of rape and sexual abuse against hundreds of thousands of innocent children. You have heard from a historian, a priest who explained just how far back this abuse goes and the reason it began. And why? Because of *greed*. To protect the Vatican's property!

"You have heard how the Vatican recruited many of its priests from the most young and vulnerable among its faithful, at a time when those young boys' sexual urges were just beginning to take control over their bodies. The Vatican did all this without the necessary instruction on how to deal with their sexual urges, all the while purposely creating an environment that fosters pedophilia.

"Sadly," he continued, staring at each of the Defense team attorneys square in the eye, "you have heard the Defense attempt to downplay confessions from some of the top members of the Vatican, and how they have allowed this abuse to continue, by forming their own secret society, a 'good old boys club,' whose one depraved and unholy mission was to protect the Vatican. How do these men sleep at night, you ask yourself?

"The better question is: How can *you* sleep at night, ladies and gentlemen," he turned to the jury, "knowing you did not do everything within your power to end this cycle of abuse—and hold accountable not just the men who orchestrated and allowed this abuse to continue, but the organization itself: *The Vatican!*

"Today," Vance said, lowering his agitated voice to a whisper, "you can end this abuse."

For a moment Vance's eyes seemed to grow foggy. A drumming sound beat in his brain. Replacing the documents on the table, his gaze burned into them.

"Ladies and gentlemen, brothers and sisters, allow me to share my own personal testimony. I took on this case because I myself have been the victim of abuse, at the hands of my own client. I took this case, hoping to be able to forgive my rapist—Father Charles Murphy, the very priest I represent, and the priest I convicted a decade ago of sexually abusing many innocent children!"

Walking to the other side of the Prosecution table, Vance stopped, looking down at Father Murphy.

"Father Charles Murphy, I forgive you, sir, right now, in this courtroom, for the abuse and torment I suffered at your hands. As God offers His free and unmerited mercy to me, as the salvation for my sins, so I offer my mercy and forgiveness to you, sir."

Murphy seemed shocked by this. But he held out his hand, took Vance's, and nodded. Not missing a beat, Vance turned back to the jury.

"Yet folks, as you heard in the Defense's closing statement, Counselor Simmons is unable to forgive this same priest—the man who wickedly and immorally abused us both. He is stuck in the purgatory of unforgiveness. While I empathize with learned counsel's decision, I say with all humility to those who have shared their testimony today, and to each of you sitting before me on this jury: Forgiveness is a battle—a battle we all face. While we may never forget, and should always hold accountable for their sins the perpetrators of any crime, we also must learn how to forgive. And maybe even understand the purpose for our forgiveness. For it was motivated by love that God provided, a way for *our* sins to be forgiven. Wasn't it Christ himself who forgave the Roman soldiers who mocked him and cursed him and nailed him to the cross?"

Vance's voice rose now. "Forgiveness, brothers and sisters, sets us free of a burden that only God Himself can make right. Truth is, forgiveness doesn't free the abuser; it frees *us*. Forgiveness, though, does not free us from holding our abusers accountable. We need to hold those liable for these horrendous acts of abuse, torture and rape. Both the men and the institution responsible. The Vatican.

"In closing, ladies and gentlemen, I ask that with the preponderance of evidence presented to you today that you to do two things: Vote to find the Vatican guilty of crimes against humanity, and issue a judgment of $100 billion—a sum so great this organization we know as the Vatican will have to sell off all its assets, and distribute the proceeds to the hundreds of thousands of children, many now grown men and women, who are still struggling with the trauma inflicted on them. Who were abused over the decades."

Vance turned to the judge, then to the Defense table, his eyes seeking out Simmons. His final words boomed.

"God will guide us to create another Vatican! One stronger and more compassionate, hopefully run by men— and this time, women—who learn from the lessons of the past. I have faith, ladies and gentlemen, that you will see this done. Thank you."

Back in his cell, four hours later, Father Murphy sat on his metal bunk, eyes staring at the floor, awaiting the verdict. His trembling fingers curled around a blue pen, granted to him by the guard, a hockey fanatic named Goose, who felt pity for the dying old man. In his lap sat a crumpled leatherbound notebook.

The rest of the lock-up was empty. Goose had clocked out, and gone home, sneaking out the back door to avoid the media circus. The second shift guard, a lady sergeant named McGill, was in the back office, writing up her report notes on the prisoner's status, and the meal he'd turned down.

Murphy had other things to do.

He fingered the worn and torn notebook Doc Dillard had mailed to him from Folsom, then flipped it open to page 194. It was blank. Murphy rubbed his wrinkled palms together, contemplating, then leaned back against the wall and started scribbling out his long-awaited comedic rewrite of the Gospels, today's chapter, Luke 23, beginning with Jesus's trial.

Eyes closed, Murphy pondered how to bring some humor to it: perhaps a few catchy jokes, Jesus popping off a few wisecracks and zingers to Pilate. He giggled, rolled up his sleeves, put the pen to the paper. After writing the first paragraph he sat back and smiled and—

And he felt a searing pain down in his gut.

Dear God, he groaned, *not now!*

Dropping the pen, Murphy rose grimly from the bunk. He leaned against the wall, rubbing his back. The pain increased, shooting through every part of him. *Fucking swell!* he groused.

God, please, he begged, *I asked you before, Big Guy, would You please make a commitment? Just death or a miracle healing, one or the other! No more of this pain!*

Murphy closed his eyes, trying to find peace in his thoughts, seeing his old cellmate Drizzle again. Drizz was the one person he always turned to, the vision he always pictured when he needed peace, relief, comfort.

"Drizz, I'm losin' it, kiddo," he whispered. "Is my time up? That wasn't a trick question," he chuckled, groaning with intestinal pains. As he listened, waiting for an answer, slowly the vision relaxed the pangs in his gut, his side, his back, his neck.

As his agony subsided, Murphy gave the vision of Drizzle a groaning thumbs-up. He bent down on one aching knee, reaching to the bunk for support. Then he cleared his throat nervously, looked to the heavens, and prayed.

"God," he whispered, "please forget about that ultimatum I gave You just a minute ago. You know how grateful I am just to be alive, for another breath, another day. Grateful that the truth is out. And now it's up to You, God." He nodded, gulping air. "I can take the punishment. You always punish the wicked—at least, that's what I've heard through the grapevine down here. It would be pointless to stop believing that now...Thank You, Lord. Amen."

Grasping his pen and his notebook from the floor, Murphy focused his attention back to rewriting the Book of Luke. He paused, stared up. "Oh, and one more thing, Big Guy. Please watch over my attorney, Vincent Vance. Only

You and he know how the kid's handling what came out in court today…"

∞ ∞ ∞

Seven blocks away, on Canal Street, Vance exited the massive Caesar's Casino, plowing through the neon doors and into the daylight. Outside it was red hot, the sun blazing down. Vance wrung his sweaty hands, leaving behind the slot machines, roulette tables, blackjack and poker games, the voice of his gambling addiction screaming in his head, as he walked away from a losing poker hand.

Leaning against the wall, Vance calmed the voice in his head, then transferred his attention to his coat pocket, pulling out of it a fistful of lotto tickets. *Okay, okay, these are the last ones,* he told himself, scratching off the play area of each ticket with his thumbnail, hoping desperately for a match. Any match. With each failed attempt he scratched off the next one, then the next, one by one tossing the losers into a nearby garbage can.

Eventually they were all gone.

Vance thought about buying some more, but even that thought faded. He barely had a hundred dollars left, had stopped worrying a long time ago about the credit card bills he'd accrued, way past broke. But he didn't seem to have any gambler's luck left, or the old bettor's edge. The edge gave him the intensity he needed to overcome a losing streak. Hell, even losing didn't give him the same rush of adrenaline anymore.

Across the street huddled a group of young women, dressed like Catholic schoolgirls, standing outside Brennan's restaurant. *Really? Street walkers, at this time of day?* Cigarettes dangling from their lips, they were obviously trying to hustle up work. Seeing them in broad daylight made Vance feel more than sad, more than depressed—he felt lonely.

After court let out, Vance had looked everywhere for Jay-Jay, without success. Since he was in New Orleans, Vance decided to visit Peaches, a used record shop on Magazine Street, guessing his old partner might be hanging out there. No such luck. He also paid a visit to the local Five Guys—Jay-Jay loved their bacon burgers and cheese dogs, and the free peanuts they gave you while you waited—then he called Jay-Jay's cellphone, letting it ring until the voicemail picked up and told him the message in-box was, as always, full. *Great!*

He could feel the pressure of the trial creeping in. The days, months of obsessive preparation. The emotions connected to his gargantuan efforts to forgive Murphy at every step. The exhaustion slammed his brain like a sledgehammer. Memories of his closing arguments faded fast, replaced with a barrage of doubts.

Needing to hear a human voice, Vance called his neighbor to check up on Fatty. There was no answer. He fixed the phone with a stern gaze, wondering who else he could call. *My Mom? Hell, maybe my sister?* "Hey, sis, how's Dad?" Shading his eyes from the sun, Vance realized, *Dear God, what's the use? They never answer my calls anyway.*

Leaning his back into the wall, he let out a deep sigh, as he felt the air around him growing hotter and heavier.

A stab of fear pierced him. *Jesus, I'm tired!* he groaned out loud, walking away from the casino in disgust. *Everyone in your life has deserted you, Vance, baby. And maybe you deserve it.* Never in his life had Vance felt so alone.

Face it, he thought, surging past the bars and tattoo parlors, *the only person who hasn't deserted you, hasn't lost faith in you, is a repulsive old, convicted pedophile — a disgraced Catholic priest, who, until this train wreck of a trial, barely had an ounce of faith left in his own Creator. And after the verdict is read, and we've lost, he'll be gone, too.*

Gone because the secret truth about the two of you is out now.

But who cares? Vance thought. *By tomorrow, the case will be over. Simmons shredded my key witness. I'd heard the man was unbeatable. What I didn't expect was that the whole thing was rigged from the start.*

His anger towards Simmons began to wane, replaced by a feeling of empathy after their truths were revealed. *How would the man move forward?* Vance thought. *How would it change him? Would Simmons hit the bottle like he had?*

As Vance kept walking, he scolded himself. *I'll never change my ways now. I'm an addict. Winning or losing this case won't change that.*

He crossed the street, slipped down an alley to find an entire boulevard of gambling houses and bars. Suddenly he wanted the relief of a drink, just one, something to dull the pain. *I'm tempted to go on one final bender,* he thought. *It's too late to throw the case now — but maybe the appeal, which Murphy will no doubt be pleading for. The guy'll be on his deathbed, still begging and pleading for one more shot, one more crack at suing the Vatican.*

His face sweating, Vance passed the grimy windows of The Saint Bar & Lounge, a dive bar to beat all dive bars. He battled the urge to stop, turn around, to enter the bar and wet his whistle, get bombed.

Hurrying back, he pressed his nose against the window, and stared at the four guys shooting pool, the line of customers lounging at the bar, laughter drifting out through the open front door, the row of gleaming bottles of Old Fitzgerald and Henry DuYore's bourbon stacked high on the wall, the air full of smoke.

A prickly sensation needled the back of his throat. *Vance, you coward! You can't do this! You can't have a nervous breakdown! Not now!*

Turning back to the street, his face blanched. For a split second, he recalled the words of his Father. *Everything can be overcome with prayer.* They were words he'd never believed in, never put any faith in. Wasn't the Almighty up to His ass in non-believers begging for a last-minute rescue?

Vance glanced back at the bar, the bottles of shimmering liquor. Too tired to think anymore, tears welled behind his eyelids. *Ask God. Ask Him for strength. Ask Him for forgiveness. Ask Him to help you escape this moment, this weakness.*

Shifting his head, he squinted in the mid-day sun. Across the street from The Saint flashed a chapel sign. Part of a homeless shelter.

He was staring in the window of the Chapel, watching two homeless men bowing before the cross, when the need to pray struck him. Before he could utter "Bless me Father for I have sinned..." his phone buzzed.

Clicking on it, he bit his lip. He felt his body temperature drop 10 degrees as he read:

Counselor Vance, this is the court bailiff.

The verdict is in.

∞   ∞   ∞

Running like a madman Vance flew between the police vans and TV news trucks, running up the courthouse steps, through the doors and the metal detectors. He exhaled in relief, wiped the cold sweat from his forehead, jogged through the crowded corridor and into Courtroom B.

He was gasping and wheezing as he arrived at the Prosecution table, the Defense team already in their seats, Simmons' lifeless eyes staring through Vance, the light in his eyes extinguished from his gut-wrenching testimony.

Vance was still on his feet and pulling notes from his briefcase when Father Murphy was escorted into court. A minute later, the bailiff opened the judge's chamber door, and O'Grady marched in. He gave the room a skeptical glance, took his seat, banged his gavel, gestured to the bailiff who admitted the jurors.

Vance sat still, barely breathing.

"Will the jury please rise and pass the verdict for reading?" O'Grady said.

Vance turned his head, eyes fixed on the sealed piece of paper as it passed from the jury foreman to the bailiff, then into the hands of the judge. Watching O'Grady flick open and read the verdict, Vance groaned, the moment pushing him over the edge. Then the judge tilted his chin up, his gaze scanning the hushed courtroom, the words taking a lifetime to come out.

"The Jury finds the Vatican guilty of crimes against humanity," O'Grady read, turning one eye to Father Murphy, taking a deep breath and then letting it out, "and hereby orders the Vatican to pay those abused by priests under its rule the amount—"

Vance closed his eyes, his mind working itself into a frenzy—

"—of $500 billion."

CHAPTER TWENTY-ONE

T EN IN THE MORNING, A week before Easter Sunday, the package arrived at the Beale Street law firm of Vance & Jussip in Memphis.

Wrapped in white butcher paper, and heavily insured, the FedEx carrier laid it on the desk of Attorney Vincent Vance, who signed for it and stood by the package staring down at it for a long time, before he called in his partner.

There was no return address, no sender's name, which both men thought was strange.

"Might be the documents for that Tampa sex trafficking case," said Jay-Jay, scratching his head.

Vance rubbed the muscle running down the back of his neck. "Might be," he calculated.

Their new firm representing abuse victims of all types had been doing well in the two years since the trial. It was satisfying for Vance to be working alongside his old mentor again, to be the spark of hope victims needed. The notoriety of the Vatican trial certainly hadn't hurt business. The flood of overdue bills had been religiously paid off after his 5% cut from the Vatican's asset sales.

"Or it could be a new printer, since ours crapped out," blurted Jay-Jay, moving to the waiting room to answer the ringing phone.

The phones were always ringing now, Vance grumbled, watching Jay-Jay sweep up piles of case files they barely had time to deal with, plopping them down on the leather couch where Fatty was napping, the little dog snoring away. The couch had been paid for by Vance's AA sponsor, a gift Vance insisted upon repaying. He hadn't touched the bottle since the verdict and AA had a lot to do with that. Kicking his gambling addiction was harder, but Vance was working on it.

"Maybe it's a package from Simmons," said Jay-Jay, hanging up the phone in the other room. "He keeps calling and asking about Portland, Oregon. Wants to set up some sort of pow-wow. He's all buddy-buddy, palsy-walsy now. Driving me nuts."

Vance chuckled grimly. He and Jay-Jay had been invited to attend the first Mass of the New Church in downtown Portland on Easter Sunday.

Hearing a loud bark at his heels, Vance looked down to see Fatty yipping at the mysterious package. "Think we should open this thing?" he asked.

"You open it," answered Jay-Jay, grabbing his Tennessee Titans hoodie off the coat rack. "I've got a court date. Plus I've seen that movie *Seven* with the severed head in the box too many times."

Jay-Jay stepped outside, Vance watching him cross the busy street to where they had parked the Honda. Looking at the package his brain tingled. *For crying out loud.* Finally he tore open the butcher paper, opened the box, found another box inside, hand-hewn out of cedar. As he cradled it out, a note fluttered to the floor.

ATTORNEY VINCENT VANCE it read, in capital letters probably banged out on an old Smith-Corona.

For a long moment Vance studied the note. Fatty rubbed back and forth at his ankles. Plucking the dog off the floor, Vance set him on the desktop. Then he read the attached paperwork, and whispered, "My God."

It was from Folsom Prison. The packing list inventory, signed by Doc Dillard, itemizing one enclosed item: HUMAN CREMAINS.

Murphy's ashes, Vance realized. He returned to the typewritten note, astounded, and read:

DEAR VINCE,

THANK YOU FOR ALL YOU'VE DONE.

LOVE, CHARLES MURPHY.

P.S.: DO WHAT YOU THINK IS BEST WITH THE ENCLOSED, SON.

JUST DON'T BE AN ASSHOLE AND PISS ON MY GRAVE.

For a long moment, Vance stood stunned, his thoughts frightening him.

Murphy's dead? Knees weak, he turned to open his laptop, searched for any news of Father Murphy. There it was: a week ago, a CBS News report from KOVR-TV Sacramento. Murphy'd died alone in his cell, having survived two years past his sell-by-date, as the old geezer would probably have wisecracked. Thinking this forced a smile to Vance's face.

With a chuckle he loosened his tie, picked up the cedar box and the dog, sat holding them both on the couch. For a beat or two his heart was filled with anguish and loss and pain. Then the tears fell, and Vance dabbed them away with his tie while Fatty licked his wet cheeks.

They sat there for ten minutes, while the office phone rang. Placing the receiver off the hook, Vance left the waiting room. He rummaged through the FedEx package for more instructions from Doc Dillard or Father Murphy. But there were only some Styrofoam peanuts, and dust. Lots of dust.

Vance stroked the back of his neck, his throat tight. He placed his hands on his hips. "What the hell are we supposed to do with this, Fatty?" he shrugged.

CHAPTER TWENTY-TWO

EASTER SUNDAY, 9 A.M., DOWNTOWN Portland, Oregon. Vance stood at the foot of The New Church of the New Vatican, previously St. Peter's Parish, a towering old Catholic cathedral on the corner of North West Park and Jackson, cradling under his right arm the box containing Murphy's ashes.

Vance shook his head in wonder. Though it was half an hour before Easter Mass began, a crowd of thousands had gathered outside, the line going into the church a full block long and growing.

For a few long minutes Vance kept a silent vigil, staring hypnotically up at the gleaming spire, the clanging church bells, and the bright new sign: EASTER MASS 10A.M. ALL ARE WELCOME HERE. GOD SAYS COME AS YOU ARE.

"I bet you're loving this," Vance said, patting the box of ashes. Then a minute before 10 he went up the stone steps, filed in with the smiling throng, displaying his invitation.

He found a seat near the back, unbuttoned his coat and gently set down Murphy's box on the pew beside him. And waited.

The church was silent. Finally a young woman in faded blue jeans and a NEW CHURCH sweatshirt rose from the front pew. Stepping to the pulpit, she admired the first glow of sunlight streaming in, placed her hands on the Holy Bible, smiled at a young man cradling his baby daughter in the front row, then addressed the congregation.

"Ladies and gentlemen of the New Church...My name is Mrs. Margaret O'Reilly, and I'm your parish priest. Welcome to your new home," she said, spreading her arms out wide as if to touch the stained-glass walls of the cathedral, "and to the first Mass of the New Vatican!

"Two years ago, after the court verdict was handed down and the old Vatican was forced to sell its assets to pay hundreds of thousands of sexual abuse victims, many thought it was the end of the Church. Little did they know the power of resurrection Jesus teaches us today, on this Easter Sunday."

Tucking the Bible under her arm, she strolled from the pulpit, stopping in front of the altar. "After that verdict, I didn't want our Church to be just a memory of hypocrisy, greed and neglect, or a memory of the Church's failure to protect the most innocent of God's flock.

"Our small social media campaign saw millions of Catholics, across the globe, send us letters, emails and donations, asking us to *not* let our small and insignificant Church here in Portland, Oregon forsake them. They wanted a Church that would truly embody the teachings of Christ.

"Their donations allowed us to purchase many of the Churches that had closed their doors: Peter's Basilica in Vatican City; Old St. Patrick's Church in Chicago; St. Patrick's Cathedral in New York City, and so many others across the world. Through God's blessing we have been able to resurrect the Church in His true image and likeness—a Church He will be proud to say He was instrumental in creating.

"Today," Mrs. O'Reilly said, raising the Bible high in one hand, "we celebrate not just Christ's resurrection from the dead, but our own rebirth as the New Vatican. A new Church truly built by you, and for all Catholics worldwide. A rebirth that does more than pay lip service to His tenets of unconditional love, compassion, equality and forgiveness, but one that embraces those tenets and commits to a life honoring them. We are a Church God will be proud to gaze down upon. And as we livestream this service across the globe, we begin our first sermon with one question:

"Why did Jesus rise from the dead?

"Of all the lessons He was teaching us, what lesson were we to learn from this one act? We know His crucifixion was dying for our sins. A lesson so powerful that we cannot forget the effect sin has on us all. But rising again?"

Raising her eyebrows, she took her thumb from the middle of the book and opened to John, Chapter 20. "The Bible tells us that Jesus died and rose again not only so that we could receive forgiveness, but something more. He died and rose so that we might have *life*. It is through His death and resurrection that we receive life!

"And we now have a new life. Resurrected as a New Church, where abuse, in any form, is a thing of the past. Where cover-ups by Church officials bring prison sentences, and where you, the parishioners, now have oversight in helping we humans in charge of this new, sacred institution, forge a new path. Our new parishioners' Shepherds Committee will protect us from the sins of the past.

"Those men who abused," O'Reilly said, her voice rising to the ceiling, "who covered up that abuse for decades, have now been dealt with. Some have been imprisoned. Some have taken their own lives. Some live in exile. And some are here today with us." Her eyes scanned the crowd, her face shining.

"Why are they here? Because today is more than just a physical rebirth of the Catholic Church; it is a day to renew and remind. Renew our vows to keep sacred the teachings of God through His only Son. And remind us that His most powerful of all teachings is one of *forgiveness*.

"So today, on this first Mass of our resurrected Church, I, Mother Margaret O'Reilly, together with my husband and fellow priest, Father Christopher O'Reilly," she said, beaming a smile at the young man seated in front, holding their newborn in swaddling clothes, "put to rest our past. We move forward with ambitions our God is proud to gaze down upon.

"Father Charles Murphy has died. A vestige of the past. Mind you though, we will not be honoring this man's life.

Let it be said: He was a monster. A pedophile. What we will do," she said, almost with a hush, "is *forgive*. For as we are made in God's image and likeness, so too do we strive to become one with Him by applying His teachings."

Once more she returned to the pulpit, looking down at her husband and baby daughter with adoration, opening her arms as if the hundreds gathered were family and friends. "In God's world, so too in ours, there is no room for revenge, bitterness and hatred. Our resolve, beginning to-day, is to live within the teachings of His Holy Name. Embrace forgiveness. Always strive to attain unconditional love in our lives.

"So let today's Mass begin—in His name and the name of forgiveness! Because, while history takes time to correct injustice, forgiveness—because it breeds karma, hastens all inequities!"

The parishioners' hearts swelled with every sacred rhythm of the Mass. What had once been a routine hand-shake became a vessel of warmth—radiating tenderness, forgiveness, and renewal. And when Mother O'Reilly offered her final benediction—"Go in peace, and carry your newfound commitment of love"—the congregation answered with an *Amen* so full-throated, so luminous, it seemed to lift the very rafters.

∞ ∞ ∞

Outside on the church steps, after the service, Vance stood hugging the cedar box, tears streaming down his cheeks. He paused now and then to blow his nose, the air turning warmer, wind whipping through downtown Portland and ringing the old church bells.

Tears and hugs seemed to be happening all around him. The priest, Mrs. Margaret O'Reilly, was hugging a 15-year-old deaf young man, hearing about his sexual assault at the hands of a priest in Phoenix, and how he was adjusting to a new life since Murphy's verdict. Other victims were weeping and running their hands over their faces while a black street musician played *Amazing Grace* on his tenor saxophone.

Oregon sunbursts fell on the downtown joggers, waving as they passed. Children in Easter outfits waved back, running up and down the cracked stone steps, then racing to embrace their parents.

Vance shook his head. A few feet away stood his old nemesis, Roland Simmons. Counselor Simmons smiled next to his son Daniel and his new daughter-in-law, swinging his arms around his ex-wife and her boyfriend, thanking them all for coming.

Ruben Sanchez stood silently listening to the ringing church bells as Stephan Parker, along with a host of other former victims, greeted each other warmly, almost as if their abuse had melted into another lifetime.

One by one they came up and shook Vance's hand, eyeing the strange box he carried.

Then Vance felt somebody tug at his arm. Turning, he found his sister Janice, his mother, his estranged son Jordan, and his father, who had been pulling at his arm from a wheelchair. For a stilted moment they looked at each other, not knowing what to say. Then his sister took Vance's hand, and squeezed it.

"Vince," she said, "dammit, I love you."

Vance blinked at her. Before he could reply, his father tugged at his arm. Vance turned his head until his eyes looked boldly into his father's. "Son, I love you, too."

Vance's eyes widened. They shifted to his son. Jordan took a deep breath but seemed unable to look at him. Sensing doubt, Vance spoke, with all the love he'd been holding inside.

"Jordy," he said, wrapping his arm around his son, eyeing him straight on, "you've always been the light in my life. I just never knew how to express it. For that, I apologize and ask for your forgiveness."

Tears welling up, Jordan grabbed his father's hand. "Always, Dad," he said.

His mother kissed Vance's neck. "Son, forgive us all," she whispered.

Vance raised his eyebrows. *Forgive us all?* Suddenly he felt dizzy. His brain getting fuzzy from the April wind that was swirling and kicking up.

The clanging of bells in his ears, Vance looked at his son. *God, he is so young!* He wondered about all the years they'd missed, the time they'd thrown away, forever lost. *Don't worry*, something in his brain spoke. *Because he's here now, ready to build something new.*

Raising his arms to embrace them, tears streaming down his neck, Vance's head felt instantly light. His old anger and guilt receding, he gazed off and across the street at the new monument under construction. Two rectangular slabs of gleaming black granite, more than twice Vance's height, pointing downtown, where the Willamette River met the heart of the city. *Victims Square,* he heard they were calling it. A quarter-mile V-shaped wall engraved with hundreds of thousands of forgotten names, serving as a reminder of a time never to be relived. A monument for generations to understand that abuse has its consequences.

Vance wiped his eyes. A silent surge of gratification swelled inside of him, recalling how his small part contributed to the death and resurrection of the Church. *And I sense this Church will be different,* he thought, his soul believing — perhaps truly *knowing* — this time it was going to maintain its integrity. Embody its commitments of forgiveness and love.

Feeling all this, he gazed at the new monument. There Jay-Jay stood, leaning against the wall, head bowed in prayer. Again Vance's eyes moistened.

Behind him the families and the victims began drifting away, until only Vance remained. He stood motionless, the sun scudding from behind a cloud, letting the wind trace the creases in his face, as he stared up at the sky. Then Vance looked down at his hands, saw the box containing Murphy's ashes. And he began to tremble with some mysterious and unspoken excitement.

As his eyes focused back on the monument, Vance sensed a shift in the Portland air, in the energy high above the granite wall. Soft white silhouettes were forming, wavering overhead in the clouds. For a moment, Vance marveled and wondered. *Am I alone in seeing this?*

High above him the silhouettes flickered, became more distinct as they stretched out, as their wavering began to drift toward the heavens, rising to Goliathan heights, whipped and stirred by the wind into strangely familiar shapes.

Astonished, his heart racing, Vance suddenly wanted to fall to his knees. He began to see a vaguely human face, a face he knew well, a face that once caused him pain and now only brought love—Father Murphy's face, streaming across the Oregon sky.

The more Vance stared, the clearer he saw other faces. First one, then another, and another. Names he had no idea he knew sprang to mind, some of them children: *Ignatius Vilardo, Shabbir Shahid, Alicia Santana, Akwasi Akoto, James Dawson, Joy de Fazio*...Name after name pulsed through his brain, the faces awakened as if from a dream. Each held a candle, their arms locked, effortlessly ascending, stopping for only a moment to allow the final shining silhouette to form and join them. *That must be Marilyn,* Vance realized, locking arms with Murphy as all made their way upwards.

As the line of souls ascended, marching toward Heaven, tears of joy welled in Vance's eyes. That's when he remembered the cedar box under his arm.

Gripping it in both hands, he opened the box, letting the first few flakes of ash float out to the horizon, far above and beyond our little world.

"So long, Murphy. I'll catch you on the flipside," Vance said. Then a final surge of forgiveness shook him, and Vance spread his arms wide. The cloud of ash burst forth from the box, floating and climbing upward, and setting Murphy free.

EPILOGUE

SIX MONTHS AFTER EASTER, THE NEW Memphis law firm of Vance, Jussip, and Simmons opened their doors, dedicated to serving abuse victims while creating a tribunal for the New Vatican to oversee any and all forms of injustice within its confines.

The monument in Victims Square, across from the New Church in Portland, was completed, listing the names of all 904,812 of the Old Vatican's sexual abuse victims.

And parish priest Mrs. Margaret O'Reilly was elected the new Pope of Vatican II.

Author's Note to the Reader

Vote Today

As a reader, you now have the unique opportunity to step into the jury box.

You've heard the testimony. You've seen the evidence. Now it's your turn to decide:

Is the Vatican guilty or not guilty of the crimes alleged?

Go to www.SuingTheVatican.com/vote to enter your verdict or scan the QR code below.

Thank you for bearing witness.

NOTES AND SOURCES

Please visit www.SuingtheVatican.com/notes for a digital version of these notes, complete with clickable links to sources, or scan the QR code below.

CHAPTER 15

(1.) **Page 198:** The United Nations Committee Against Torture (CAT) monitors the implementation of States Parties' obligations under the UN Convention Against Torture. CAT was created in accordance with article 17 of the UN's Convention Against Torture.

CAT, along with other UN human rights bodies, has strongly condemned sexual abuse within religious institutions, particularly in the Catholic Church, recognizing it as a form of torture and of cruel, inhuman, or degrading treatment under international law. Their stance is based on multiple reports, investigations, and hearings that have examined the Church's role in covering up and mishandling cases of sexual abuse. CAT states:

• If the abuse is systematic or particularly cruel, it may qualify as torture or inhuman/degrading treatment, especially if the state is complicit or negligent in its prevention.

• Article 2 and 16: Require states to prevent acts of torture and other cruel treatment by public officials and that failure to prevent or punish sexual abuse in institutional settings, especially involving state or church complicity, can be prosecuted under CAT.

Additional Findings & Statements by the UN Committee Against Torture and other United Nations findings:

• 2014 Review of the Vatican

The Committee Against Torture conducted a review of the Vatican's compliance with the Convention Against Torture in 2014. It criticized the Vatican for failing to properly investigate and prevent sexual abuse of children by clergy. The Committee asserted that sexual abuse by clergy members could amount to torture under international law, particularly when church officials concealed or enabled such abuse. It condemned the systematic cover-ups and the Vatican's failure to report abusers to civil authorities.

• UN Committee on the Rights of the Child (CRC) Report (2014)

In a separate 2014 report, the UN Committee on the Rights of the Child (CRC) accused the Vatican of enabling widespread sexual abuse of children by priests and failing to take sufficient action. It called on the Church to remove abusers, hand them over to law enforcement, and provide justice for victims. The report criticized the Church's practice of transferring priests to different parishes instead of removing them from ministry.

• Convention on the Rights of the Child (CRC) – 1989

Article 19: States must take "all appropriate legislative, administrative, social and educational measures to protect the child from all forms of physical or mental violence, injury or abuse, neglect or negligent treatment, maltreatment or exploitation, including sexual abuse."

Article 34: Requires states to "undertake to protect the child from all forms of sexual exploitation and sexual abuse."

• UN Special Rapporteur on Torture (2015)

Juan E. Méndez, then UN Special Rapporteur on Torture, affirmed that clergy sexual abuse could constitute torture, especially when institutions failed to prevent it.

• UN High Commissioner for Human Rights in Various Reports

The UN Human Rights Council has highlighted sexual abuse in religious institutions as a violation of human rights. It has urged governments and religious institutions to provide transparency, prosecute offenders, and support survivors.

(2.) Page 199: International criminal tribunals are special courts established to prosecute cases arising under international criminal law. These tribunals have jurisdiction over crimes of torture, sexual abuse, crimes against humanity, among other international crimes.

One key legal instrument that addresses this is the Rome Statute of the International Criminal Court (ICC), which includes sexual violence as a war crime and a crime against humanity. Under the Rome statute, Article 7 explicitly includes rape and sexual slavery as crimes that can be prosecuted as 'crimes against humanity' when committed systematically.

Also, The International Criminal Tribunal for the former Yugoslavia (ICTY) and other international tribunals have classified rape and systematic sexual abuse as forms of torture or crimes against humanity under international law.

For these specific rulings and legal references, you can consult the official websites of:

• International Criminal Court (ICC) - www.icc-cpi.int

• International Criminal Tribunal for the former Yugoslavia (ICTY) - www.icty.org

These sites offer detailed documents, rulings, and discussions of how sexual violence is addressed as torture within the framework of international human rights law

(3.) Page 199: Amnesty International https://www.amnesty.org is a global non-governmental organization (NGO) with over ten million members and supporters and that focuses on the protection and promotion of human rights. Founded in 1961 by British lawyer Peter Benenson, its mission is to ensure that human rights are respected and protected for all people, regardless of their nationality, religion, or any other status.

Key areas of focus of Amnesty International as it relates to this book:

• Ending Human Rights Abuses: Amnesty works to end various forms of abuse, including sexual abuse and other forms of torture.

• Campaigning for Justice: The organization campaigns to end child sexual abuse, often focusing on instances where governments or powerful institutions fail to take action.

•Reports and Investigations: Amnesty is well-known for its research and documentation on human rights abuses. Its reports often bring attention to violations that might otherwise go unnoticed or unreported.

• Campaigns Against Torture: The organization has played a key role in advocating for the prevention of torture and sexual abuse, working to hold perpetrators accountable.

Amnesty operates in more than 70 countries, with millions of supporters, members, and activists who take part in their efforts to promote human rights. The organization's approach includes research, campaigning, lobbying, activism, and public education.

Their reports, campaigns, and advocacy work often shine a light on state-sponsored abuses or institutional violence, including churches and governments involved in widespread violations.

Amnesty International has addressed the issue of sexual abuse within the Catholic Church, particularly regarding the Vatican's failure to adequately address the widespread cases of childhood sexual abuse by clergy members. The organization has called on the Vatican and other religious institutions to be held accountable for enabling or covering up such abuses.

(4.) Page 204: https://www.theguard-ian.com/world/2010/mar/25/pope-us-priest-children-abuse

(5.) Page 205: https://www.bishop-accountabil-
ity.org/reports/1985_06_09_Doyle_Manual/
https://www.bbc.com/news/world-44209971

(6.) Page 207: https://www.amazon.com/Sex-Priests-Se-
cret-Codes-Catholic/dp/1566252652

(7.) Page 209: https://www.bishop-accountabil-
ity.org/news2008/01_02/2008_01_08_Doyle_VOTFAnd.htm
https://www.bishop-accountabil-
ity.org/news2008/01_02/2008_01_29_VOTF_OpenLetter.ht
m

(8.) Page 214: https://en.wikipedia.org/wiki/Truth,_Jus-
tice_and_Healing_Council
https://www.washingtonpost.com/national/reli-
gion/australians-suggest-celibacy-played-a-role-in-clergy-
abuse-scandal/2014/12/12/5ad2792c-8238-11e4-b936-
f3afab0155a7_story.html
https://www.tjhcouncil.org.au/me-
dia/39435/30549468_2_TJHC-Towards-Healing-
submission-30-Sep-2013.pdf

(9.) Page 214: http://www.tjhcouncil.org.au/catholic-
community/the-catholic-church-and-the-royal-commis-
sion.aspx

In December 2017, the Royal Commission into Institutional Responses to Child Sexual Abuse in Australia released its Final Report, which included an examination of

the Catholic Church's practice of clerical celibacy and its potential connection to child sexual abuse. The Commission found no causal relationship between celibacy and such abuse but recommended that the Church consider making celibacy for diocesan clergy voluntary. This suggestion aimed to address concerns about the adequacy of preparation and support for a celibate lifestyle among clergy.

In response, the Australian Catholic Bishops Conference (ACBC) and Catholic Religious Australia (CRA) issued a joint statement acknowledging the Commission's findings. They noted that while celibacy itself was not identified as a cause of abuse, insufficient training and support for celibate living might have contributed to instances of abuse. The Church emphasized the importance of proper information and ongoing support for clergy committed to a celibate life.

The Vatican also addressed the Commission's recommendations. In a communication dated February 26, 2020, the Holy See reiterated its commitment to child protection and acknowledged the need for continuous improvement in Church practices. However, the Vatican did not indicate any immediate changes to the discipline of clerical celibacy.

For more detailed information, you can refer to the following sources:

• Royal Commission's Final Report: Royal Commission into Institutional Responses to Child Sexual Abuse

https://www.childabuseroyalcommission.gov.au/final-report

• Australian Bishops' Response: Vatican News - Church in Australia responds to the Royal Commission https://www.vaticannews.va/en/church/news/2018-08/australia-bishops-catholic-religious-royal-commission-response.html

(10.) Page 223: https://www.ketv.com/article/the-church-must-become-like-the-grieving-mother-cupich-says-as-leader-of-abuse-summit/26475654

(11.) Page 223: https://www.vatican.va/archive/cod-iuris-canonici/eng/documents/cic_lib6-cann1364-1399_en.html

(12.) Page 225: https://www.ny-times.com/2018/12/19/us/illinois-attorney-general-catholic-church-priest-abuse.html

In December 2018, the Illinois Attorney General's office released a report focusing on the Catholic Church's handling of sexual abuse cases in the state, with particular emphasis on the Archdiocese of Chicago. This report was part of a broader investigation led by then-Attorney General Lisa Madigan, which aimed to hold the Church accountable for its handling (or mishandling) of sexual abuse cases.

https://illinoisattorneygeneral.gov/Safer-Communities/Responding-to-Sexual-Assault/assets/Catholic_Church_Preliminary_Findings.pdf

The 2023 final report from the Illinois Attorney General, Kwame Raoul's office:

https://clergyreport.illinoisattorneygeneral.gov/download/report.pdf

Key points from the Report on the Archdiocese of Chicago:

• Failure to Investigate: The report accused the Chicago Archdiocese of failing to investigate allegations of abuse thoroughly. The Illinois Attorney General found that many allegations were not fully examined or documented, and the Archdiocese had not always taken appropriate action to protect children or support survivors.

• Underreported Abuse: The report highlighted that the Archdiocese of Chicago, along with other dioceses, often underreported abuse cases, leaving many instances of alleged abuse unaddressed. The Attorney General's office estimated that the number of clergy members accused of abuse was likely much higher than the publicized figures.

• Neglect of Victims: The report emphasized that survivors of abuse were not always given the help or support they needed. Many victims came forward but were not given a proper response, and the Archdiocese sometimes downplayed or dismissed their allegations.

• Documenting Accused Priests: The Illinois Attorney General's report included the publication of a list of clergy members who had been accused of sexual abuse, some of whom had remained in active ministry despite the allegations. The report also pointed to the lack of transparency regarding these individuals' backgrounds.

• Call for Greater Transparency and Action: The Attorney General's office called for the Archdiocese of Chicago and other dioceses to release more information about accused priests, be more transparent in their investigations, and do more to assist victims in coming forward.

(13.) Page 228: https://en.wikipedia.org/wiki/Meeting_on_the_Protection_of_Minors_in_the_Church

https://www.khou.com/article/news/cardinal-dinardo-accused-of-mishandling-case-of-sexual-misconduct-involving-onetime-deputy-and-wealthy-benefactor/285-1ea33eb1-2e3e-4204-b36f-05f0381a487e?utm_source=chatgpt.com

https://www.nbcdfw.com/news/local/woman-accuses-top-us-cardinal-of-dismissing-sex-abuse-case/231835/?utm_source=chatgpt.com

https://www.americamagazine.org/politics-society/2019/06/04/woman-accuses-top-us-cardinal-dismissing-sex-abuse-case?utm_source=chatgpt.com

https://www.cbsnews.com/news/cardinal-daniel-dinardo-head-of-u-s-catholic-bishops-kept-2-priests-accused-of-abuse-in-active-ministry/?utm_source=chatgpt.com

CHAPTER 16

(14.) Page 241: https://www.americamagazine.org/issue/534/article/11th-century-scandal

(15.) Page 241: https://www.americamagazine.org/issue/534/article/11th-century-scandal

(16.) Page 244: https://www.yahoo.com/news/latest-pope-demands-bishops-act-now-end-sex-082524470.html

In his 2018 speech at the Vatican summit on the protection of minors, Bishop Crisostomo Santos addressed the issue of covering up sexual abuse within the Church with a call for accountability. He argued that the cover-up of abuse by clergy members was as grievous as the abuse itself. He expressed the need for the Church to confront this issue with full transparency, urging that bishops and other Church officials who shield or protect abusers should be held accountable. Bishop Santos even suggested that bishops who facilitate cover-ups could face imprisonment, stressing that the law should not exclude anyone from accountability, regardless of their position in the Church. He emphasized that the protection of victims and the prevention of future abuses should be the Church's top priority, and that justice must be pursued without exception.

(17.) Page 252: https://www.ncregister.com/blog/theodore-mccarrick-dismissed-from-the-clerical-state

(18.) Page 252: https://www.cityclub.org/forums/2002/04/26/cardinal-theodore-mccarrick

(19.) Page 254: https://www.bishop-accountability.org/bishops/global-list-of-accused-bishops/

(20.) Page 255: https://www.bishop-accountability.org/docs/brooklyn/Ferraro__Rev_Romano/2009_06_10_Sipe_Ferraro_Affidavit.pdf

(21.) Page 257: https://www.bishop-accountabil-ity.org/resources/resource-files/timeline/2003-02-23-Sipe-ViewEyeStorm.htm

(22.) Page 259: https://www.newsweek.com/child-sex-conviction-pope-francis-former-treasurer-overturned-aus-tralian-high-court-1496464

CHAPTER 18

(23.) Page 278: The Vatican Secretary of State, along with two other high-ranking Vatican officials, have been accused in the International Criminal Court (ICC) of covering up sexual abuse crimes by Catholic priests. These accusations include failing to prevent or punish perpetrators of rape and sexual violence against children, as well as engaging in a systematic and widespread practice of concealing these crimes globally.

The Center for Constitutional Rights (CCR) and the Survivors Network of those Abused by Priests (SNAP) have filed submissions with the ICC, urging it to investigate these high-level Vatican officials. The accusations are based on the concept of "command or superior responsibility," which holds leaders accountable for failing to prevent or punish crimes committed by their subordinates. This legal concept is often applied to situations where superiors either neglected their duty to stop the crimes or actively covered them up (Center for Constitutional Rights: https://ccrjustice.org/home/get-involved/tools-resources/fact-sheets-and-faqs/fact-sheet-seeking-justice-icc) (Church and State:

https://churchandstate.org.uk/2023/04/the-global-scandal-of-sexual-abuse-in-the-catholic-church-a-widespread-problem/).

The Center for Constitutional Rights (CCR), on behalf of the Survivors Network of those Abused by Priests (SNAP), did formally request in September 2011 that the International Criminal Court (ICC) open an investigation into Pope Benedict XVI and three top Vatican officials (Cardinals Bertone, Sodano, and Levada) for crimes against humanity related to child sexual abuse and systematic cover-ups.

However, the ICC prosecutor reviewed the 71-page complaint (submitted with over 20,000 pages of supporting materials) and, in May 2013, declined to pursue an investigation at that time. The decision was based on jurisdictional limitations—such as temporal and subject-matter jurisdiction—not due to a factual dispute over the allegations The prosecutor did leave the door open to reconsider if "new facts or information" emerged.

See the following statement in the first URL below: Pamela Spees, a senior staff attorney with the Center for Constitutional Rights who brought the case to the ICC, said the court identified several jurisdictional hurdles and "left the door open to reconsider" its decision.

https://www.ncronline.org/news/accountability/international-criminal-court-declines-pursue-crimes-against-humanity-case?utm_source=chatgpt.com

https://ccrjustice.org/home/get-involved/tools-resources/fact-sheets-and-faqs/fact-sheet-seeking-justice-icc

https://ccrjustice.org/home/press-center/press-re-
leases/clergy-sex-victims-file-international-criminal-court-
complaint-case?utm_source=chatgpt.com

https://ccrjustice.org/home/what-we-do/our-
cases/snap-v-pope-et-al?utm_source=chatgpt.com

(24.) Page 279: Amnesty International's latest human rights report highlights widespread evidence of child sexual abuse by members of the Catholic clergy over decades. The report points to the Vatican and its officials as responsible for a persistent failure to seek redress for the victims, label-ing these as crimes against humanity. This failure includes systematic cover-ups, moving offending priests between parishes, and lack of proper punishment, all contributing to an environment where abuse could flourish unaddressed and unpunished.

https://home.crin.org/issues/sexual-violence/australia-
case-study-clergy-abuse)

https://archive.crin.org/en/library/publications/holy-
see-child-sexual-abuse-report.html

(25.) Page 280: Cardinal Bernard Law was indeed given a prominent position in the Vatican after resigning as Arch-bishop of Boston in 2002, amid revelations of his role in cov-ering up sexual abuse by priests. Pope John Paul II ap-pointed him as the Archpriest of the Basilica di Santa Maria Maggiore in Rome in 2004. This appointment was contro-versial and perceived by many as a "cushy job" or a com-fortable reassignment despite his involvement in the abuse scandal. The decision to appoint Law to this prestigious position, rather than disciplining him, drew significant criticism from victims and advocates for accountability within the Church.

https://en.wikipedia.org/wiki/Bernard_Francis_Law

https://www.bishop-accountability.org/bishops/removed/

https://www.catholicnewsagency.com/news/1219/cardinal-law-given-a-ceremonial-post-at-the-vatican?utm_source=chatgpt.com

https://en.wikipedia.org/wiki/Bernard_Francis_Law?utm_source=chatgpt.com

(26.) Page 26: 282: In 2019, during a summit convened by Pope Francis to address sexual abuse within the Catholic Church, several important new reporting rules were implemented. These rules were aimed at increasing accountability and transparency in handling allegations of sexual abuse by clergy.

The issue of *America Magazine* reported on the 2019 summit convened by Pope Francis to address the issues of abuse and cover-up within the Church was published in February 2019. The article covered the Vatican's Sexual Abuse Summit, where the Pope and senior Church leaders discussed how to address sexual abuse, the protection of minors, and the Church's failures in handling these crises.

https://www.americamagazine.org/faith/2019/02/21/pope-francis-presents-21-point-road-map-guide-discussion-abuse-summit

(27.) Page 283: Richard Sipe's statement to Pope Benedict XVI in 2008 highlighted the systemic nature of the sexual abuse crisis within the Catholic Church in the United States. Sipe emphasized that the abuse was not only due to unsuitable candidates for priesthood but also stemmed from the behaviors of superiors, including bishops and cardinals. He provided specific examples, such as Bishop Thomas Lyons, Abbot John Eidenschink, and Cardinal Theodore McCarrick, who were involved in or covered up abuse.

Sipe argued that the problem was systemic and deeply rooted in the Church's hierarchy, with sexual abuse being perpetuated and covered up by those in power. He urged Pope Benedict XVI to listen to the stories of victims and take decisive action to address the crisis, suggesting that such abuses compromised the Church's integrity and harmed countless individuals.

https://www.bishop-accountability.org/news2008/03_04/2008_04_21_Sipe_Statement-For.htm

(28.) Page 283: The Vatican ratified the UN Convention Against Torture and Other Cruel, Inhuman or Degrading Treatment or Punishment on June 22, 2002. This treaty obligates signatory states to prevent and punish acts of torture and other forms of cruel, inhuman, or degrading treatment or punishment.

https://www.ohchr.org/en/instruments-mecha-nisms/instruments/convention-against-torture-and-other-cruel-inhuman-or-degrading

https://en.wikipedia.org/wiki/United_Nations_Con-vention_Against_Torture

https://www.catholicculture.org/culture/li-brary/view.cfm?recnum=4560&utm_source=chatgpt.com

(29.) Page 284: The United Nations Committee Against Torture (UN CAT) began an investigation into the Vatican's handling of sexual abuse cases around 2014. This inquisition was part of the broader scrutiny faced by the Vatican for its failure to address and prevent the systemic sexual abuse of children by clergy members. The investigation was prompted by reports and evidence of widespread abuse and the Vatican's consistent efforts to cover it up rather than take corrective action.

In its concluding observations in May 2014, the UN CAT criticized the Vatican for not fulfilling its obligations under the Convention Against Torture. The committee found that the Vatican's failure to prevent and punish rape and other forms of sexual violence amounted to torture and cruel, inhuman, and degrading treatment. This scrutiny included the Vatican's practices of relocating abusive priests rather than reporting them to civil authorities and failing to provide proper monitoring and accountability.

https://www.voanews.com/a/un-torture-watchdog-urges-vatican-to-pursue-sex-criminals/1920950.html https://www.omct.org/en/resources/statements/un-committee-against-torture-criticises-holy-see-over-child-sexual-abuse

(30.) Page 284: The UN and CAT explicitly rejected the Vatican's claim that its treaty obligations are confined to Vatican City, affirming that they in fact "extend to Holy See officials worldwide, wherever they exercise effective control."

https://www.omct.org/en/resources/statements/un-committee-against-torture-criticises-holy-see-over-child-sexual-abuse?utm_source=chatgpt.com

https://www.theguardian.com/world/2014/may/23/un-committee-against-torture-vatican-sex-abuse-scandal?utm_source=chatgpt.com

(31.) Page 284: The 2017 report by the Royal Commission into Institutional Responses to Child Sexual Abuse in Australia is a comprehensive and detailed examination of how various institutions, including religious organizations, handled allegations and incidents of child sexual abuse. The report revealed systemic failures, highlighting that institutions often prioritized their reputation over the welfare of children.

https://www.abc.net.au/news/2017-02-07/royal-commission-into-sexual-abuse-/8246584?utm_source

The final report called for a national redress scheme to compensate victims and urged significant changes in institutional policies and practices to prevent future abuse.

(32.) Page 289: Attorneys who specialize in the Foreign Sovereign Immunities Act (FSIA) are legal professionals who typically focus on cases involving foreign states and their agencies or instrumentalities, as well as issues related to sovereign immunity, international law, and complex jurisdictional questions.

https://en.wikipedia.org/wiki/Foreign_Sovereign_Immunities_Act

https://www.fjc.gov/sites/default/files/materials/41/FSIA_Guide_2d_ed_2018.pdf

(33.) Page 291: https://www.law.cornell.edu/uscode/text/28/1605

https://travel.state.gov/content/travel/en/legal/travel-legal-considerations/internl-judicial-asst/Service-of-Process/Foreign-Sovereign-Immunities-Act.html

1605(a)(5) - money damages are sought against a foreign state for personal injury or death, or damage to or loss of property, occurring in the United States and caused by the tortious act or omission of that foreign state;

1605A - money damages are sought against a foreign state designated as a state sponsor of terrorism for personal injury or death that was caused by an act of torture, extrajudicial killing, aircraft sabotage, hostage taking, or the provision of material support or resources for such an act, if such act or provision of material support or resources is engaged in by an official, employee, or agent of such foreign state while acting within the scope of his or her office, employment, or agency.

https://www.fjc.gov/sites/default/files/materials/41/FSIA_Guide_2d_ed_2018.pdf

(34.) Page 294: https://www.reddit.com/r/worldnews/comments/9ajxhf/pope_francis_refused_to_address_accusations_that/

https://www.reuters.com/article/us-pope-ireland-abuse-plane/pope-says-will-not-respond-to-allegations-of-abuse-cover-up-idUSKCN1LB0OQ/

https://www.theguardian.com/world/2019/feb/24/pope-francis-calls-for-all-out-battle-against-abuse-of-children

https://www.washingtonpost.com/world/europe/the-pope-ignored-them-alleged-abuse-of-deaf-children-on-two-continents-points-to-vatican-failings/2019/02/18/07db1bdc-fd60-11e8-a17e-162b712e8fc2_story.html

(35.) Page 296: At the age of 15, Gabriele Martinelli was reportedly given the unusual authority by the rector of the seminary to hand out papal assignments. This is a significant position of power for someone so young.

Here are several reputable sources that detail the case of Fr. Gabriele Martinelli, a former seminarian accused of sexually abusing younger boys at the Vatican's youth seminary:

1. AP News (October 6, 2021)

"Vatican court absolves former altar boy in sex abuse trial" covers the Vatican tribunal's initial verdict that acquitted Martinelli of some charges, citing lack of evidence of coercion, and provides context on how allegations emerged publicly in 2017.

2. AP News (Trial reports) "Priest in Vatican youth seminary trial denies abuse claims" provides details from Martinelli's criminal trial where he denies the allegations and offers insight into courtroom exchanges with prosecutors.

3. Washington Post (January 23, 2024) "Vatican court convicts former altar boy who served the pope" reports that a Vatican appeals court overturned the earlier acquittal, finding Martinelli guilty of "corrupting a minor" and sentencing him to 2½ years in prison.

4. AP News (October 14, 2020)

"Ex-Vatican altar boy testifies in seminary sex abuse trial" features testimony from the alleged victim (identified as L.G.), describing how Martinelli allegedly abused him in the Vatican's St. Pius X seminary between 2007–2012.

5. NCR & Vatican News (January 23, 2024)

"Vatican appeals court finds priest guilty of 'corrupting a minor'" details the appeal court's ruling, its legal rationale, and the 2.5-year sentence handed down against Martinelli.

• 2013: The Pope and several Cardinals received a letter alleging that Martinelli was sexually abusing other younger boys at the youth seminary.

• 2014: A letter from the third-ranking Vatican official referenced these allegations and stated that the Pope was aware of the case. This indicated that high-ranking officials, including the Pope, were informed of the accusations against Martinelli.

- 2017: Despite these serious allegations, Pope Francis ordained Gabriele Martinelli as a priest. This case is part of the broader issue of sexual abuse within the Catholic Church, which has involved numerous allegations and instances of abuse, often accompanied by accusations of cover-ups or failure to act by Church authorities.

CHAPTER 19

(36.) Page 310: Code of Canon Law in 1917 as it relates to celibacy: The 1917 Code of Canon Law was the first comprehensive codification of Church law in the Roman Catholic Church and governed the life and practices of the Church until it was replaced by the 1983 Code of Canon Law. Regarding celibacy, the 1917 Code outlined rules and expectations for clergy, particularly in relation to their commitment to celibacy as a part of their vow of chastity.

Clerical Celibacy (Canon 132, 1917): The 1917 Code made it clear that all clerics (ordained ministers in the Church, including bishops, priests, and deacons) were bound to celibacy. Celibacy was considered an essential aspect of the priestly vocation, and clerics were prohibited from marrying. This vow of celibacy was a serious obligation for those entering the priesthood.

The 1917 Code required that clergy members must remain celibate, meaning they should abstain from all sexual activity and marriage. If a priest or deacon violated this vow, they were subject to penalties, including the potential for laicization (removal from the clerical state).

https://www.britannica.com/topic/canon-law/The-Codex-Juris-Canonici-1917?utm_source=chatgpt.com

(37.) Page 313: Bishop-Accountability.org is a non-profit organization and website dedicated to providing detailed information about the sexual abuse crisis within the Catholic Church, focusing on holding Church leaders accountable for their role in the abuse and cover-ups. Founded in 2003, the organization collects and publishes publicly available documents, records, and information related to sexual abuse by clergy members, as well as the actions (or inactions) of bishops and other Church officials in handling abuse allegations.

Key features and missions of Bishop-Accountability.org:

• Database of Clergy Abuse Cases: The website maintains an extensive database of priests, bishops, and religious figures accused of sexual abuse. This database includes information on clergy members from around the world, with a focus on those cases that have been reported in the media or documented in legal proceedings.

• Documentation and Transparency: The organization aims to increase transparency about abuse cases and Church leaders' responses to allegations. They provide access to key court documents, news reports, and internal Church records that reveal the extent of the abuse crisis and how the Church managed (or mishandled) abuse cases.

• Focus on Bishops' Accountability: A significant aspect of the organization's work is holding bishops accountable for their role in either directly abusing minors or covering up abuse by other clergy members. It focuses on tracking how bishops have responded to allegations, whether they took appropriate action to protect children or whether they allowed accused priests to remain in ministry.

Bishop-Accountability.org plays an important role in the ongoing effort to bring justice to victims and hold the Church accountable for its handling of sexual abuse cases. It is widely regarded as an authoritative resource for survivors, journalists, researchers, and anyone seeking detailed information on the topic.

(38.) Page 314: SNAP, or the Survivors Network of those Abused by Priests, is a non-profit organization that advocates for and supports survivors of sexual abuse by clergy members, particularly those who were abused within the Roman Catholic Church. Founded in 1988, SNAP's primary goal is to provide support and advocacy for survivors, raise awareness about the widespread issue of clergy sexual abuse, and push for accountability within the Church.

ACKNOWLEDGEMENTS

This book would not have been possible without the patience and dedication of Sam Severn. His gift of mentoring writers across the globe has allowed the words in this book to flow from my soul.

Thank you, Sam, and may God bless you for the amazing talent He provided you with.

www.ingramcontent.com/pod-product-compliance
Lightning Source LLC
Chambersburg PA
CBHW070202120726
47909CB00001B/218